# Curse of the I

## Keepers of the Stones, Book One

## Tara West

Artwork by Bob Kehl.
Edited by Vickie Johnstone.
Special thanks to my beta readers, Janet Michelson and Shéa MacLeod for catching those last minute oopsies.

# Curse of the Ice Dragon

Born with mark of the Mighty Hunter, Markus saves his village from the brink of starvation-for whenever he releases an arrow, his aim is true. But despite his skill and strength, Markus is unable to confront his tyrannical father. Shamed by his cowardice, he distracts himself by needlessly shooting the forest creatures.

When Markus takes no heed of the village prophet's warning that his actions will attract The Hunter's Curse—for every animal Markus kills, his loved ones will suffer the same fate—the Sky Goddess unleashes her ice dragon.

Now, Markus must flee the dragon without killing it ... or his beloved brother will be the next to die.

# Dedications

This book is dedicated to my nephews, Mark and Alex, for inspiring the characters in my story.

I'd like to offer special thanks to my husband for his archery expertise and for his unwavering faith in my writing career.

Bob, I'm probably biased, but this is the best fantasy art ever!

And finally, thanks to all of my readers who've enabled me to become a full-time writer.

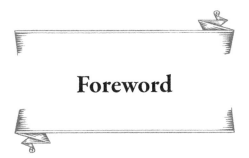

# Foreword

A thick mist coated the night sky with an unforgiving chill that stretched across the horizon for miles. The soft blanket of snow had turned to ice, leaving the ground barren, cold and unforgiving. All was quiet beneath the frosted pines. Even the glaciers surrounding the cragged peak of Tehra's Ice Mountain seemed immobile. No soft winds carried the sounds of animals on the breeze. The only sign of life resided in a small log hut, nestled in a deep valley beneath the mountain. A fire kindled within, but life there was stagnant. Breaths were stilled as faces resembled stone masks of worry.

A babe's cry broke the silence.

The mother, having used the last of her strength for the final push, slumped against the sweat-drenched furs and fell into a deep slumber. Cradling the infant in a worn, but thick pelt, the midwife placed the bundle in the gnarled hands of the old prophet.

The child's cherubic face, crimson-flushed from crying, was almost perfect in form and proportions. The only mar on his features was a scar, tracing from the corner of a tiny ear to the tip of his brow. It resembled the shape of a half-moon or a hunter's bow waiting to be drawn.

"The boy has the hunter's mark."

The many lines surrounding Dafuar's pale stone eyes belied his age. The ancient healer and prophet was older than any of the villagers, and perhaps even older than the village itself. For his longevity alone, people sought his knowledge, but they also feared him, for many of his dark prophecies had come true. After he'd predicted the great famine, the villagers avoided him, fearing he'd not only prognosticated, but precipitated starvation and death.

To some, Dafuar was a bad omen.

But Rowlen refused to cower to foolish fears. He was a man, strong and brave. He'd brought Dafuar to his hut this night, hoping the prophet would

3

bless the birth and cast a spell to ward off the sickness that had plagued his firstborn son.

A smile cracked the hardened shell that coated the grim lines around Rowlen's face. "Then the village shall celebrate, for my son will keep them well fed."

Dafuar shook his head. "He must be taught humility or he will wield his power with destruction."

Rowlen laughed, his booming voice shaking the stagnant air. "My son will be a great man, a fierce hunter."

"A hunter need not be fierce to feed his people. His skills must be tempered with kindness and compassion." Dafuar's eyes softened, saddened, before he closed them altogether.

Rowlen knew Dafuar was lost in distant memories; knew he would soon conjure up the old tale about the cursed hunter who was killed by the breath of the beast. The prophet had served him well this night, but he had no time for the old man's foolish fairy tales.

"Compassion is for the weak, old man. I have no use for weak words — or weak sons." He shot a menacing glare at a small child crouching in the corner of the room.

The child blinked once, and then did not stir. He would have been invisible to the naked eye, so small and quiet was he, were it not for the blinding tufts of pale blond hair that curled around his nightcap and wide, watery eyes that shone with both longing and fear.

Scowling, Rowlen turned his back on his eldest son.

Only then did the boy resume the ragged rise and fall of his chest. Struggling for each breath, he silently coughed into his palm, having learned to conceal any sign of his infirmity.

The boy whispered his thanks to the Goddess that this night he had been given a brother. In his short lifespan, he'd been blessed with neither strength nor skill, but he had been gifted with a wisdom and compassion beyond his four years. He prayed his brother would be compassionate, too.

He'd give his last dying breath to make certain the babe did not grow up to become a monster.

# Chapter One

*The Bond of Brothers*

"WAIT UP! YOU KNOW I cannot run as fast as you!"

"We must hurry before Father whips us for delaying his supper!"

Markus threw a glance behind him, before coming to a halt. Alec had once again slowed their progress. Tossing his sling and the rabbit carcasses to the ground, Markus went to help him. Although the onset of spring had thawed most of the perilous icy freeze, his brother's condition appeared to worsen with each melting snow cap.

Alec clutched one hand to his chest, using the other to steady his slender frame against a pine tree. "We both know I will be the one whipped, not you."

"Even more reason to make haste." Markus grimaced, knowing his brother's words were true, but he could not understand why Alec was always the victim of their father's heavy hand. Father had only struck Markus once, and that had been long ago.

Mayhap Father knew that if he beat Markus, he'd risk injuring his drawback arm and then there would be no more venison stew for supper.

Even so, he hated seeing his brother abused. The red and purple splotches on Alec's pale arms and back were daily reminders that Markus was the favorite child. He should have been grateful that it was Alec who attracted their father's wrath, but watching his brother degraded and hurt unleashed strange emotions inside him. Anger welled up in his heart every day he witnessed Alec's torment.

Anger at their father.

Anger at himself.

Was it not Markus's destiny to be a mighty hunter and a fearless leader? Hadn't he already been providing the village with most of the meat for their tables? Yet, when it came to his father, why hadn't he the courage to stand up to him and defend his brother?

Although Alec was almost twenty winters, and by all accounts old enough to be a man, he had the physique of a juvenile boy and was not strong enough to live on his own. Thus he was forced to endure their father's wrath in exchange for a warm bed and food.

Hardly a life worth living.

Markus promised himself that when he came of age, he would make it up to his brother. They'd live in a hut of their own and he would hunt for Alec, giving him all the choice meats. Alec would grow stronger then and recover from his sickness.

Until then...

"Do you wish me to carry you?" Markus asked. Standing over a head taller, he looked down as Alec coughed and wheezed through the rattle in his chest.

Alec looked up, glaring. "Carry me? Don't be foolish. You cannot carry me and your kill."

But carrying Alec would be easy work. By his thirteenth birthday, Markus had been blessed with the strength and size of a full-grown man. Now, almost three years later, he could toss his brother's hollow bones over his shoulder in one sweep.

"I've carried stags heavier than you," Markus laughed.

Pale orbs beneath Alec's sunken sockets darkened. "I just need a moment to catch my breath."

Sometimes Markus marveled how Alec had lived so long as to reach his nineteenth birthday. Each night, Markus had sent a silent thanks to the Goddess for his brother's fortitude, for he truly did not know how he could go on living without Alec by his side.

Leaning against the pine tree, Markus's voice softened. "One moment, then we must go. It is nearly time to eat, and I've not skinned the rabbits."

A wolfish grin spread across Alec's face. "Had you not stopped to spy, we would not be delayed now."

Markus felt a rush of heat burst forth from his chest and inflame his face. Dianna was his one weakness, and he silently cursed his brother for alluding to her. "I was not spying."

Alec burst out laughing before he was forced to give into a fit of coughs. Once his coughing had subsided, he looked at Markus with a hint of mischief in his pale eyes. "What would you call it then?"

Folding his arms across his chest, Markus exhaled a breath of frustration. What was it about that girl that confounded him so? Despite all of his efforts to help her, she refused, paying him no more heed than the mold growing beneath her boot. Out of all the villagers, she should have desired his hunting skills the most. Her parents had been killed in an avalanche the previous winter, leaving Dianna and her brother to fend for themselves.

"She is stubborn. I was just making sure she and her brother do not starve."

Alec shook his pale head. "I saw the skin of a doe hanging from a nearby tree."

"A small doe."

Alec shrugged. "'Tis all they need."

"I could have killed a bear for her!" A surge of anger infused Markus's skull. Pushing away from the tree, he picked up the rabbits and marched toward home.

Girls were so foolish. Why did men see any use for them?

"They've no need for that much meat," called his brother from the distance, while coughing through his words.

Storming through the darkened forest, Markus easily dodged the perilous, winding roots that snuck up from the ground, threatening to trip the hapless wanderer. But he'd traveled this path since he was old enough to draw back a bow. He knew he should slow his pace, but anger fueled his movements, and he was in no mood to be ribbed by his brother. It was not in Alec's nature to tease him, unless the topic strayed to Dianna.

"She wastes her time on the hunt when all she needs is to ask me," he growled, trudging heavily along the well-worn path to their hut.

"Mayhap she likes the hunt."

Markus whipped around to face his brother, who had remarkably kept up with his fast stride. "She's a girl," he spat. "Girls do not like hunting!"

Alec leveled him with a smug smile. "Is that so?"

Markus wasn't sure he liked his brother's cocky attitude. Alec was the more intelligent of the two, for sure, and he didn't want to be reminded of his superior wit. "What do you know about girls?"

Markus wished the venomous words back as soon as they'd slipped off his tongue. Despite Alec's every effort, girls refused to pay him any heed. Maidens wanted strong husbands who could keep their family well fed. That's why Markus had no shortage of admiring females. They practically flung themselves at his feet—well, all except Dianna.

"More than you, it would seem." Alec snickered, ignoring his brother's attempts to silence him.

"You should've let me kill that stag," Markus grumbled, as he spied the clearing through the trees. "I would've left it at her door."

"It is a good thing Father does let me go on your hunts, otherwise you'd have killed the whole forest by now! Do not waste the lives of our woodland creatures."

Markus rolled his eyes at the change in his brother's tone. Sometimes he acted more like a parent than a sibling. "I do not need another lecture from you on the preservation of species."

"Where are those damn boys?!"

The familiar roar sliced through the frigid air, sending shards of ice-cold fear to the marrow of Markus's bones.

Why did his father affect him that way?

Why did he allow his father to affect him that way?

"We're here, Father," he called back, regretting the crack of fear that broke through his strained voice.

Trudging through a new growth of snake moss, he led the way toward their small hut. A fire kindled through the smoke hole, and freshly washed shirts and trews dangled from a weathered rope. A small patch of newly plowed soil graced one side of the hut. Beneath the majestic backdrop of the snowcapped mountain peak, all would have seemed perfect on this tiny plot of land.

Save for him.

Almost as wide as a great snow bear (though not as tall, for a snow bear was easily twice Markus's height) and twice as mean, Rowlen had no patience for anything save brewing his many pots of ale. His mouth was draped with a permanent scowl and an acerbic bite of condescension seemed to linger at the end of every word that dripped off his venomous tongue. Eyes darker than stone reflected the contents of his heart—cold and impenetrable. The only things harder than his heart were his meaty fists when they pummeled Alec—almost a daily occurrence.

When he was little, Markus learned to recognize the loathing gleam in his father's eyes just before he was about to strike; knew the exact time to run. When there was no place to hide, Alec would shield Markus's body with his own. Though it didn't matter; Rowlen was only after Alec's blood.

As he grew older, Markus became more aware of rumors circulating about him. He'd been born with the mark of the great hunter. He would free their people from starvation. Over the past few winters rumor had turned to reality. As if by a miracle, the more he honed his skills, the more the animals flocked to the forest.

At first their father was proud, boasting to the whole village how his son had saved them from famine. And for a short while, Rowlen was happy. With their father's lighter mood, Alec was spared his cruelty. But his mild temper was short-lived and the abuse would begin again.

Markus blamed himself—he thought mayhap Father wasn't pleased with his hunt. Mayhap if he harvested more animals, Father would spare Alec. But now it seemed that with each fresh kill, Rowlen used Markus's success against Alec, chiding his oldest son for his incompetence.

Dropping an axe on top of a pile of wood, Father strode over to them in long, heavy steps, never tearing his fiery glare from Alec's feeble frame. "Do you purposely mean to make me wait for my supper?"

"'Tis my fault, Father," Alec said, coughing into his hand. "I had to stop for breath."

Markus's limbs turned to ice and his eyes darted to his father, bracing himself for his angry reaction. Great Goddess! Why had his foolish brother taken the blame upon himself?

Rubbing one thick hand through his scraggly, graying beard, Rowlen eyed Alec with a sneer. "I do not know why I allow such a weakling to attend my son on the hunt."

"Do you forget I am your son, too?"

Markus felt the anger in Alec's shaky voice and could only stare at him in awe.

"How dare you speak to me that way!" Rowlen raised his hand to strike.

"Father, wait!" Markus jumped between the two men, surprised at his own act of courage. "I need Alec to help me skin the rabbits."

Growling under his breath, Rowlen lowered his arm. "Put him to work, son. He is of no use to me."

Markus turned, and with a shaky hand he grabbed his brother by the elbow and led him to the skinning shack. Still puzzled at how he was able to stand up to Father, his elation was short-lived. This meager defiance meant nothing when so much damage had already been done. When so much violence was still to come.

What would he have done if Father had pushed him aside and struck Alec? Would he have defended his brother? Probably not. His quivering innards reminded him that he was a coward.

After they had reached the shack and lit the oil lamp, Markus turned to his brother and grumbled, "Why do you lie for me?"

Had Alec not lied, Markus would not have been forced to defend him. For that he was angry, but most of all, he was angry with himself for his cowardice when it came to standing up to their father.

Alec dropped his shoulders, a wry grin crossing his face. "I don't know."

"I wish you'd stop," Markus growled, before turning his back on his brother and tossing the rabbit carcasses on the skinning table. Pulling the boning knife out of his belt, he grabbed a rabbit and pierced the animal just below the belly.

"Why?" Alec hissed at his back. "So he can beat you?"

"Well, don't provoke him then." Markus bit his lip before he said too much, before he admitted his fears. He sliced the blade up to the rabbit's neck and the blood from the exposed flesh warmed his shaking hand.

Taking a deep breath, Markus forced himself to relax, putting all of his effort into skinning the rabbits and trying to block out the memory of his father's face and the sound of his voice. For a brief moment, he savored the stagnant air, smelling of blood from all of the animals he had slaughtered on the weathered, red-stained skinning table. The pungent odor of the freshly killed rabbit carcasses blended with the old blood. To some the smell would've been overpowering, but to Markus, the stench brought an unexplained sense of peace.

"If he'd acknowledge me as his son, and treat me as a human, then mayhap I wouldn't."

Markus sighed. His brother's words refused to allow him to push the image of Father from his mind. Besides, Alec was right. Why did Father hate him so? It was not Alec's fault that he'd been born with an infirmity and Father's daily beatings did nothing to improve his condition.

But at least Alec had the one elixir that neither Markus nor Father could lay claim to—Mother's gentle touch, her soft, soothing voice and tender smile.

"It is no special honor." His throat tightened with emotion. "At least you have our mother's love."

Markus ripped open the rabbit's flesh at each extremity with brutal strokes, slicing his way toward the belly before hacking off each foot. After cutting off the tail, he pulled the pelt of the rabbit up over its neck.

Father had repeatedly told him it wasn't mannish to savor the soft caresses of a woman, but how he longed for Mother to brush her fingers across his cheek, to hold him and stroke his hair as she did with Alec. But Markus's hair was as black as the night sky and coarse, like straw, unlike the soft, pale wisps of his brother's. And he was far too large to fit in the cradle of their mother's arms, while Alec could still fold his slender frame into her lap without crushing her.

Of course, Mother only showed affection to Alec when Father was in the barn, drowning himself in brew. Alec would come into the hut with a fresh bruise, his eyes pooled with moisture and Mother would open her arms to him. Markus had no choice but to turn away, an aching in his heart, for he never knew that kind of love from his mother.

"She loves you too, brother," said Alec, placing a steady hand on his shoulder. "Father forbids her from showing it, is all."

Markus exhaled a long breath, choking back the rising tide of anger. "That, I cannot accept."

"The Great Hunter cannot be fierce if he is coddled." Alec mimicked their father's stentorian tone.

In one swift stroke, Markus chopped off the head of the rabbit. It rolled down the gentle slope of the table and landed in a bucket. Blood pooled from the empty cavity.

"I wish I never had such skill. I wish I was more like you." Tossing the blade aside, Markus turned toward Alec.

Eyes narrowing, Alec's gaze intensified. "Do you wish for every breath to be a struggle? To be weak and infirm, and hardly a man even at nine and ten winters!"

"You are the strongest man I know, Alec. It takes strength and courage to stand up to our father. And your kindness to me..." His voice quavered as he dropped his gaze. "I do not understand."

"You are my brother." Alec gripped Markus by both shoulders, looking up into his face with a pained expression. "What is there to understand?"

Markus shrugged and swallowed the lump in his throat that seemed to originate from a hollow pit in his belly. "He beats you, even for my mistakes. A lesser man would despise me."

"You have good in you, despite our father's best efforts to make you a monster."

"I do not stand up to him as you do. I do not defend you as I ought."

"You might be as strong as an ox, but you are a lad still. Your time will come, brother." Alec's voice cracked before he coughed into his hand for several interminable seconds. Finally, Alec righted his posture and looked at Markus with a glazed-over expression. "On the night you were born, I made a promise to the Goddess that I would teach you compassion. A promise I will give my last dying breath to uphold. This is why I scold you when you kill more than you can eat. A kind hunter respects those animals he kills and does not take their lives unnecessarily."

Markus turned back to his kill. Picking up the knife, he cut through the meat of the rabbit before ripping open the ribcage with the tip of his blade. "Aye, brother, but when I see an easy target, I cannot stop the blood that pumps through my veins, driving me to kill the beast. It is a feeling I cannot explain."

With a hand on Markus's back, Alec breathed at barely a whisper. "You must not surrender to your impulses."

Repressing the urge to laugh at his brother's request, Markus pulled down the animal's innards before ripping them free of its body. A smile crossed his face as the gutting was finally finished. All that was left were meat and bones for the stew.

"I cannot help it." He shrugged before tossing the organs in the bucket.

Alec stood speechless behind him, leaving nothing between them but the wheezy sound of his strained breathing and the odor of fresh blood.

Finally, he cleared his throat. "Killing comes too easily to you, Markus. It would seem your gift is more of a curse."

# Chapter Two

**M**arkus stalked his prey with little effort. Their tracks had been fresh when he'd come upon them in the late hours of the morn. He'd swiftly circled them downwind, just below the sloped field of overgrown grass in which they'd been grazing. Mountain goats, two large billies and several ewes. They'd make a fine addition to the festival tonight. The people would be in awe when he hauled their carcasses into town on his father's cart. Dianna would also be there, helping the other women with the preparations for the event.

It was a festival in honor of him, The Mighty Hunter, for saving the town from starvation. Tonight there would be dancing, and Dianna wouldn't dare refuse the guest of honor when he sought her for a partner. She was such a beauty—hair pale and smooth, just like his mother's, hung nearly to her waist. Although she usually wore it tucked into a woolen cap, he'd seen its length once, cascading down her back like soft falling snow.

He wondered if she'd wear her hair down tonight, and how she'd feel in his arms when they danced. If only she'd look up at him with something other than scorn reflecting in her wide, emerald eyes. He'd give anything for a glimpse of her smile.

Eyes locked on his target, Markus silently drew back his bow. The muted thwack of the string releasing was the only warning the large billy goat received before the arrow struck the center of his lungs. By then, another arrow had been fired, and another. Both billy goats and a large ewe were down, and the rest began to scatter in panic, but a newborn lamb had been trampled in the confusion. He lay on his side, crying out for his mother. Markus knew she'd return, and when she did he would shoot both mother and lamb.

His chest swelled with pride; four large goats and a succulent little lamb for dinner. He would be sure to save the lamb for himself and Alec. Mayhap if Dianna agreed to sit with him, he'd share the tender meat with her, too.

PERCHED ON THE ORNATE throne the townspeople had carved for him in the shape of a snow bear, Markus watched the joyous dancers with a scowl. He should have been honored, but instead he stewed in his misery. Though many mothers offered their daughters as partners, he was in no mood to dance.

Dianna had refused him.

Protesting that she could not leave her brother without a partner, she danced with the boy for the first three songs. All the while the boy glared at him over Dianna's shoulder. Markus thought he should teach the pup a thing or two about manners.

And where was Alec? His brother's chest had felt especially heavy today, so he stayed behind while Mother prepared him a special brew. But they both should have been here by now. Unless Father...

Markus tried to purge the image of Father beating Alec from his mind. It would be in Father's nature to beat Alec until he was too sick to attend the festival because he was so ashamed of having his infirmity paraded about the village.

Markus silently cursed himself for going ahead of his family, but Father had insisted that The Mighty Hunter couldn't be late to his own celebration. Markus tried to shake off such dark thoughts by once again focusing on the dancers.

On her.

Dianna had chosen the trews of a man over the traditional dress. And although the women whispered behind her back, and many men gawked like filthy dogs, she paid them no heed. He'd crossed her on the hunt once when she was wearing those same tight, doeskin breeches. Did she really imagine herself to be a mighty huntress? Had she dressed as one to mock him at his celebration?

His gaze shifted to her hair. She'd worn it down in one long, pale braid. The tip of the wispy tendrils swayed against her rounded bottom as she moved to the music.

Markus shifted uncomfortably in his seat as a strange feeling stirred in the pit of his belly at the thought of holding her in his arms. He tried to focus on something else, averting his gaze to anything but her.

Although the hall was dark, the muted flames of candles draped from overhanging branches cast a soft, shadowed light across the dance floor. As tradition dictated, most of the men had shaved their beards, signifying the end of winter, and their hair was tied behind their necks with leather bands. The women clutched the sides of their long woolen dresses, lifting the hems just high enough to reveal brightly colored, wooden shoes.

As the dancers stomped on the planks of the floor, sound waves reverberated through Markus's entire body. But, while the room shook, it did not crumble, though the floor was suspended several feet off the ground, nestled inside the mighty branches of the Lyme tree.

Markus wondered briefly if their dancing would trigger an avalanche. But his village of Adolan was situated far enough beneath the snowcapped peak of Ice Mountain that they need not fear a slide. This was why some villagers from Kicelin, which sat perilously near the base of the mountain, had journeyed here tonight. They would not be able to dance again for many days to come.

From the corner of his eye, Markus saw his family enter. Rowlen was first, glancing about the room before spotting a group of men in the rear, already drinking heavily from their cups. Father rushed upon them without a second glance at his family, hollering and hooting in their midst while they passed him a large tankard of ale.

Mother followed silently into the room, her eyes downcast. She pulled Alec behind her to sit quietly in a dark corner at the end of a long table. Alec's entire frame seemed to turn inward like the branches of a pine tree, bending under the weight of heavy snow.

A hollow ache settled in the pit of Markus's stomach, slicing its way up to his chest. Alec had not pulled down the hood of his cloak.

What had Father done now?

Pushing himself off his throne, Markus made his way down the wooden dais and toward his family. Alec was slumped over in his chair while Mother gently stroked his back. His brother was injured. Mother always coddled him after Father's abuse. The dread that had struck Markus's chest began to spread through his body, icing over his limbs. What new bruise would he find when he gazed into his brother's pale face?

His mother caught his eye first; her pain-stricken gaze bore into him. The eyes of her once beautiful face were sunk low, as if receding into the hollows of her skull. Even though he provided plenty of meat for the family, she barely ate, and the bones of her frail body nearly poked through her skin.

Her stony gaze held his for a long moment, longer than he'd ever held her attention. An uncomfortable ache crept into Markus's heart. While he had always wished for his mother's tenderness, he did not like the weight of her stare now. Narrowing her eyes, she finally turned away. At that moment, Markus felt his mother's hatred in his bones.

But why?

What had he done to her, other than try to win her affection? To make her notice him, love him. Swallowing the rising tide in his throat, he fought the burning ache of tears in the corners of his eyes. He was a man, a mighty hunter—he would not cry.

Walking over to Alec, he placed a gentle hand on his brother's feeble shoulder and bent down to his hooded face. "Let me see, Alec."

His brother dropped his head. "Not now, Markus."

He tried to squeeze all emotion out of his voice. "Would you not sit with me? I am lonely up there on my throne."

Alec sunk lower in the seat. "I prefer my spot down here with Mother."

Biting back a curse, Markus turned away from his family, the familiar anger welling up inside his chest. He was not the cause of his father's cruelty, so why were they punishing him? Had they come to his celebration only to sulk and glare? What were they expecting him to do? He might be skilled with a bow, but he was no match for Rowlen.

Still, he could not purge the guilt that seemed to eat at his soul. If anyone had a chance against Father, he was bigger than Alec by far. But this was Markus's celebration. He could do nothing now.

Stalking through the crowded room, Markus grabbed his cloak off a hanging branch and walked out into the crisp evening air. He needed to be outdoors, the only place where he felt truly at peace. With heavy steps, he made his way down the long plank until the brittle, dry grass crunched beneath his boots. Looking heavenward, he marveled at the brilliance of the sunset. Many colors painted the sky, the hues ranging from orange to deep crimson, in sharp contrast to the dark ache in his heart.

After several strides across a short field, he found himself beneath another lyme tree, which the villagers called the sapling, for she was small compared to the massive lyme tree where they held their festivals. But, to Markus, the sapling was beautiful, standing at least ten men tall, with a canopy of branches that could shelter an entire village.

The eve was still young, and no amorous couples had found their way beneath the tree's secluded darkness. Of that he was glad, for all he really wanted was to be alone. Exhaling a sigh of frustration, he slumped against the wall of the great trunk, hanging his head between his knees.

*Thwack!*

Markus's head jerked at the instant, dizzying pain in his right ear. Instinctively, he placed a hand to his head and felt the warmth of blood trickling just below his lobe. He was too dazed to dodge the second attack as something pelted him on the top of the head. Then he ducked as a third object banged off the side of the tree.

Jumping to unsteady feet, Markus drew his boning knife and turned to his assailant.

The boy, Dianna's brother, Desryn, stood before him, clutching a fist-full of rocks. A grimy face and a tangled mop of muddy-hued locks, he was less than half of Markus's size and could be no more than ten winters old.

Desryn's mangy, black hound growled at Markus from between the boy's legs. With stubby legs, a long snout and a limp, bushy tail, the mutt looked more like an over-sized rodent.

"She does not want you, so let her be!" Desryn squealed before hurling another rock.

"You speak nonsense, you little imp," Markus growled, "and when I get hold of you I shall teach you a lesson!"

Desryn's little dog stood beside his master and barked with all the tenacity of a rabid fox.

"Oooohhh, The Mighty Hunter!" the boy taunted. "I'm quivering in my boots!" His eyes narrowed before he pelted yet another stone at Markus.

This time, Markus was ready and easily deflected the object with his knife. "Do you think mere rocks can best me?"

"I see the way you stare at her," Desryn hissed. "You are a filthy dog, just like your father!"

Markus's limbs froze, and for a second he thought his heart stopped beating. Rage infused his skull to the point of bursting. He was not like his father. He would never be like his father. With one swift movement, he unleashed the blade, his aim striking true. The boy's scream pierced the night sky like the whelp of an injured rabbit.

Turning his back, Markus walked across the field, leaving Desryn with his frayed locks pinned to an overhanging lyme branch. The only way of releasing him would be to cut through his tangled web of hair.

"Good," Markus mused to himself. "Now his sister will have to groom him instead of wasting her time on the hunt."

He had only taken a few strides when Dianna came bounding toward him, her long, pale hair falling undone and whipping in the breeze. She was so beautiful, just like drawings he'd seen of the Sky Goddess, Madhea, flying through the clouds with soft flurries of snow trailing in her wake.

With wide eyes, Dianna looked up at him before peering behind his shoulder at her pinned brother. She gasped, both hands flying to her mouth.

At that moment, Markus's heart sank to his stomach.

"What have you done!" she cried.

Markus didn't deflect the small fist that crashed into his chest. But, gasping at the pain that seared through his lungs, he instantly regretted his decision. Her strike was powerful, even for a girl.

Dianna quickly skirted around him and rushed to her brother's side, pulling the blade free. "Are you hurt, Des?"

The boy said nothing, but only fell into her arms in a heap of sobs.

Eyes colder than a winter ice storm turned upon Markus. "Haven't you killed enough this day?" Dianna's voice broke into a shrill scream. "Now you must prey upon defenseless children?!"

Although he'd been sorely tested this night, nothing could bring him lower than the look of hatred in Dianna's eyes.

Markus threw his arms wide. "He pelted me with rocks!"

The child cried louder.

Judging by the mar on Dianna's brow and her deepening scowl, Markus knew he would not win against the child's false tantrum. He heaved a frustrated groan.

Clutching the child to her chest, Dianna's face reddened, her eyes shining with the gloss of unshed tears. "You should be ashamed!"

Markus hung his head, not knowing how to answer her retributions. Though he was not sorry for teaching the boy a lesson, he'd never intended to make Dianna cry. His heart had been broken enough times whenever he'd found his mother sobbing over Alec. He hated Father for making Mother cry, and now he hated himself.

"It is you who should be ashamed, foolish female, trolloping about the woods in men's trews!"

Markus cringed at the familiar, garbled slur of his father's baritone when in a drunken rage. Cursing, he turned to find that a mob of villagers had gathered around them, his father at the head, still clutching a tankard of ale as if it was his lifeline. The rowdy looking bunch reminded him of a pack of marauders, with a monster for the henchman.

Ice-cold fear pricked the hairs at the back of Markus's neck and threatened to splinter his brain. Swallowing the lump of granite that had formed at the bottom of his throat, he found the nerve to speak. "Father, please, this is my battle." He did not want Dianna to be the victim of his father's wrath.

Heedless of Markus's plea, Rowlen stepped past him, bridging the gap between Markus and Dianna. "This night is to honor my son and I'll not have you ruin it for him," he bellowed.

Many among the crowd voiced their agreement.

Markus stepped to the side of his father, so he could better view Dianna, mayhap defend her if needed. But what could he do against his father? He felt as helpless as a pebble trying to crush a glacier.

Dianna cupped her brother's chin and their gazes held for an eternal moment. The boy nodded, and they both rose, Dianna in front. Stance wide, arms crossed, she stood her ground in the most beautiful act of defiance Markus had ever witnessed.

Tilting her chin, malice shone in her eyes as she leveled her stare at Rowlen. "What care I for honoring your son? He has done nothing for me. I feed my own family."

"It is time you learned your place and left the hunting to the *real men*." Father ended on a deep, sinister chuckle.

Glancing toward Markus, he winked, before turning to the crowd and raising his tankard.

The men cheered. The women whistled.

Markus wanted to scream.

"Tell me then, do *real men* beat their afflicted children?" Though she spoke through clenched teeth, her strong voice carried far.

The townspeople behind him gasped and murmured amongst themselves.

Father choked on his drink, purging out a great deal through a roar. Markus's mind hollowed and he could not think clearly. He only knew that Dianna put herself in great peril by goading his father so.

She merely smiled, tilting her chin higher. "I know how you treat your eldest son. You, sir, are a monster, not a *real man*. And I will not honor 'The Mighty Hunter' who will grow to be just like you."

Her words came out on a hiss, searing the distance between them like arrows of fire, burning straight into his heart.

Though she spoke to Rowlen, her venom was meant for Markus. Did she truly think he would become like his father?

"You lying little shrew! I should tan your hide!" Father clutched his ale until his knuckles turned white. The veins on his neck swelled like raging rivers after the winter's thaw.

Shaking her head, Dianna laughed, clearly unaffected by his growing rage. "Perhaps you should, and save Alec from some of your cruelty."

Pointing into the crowd, Dianna moved forward, whipping past Rowlen before he could react. "See him there, cowering behind his mother. Ask him to pull down his cloak and then see if I'm lying."

"He will not." Father's voice cracked and rose in pitch. "He is unwell and needs his cloak to shield him from the night air."

She spun on her heel, shouting at Rowlen with clenched fists. "It would not hurt him to show his face, and well you know it!" In an instant, she'd turned back to the crowd, her spine rigid as she marched toward Mother and Alec.

He knew not how his feet propelled him, but Markus raced after her into the parting sea of spectators. Whatever she was trying to do, he had to stop her. No good would come to her if she exposed his father.

Mother, with Alec behind her, had both reacted as one, backing up several paces as Dianna advanced, but they were no match for her quick strides. Mother made a strangling, garbled cry, and turned to shield Alec in her arms.

"You must not do this," Markus pleaded, regretting the harsh tone in his voice, but he had to make Dianna understand the danger in crossing his father.

Behind him, Markus heard a bellow of rage, sounding like a warrior descending into battle. He turned to see several large men attempting to restrain Rowlen. A chill swept up Markus's spine at the demonic gleam in his father's eyes. The monster would have Dianna's blood for this.

Dianna's lips narrowed into a grim line, her eyes glowing with determination. With a firm, but gentle tug, she pulled Alec free of his mother's embrace. At the same time, his hood fell away for all to see. An eerie stillness fell about the place. For a moment, even Rowlen had gone quiet.

Silent tears streamed down Markus's face at the sight of his brother. Never before had Father beaten him so badly.

One dark, swollen eyelid would not open—sealed shut by some invisible, binding force. He wondered if his brother would ever see out of that eye again, such a massive bloody mess it was. The other eye was only partially visible, and Markus suspected it must be a burden for Alec to keep it open as a cut ran deep through his eyebrow and mid-way to his forehead.

How had Alec been able to attend the festival at all with such an injury?

Below Alec's eyes, his nose was encrusted in a hard coating of dark blood and one side of his lip was swollen to three times its normal size. Many black and purple splotches coated his pale face, making him look as if he'd been beaten by the plague.

As those around him gawked at his injuries, Alec hung his head. He did not speak and no emotion could be read in his grotesque features. Only a single tear swept down his nose and shattered in the hard grass at his feet.

Holding Alec's hand, Mother wept by his side. Markus stepped up to Alec, and with the gentleness of swaddling a new-born babe, he lifted the hood back over his brother's head, shrouding his features once again in darkness.

Soon the people began to whisper while some men grumbled, and many women gave way to tears.

Dianna did not cry. Fists planted at her sides and her stance wide, her icy gaze was on Rowlen.

Three men still held him, though he had stopped fighting to break free. Rowlen's eyes belied the vehemence of a thousand whipping ice storms. These men held him now, but they would not hold him always. What then? How long before Dianna suffered the monster's revenge? What could Markus do to prevent it?

After a long, tense moment, Dianna turned to the people, clearing her throat to speak. "I happened upon them at Danae Creek one eve while I was stalking a lone elk. This monster pounded into his sickly son while the poor boy begged for mercy. All the while 'The Mighty Hunter' cowered behind a tree like a frightened mouse."

Markus's heart plummeted. No wonder she scorned him. She knew him for a coward.

"You filthy bitch!" Father roared, his rage-infused face taking on the hue of an overripe apple. Markus thought he saw the branches of the lyme shake from the tremors of Father's fury.

Dianna dismissed his words with a flick of her wrist. "Needless to say, they spooked my prey." Turning her cold gaze back to Rowlen, she tilted her mouth in an impish grin. "You are lucky to be alive this night. I almost turned my arrow upon *you*."

What kind of foolish female was she? Had she a wish to join her parents in the afterlife?

"She lies!" But Father's words were said with less conviction.

The villagers shook their heads, their faces draped in heavy scowls. They were not convinced of Rowlen's innocence, either.

"My brother was with me and can bear witness." Dianna motioned to Desryn, who had come up through the crowd. He had managed to crawl between the villagers' legs to reach his sister while his mutt trailed behind him.

Stepping up beside her, Desryn inflated his chest and wagged a finger at Rowlen. "I saw it. I saw the whole thing."

"My son is sick," Father cried out beneath his sweat-drenched brow. "These bruises are part of his ailment. This shrew thinks to be a mighty huntress. She is merely jealous and wants to steal Markus's glory."

"Is that so?" Dianna turned her focus upon Markus. "Tell me, *Mighty Hunter*, do I seek to steal your glory this eve or is your father really a monster?"

Markus thought his legs would buckle under the weight of her stare. She was asking him to bring Father's wrath upon his head as well.

She was asking him to be brave.

The eyes of the village were upon him. What would they expect The Mighty Hunter to say? Did they want the truth? Did they want to know that the hero who had saved them from starvation had cowered behind a tree while his brother was brutally beaten?

What would Father do if Markus told the truth? Would he turn his heavy fists upon him now? Markus's throat went bone dry, and then constricted until his breath came in shallow gasps. His limbs, which had once felt as heavy as stone, now shook like the feeble branches of a fig tree. For the first time, he realized how his prey must have felt during that fatal second when they saw his arrow tunneling swiftly upon them.

All the while, the townspeople anxiously awaited his answer, their eyes wide.

"Tell them, son," the monster bellowed as he resumed his struggle against his captors. "Tell them I am a good father."

"You are no father to me!" Markus cried, before he barreled through the crowd and into the overgrowth of trees behind them.

He was not mighty. He was not brave. He was humiliated. He was terrified. But most of all, he was angry. Angry at Dianna for exposing him, angry at Father for hurting his brother, and angry at himself for the feeble coward he'd become.

# Chapter Three

A small campfire kindled beneath the heavy overhang of several towering pines. A lone hunter sat near the blaze, warming his fingers as the chill from the darkening sky seeped into his bones. Although he was far from his family's hut, this was where Markus felt most at home. The forest was his salvation; the place he could go to escape his father's dark moods. The quiet moments he spent by the fire after a successful hunt were his most cherished times. He could recount the day's hunt, remembering the adrenaline pumping through his veins just before he released his arrow, always striking true.

That night's hunt had been fruitful: an elk, a hawk and one pesky squirrel. The elk carcass hung on a nearby tree, blood dripping from the hollow cavity. Markus planned to harvest the choicest meats for his family. The hawk had been stripped, his breast roasted on a spit above the fire. The squirrel, however, served only to amuse Markus as he desired a guest to accompany him this dark night. The bushy-tailed animal sat across from him, his body propped up by a few small rocks, so he looked as if he was resting his bones beside the fire. Dried spatters of blood had emptied out of a hole in his chest.

Though he did not always eat the entire carcasses of the animals he harvested, Markus would usually make use of the parts he needed for the hunt – sinews to fasten a broadhead to the shaft of an arrow and for stringing his bow, feathers for fletching the veins upon his arrows, and leather to protect his fingers when releasing the string.

Markus liked to sit by the campfire and work with his tools. Tonight he was engrossed in flint-knapping stone, carving broadheads out of mere rocks. Sharp broadheads and a perfect aim were what made his arrows so deadly. He'd pour all of his energy into crafting one tip well into the dawn. To focus on this simple act of carving stone took all of his concentration, leaving no time for dark thoughts of his father.

He was particularly determined to drive any dispiriting thoughts from his mind, knowing that when he returned home at dawn he'd have to face Alec's pain, Mother's scorn, and Father's wrath. Mayhap it was because he was so engrossed in driving away his demons that Markus did not hear the footfall until the man was already behind him.

At the snapping of a twig, Markus leapt up from his log, knife in hand. He was met by the familiar, weathered eyes of the healer. Markus lowered his guard and sheathed his knife, having been used to visits from the old man on the many occasions that Alec was unable to rise from his bed.

Looking into the smiling face of Dafuar, Markus was reminded of a weathered map, as many tributaries were etched in his leathered features. Markus wondered the age of the healer whom some called a prophet. His father had told Markus that Dafuar had been there at his birth and foretold he would be a mighty hunter. Though none knew Dafuar's age, he was rumored to be as old as Ice Mountain. As a boy, Markus had always thought each line on Dafuar's face represented a year, but the healer would never sit long enough for him to count them all.

Now the white-haired man had come to him this night. Markus hoped Dafuar would sit with him by the fire and mayhap recount stories of old that would chase away the gnawing fear welling in his heart.

Dafuar's soft eyes held Markus's for a long moment before his gaze dropped to the fire, the sharp edges of his face cutting into a deep frown. Without waiting for an offer, the healer took a seat beside the squirrel, pulling up the hem of his robe and stretching his bony legs beside the fire. "This squirrel's offenses must have been great."

Markus gave pause, reflecting on the healer's words and actions. Simply being ancient did not give the healer the authority to judge Markus.

"I am a hunter. It is my job to kill animals," replied Markus, settling on a log opposite the old man.

Dafuar turned to the sitting squirrel with a grimace. "Do hunters not skin animals as well?"

Waving away the healer's words with a flick of the wrist, Markus could not shake his growing annoyance at the condescending tone in the old man's voice. "I am not in the mood for squirrel tonight."

The healer's bushy brows rose and he rubbed his pointed chin with a gnarled hand. "A hunter takes a life to feed himself and his people. If you do not eat what you kill, you are no hunter."

"I am the greatest hunter in all the land," Markus barked. "I have killed up to ten animals in one hunt."

Had Dafuar come to seek companionship or pass judgment? Markus had had enough aggravation for one day.

"I have not heard of so many deaths since the last plague." The dark stony depths of the healer's eyes seemed to pool over with the reflection of distant memories. "Perhaps that is what you are, a sickness of some kind."

Markus bit back a curse, his patience growing as taut as a newly strung bow. "I am no sickness, but I am growing ever sick of you, old man. Do you seek my fire for warmth or for foolish jests?"

Dafuar's eyes grew darker still, the lines around his mouth drawing into a grim line. Bending his crooked frame toward the fire, shades of the burning embers cast an eerie glow upon his face. "I seek your fire tonight to warn you."

Markus's heartbeat stilled as he choked out the question. "Warn me?"

"Aye." The healer nodded. "Of Madhea's great ice dragon."

Shaking his head, Markus considered the prophet's words. Ice dragon? Was the old man daft? Had his mind finally withered to dust? He thought mayhap Dafuar had sought to warn him of some new evil deed by his father, rather than feed him some silly tale of a mythical dragon. He had heard stories of an ice dragon from his brother. Alec had told Markus that Madhea imprisoned the dragon beneath an impenetrable tomb of ice. The last time Madhea released her monster was hundreds of years ago, when it destroyed an entire village for blaspheming the Goddess.

With widened eyes, Dafuar sat upright; his face seemed transfixed by a spell. "The dragon is called Lydra—a monster so fierce and foul, few men have seen her and lived to tell."

"Is that so?" Crossing his legs at the ankles, Markus folded his arms across his chest. "Tell me more of this Lydra."

The healer threw his arms wide. "More than twice the girth of a snow bear, she stands five men in height."

Chuckling beneath his breath, Markus could not contain a smile. Though the old man was irritating, he was amusing. "And does she breathe fire like a dragon?"

Dafuar's stare became blank, expressionless. "Not fire, ice, colder than the darkest winter storm." He raised a bony finger to the deep lines that cut channels into his left eye. "The fire is in here."

Markus's smirk widened. "Her eyes?"

"Aye, red and glowing like the molten depths of hell." The healer almost hissed the words, as though he was actually recalling the memory of a real ice dragon.

"I see." Markus decided to humor the healer and go along with the jest. "So, do you wish me to fell Lydra with my bow?"

Dafuar shook his head. "I'm afraid you cannot."

"You are mistaken," said Markus. Jutting out his chin, he thumped his chest with a fist. "There is no fowl or beast I cannot kill."

The healer cast his gaze heavenward before fixing Markus with a penetrating glare. "I am sure you are able to kill her, but you *cannot* kill her."

Shifting in his seat, his rising irritation infused his skull. This so-called prophet was too odd for his liking.

"Do not speak to me in riddles," Markus growled. "Speak plainly or warm your bones elsewhere."

Dafuar reacted by closing his eyes, mumbling what sounded like an incantation.

Was this some strange spell? Or had the healer come to him tonight to play tricks on him? Either way, Markus had had enough. Rising to his feet, he was going to make Dafuar leave by force.

He gasped as the old man's eyes shot open. Deep within his sunken orbs, Markus thought he saw red. Dafuar's incantations grew louder, until Markus could finally discern the lyrics of a poem.

"One fell shot from the bow
And many will know Madhea's curse has descended
Omens will fall to family
And all the cruel hunter has befriended
For each life he claims
His kin suffers the same death by similar strand

For she will allow no beast nor fowl
To be hunted by his hand
To the hunter who reaps his fill of kill
And nary none from need
Beware her beast who wakens to feast
On avarice and greed
Eyes that glow like burning coals
In the embers of demon's fury
Breath so cold, Lydra freezes the souls
Of any at her mercy
Sad is the tale that is known so well
The hunter who slaughtered with pleasure
His heartless crime was recompensed
For discarding the forest's treasure"

Once again the healer closed his eyes, and when they reopened he shook his head and blinked several times, acting as if he'd woken from a dream.

Markus remained standing, his feet like granite stones planted firmly on the ground. Fear had sent ice through his limbs and weighted his body to the spot. Had Dafuar really had some kind of vision? If the man's intentions were to spook him, he'd clearly succeeded.

With clenched fists, he spoke through gritted teeth, "Your parables are not amusing."

Dafuar's shoulders slumped, and he cast his gaze upon the logs of the fire. "I do not speak to amuse. Beware the hunter who kills for the sake of killing. The Goddess will unleash upon him a curse. For every animal he slaughters, one he cares for will die the same death."

"Nonsense!" Markus roared.

The prophet sighed. "She shall free Lydra, her great dragon, from her icy prison. The hunter will become the hunted. And, though The Mighty Hunter possesses the skill to pierce the solid scales of the dragon, if he fells the beast, the one he loves most will breathe his last breath."

Markus finally found the courage to move, marching up to the healer, bearing down upon him with a scowl. "It is a fool's tale you weave!"

"It is a fool who does not heed my warning," the healer responded, rising to his feet.

His elderly body seemed more fragile than when he'd approached the fire. Dafuar resembled the twisted root of a tree, fighting the confines of his worldly prison. With his features hung low, his aged eyes belied his sadness.

Turning a weak smile upon Markus, the healer placed bony fingers on his thick shoulder and patted once, before his hand fell to his side. "I thank you for the warmth of your fire, Mighty Hunter. These old bones have rested too long."

Without another word, Dafuar walked away slowly, rhythmically, as if marching to the drum of a funeral procession. Into the night he went, until his ancient form was shrouded in darkness.

# Chapter Four

"**D**amn that healer! Damn Father! Damn everyone!"
Following the direction of the wounded hare, Markus stomped through the tangled overgrowth of roots and leaves, chasing after the piercing screams of his victim.

Dawn had barely broken and only a few shards of light had pierced the dark canopy of tree branches. But Markus did not need the light. His hunter's eyes could see through a winter storm in the dead of night. Besides, the rabbit had left a thick trail of blood for him to follow.

Damn the stupid animal!

Markus dodged branches and hacked through bushes. How had the little beast managed to hop so far with his entrails lagging a foot's length behind him? He'd never aimed his arrow at the stomach before. How interesting it would be, he thought, to see how long it took an animal to die.

Too long.

Reminding himself to always aim for the lungs, Markus swore as overgrown vines and limbs swatted him in the face. Never had the forest vegetation seemed so thick. It was as if the trees had extended their limbs to prevent him from catching his prey. If the animal was not dead now, he would be soon enough.

As blood poured from its bulging entrails, the shrill screams of the hare weakened. Finally, Markus was upon him. The rabbit had dragged his body out into a clearing. Lying there on his back, one leg thumping against the cold ground, eyes wide, ears twitching, the cords of his entrails hung beside him in a pool of blood.

When the rabbit turned his gaze on Markus, the funny creature screamed louder than before. By the Goddess, the pitch was almost deafening. Shaking his head, Markus covered his ears, deciding to wait out the animal's death. Aye, shooting animals in the lungs was by far much easier and faster.

Markus needed to do this. Watching the beast suffer made his own problems seem much less significant. If the rabbit could endure the agony of death then he could face a beating from his father. Besides, he needed a way to vent his frustration—his rage. Dianna had scorned him and the whole town knew him for a coward. Though he knew he was more to blame than anyone for not standing up to Father, he couldn't exactly shoot himself in the stomach.

What better way to relieve vexation than killing a stupid rabbit?

"Markus, what have you done?" A voice behind him rasped.

Whipping around, Markus locked eyes with Alec.

Beneath bruised eyes, a swollen lower lip and several purple splotches on his face, Alec fixed Markus with a familiar scowl; the one he always used when he was about to lecture. Eyes narrowing, nostrils flaring, Alec's mouth set in a grim line.

All the while, the animal continued to scream.

Markus shifted on his feet under the pressure of his brother's glare. "I shot a rabbit. What does it look like I've done?"

"Brother, he suffers." Alec raised his palms, pleading. "Will you not put him out of his misery?"

Thinking of the arrows in his quiver, Markus did not want to bloody another newly polished broadhead. Looking over his shoulder, he spied a large rock near an overgrowth of bushes. Pulling it free from the dirt, he stepped up to the wounded rabbit and raised the rock above his head.

In one heavy blow, the animal's head was smashed.

The forest was quiet once more. Save for the shrieking in Markus's ears. Shaking his head, he struggled to clear the echo of the rabbit, which had seemed to penetrate his skull. After a long moment the screams stopped and he exhaled a sigh of relief.

He had heard many grunts and groans after felling an animal, but none like this. No kill had ever been so... strange.

The blood loss of the rabbit could have filled three buckets. And its endurance? It hopped through thick brush and tangled roots for several steps with its guts trailing behind.

What of its screams? Shrill and harsh, sounding almost like his mother the night she birthed a still-born child.

It was not like he felled a beast.

But like he felled a human.

Alec cleared his throat, pulling Markus from his reverie.

Markus looked into his brother's eyes, and was met with the same hardened glare. Why was he always so determined to judge?

"Do not look at me that way, Alec."

Placing a hand to his chest, Alec's breathing came in short gasps. "Who is this monster you've become?" He spoke on an exhale.

A sudden realization struck Markus. Was his brother feigning his illness like Dianna's brother had feigned injury last eve? Was he passing judgment, knowing Markus would take pity on his infirmity and bear his censure?

Not today.

Hunting was his calling, his gift. Markus should not be ashamed because the Goddess blessed him and cursed his brother. "I am no monster." Arms folded across his chest, Markus raised his chin. "I am a hunter. I've always been a hunter."

Alec shook his head, his widened eyes glossing over with pools of moisture. "A hunter need not be cruel." Alec ended with a wheezing cry, sounding as though he, too, had felt the rabbit's suffering.

Markus's confidence faltered and his gaze dropped to the ground. How was it that Alec always managed to shame him? "I did not mean to disembowel him."

"Your arrow always strikes true," Alec cried. "You could have ended his life swiftly."

Enough! The rage infused his skull once again. Why was Alec always determined to make him feel of less consequence than dirt? It was time Alec swallowed the same medicine.

"You've always been jealous of my skill, that I can feed an entire village while all you do is snivel and cough in your bed."

Alec's jaw dropped. Pain flashed in his eyes before he turned his back on Markus. "Jealous? No," he spoke on a hoarse whisper. "Disappointed? Aye. All that I have taught you was out of love, Markus, not jealousy."

"Damn it, brother!" Markus yelled, grabbing Alec by the shoulder and spinning him around. "Must you always be so good? Must you always pretend to be better than everyone around you? Now I see why our father strikes you!"

In an instant, Markus regretted his words.

Tears welled up in Alec's bruised eyes as his lower lip trembled. "I see your impulse to wound is no longer limited to hunting. The venom of your words struck my heart with more pain than any arrow."

Spinning on his heel, Alec marched down the shaded path to the hut.

Markus trailed after him, feeling like the whole world was sinking beneath his feet, the image of Alec's watery eyes etched in his mind. Why did he allow his anger toward Alec to spiral out of control?

"Alec, wait," he called at his brother's retreating back. "I did not mean it. I was only angry, is all."

Even through the coughing and wheezing, Alec did not slow his pace. "Do not try to take back your words now, Markus," he called over his shoulder.

But Markus refused to let up. He would hate himself for all eternity if his hasty words turned his brother from him. Alec was the only good thing he had left in this world, and he would not give him up without a fight.

Looking ahead, Markus saw that the path through the forest was almost at an end. They would soon reach the hut and he knew he would have to deal with his father, leaving him no time to settle things with his brother. In several long strides, he caught up with Alec.

Reaching out, Markus sought to turn his brother around and make him face him, listen to his apology and see the sincerity in his eyes. But he froze at the unmistakable sound of his mother's shrill scream, which sliced through the air with the explosive force of an ice glacier being crushed by a giant's fist. Alec stopped suddenly, glancing at Markus with wide, frightened eyes.

Their mother screamed again, this shrill more terrifying than the first. The brothers raced toward the hut.

That his mother was in agony, Markus had no doubt. What had happened? Had Father struck her? No, she would not have cried out with such force. Maimed her? Or mayhap she was under attack by a snow bear. A million possibilities raced through his mind as he bolted toward the sound of his mother, passing his brother with long, urgent strides.

As soon as Markus was out of the clearing, he drew out his boning knife, keenly looking around for some sign of his mother's attacker. A plume of gray rose up from the smoke hole in their hut. Since it was morn, Mother would be inside, preparing porridge to break their fast.

Crouching down, he crept swiftly, but silently, up to the hut and peered into a small, open window. His mother was on a cot, curled into the fetal position, and his father was standing over her.

Markus's heart leapt into his throat, every muscle in his body tensed, and his veins surged with ice-cold rage.

Monster!

This time, Markus had no second thoughts. No longer would he cower while Father abused the family. He slipped his quiver and bow to the ground, then clenched his knife and braced himself for battle. Thrusting open the door, he stormed into the hut, knowing that he would be placing himself in the pit of his father's wrath.

"What have you done to her?!"

Father spun around, red rage shining through his hooded eyes. "I did not touch her!" he bellowed.

He'd seen similar aggression in his father's eyes whenever he beat Alec, but never before had a look conveyed such anger as the one his father was giving him now. Gripping the knife tighter, Markus knew the weapon was his only lifeline. Though his legs felt as if they were about to give way, he would not stand down.

All the while, Mother cried out behind his father. Markus knew he could not go to her and render her the care she needed unless Rowlen stepped aside, or he forced him to. Markus braced himself for an attack.

At the sound of the door whooshing behind him, he knew Alec had entered the hut. He was only vaguely aware of his brother's thin shadow slipping past him and kneeling at Mother's cot.

Sneering, Rowlen turned to Alec and Mother. Markus held his place, knife at the ready in case his father unleashed his wrath upon his family again.

"Mother!" Alec cried. "What has happened?"

All color had drained from her already pale face, making her look as transparent as a sheet of ice during the spring thaw.

"The prophecy," she breathed.

"What prophecy?" Alec implored.

Removing her hand from her stomach, she wagged a shaky finger at Markus.

Alec cried out.

Father cursed.

Markus sucked in a gasp as his gaze was drawn to his mother's center, at the widening, crimson bullseye on her stomach, and to the blood dripping off her quivering arm and hand.

"Dafuar told me your brother would bring a curse upon our heads for his cruelty." Her hand dropped back to her stomach, cradling the wound there.

"What?" Alec choked on a sob. "When did he tell you this?"

She looked at him with glazed-over eyes. "On the eve of your brother's birth."

"Why did you not speak of this to me, woman?!" Father bellowed.

Mother did not pay him heed. Her gaze was locked with Alec's, and she lifted a limp hand to tenderly caress his cheek while offering him a weak smile. But in that smile, Markus read her true meaning, that she loved Alec, and only Alec, with every last breath in her body.

Her hand dropped, her eyes sinking into their sockets, while her mouth fell agape. She was gone.

Markus thought his ribs would crush from the weight of the stagnant air that smelled and tasted of his mother's bloody death—of his bloody curse. He knew now that the healer's words were true. He had killed his own mother and he feared the worst was yet to come.

"You fool! She was all the good I had in this world and now she's gone!"

Markus jerked as his brother advanced upon him, white hot rage shining through the depths of his blood-shot eyes.

Markus held out his hands, pleading through a constricted throat. "I didn't mean for this to happen."

"I warned you of your greed, of your brutality!" Alec backed Markus into a corner; his hands were fists at his sides, looking ready to tear Markus in two. "Now look at the monster you've become! You are no better than him!" Alec waved a hand at his father, casting him a heated glare through his tear-soaked face.

"Hold your tongue, you filthy maggot!" Father reached out with one long, powerful arm, and grabbed Alec by the front of his shirt. In the next instant, he dragged Alec out of the door and threw him in the dirt.

Markus was right behind, racing to Alec's side. Father rolled up his sleeves, scowling like a demon. "Move out of the way, Markus," he growled, while never shifting his hateful glare from Alec's face.

"Go ahead and kill me this time," Alec spat. "I've nothing to live for now."

Markus did not need to think twice about his next move. He rounded on his father, slamming a fist into his father's jaw with a primal roar.

Father staggered back, his eyes wide with bewilderment.

Markus attacked again, feeling his knuckle bones crack as his fist struck Father's nose. But his mind did not register pain. Only hate.

Covering his bloodied face with one beefy hand, Father moaned, staggering backward until he tripped on the threshold to the hut. He landed on his haunches with a thud, just inside the doorway.

But Markus was not finished. Stalking his father, he laughed bitterly at his retreating form. Father had scooted into a corner of their small hut and lay curled up on the floor beside the cot that held Mother's lifeless body.

"My brother is no maggot," Markus said through a clenched jaw. "He is brave and strong. You, old man, are the lowest, dirtiest filth I've ever known and if you ever strike him again I will kill you!"

Vaguely aware of the flood of tears that were cascading freely down his face, Markus paid them no heed. No longer would he hide his emotions because Father thought them unmanly. Turning, he climbed up the small ladder to the alcove above, which he and Alec had shared to sleep in each night. Grabbing his hunting satchel, which was nothing more than an oversized quiver, always kept ready with supplies and arrows, Markus hurried back down the ladder and out of the hut. Then, he spied his bow beside the door and slung it over his shoulder. He stuffed his new arrows into his satchel as well.

Alec was still lying in the dirt, weeping into his shirt sleeve. Markus's heart clenched and a new flood of tears constricted his throat with raw emotion. Alec did not deserve this. More than anything, Markus wanted to offer his brother a hand and tell him that everything would be alright.

But it wouldn't. Their mother was gone. Alec would never forgive him and Markus would never forgive himself. With one final look at his brother, Markus marched toward the forest. He had to make haste before he brought the dragon to Alec.

"Where are you going?"

Markus froze in his tracks at the sound of Alec's pleading voice. Turning back, he lowered his gaze to the dirt. "I have to leave."

"No, you don't," Alec cried, staggering to his feet. Wiping away a new wave of tears with the back of his shirt sleeve, he spoke with a shaky voice. "It was an accident, Markus. You did not know she would die."

A bitter-sweet sense of relief washed over Markus. He still had his brother's love. And though he did not deserve it, he would cradle that love in his heart for whatever time he had left in this world. It was comforting to know that when the dragon defeated him, at least one person would mourn his death.

But he did not want Alec to suffer his fate.

Looking into his brother's pain-stricken eyes, he swallowed down the lump in his throat. "There is another part to this curse, Alec. A beast will follow—Madhea's ice dragon, Lydra. She will hunt me, and if I kill her you will die next."

His brother held his feeble frame erect, clenching his fists by his sides. For a moment, he almost looked like a man; a strong man who could defend his brother. "Then I will kill Lydra for you."

A wave of fresh tears threatened the backs of Markus's eyes. He knew his brother would not survive a confrontation with a dragon. "You cannot draw back a bow, Alec."

Exhaling a groan, Alec cursed before coughing uncontrollably into his hand. Markus wanted to go after Alec and carry him to his bed while Mother prepared a potion. But she was gone now and each moment he wasted here brought the threat closer to his brother. It took all of his willpower to turn on his heel and continue back into the forest.

"Wait!" Alec called out between coughs. "Where will you go?"

Markus turned back to see Alec closing the distance between them. Alec's body trembled and swayed as he tried to hurry, making him look like a willow being whipped about in the breeze.

"I don't know," Markus sighed, knowing he needed to get away from his brother while wishing he could remain by his side. "Somewhere far, where the dragon cannot hurt you or the villagers."

Alec threw up his hands. "We must go to the old prophet and see if there's a way we can break the curse."

Shaking his head, Markus struggled to stay strong when all he wanted to do was fall into his brother's arms. "I am wasting time even as we speak. The monster will be upon us."

"Markus, look out!" Alec screamed, his eyes wide.

Ducking for cover, Markus instinctively rolled as he felt a heavy weight soar over him. Markus had thought it was the dragon, but his jaw dropped at the sight of his father sprawled out in the dirt. With amazing speed for a huge, drunk monster, Father regained his footing and came after Markus, a glint of metal flashing in his right hand.

Father was going to kill him. By the Goddess, he'd truly gone mad.

Backing up several paces, Markus reached for his blade, never removing his gaze from his father's crazed eyes.

"You ungrateful sack of cow dung!" his father roared. "I will kill you and your weakling brother for bringing shame upon the family!"

Feeling the weight of a wide pine behind his back, Markus knew he had no option but to defend himself. He gripped his blade firmly, readying himself for the attack. "Not if I kill you first!"

"Do you think to stop me?" Rowlen growled through a menacing chuckle. "I have heard the tale of this hunter's curse. If you kill me, your brother will die! The beast will not return to her tomb until you are dead. I must kill you, Markus, or we'll all be slaughtered!"

A war-like cry tore from Father's throat as he lunged, the blade in his hand poised and ready to strike Markus's heart.

Markus knew he ought to defend himself, shield himself from his father's attack, but his brain and limbs went numb, and he felt as helpless as a lamb before the slaughter. Then an odd thought struck him and he understood why all of those stupid animals stared at him with blank expressions just before he released his arrow.

Marveling at this thought, Markus was barely aware when his father sank face down into the dirt at his feet. Grunting once, Rowlen's body went limp. The long silver blade of Alec's boning knife protruded from his back.

"Markus? Are you alright?"

Coming to his senses, Markus saw Alec standing in front of him, clutching him by the shoulders. Had the weak, sickly Alec done this to their father?

"H-how did you...?" Markus stuttered.

"It was the only way." Tears pooled down Alec's bruised face, but he spoke with little emotion. "You cannot kill, brother."

Markus simply stared at Alec, in awe of the man he'd become. Markus, The Mighty Hunter, couldn't even defend himself, but his brother had saved him.

Without speaking, Markus embraced Alec. Silently he wept, and though he could've easily crushed his brother's bony frame, he felt Alec's strength surge through him. He marveled at the warmth filling his heart as Alec clutched his back tightly. He wondered if he'd ever have a chance to hold his brother again.

A deafening roar from overhead broke the moment.

Lydra!

Markus's stomach roiled as his legs nearly buckled beneath him.

Alec's battered features sprung to life. "Run, brother," he commanded, pushing Markus away from him. "I will summon the village hunters. We will find a way to stop this beast."

"And if you cannot?" Markus wiped the tears from his face with the back of his hand, knowing he probably wouldn't survive to see sunset.

"I never gave up hope on you. I ask that you do the same." Alec's jaw hardened, grim determination set in his pale eyes. "I will find a way."

In that moment, Markus knew Alec would do everything in his power to save him. Alec would be strong for him and he, too, must be strong in return.

Focusing on Alec's pale features, Markus called to memory a vision of his brother's smiling face before the bruises and cuts. He wanted to hold that picture dear in his heart, the final memory of the one he loved most.

"I love you, Alec," Markus spoke through a tightened chest.

Suddenly the forest stilled and a shadow swept above them. The temperature rapidly dropped, as if all of the warm air was being sucked into a giant abyss.

Alec gasped, looking upon Markus with a renewed urgency. "And I have always loved you. Be strong, brother, and please do not die! I could not take another breath knowing you were gone from this world. Go, now!"

Turning, Markus propelled his feet forward, running faster than he'd ever run before. Calling to memory all of the mistakes his prey had made when he bore down upon them, he would carry with him those lessons. The Mighty Hunter had now become the hunted, but he wouldn't give up without a fight. He would use every resource of his hunter's intuition to preserve himself without felling the beast. He had to find a way to survive, not for his own sake, but for the sake of his brother.

# Chapter Five

**M**arkus ran for his life, dodging the pine needles that rained down while deafened by the thunderous flapping of the beast's giant wings overhead. The roar of the beast as her underbelly scraped the tops of the pine trees rattled Markus's insides and filled his chest with a dread that shook him to the core.

And the icy chill that followed the beast!

Had he not been running, had his heart not been racing, Markus would have surely frozen to death. His teeth and extremities were already sore from the stiff cold permeating the air.

Still, Markus counted his good fortune—the forest was too dense for the monster to land.

Through the dim shards of light, Markus could make out a clearing up ahead. How long had he been running? He had no idea, but he could tell by the heaviness in his stride and the hollow growl in his stomach, that he was in need of nourishment and rest. Neither of which he would get for a long time. While running for his life, Markus had come to a realization. He now knew the only way to break the curse was to appeal to the Goddess herself and beg her forgiveness. But to reach her, he'd have to scale Ice Mountain.

Traversing a monolith of ice would be difficult enough, but impossible with a dragon in pursuit. He had to shoot Lydra. Markus would not survive the climb to the snow-capped peak if the beast could scoop him up like a hawk picking off a mouse.

The only way to survive would be to bring the monster to his level—fell the beast with a shot to the wing. He had already reasoned that injuring an animal would not bring on the curse, but if it did then perhaps Alec would only suffer a broken arm. Markus shuddered at the thought of hurting his brother, but he was left with no choice. He knew that if he was killed by the dragon, Alec would not survive the next winter alone.

Markus could now see the clearing. Pulling his bow and arrow free, he armed himself as he ran. Once the tree line broke, Lydra would be in plain view. Markus knew the beast flew swiftly. Many times during their long chase, he had almost been beaten to the ground by the rushing current from the dragon's flapping wings. He knew he would only have one shot at such a powerful monster. If he missed, his life would be over.

His heart beating wildly in time with each step, Markus's vision tunneled and he felt as if he were racing through a nightmare. Rushing out into the clearing, he stumbled and was almost knocked to the ground by the powerful beating of the beast's wings overhead. Turning swiftly, he fell backward on the ground at the sight - his first true glimpse of Lydra.

Great Goddess!

Her body was twice the size of a snow bear, with the wingspan of at least ten men. Icicles hung off her extended jowls and razor-sharp teeth. With a hide the hue of ice, the glinting sunlight reflected off her shimmery scales, creating blinding prisms of color. But it was the beast's eyes that horrified him the most—blood red and glowing, as if the fiery pits of hell burned in their depths.

Fighting back the urge to shield his eyes, Markus drew his bow. Just as Lydra reared back her head and a cloud of icy air rushed from her lungs, Markus released his arrow.

Always striking true.

Lydra howled with a blood-curling intensity that shook the ground. The monster's body dipped, and she struggled to remain airborne with her tattered wing. Watching in awe, Markus scurried back several paces, his mind numb from terror. He knew he should run, but fear and morbid curiosity rooted his body to the ground.

*Run you fool! What if she should fall on you!*

Markus cursed himself for his slow reaction, for acting the part of the witless animal, watching and waiting for the brutal hunter's strike. Only this was no ordinary hunter, but a dragon that could devour him in one gulp.

Jumping to his feet, Markus bolted, just as the beast fell to the ground with a thunderous clap. Almost losing his footing from the tremor, Markus turned his head to see the dragon rolling to one side, cradling her injured wing. He knew not where he gathered his courage or strength, but, turning his back on the beast, he ran toward the treacherous base of Ice Mountain where even more danger awaited.

But one question loomed above him, taunting him and frightening him, just like the powerful, frigid threat of the ice dragon—how would he earn Madhea's forgiveness?

MARKUS WAS SEVERAL hundred paces ahead of the dragon now. Just as he had hoped, Lydra had delayed her pursuit to nurse her injured right wing. At this point, Markus had reached the rocky base of Ice Mountain. Looking up at the towering precipice above him, he swore to himself when he realized he'd forgotten to bring his climbing boots and pick.

Not that they would have done much good. His father had rarely been sober enough to teach him how to climb, and his one attempt had ended in failure. But, how could he climb without the proper gear? Looking through his sack, the only useful item he could find was some rope. Straining his neck, Markus tried to see to the top of the mountain, but it was shrouded in cloud. How long would it take him to scale it?

Then a thought struck him. The town of Kicelin was half a day's hike along the base of the mountain. He could get supplies there and continue his journey. But, doing that would lead the dragon directly to the village. Weighing his options, Markus knew he had no choice. If he picked up his pace, he could place sufficient distance between himself and the dragon to be able to leave the village quickly, enough to divert the beast. It was the only way.

KICELIN LAY BELOW THE north face of Ice Mountain. An almost permanent gloom seemed to hover over the village, isolated as it was from the warmth of the sun by the long shadow cast by the great peak. Although the small hamlet was in sight, he knew it would take almost an hour to reach it. Traversing across boulders was tedious business—and treacherous.

The rocks were increasing in size, some the width of a full-grown boar. To make matters worse, many were slick with black ice, which had yet to thaw with the onset of spring. The ice blended so perfectly with the large blocks of granite that Markus had no idea which stone was friend or foe, so he had to tread on all of them with care. Not an easy task with a dragon in pursuit.

Markus had put nearly a thousand paces between himself and Lydra. Casting a furtive glance behind him, he spotted the monster in the distance, her glistening scales a sharp contrast to the rocky boulders at the base of the mountain. The dragon was obviously dependent on her wings for balance and was having a difficult time crossing the terrain.

Crouching forward, Lydra dragged her injured wing, stumbling over it as she walked. She kept her good wing tucked into her body. Every so often she'd stumble, crying out whenever she was forced to use both wings to steady herself.

Each time the dragon roared in pain, she shook the ground beneath Markus, forcing him to dodge avalanches of loose pebbles from above. His satchel had worked quite well as a shield until one errant pebble nicked him on the ear. The force of it nearly knocked him flat on his face, and he had to pause until the dizziness subsided. He marveled at the sharp and severe pain that could be caused by one tiny stone.

Markus wondered at the sagacity of his plan to climb Ice Mountain with the ever-looming threat of an avalanche. If one small piece of granite could cause so much harm, what would he do if he were caught under a powerful rush of ice and snow? But it was too late to back out of his plan now. At least until he thought of another.

The dragon's last stumble, coupled with Markus's steady headway, had lengthened the distance between them. Amazed at his speed, Markus would have grinned from ear to ear at this accomplishment in the past, but a dark depression had been settling in his heart the farther he traveled from home, and from Alec. He did his best to push away dispiriting thoughts, but his mind constantly wandered to that fateful shot into the rabbit's belly. If he hadn't been so foolish, if he had listened to the old prophet, his mother would be alive and the dragon would not be pursuing him.

Consumed with self-pity, Markus did not notice the large gap between two boulders until it swallowed his foot, and he came down heavily on his leg at the sudden shift. Wincing at the pain that coursed through his ankle, he was grimly reminded to heed the task at hand. Traversing these massive rocks was not easy, especially when he wasn't focusing on his surroundings.

Sitting on the edge of a boulder, Markus wrenched his foot out of the stone's grasp. Another spasm of pain shot through his foot and speared his calf.

Boar's Blood!

He could not afford an injury. Twisting his foot from side to side, he noted how the pain intensified when he bent it to the left. He would simply have to favor the right side and scale rocks with a bent foot. Biting his lower lip, he tried his best to block out the throbbing pain. It would do him no good to wallow in misery now. He was already miserable enough.

"Hey, ho!"

The voice startled him. Instinctively, he looked up while reaching for his boning knife. He swore under his breath. What good would a knife do him now he was cursed?

He breathed a sigh of relief as Zier, the dwarf trader, approached. A mountain of animal skins and other various goods dangled from a large pack atop his broad back. The stocky, red-bearded trader visited Markus's village frequently during the warmer season, trading pelts and just about anything else for fruits and grains.

Markus wondered how he had failed to notice Zier's approach earlier, and derided himself for losing focus once again.

"Put away your knife, boy hunter," the man chuckled. He thumped his chest. "It is only Zier!"

Markus could not help but feel annoyance at Zier's jubilant expression when his foot throbbed, and he was fatigued and famished. But the trader seemed oblivious to his suffering.

Reminding himself to reign in his temper, Markus fixed his gaze on Zier. "A hand up, please."

Holding out his hand, Zier's smile lit with amusement. "Twist your foot, son?"

"Aye," Markus grumbled, pulling himself up.

Zier did not pull, yet Markus knew his movements were restricted by being laden with so many goods. Zier's body always moved stiffly under so much weight, making him resemble an extension of his furs.

"These rocks can be tricky." Zier nodded at the dark crack from which Markus had dislodged his foot. "Many do not see the ice until they are flat on their backsides or worse."

"Aye," Markus muttered again as he scowled down at the dwarf, afraid to say more lest he berate the trader for his indifference.

Zier fixed him with a quizzical stare. "Why so few words?"

Exhaling, Markus rubbed a shaky hand across his sweat-drenched brow. Until this moment, he had not realized how much his limbs shook, but he felt the tremors in the marrow of his bones. Throwing a glance behind him, he swore, seeing how quickly Lydra was bridging the gap between them. "I must make haste."

"Why? What brings you so far this side of the mountain, boy?" As Zier spoke, his voice faltered as his gaze trailed to the spot where Markus had been staring. "Great Goddess!" he exclaimed. "What is that creature I see in the distance?"

"A dragon." Markus sighed.

Zier's eyes widened as he backed up with jerky movements, nearly stumbling on a rock behind him. "Let us move, boy. Methinks it pursues us."

"Nay, trader, she pursues me." Markus shook his head, still hardly believing his present fate. "I must be off."

"What has happened?" Zier's words rushed forth as if they were carried off by a great current of air. "Why does she pursue you?"

"Madhea's curse of the ice dragon," Markus groaned, feeling his insides churn as the truth of his plight settled in the pit of his stomach. "I've no time for more words."

He proceeded to limp toward the town of Kicelin, passing Zier who stood spellbound with one hand splayed across his chest.

Cursing under his breath, Markus bit back a sardonic laugh. He had thought to level his chances against the dragon by injuring its limb, but, once again, the monster was at an advantage.

"Do not tell me you go to Kicelin!" screamed Zier. "My daughters live there!" With quick movements, the trader had advanced upon Markus, grabbing hold of his elbow.

"I've no choice, trader!" Markus barked, while jerking his arm out of Zier's grasp. "I need supplies if I am to reach Madhea at the peak. I must beg for her forgiveness. It is the only way."

Feeling the strained crack in his voice, Markus broke off and lowered his head. His mind and soul were fraught with emotion, and he didn't trust himself to say more. An overwhelming sense of despair hovered over him, threatening to swallow him whole.

Having had such a difficult time traversing the boulders at the base of the mountain, how would he cross the ice? How could he hope to conquer Ice Mountain? Visions of Alec alone in the hut, suffering starvation and sickness, filled his heart with dread as he choked back a lump of bitter bile.

He had to climb the mountain. He must not fail.

Glancing back at the dragon, he was relieved to see that the beast had stopped to nurse her injured wing. Dipping her extended jowls into the crook of it, she licked her injury like a feline cleansing her paw. The beast made an eerie sight. As she buried her face beneath the translucent flap, the crimson glow from her ominous eyes shone through the curtain of icy membranes.

"What supplies do you need?" Zier had dropped his pack and was rummaging through a layer of furs. His face draped in a heavy scowl, he was scattering pots and hunting knives with erratic movements.

Markus had not realized the trader had acquired quite so many goods. "Ice picks and spikes for my shoes," Markus blurted, while mentally trying to recount what he and his father had used the one time they'd gone climbing. He shivered beneath his buckskin cloak as a cold wind blew from the north. "And a fur would be nice."

"Here! Take these and go!" said Zier, shoving an armful of supplies at Markus.

At that moment the ground shook and the dragon roared. The beast had slipped again.

"Shield yourself!" Markus yelled while pulling his sack over his head.

Zier ducked behind a large metallic disk. Alec had once told Markus about a great army from below that had passed through their mountain centuries ago. On their way to battle another army, they carried large, circular shields of metal, which they used to protect themselves from arrows. Markus thought such a disk could come in handy when being pelted with falling rocks.

The gravel hit them in a rush and there came the pinging sound of rocks deflecting off Zier's shield. As soon as the rocks stopped falling, Markus began to shove the supplies into his pack. He looked over at Zier, who was hastily repacking his own goods.

"What was that disk you used to cover yourself?"

"Nothing," Zier mumbled.

"Do not say nothing," Markus snapped. "It resembled a shield."

"Only a scrap of metal." Zier shrugged, his eyes widening as he glanced past Markus.

Markus did not want to look. He knew by Zier's expression that the dragon was advancing again.

"Then let me see it." Unable to keep the tension from his voice, Markus held out his hand.

Zier's features twisted as if his face was tying itself in a knot. "The shield is mine and not for trade." Zier pulled the disk to his chest like a child defending a toy.

The fine details on the copper-colored plate did not escape Markus's notice. It was etched with a strange looking, rotund fish, sprouting a stream of water. Markus knew the beautiful object was a prize to Zier, as it would be to any man, but he had greater need of it. If it could deflect rocks, mayhap it could deflect the dragon's icy breath.

Zier carefully wrapped the shield in a large pelt and draped it over his back. His lip turned down in a pout. Then he raised his chin and shot Markus a challenging glare.

Markus nodded. "Mayhap the village has a shield?"

Zier's entire face dropped. "No!" He scowled, and then swore, before slinging the disk off his back. "Here, take it!" he cried, shoving the shield toward Markus.

"Thank you, Zier."

Taking the shield in his hands, Markus was surprised by the weight of it. He was grateful at his advantage in size, for he had to hold the object with a heavy grip. "I shall return it to you when I'm finished."

Zier's face was ashen as he looked past Markus in the direction of the advancing dragon. "No! Stay away from Kicelin. I've heard tales of this curse. You will not bring Madhea's wrath upon our village."

Markus shook his head. Once he'd won Madhea's forgiveness, all danger would be gone. "But I must repay you when I return."

A deep, bitter laugh resonated from Zier's heavy chest. Casting woeful eyes upon Markus, he reached up and squeezed his shoulder with a thick, stubby hand. "You shall not return, lad."

Dropping his hand, the trader turned without another glance, hauling his heavy-laden body across the rocks with amazingly quick movements.

Markus's heart seemed to plummet with Zier's retreating steps. If it were not for the advance of the beast, he would have no more will to continue, but the ever-looming threat of the dragon pushed him onward and upward.

What new threats lie in wait for him once he scaled the north face of Ice Mountain?

# Chapter Six

Markus stood on the precipice of fate. The mighty glacier lie before him; an endless, unforgiving barrier of ice and snow, mixed with hidden pockets of deep crevasses, which could trap and suffocate the hapless wanderer who mistook one for stable ground. Almost as foreboding as Ice Mountain itself, the glacier stretched as far as the horizon and disappeared beyond the mist. An ocean of frozen ice, it divided Ice Mountain from other smaller, lesser peaks. None in his village had ever ventured to the other mountains, for to do that would involve either travelling a great distance across the glacier or scaling and crossing Ice Mountain.

For now, Markus only needed to traverse a small section of the glacier to get back on solid ground. From there he could begin the ascent of the mountain. If he was careful, he could cross over the corner of the glacier and get back to the mountain before the sun set.

*Look for animal tracks and walk in them.*

That was the one sage piece of advice that Father had offered him the one time he'd taken him to this spot, but Markus could not see any animal tracks now. Perhaps they'd heard the roars of the advancing beast and gone into hiding.

Casting a glance over his shoulder, he caught the prism of blinding colors reflecting the mid-day sun off Lydra's scales. Again, the monster was too close for his liking.

The only good to come of this was the stinging chill from the snow, which seeped through the hide of his leather boots and numbed almost all the pain of his injured ankle. He was able to walk on it again though awkwardly. But, how was he to scale the mountain with such boots? Why hadn't he thought to ask Zier for a spare pair? No use berating himself for his mistakes now. He was sure to make many more on the ascent.

With a tentative step onto the vast, frozen wasteland, Markus gingerly made his way across the ice, pick in hand in case he fell through a crevasse. Scaling ice was difficult enough without a monster in pursuit, but he felt comforted in the knowledge that the dragon would not possibly be able to sustain her weight on the ice. If the beast continued to pursue him, she would surely fall through and he would be spared her threat.

Markus smiled at the thought of Lydra plummeting into the abyss. He'd seen it happen once to a herd of elk that had chanced upon a lake during the first freeze of winter. A young hunter then, he had been stalking these animals one morn when they caught scent of him and rushed onto the frozen lake. Foolish they were to try to cross. They would have fared better facing down his arrow. In an instant, the elk all perished, sucked down through a break in the ice.

Walking gingerly, yet swiftly with numbing feet was proving a difficult task. Markus tried to stay on the higher ridges, avoiding the pits of sunk-in snow. Mayhap traversing the glacier with the thaw of winter was safer. After all, he could clearly see the sinking snow holes, which he knew to be crevasses. His walk became brisker, more confident. The dragon would not be able to maneuver this glacier with her large, clumsy body.

Casting another glance behind him, Markus almost stumbled over his own feet. He gazed in horror at Lydra sitting perched at the cusp of the glacier, blowing a long curtain of ice in front of her. With a deep intake of breath, the beast's chest ballooned before she blew out another stream of ice, frost dripping off her fangs with each hiss of air. She was making the path thicker and impenetrable.

She was building a bridge across the glacier! Looking up from her perch, Lydra leveled Markus with a crimson, sinister glare.

Swallowing a lump of fear, Markus struggled to breathe through his constricting lungs. This was no dumb animal. Nay, Markus was the fool. He had considered himself safe on this glacier, but he had proven himself to be no more intelligent than an elk.

Lydra did not try to traverse the ice bridge on clumsy legs—she used her belly instead. The shimmery scales that coated her distended stomach must have been smooth as well, for she slid seamlessly along the surface. When she reached the end of the bridge, she stopped herself with the tips of her long fangs and stood up before blowing yet another bridge of smooth ice across the glacier.

Turning, Markus picked up speed, knowing that with his weighted, frozen feet, he put himself at greater risk of falling through the ice. But he had no choice. The dragon would be upon him before he crossed to the mountain. With his quickened pace, he narrowly missed several crevasses. The dragon had come so close to him now that he could almost feel its frozen breath at his back.

Up ahead, Markus spotted what would either be his salvation or demise—a ditch in the ice so huge that no ice bridge blown across it could sustain Lydra's weight. Only now he wondered how he would be able to cross it himself.

Recalling the supplies in his sack, Markus thought of a plan. If he tied a rope to his pick, could he swing across? Running to a halt, he nearly fell into the wide fault in the ice. Though he'd seen the gully from a distance, he was not expecting the edge to be so sharp, so sudden.

Peering past his toes, which dangled dangerously at the precipice of the drop, Markus knew this was no gully. The glacier itself seemed to be cracked in two. Backing up, he let out a low whistle at the sight. The crevasse spanned the width of ten men, but it was its depth that made him gasp in awe. It appeared to have no bottom. A thought struck him that if Lydra were to fall into this hole, she would be trapped for a long time, mayhap forever.

Pulling the rope out of his sack, Markus secured it to his pick. Tightly gripping the other end of the rope, he tossed the pick across the crevasse, cursing when it lodged into its target, but failed to hold. A glance over his shoulder made him shudder—the dragon was closing the distance between them.

As quickly as he could, he pulled the dangling pick back up the ledge, swearing as it jammed in a pocket of ice. He jerked it through and swung again, this time aiming for a small rock protruding from the side of the wall. The rock dislodged and the pick tumbled down with it. Pulling it back yet again, Markus fought to calm his shaking limbs, but he was nearly out of time. The dragon was almost upon him—so close he could see the outline of each shimmery scale and read the malice in Lydra's eyes.

If the pick failed to hold this time, his life would be over. But the pick was too difficult to wield. If only it were an arrow...

Great Goddess!

With only moments to act on his new idea, Markus cut the rope free of the pick, which he threw into his satchel, and pulled his bow and arrow from its quiver. Seizing the rope, he tied it to the center of his arrow, and then tied the opposite end around his waist. Markus aimed at a thick ice slab on the top of the opposite ridge before pulling back the bowstring and releasing...

Always striking true.

His arrow made solid purchase with the ice. The dragon was so close upon him now that the air around him seemed to thicken with a stagnant chill. Looking behind him, Markus realized he was only a few paces away from the tip of the dragon's ice bridge. The beast was on her belly, jowls extended.

Markus's mouth fell agape at the awesome sight of the giant monster racing toward him. He wanted to flee, jump over the ledge and free himself from the beast's wrath, but his mind was transfixed by the demonic gleam in Lydra's blood-red eyes.

*Would she eat me or freeze me?*

Just as Lydra was upon him, he almost thought he heard a sinister chuckle resonate from the monster's chest. Only then did Markus find the will to jump. The dragon's icy breath whooshed swiftly behind him, and the sound of ice shards shattering in the air filled his head like sharp bursts of cold explosions.

As Markus's body slammed into the opposing wall of ice, the mighty dragon roared and then tumbled behind him. He heard a sickening thud as Lydra hit the bottom of the crevasse. Markus's brain rattled at the tremors caused by the heavy beast and the air around him exploded with a chill that swept through his bones. He covered his head as an onslaught of ice pellets rushed past him.

Once the ice had stopped, Markus breathed a sigh of relief as he peered down into the bottomless pit where the dragon had fallen. He could not see Lydra through the dark gloom, but he heard her cries of anguish. The monster was injured, and if she ever found her way free, she would be sure to seek revenge. Even more reason for Markus to reach the Goddess at the peak of Ice Mountain.

Grabbing hold of the rope, he planted his feet on the wall and began to haul himself out. Then came a thunderous crack! Louder and more ominous than the fury of a hundred winter storms, the sound filled his ears and reverberated through his skull.

Avalanche!

Instinctively, his eyes shot up, just in time to see the weight of nature's frozen fury crashing down upon him. He closed his eyes against the terror, while shards of ice and snow flew in his open mouth and crammed up his nose. Coughing and choking on the burning, bruising weight, Markus desperately clutched his rope, his lifeline, as he tried to press his body against the wall. It was useless.

The onslaught of snow and ice rushed over him, whipping his body against the crevasse wall. Markus felt crushed under the frigid weight; his head and neck ready to explode from the jarring pain. He was as helpless as a mouse being playfully tossed about in the clutches of a wolf.

Just as he thought his entire body would burst from the torrential torment, the rush abruptly ended. Coughing and choking on the melting ice, Markus purged a great deal out through heavy heaves of his burning lungs. Rubbing ice crystals off his stinging eyelids with the backs of his frozen fingers, he finally opened his eyes. Looking up, he was horrified to see that the ice-crusted rope holding him was frayed in several spots. At any moment the rope would snap.

*Thwack!*

A scream had barely escaped his lungs when he found himself landing on his own two feet. Disoriented and feeling like he weighed a thousand stones, he stumbled backward onto his buttocks.

Why did he feel so heavy? Peering over his shoulder, he recognized the problem. His shield was piled so full of snow that it lay flat, cutting against his satchel, with the frayed ropes holding it in place ready to snap in two. Shrugging off his pack and shield, Markus breathed a sigh of relief as he could move again with ease.

Perhaps his added weight had caused the rope holding him to fray. Looking up, Markus saw that the rope had ripped apart, but he'd only dropped a short distance. For a few moments he sat there, trying to adjust to the shock of what had just happened and make sense of his present situation.

Oddly, he couldn't remember anything. His mind simply went blank. Rubbing his brow with a shaky hand, the horrifying events of the day began tunneling back. The curse, his mother, the dragon!

With a sharp exhale of breath, he yelped, jumping to his feet, and immediately hissed at the pain that seared through his injured foot. The throbbing had returned. His hands, ribs and chest felt battered and bruised. While favoring his right leg, Markus turned in a full circle, scanning the horizon for the dragon.

Nothing!

The deep, dark ice crevasse and the monster were gone, buried under the weight of the avalanche. Markus exhaled a long, low cry of relief, releasing all of his pent-up fear and tension in one shaky breath. The monster was back where she belonged: imprisoned beneath the ice.

The heavy ice would not thaw until mid-spring at the earliest, leaving Markus to scale the mountain without threat from the dragon.

Hopefully.

But first, he had to find a way out of the gully. He was standing on a shallow pit, one he could easily scale if he had a proper rope. Markus wanted to scream at this new misfortune, but he feared the sound might trigger a fresh wave of brutal snow. He didn't know if he could survive another.

The distance to the top of the gully was about ten men in length. He could probably climb such a short distance with just his ice picks. But to scale a wall of ice without rope, he'd need to plant more weight on his feet. He was prepared do it if needed, but each step upward would be sheer misery with an injured foot.

With a hand shielding his brow from the rising sun, Markus scanned the horizon. The height of the walls surrounding the gully dipped as it curved and angled down toward the bottom of the glacier where it met the base of Ice Mountain. It was like a giant frozen river; a solid, wavy slide of ice and snow that was smooth, almost like the bridges the dragon had created to glide across. If only he, too, had a slick underbelly to slide down the gully.

Eyeing the shield lying at his feet, an odd thought crossed his mind. Picking up the disk, he shook off the snow and ran his numbing fingers across the surface. It was smoother than any stone broadhead and slicker than the crude sled his father had fashioned out of pine wood. For the first time that day, Markus smiled.

After beating ice crystals off his satchel and shield, Markus gnawed on his lower lip, contemplating how best to mount the shield. Sliding his arms into his satchel, he decided the best action was to lean back into the disk and push off with his hands. It appeared simple enough.

His bottom had just touched the smooth surface of the shield's inner wall when the ground slipped from beneath him. It was so spontaneous, he barely had time to lift his legs and clutch the sides of the shield.

He was off!

A gasp of shock ripped from his chest as he barreled down the winding serpent of ice. The disk flew down the gully, catching the air as it struck odd bumps along the ground. Markus would land each time with a sharp thud, and then spin twice or thrice before resuming his wild, rapid descent.

Despite the threat of avalanche, Markus could not control his screams of terror, fueled by the rush of adrenaline that pumped through his chest. Whips of wind sliced into his cracked lips and burned his forehead and cheekbones. From clutching the disk so tightly, his whitened knuckles mirrored his snowy fortress.

Sliding, slipping, spinning, Markus barreled toward the rocky bottom of the frozen river. Sucking in a huge gasp of air, he braced himself for the inevitable crash. The slick surface ended suddenly, and he was hurled onto the rocky terrain, bouncing and jarring in the shield until he came to an abrupt stop.

Markus had expected a violent ending—to be flipped and have his body ripped open when he was tossed against the jagged rocks. Laughter bubbled from his chest as he sat in his disk for a long moment, too stunned to move. He laughed until his sides hurt and tears streamed from his eyes. He knew not why his present fate was so funny, but it felt good to enjoy a moment of mirth before reality set in.

And it did, all too soon.

Some of the clouds surrounding the base of the mountain had dispersed. Craning his neck, Markus was able to see a great distance upward. He could not possibly survive such a climb.

With a heavy heart, he crawled out of his metal shell, rising to his shaky legs. Then he noticed his clothes were soaked through, his body chilled. He would have to find shelter to shield himself from the night air or he would surely freeze to death.

As if by a miracle, a crude hut appeared in the distance. Slinging his shield across his back, Markus limped toward the shelter. Hopefully, he would be able to build a fire inside for he would need dry clothes for tomorrow's climb.

MARKUS WHISPERED THANKS to Madhea after settling down in the shelter. He must have done something well this day to please her, for this hut seemed made for him. Then he remembered that Father had brought him here before they ascended the mountain.

"It was built especially for the fools who tried to scale Ice Mountain," Father had said.

The warm, dry hut was already supplied with a small bundle of firewood. He remembered that it had been stocked with wood the last time, and the following morning Father had sent him out to get more to leave behind when they left.

Even though he knew he must make haste, Markus would have to stock the hut with more wood before he left in the morning. He would not want another cold, wet climber to find a barren shelter. Wrapped in the fur that Zier had given him, Markus sat on a log inside the hut, stripped of all his clothes, and hung them above the fire. Hopefully, they'd be dry by morning. Another surprise awaited him inside the hut; one he knew must have been a gift from fate. Someone had left behind a rope. Though old and caked in dirt, it was solid and thick.

As Markus gnawed on strips of meat and drank from a small pot of water, he contemplated the day's events. Although he was trying his best to cast out the heavy gloom that had settled in his heart, he could not block out the painful memory of his mother's death. She had paid bitterly for Markus's foolish actions.

Perhaps the Goddess had taken pity on him. Had she saved him from the avalanche and crashing his shield? Mayhap she even provided the rope.

Markus could only pray that through his relentless fight for survival, he had somehow won her favor. He would need her guidance if he was to survive the climb to the peak.

# Chapter Seven

U nder the mystic glow of pale lights, Madhea sat on her ornate ice throne, looking down into the swirling mists. Try as she might, she could not summon forth an image of her dragon. Lydra was lost for now, trapped under the crush of heavy snow. The foolish beast had failed her.

Cursing, she slapped the vortex of spinning vapor, scattering wisps of clouds across the stones. Madhea was tired this night and her magic was draining, but she needed to know what had become of the boy. With one final attempt, she spun her hand around the circle of stones beneath her, calling forth her vision spell until a faint image of the boy hunter appeared.

He looked too much like his father, with coarse midnight hair and a thick, square jaw. Her wingtips twitched and hummed as her mind conjured up images of the one night she'd spent in the cradle of Rowlen's strong arms.

*Rowlen, why did you leave me?*

"Lydra is trapped, My Deity." Her servant, Jae, a beautiful girl with long coppery curls that fell just below her waist, stood at the threshold of the throne room, her feet obscured by a soft fog rising from the floor.

"Yes, I know about the dragon," Madhea answered flatly, as her wings drooped at her sides. Unable to mask her annoyance, Madhea waved away the servant with a flick of her wrist.

Jae stood grounded to the spot while she leveled Madhea with the direct gaze of her tapered amber eyes. The girl was bold. Her insolence would have to be dealt with—soon.

Madhea knew it was her beauty that made the servant so. She too had been that way once, when the allure of her ivory hair and vivid green eyes were matched by no woman. Madhea had been a youth then, though it seemed only a few winters ago. But, once her heart had been shattered into a thousand splintering ice crystals, her beauty died with it. Her death from within, from the plague that ate at her soul, crept outward, gnawing at her flesh until naught was left but the wrinkled skin of an old woman.

But Madhea had had her revenge—the curse she put upon Rowlen's heart before he descended. His young bride and sickly son did not know he would return a monster. Now that he was dead, the last remnants of Madhea's heart had withered to dust. But she would mourn silently. The Elementals need not gain another reason to doubt her powers.

"Do you wish me to release the pixies?" asked Jae, waving a hand toward the dark, deep void in the wall behind Madhea's throne. Upon hearing their names, an eruption of squeals began. Thousands of pixies, each no bigger than a child's fist, screamed from behind an iron grate for their release.

"No, girl." Madhea leered at her servant from beneath pale lashes and silenced the pixies with a wave of her hand.

Jae's eyes bulged. "My Goddess, please do not tell me you will waste *your* magic."

"Do you dare tell me what to do?" Rising, Madhea slammed her fists against the stones.

The girl worried for nothing, brainwashed by the Elementals of the ice coven. Madhea knew her magic was not waning. The ice was not melting. Her towering pillars of frozen crystallites had withstood over ten thousand winters and they would protect them for thousands more to come.

"Forgive me, My Goddess." Casting her gaze downward, Jae bit her lower lip.

Sighing, Madhea sank into the furs lining her throne. She was tired and needed rest. By morning, her magic would be revived. "Why should I release the pixies or use *my* magic?"

Narrowing her eyes, she looked down at the circle of stones as the boy's image faded away. "I give him no more than another day. The boy hunter will not survive *my* mountain."

"USELESS GLOVES!" MARKUS cursed as he tossed the soft doeskin leathers off the ledge, watching as they disappeared through the clouds and into the abyss. He had once admired them for their supple, smooth texture, and they had taken him nearly a fortnight to make. He remembered fondly how he sewed each stitch with care; something not easily done with large, clumsy fingers. But they were no good to him now.

The gloves had nearly cost him his life. The slick leather gave him no purchase when he was pulling himself up on an equally slick rope. Had it not been for the knot he'd tied at the end of it, he would've slid right off. Luckily, he'd been able to lower himself onto a ledge below, only banging his shin twice in the process.

The rope dangled now just above Markus's head. He would pull himself back up once he'd caught his breath. His body was already numbing to the pain inflicted on him by the mountain.

Cuts and bruises mattered little to him now. He had barely flinched when he'd crushed his knuckles with the blunt end of his ax. That had been just another foolish, clumsy mistake.

Markus had only started the climb this morn, so he knew he'd make many more errors of judgment. Exactly how far he'd scaled he knew not, for a low mist had settled on the mountain, blocking out the mid-day sun and obscuring his vision past an arm's length, making the climb more treacherous than before.

But he had to continue. Stopping only gave him time to think. His thoughts were turning much darker, much more dangerous than the climb. How easy it would be to jump over the ledge and end his life. No more curse, no more dragon, no more memories of Father. Besides, he wasn't man enough to scale a mountain. He would slip up again. Mayhap next time he wouldn't have a ledge to save him. How many more mistakes would he make before he lost his life?

Why not end it swiftly now?

How foolish he'd been to think he could ever reach Madhea. Biting back a sardonic laugh, his father's words reverberated through his skull: *Only fools scale mountains.*

This was what Father had told him three winters ago when he'd first asked for climbing lessons. Markus had wanted to learn, not for the glory and thrill of the climb, but because Mother had once told Alec that climbing had been Father's passion. Foolishly, Markus had thought if Father climbed again, it would lighten his mood and he would no longer beat Alec.

They'd spent the first day waiting out a blizzard, cramped in a crude shelter they'd dug in the snow. On the second day they made little headway, as Markus was barely a juvenile and had hardly enough strength to pound a pick through thick ice.

By the third day, they had been stalled by another blizzard. Father had drained the last of his brew, so it was time to descend. They'd made it home on the fifth day.

Alec had been spared Father's cruel beatings for five days. But, the monster more than made up for it later by taking his frustration with the mountain out on Alec. Markus then hated himself for suggesting the climb. Never again had he asked Father for lessons.

Now Markus was stuck on the side of a mountain with little skill and only crude essentials for climbing. A cold, relentless wind slapped his face, gnawing into his flesh like a wolf with a bone. Soon it would be nightfall and he would need to find a ledge wide enough to sleep on. Would the fur that Zier provided him be thick enough to ward off the night's chill?

A thought struck him that mayhap he had needed those gloves if for no other purpose than for added warmth while he slept.

*Damn! What else could go wrong this day?*

As if the mountain was answering his thoughts, Markus heard a sharp crack and his body shook. He was nearly thrown off his perch by the sudden tremor below him. The ledge was unstable.

Looking above his head to where the rope had been hanging, Markus cried out in desperation. It was now more than an arm's length away. The ledge was sliding!

Instinctively, he lunged for the side of the mountain, grabbing cracks in the ice without the aid of a pick or rope, or any lifeline. The brittle ice sliced through his bare hands as he clawed against the surface, trying desperately to pull himself toward the rope while the ledge crumbled beneath him.

'Twas no use.

The ice was too slick. Blood gushed from his fingers, spilling onto the wall as he slid awkwardly down the face. 'Twas only a matter of time before the ice purged him from the mountain. How far he would have to slide before landing he was uncertain, for he'd no idea of the distance he'd traveled. But he knew the drop would be far enough to crush his bones.

Then, as if stuck in a waking dream, Markus lost hold of the mountain, and he slipped into oblivion. He reached out, grasping at emptiness before the image of his brother's pale face flashed through his memory. With Alec's name on his lips, he cried out as the agony of his loss shot daggers of pain through his extremities. Death was certain.

Closing his eyes to the horror, he jarred against a hard surface and a sickening crack ricocheted through his skull. Then his world darkened.

DESYRN'S LIMBS TREMBLED as he watched the older boy's chest rise and fall in erratic waves. The only sounds in the cabin were the fluid rattle of the boy's strained breathing and the heavy beating of Desyrn's own heart. He still couldn't believe they were inside the monster's home, beside the darkened hearth of their sworn enemy, Rowlen Jägerrson, father of the boy hunter who brought on Madhea's curse.

Desryn, known simply as Des to his friends, and his sister had already found cruel Rowlen's corpse, lying face down in the dirt. Spotting the giant winged dragon flying over the forest, breaking trees apart with its massive talons as if they were mere twigs, they had suspected the boy hunter to have been killed as well.

When the two siblings came across a fresh gravesite with a wreath of flowers, they realized the mother had been killed by the curse, leaving the sick boy alone. It had been Des's idea to go inside and look for the boy, and after much pleading, his sister reluctantly agreed.

"Does he breathe?" Des whispered over his sister's cloaked shoulder, as he gawked at the boy's bloody and swollen arm.

Dianna placed a slender hand on the side of the injured boy's neck. "Aye, Des, but barely. I doubt he will survive the night."

"Unless you save him," Des begged. "We could bring him back to our hut while he recovers."

Though he could not make out his sister's features beneath her hood, Des could tell by the sudden stiffness in her shoulders that she was displeased with his idea.

"And when his arm is miraculously healed and he is no longer plagued with sickness, then what? I will be marked as a witch," she replied with a barely audible hiss.

"They will not know it was you."

Dianna turned to face Des and pulled down her cloak, revealing vivid, emerald eyes that shone even in the darkness, as if a fire blazed beneath their depths. She reached out and clasped his hands within her own. Even in the cool night air, Dianna's palms were always warm, as if she were impervious to the Elements.

Squeezing her brother's hands until warmth flooded his body, she replied, "I cannot take that risk. What if the villagers sacrifice me to Madhea? Who will look after you then?"

Des shook his head. "Almost everyone thinks the boy got sick because of his father's beatings. They will think his father's death is the reason why the boy healed."

Dianna chewed on her lip before casting an anxious glance at her brother. "But what if this boy betrays me? What if he says I used magic to heal him?"

Des's heart hammered in his chest at the thought. What would he do if the villagers sacrificed Dianna to the Goddess? They had worked so hard to conceal her secret. Would their act of kindness be met with betrayal and cruelty? No, he refused to believe this sick boy was anything less than kind. He had witnessed the compassion that the boy had bestowed upon his undeserving younger brother, the cruel hunter who butchered animals. Des knew in his heart that this boy would show himself and Dianna the same understanding.

Des turned up his chin and met his sister's direct gaze. "He will not betray you."

She arched a brow before casting Des another wary glance. "How can you be sure?"

"I just know, Dianna. Please, you cannot let him die."

# Chapter Eight

*People of the Ice*

Markus awoke to a chill that filled his lungs with each shallow intake of breath. Like a stale wind tickling his skin, the cold air encompassed him. Yet he was somehow comforted by an unfamiliar heat that had settled in the marrow of his bones, warming the empty ache in his chest and the hollow of his stomach. It was unlike any feeling he'd known before. Then he realized he must be dead.

Opening his eyes slowly, Markus's blurred vision could just make out the faint, warm glow of candlelight. A soft silhouette brushed past him. He struggled to raise himself on one elbow and follow the direction of the shadow. A girl had her back to him, and through his clouded gaze he could see she was stirring a pot of steaming liquid.

As the room came into focus, he thought that if he wasn't dead, he certainly must be dreaming. The girl's smooth arms, tinted a soft shade of blue, seemed to glow. Her hair fell in a shimmery cascade down her back, resembling a curtain of ice reflecting the light of the moon. Turning abruptly, her pale gaze found his.

Markus knew by the wild beating of his heart that he was not dead, for her beauty awakened him. The girl drifted toward him as though she was carried on the wind. Though her eyes were the shade of a clouded sky, a soft smile belied her kindness.

Markus felt no reason to fear this girl, but he could not overcome his shock. Her hair! He had thought his eyes were playing tricks on him, but now he was almost certain that it was in fact ice. Never before had he seen hair so pale as to be translucent.

Markus tried to sit up, but his head shook with a sudden wave of dizziness. Closing his eyes, his hand flew to his throbbing head and he winced at the pain. Feeling bandages there, he realized he must have been injured, and then he noticed another sensation. Why he had not noticed it before, he did not know, but his left arm throbbed. A dull, deep ache trailed from his wrist up to his shoulder. He tried to move it, to no avail. It was as if someone had placed a heavy weight upon him. But why?

"Do you know Ryne?" asked a smooth whisper.

Markus looked up to see the girl standing there, near enough for him to breathe in her crisp scent of cool spices.

"Leave the boy alone, Ura," echoed a strong voice from the other end of the room. "He is barely awake."

Markus's eyes widened. As the throbbing of his temple ebbed, his vision returned to normal. The girl stood close by, wringing her delicate hands as her lower lip trembled. One look into her wide, watery eyes and Markus knew she was on the verge of crying. A strange thought crossed his mind: would she cry ice, too?

A single tear slipped down her cheek, and Markus berated himself for his indifference.

Her voice shook as she whispered to him, "Have you seen my brother?"

The girl's compassion for her sibling struck a tender cord with Markus at the vague recollection of Alec's soft smile. It was odd how long ago it seemed since he had last held him.

A large man in a hooded cloak appeared and shooed Ura away. "Go now, girl. Let the boy rest."

As she rushed out of the room through a skin draped over the doorway, Markus noticed the strange texture of the walls—they looked like ice. By the Goddess, he had to be dead! Then Markus had the vague recollection of falling from a frozen ledge, but what had he been doing scaling a mountain?

*Madhea's Curse of the Ice Dragon!*

After bringing on the bloody curse, he had killed his mother and been forced from his beloved brother.

"Alec!" Markus cried.

"There is no Alec here, land dweller."

Land dweller? Markus looked into the man's hooded eyes, unable to read any expression beneath the shadow of his pale, fur cloak. Struggling again to sit, Markus managed by placing all of his weight onto his good arm. "Where am I?"

"You are safe," replied the man, gently patting his good arm. "I am Jon. My daughter and I will care for you."

Through the dim shadow shading the man's lips, Markus could make out a smile. Jon was unusually tall, towering over him like a pine, but Markus knew this man was kind. Odd how he could sense it, but he just knew. Just like the girl, Ura, Markus had no reason to fear Jon.

But why did he feel so safe, so strange? Surely, he had to have passed over to the afterworld? "I am not dead?" he blurted out while struggling to comprehend his surroundings.

"No, you're not." Jon's laughter was rich and deep, but not overpowering like the bark of his father. "You fell, but the break in your arm will mend. Don't you remember?"

Markus shook his head, murmuring "No," and instantly regretted the movement as a wave of dizziness overcame him. Moaning, he laid his head back against soft padding.

"Oh, yes," Jon chuckled, "you bumped your head, too. Don't worry, your memories will come back to you eventually. You will have ample time to think while your arm mends." Then his tone turned more somber. "I only hope that this Alec isn't out there looking for you."

"He couldn't be looking for me," Markus muttered.

Closing his eyes, he called to mind the image of his brother before their departure, remembering Alec's bruised face and frail body. His brother would not have the physical strength to come looking for him.

It was all for the best. Markus would not want Alec to risk his life on the mountain. He tried to block out the mental picture of Alec sitting alone in their hut, grieving for their dead mother with no one to console him. Markus's heart was weighted by a thousand stones; his carelessness had brought so much suffering upon his family.

When he reopened his eyes, Jon was still looming above him. The lines of his mouth turned down as he spoke. "Do not let your thoughts trouble you. You must rest now if you are to recover."

Thinking how nice it would be to rest his bruised bones in this soft bed, Markus almost accepted Jon's offer, but Lydra was still out there, somewhere.

As soon as the beast freed herself from the ice, she would hunt for him again. By staying in this place, Markus would endanger not only himself, but Jon and his daughter as well.

"I cannot stay," he replied.

"I'm afraid you have no choice." Jon nodded toward the arm that Markus cradled against his chest. "Your arm is broken. You cannot climb."

"But, I bring grave danger to you and your daughter." Markus regretted the words even as he spoke them. He did not want to lose his shelter, but his foolishness had already cost him his mother's life. He would not be responsible for any more deaths, save his own.

Jon sat down in a chair beside Markus and rested a strong hand on his shoulder. "What danger do you speak of, land dweller?"

Markus's gaze shifted to the weight of the stranger's hand. It was such a simple gesture, so why did the man's touch feel so foreign to him?

Markus turned his head away, unable to make eye contact with the man who was touching him so closely. He knew the gentle pressure of Jon's hand was nothing to be ashamed of, but he couldn't escape the feeling that it wasn't manly to accept his affection. Markus had only shared this kind of closeness with Alec, and only when Father was not looking.

Clearing his throat, Markus kept his stare transfixed on the shimmery wall beside his bed. "Madhea's ice dragon," he replied. "When she frees herself from the avalanche, she will come for me. I must reach Madhea before the dragon awakens."

Jon laughed through a groan. "You seek the Ice Witch?"

Turning abruptly, Markus looked at the man's hooded form. Through the shift in the shadows shrouding Jon's face, he could make out the glimmer of pale eyes beneath the cloak. Who was this man and why had he called Madhea a witch?

"Ice Witch?" Markus vehemently shook his head. "No, I seek the Goddess."

"Then the witch has you fooled. Madhea is no goddess."

Markus's veins ran cold, for he knew Madhea was to be respected and feared. Jon risked danger by blaspheming her. "Do not speak so. Do you wish her to bring a curse upon your head?"

Laughing heartily, Jon pulled down the hood of his cloak, revealing the same pale blue skin and transparent hair as Ura. Even more startling were his eyes, which were of the brightest azure, shining like iridescent ice crystals and illuminating the deep lines around his eye sockets.

"I am an ice dweller," he spoke through a smile. "Her magic cannot harm me."

Unable to contain his amazement, Markus's jaw slackened as his mind struggled to make sense of the sight before him. As a child, Alec had amused him with stories of the Ice People, but he thought them only fables.

"Her magic cannot harm you?" Markus barely breathed the words.

"No, boy," Jon shrugged, "as long as I dwell within the ice, she cannot turn my home against me."

"I don't understand."

"The witch uses the energy from the ice to draw forth her magical strength. Just as the ice can harvest magic, it can also repel it."

Holding open his arms, Jon pointed all around them. "As long as we live within the fortitude of these walls, she cannot harm us."

"Ice walls?" Shaking his head, Markus focused more clearly on his surroundings. The walls did look solid and had a most unusual glow. Indeed, they were made of ice! "I must have bumped my head hard on that fall," he mumbled to himself.

Jon's pale brows rose. "Have you never heard of the Ice People?"

"Aye." Markus shrugged. "But those stories were only fables."

"No, my boy," said Jon, looking at Markus with a glow in his eyes and mirth in his smile, "you have fallen into Ice Kingdom."

THE GIRL WORKED QUIETLY around him, mayhap thinking he had gone back to sleep. But how could he? It was impossible to sleep when he had so many unanswered questions.

Ice People? He had thought them only a fantasy, but now he found himself dwelling in a kingdom made of ice. Markus had so many questions to ask Jon, but the kind stranger had left, insisting he rest.

Watching the girl through cracked eyelids, he considered these people who dwelled beneath the ice. So far, they were kind and Ura was exceptionally pretty, even more so than Dianna. Ura wore a belted tunic and breeches made of ivory fur, so she looked as if she was draped in the pure crystals of winter's first snow. Unlike Dianna, she had an air of femininity in her walk and manners. Odd how he had difficulty recalling the memory of Dianna's fair face now.

But there was one image he would never forget, no matter how hard he tried to purge it from his mind; that of his father's twisted features the moment when Alec's blade pierced his back.

How long it would take his arm to mend, Markus knew not, but he would surely go insane if he was left with naught to do but dwell on his father. That man had been a curse. For as long as he could remember, Markus had wished his father dead. Now he felt no remorse for his passing, only hatred.

Hatred toward his father for the life of abuse he inflicted on Alec and hatred toward himself for waiting almost sixteen years to stand up to the monster. What good had it done him in the end? It was Alec who'd saved both of their lives. His feeble brother had always bested him in intelligence and now he was stronger, too. What use was he to his brother now? It had taken less than a day for the mountain to defeat Markus. How could he reach the Goddess with a broken arm? Who would hunt for Alec while he was away?

"Your thoughts trouble you."

Ura's soft whisper pulled Markus from his dark reverie. In the next moment, he opened his eyes, only to be lost in her silvery gaze and pale skin. She resembled a beautiful flower in full bloom, preserved beneath a sheen of ice.

Markus could not help but smile. "How did you know I was awake?"

Seating herself in the seat beside Markus's bed, she flashed a sideways grin. "I could see movement beneath your eyelids."

He pulled himself up until his back was resting against the soft furs padding the frame of his bed. "Sleep eludes me when I have so many unanswered questions."

Toying with her fingers, Ura batted pale lashes. "Yes, and I have one for you."

"Ask me anything," he breathed, but Markus was only vaguely aware of what he said, so spellbound was he by her graceful movements. Never before had he met a girl like Ura.

"Have you seen Ryne?" Her question ended on a sob. The girl turned her gaze down while fisting her hands in her lap.

Markus's chest tightened, feeling Ura's loss as deeply as his own. He remembered that Ryne was her brother. "I do not know. What does he look like?"

"He looks like me, only he is a boy." She paused, rolling her eyes while gnawing on her lower lip. "I mean a man, a young man."

Markus wondered why Ryne would venture above the ice if Jon had said they were only safe from Madhea's wrath within these frozen walls.

"Where did he go?" he asked.

Ura's gaze shot upward. "Above the surface, mayhap to your village," she replied, the sadness in her eyes casting a shadow over her soft smile.

"I'm sorry, Ura. I have not seen him."

Although his fingers were still sore, laced as they were with cuts and bruises from the climb, Markus reached out and gently squeezed the girl's hand.

Ura made no effort to pull away, but rather turned her palm upward and clasped her slender fingers in his. "Are you sure?" she asked, blinking back glossy tears.

Markus was lost in a vortex of emotions. The haunting sorrow reflected in the pools of her eyes was proof that Ura longed for her brother. Markus understood her pain and knew her love for Ryne was strong. He wished he could climb from his bed and hold Ura to soothe her anguish; not only out of empathy for her sorrow, but because thoughts of holding her close made Markus's heart pound in erratic need.

Choking back the surge of emotion that welled inside his chest, Markus tightened his grip on her small hand. "Surely I would remember him if I had."

"Yes." She nodded, before pulling away. Abruptly rising, she turned her back to him.

After they'd broken contact, Markus's chest felt suddenly hollow and devoid of love. What influence did Ura have over him that her touch would cause him to go mad with emotion in an instant?

His gaze traced the lines of his empty palm and he curled his tattered fingers inward until his hand made a fist. He tried to recapture the warmth he'd felt from her touch, but he didn't feel anything. Had she used some kind of magic?

Mayhap he'd just bumped his head too hard on that fall and this was all just in his imagination.

Sitting back down, Ura wiped her eyes with the backs of her hands. "Now it is your turn to ask me questions."

Shifting in his bed, Markus struggled with what to ask her first. He decided the best route was to start at the beginning.

"How did I get here? I mean, when I fell, what happened?"

Blinking once, she tilted her head. "Do you not remember?"

"I only recall falling and hitting something hard." The dull throb in his skull was a constant reminder of that.

Exhaling, she brushed slender fingers across her pale brow. "You fell through a thinning ice shield and landed on a dragon's tooth."

Markus wondered at these strange words. His father had not mentioned them on their climb. "Ice shield, dragon's tooth? I don't like the sound of that."

Covering her mouth, Ura muffled a short burst of laughter. "I will explain about dragon teeth first. Rising from the floors of our kingdom are giant, jagged columns of ice, or dragon teeth. Those are what we scale to reach the ice ceilings."

Her voice turned more somber. "You were fortunate in landing on the tallest tooth in Ice Kingdom—and the widest. It was why you were not impaled on *that* tip, which is nearly two men in width."

"Aye," Markus nodded, feeling a sickening sensation in his gut at the thought of his lifeless body falling on top of a giant, spiky tooth.

Her gaze turned heavenward. "The ice shields protect our kingdom from the heat of the sun and the magic of the Ice Witch." Glancing suddenly downward, Ura's jaw tensed and she began to twist the hem of her pale gown with her fingers.

Markus read fear in her movements. "If the shields are thinning, how are you protected from Madhea?" he asked.

Her head jerked and something akin to fire shone in her pale eyes. "We have climbers assigned to repair the ice."

Sensing that Ura was sensitive to any criticism of her home, Markus thought it best to cease his questioning, but if they were not safe from Madhea, he had to know. "So, this ice through which I fell had not been repaired?"

"Not yet," she spoke through a thinning smile.

Clearing his throat, Markus prepared his next question. He would not be daunted; he had to know. "What if the ice is not repaired in time? Can Madhea harm us with her magic?"

Ura threw up her hands. "Why do you ask so many questions about our ice?" She leveled him with a heated gaze that would melt the thickest glacier.

"I'm sorry."

Markus had pushed Ura too far. He had not meant to upset her, but he did not wish to live in denial. If the ice was not impenetrable, he would be putting all their lives in danger by staying.

Standing, Ura turned from him, her back rigid and fists clenched. "Some say it is growing unstable," she said toward the wall in a strong whisper. "That is why Ryne left. The debates have caused much dissension in our kingdom."

Markus swallowed. What if Ice Kingdom was not the strong fortress that Jon described? "And, what of your thoughts, Ura?"

Spinning on her heel, she strode back to his bed, flashing him a warning glare. Gone was sweet Ura. Harsh lines had replaced soft features. She was no longer a girl, but a woman torn.

"My thoughts are that you must not speak of it again," she spat. "The hour is late. I must finish Father's supper, land dweller."

Turning away, she marched across the room with rigid steps and lifted the flap to leave.

"My name is Markus, Ura," he called, refusing to let their talk end with enmity between them. He knew not how it had happened so quickly, but he needed this girl's friendship. He did not wish to lose it.

Exhaling a deep groan, Ura turned, brushing a palm across her forehead. "You must get some rest, Markus." A slight smile lifted the corner of her mouth. "I will bring your broth soon."

$$\times$$

"WAKE UP, MARKUS."

Her breath was a brisk rush of air on his cheek. Markus wanted to stay tucked beneath the warm furs, breathing in the spicy scent of her; feeling the cool aura of her lithe form beside his bed. He knew he could not pretend to be asleep for long, tempting as it was to fake slumber while the icy-haired beauty kept vigil by his side.

Reluctantly, Markus opened his eyes, blinking slowly as his vision adjusted to the pale light. "I am awake."

"I know," said Ura, flashing a sideways grin. "It is time you ate."

She sat down on a narrow chair beside him. Her long, sheer tendrils were pulled back in a knot at the nape of her neck. Markus wished she would let her hair down, so he could better view the pale sheen of her locks.

Ura held an ivory colored slab on her lap. It was the same size as the wooden tray his mother had used when she needed to carry Alec's medicines and broth to his bed. Ura picked up a pale-colored bowl off the slab and blew on its rising vapors.

Markus's senses were accosted by a strange odor that was pungent, yet sweet, and his gut reacted swiftly; rumbling and pounding against a hollow drum. Despite the odd smell of the broth, Markus knew he must eat. Licking his lips, he pulled himself into a sitting position.

Wincing at the dull pain that settled in the back of his skull, Markus slowly lifted his good hand to feel the tender spot and was struck by a wave of dizziness. A hard knot, about the size of a robin's egg, was the source of his misery. Grimacing, he pulled his hand away, realizing he would not be able to rise from his bed with such an injury.

Ura leaned toward him with the bowl in her hand, scooping up the liquid with an ivory-colored spoon. It was then that Markus was able to peer into the bowl.

Green slime! His need for food was replaced by the urge to vomit.

"What is that?"

"Broth." She smiled serenely, unaffected by the long trail of snot dangling from the hovering spoon. "You will like it."

Markus knew not what possessed him—mayhap it was the softness in her eyes when she smiled or that he was just a bloody fool—but he opened his mouth and let her feed him.

He gagged the moment a slimy tendril slid down the back of his throat. Like swallowing the entrails of a squashed slug! The taste was even fouler than the feel of it; a sickly-sweet blend of rotten eggs and fermented wine.

"Blah!" he gasped, reaching for the goblet on the slab. He drank until the water was drained, though he could not drink enough to purge the terrible taste from his mouth. "That is horrible!"

"What?" Ura's pale eyes darkened as she jutted the bowl just below his chin, nearly sloshing the contents on his chest. "How dare you insult my food!"

"I'm sorry, but I cannot stomach this slime." Grasping her slender wrist, Markus eased Ura and the offending broth away.

"You must eat if you want to get better." Her pale gaze was steady, unrelenting.

"If I eat this, I may get worse," Markus said, and involuntarily belched, nearly choking on the fumes of his bitter breath. "Have you no venison or hare?"

Her lips turned into a pout, Ura's gaze fell on the bowl of steaming liquid that she placed on the slab. "I've not heard of those plants."

"Not plants," he said, shaking his head, "meat."

"Meat?" With one slender brow arched, the girl looked at him with a quizzical expression.

"Aye." Markus nodded. "From animals."

"Oh!" Her lips formed a perfect ellipse as her eyes flashed with recognition. "We are out. Father and some others have gone to catch lazy-eyed serpents. They will return on the morrow."

He shuddered at the image of slurping down slimy, cross-eyed snakes. "Lazy-eyed serpents?"

Ura nodded, while setting down the slab on a nearby stool. "They are good, soft and sweet."

Markus repressed a grimace. How could these Ice People stomach such foul fare—food that did not even require chewing? "Do you have nothing tough and leathery?"

"Leathery?" Blinking once, Ura tilted her head, her pale lips turned down. "I don't understand."

Groaning, Markus coursed a hand through his hair, clenching a fistful at the roots. How could he make the girl understand what real food should taste like? Then an idea struck him: he had packed some dried meat for his journey. Though not as good as the fresh-salted leg of a roasted boar, surely anything was better than booger broth.

"Did my satchel survive the fall?" he asked.

"You mean the heavy brown bladder you wore on your back?"

Markus repressed a laugh. It was not a bladder, but made from the fine skin of a large buck he had shot the previous winter.

"Aye," he answered, in no mood to teach Ura the difference between bladders and buckskins. "Would you fetch it here?"

Ura walked to the foot of Markus's bed and lifted a thick white fur, revealing a large, snow-colored box. Markus could tell by the intricate carvings on the top that it was a chest of some kind, but how odd the color and smooth-looking texture, just like the slab and bowl. Perhaps it was made of a pale rock that only formed underground.

Ura pulled out his satchel and handed it to him. Markus relished the feel of the bag in his hand. He was relieved to see it had survived the fall. Opening it was trying work with one good arm, but he managed to loosen the strings and find what he needed - meat! His mouth watered as he shook the dried venison from the folded parchment. The bundle fell into his lap and he scooped up a large piece, eagerly biting off the end.

"Mmm, real food," he sighed as he chewed. "Here, taste this." He offered Ura the sawed-off end of his dinner.

Making a face and wrinkling her nose, she took the venison with the tips of her fingers. Turning the meat in her palm, she examined it with a scowl, as if searching for some unforeseen poison. Finally, she ripped off a small piece, placed it on the tip of her tongue and closed her mouth.

Markus watched the movement in her jaw and slender throat while waiting for her reaction.

"Ugh! This is horrid," she said, wiping the offending residue off her tongue.

Markus wondered if she had even tasted his offering. "Have you gone mad?" he asked, trying not to laugh at her comical face.

Ura grabbed a goblet of water and took several gulps. "Those spicy sticks will not make you well." She wiped her mouth with the back of her hand. "Eat your dragon weed!"

"Dragon weed?" Markus chuckled. "Is that what you call that snot?"

Hands on hips, the girl scowled at him. "You are a very ungrateful, insulting man."

A rush of heat swept through Markus and settled in his face, causing him to turn his gaze down. She had called him a man. Aye, yet he was anything but. A real man protected those he loved.

"I am not a man, Ura."

"Oh, you look a man to me."

The burning in his face intensified. Was she in earnest or was she mocking him? Had she seen through his ruse and known him for a coward? Or had she truly been fooled by his size?

Markus swallowed back a knot in his throat. "I am not quite sixteen winters." He spoke with little conviction. He knew age was not all that mattered. Alec had once told him the mark of a man was in the strength of his heart.

Markus chanced to gaze at Ura's pale features. She was eyeing him through slitted eyes, her slender arms folded across her chest.

"Well then," Ura replied, flashing a complacent smile, "since I am a year your elder, I say you must eat your dragon weed." Picking up the bowl, she held it beneath his nose.

At once, Markus was annoyed. Was this just a game to her? Had she not seen how her words troubled him?

"If you like it so much, you eat it!"

What happened next was truly by accident. Markus pushed the bowl away without thought or realization of his own strength.

Ura screamed as she lost her grip on the bowl and it toppled over the bed, splattering goo all over the shimmery wall and floor.

"Oh, look what you've done!"

The lump in Markus's throat fell to his stomach with a thud. How could he have acted this way? "I didn't mean to spill it."

Ura's gaze swept across the slop. "You've made a mess everywhere!"

"I'm sorry, Ura."

Growling, she bent over the spill and scooped the slime into the bowl with a cupped palm. "It is not easy cleaning dragon weed off of ice."

Markus tossed the meat into his satchel and pushed the furs off his legs, heedless of his throbbing skull. "Let me help you."

"No! You must rest!" She stood up and pointed a pale finger, silently commanding him to stay in bed. "Eat your meat and leave me to this."

But Markus no longer had the stomach for food, so angry was he with his own foolishness. He had made a mess of things with his brutish strength and, even worse, he'd upset Ura.

Markus wondered if he was to live his life acting on anger without thinking, striking out without a care for others. Was he destined to become like his father?

# Chapter Nine

U ra sat cross-legged on warm furs while adding shards of ice to the cooking pot. The chamber where she prepared the family meals was small. Thick pelts padded the ice walls around her, offering warmth and comfort. But, tonight she did not feel comforted and the cooking chamber seemed even more cramped than before. Thoughts troubled her, from which she had no means of escape.

Silently, she leaned over the pot of herbs and added another stick of jagged ice. It melted, but ever so slowly. She focused again on the pale warming stone beneath the pot, willing it to heat her brew. The stone turned the hue of amber and then all color faded.

Ura bit her lip, silently swearing. She had lost her focus — again. All thoughts trailed back to that foolish brute from above. When last she checked, he was asleep, and Ura hoped he would not wake until Father returned. Was he boy or man? She only knew that no one had ever affected her this way. No one had ever made her pulse jump with just one touch.

How could this land dweller, nearly the size of a snow bear, with eyes and hair blacker than the murky depths of Mystic Lake, move her in this way? She was not meant for this man-boy. She was not meant for anyone.

Ura had seen her destiny and love had no part in the horrible fate that awaited her.

"Where is your land dweller?"

Ura's head spun. How dare Bane sneak up behind her while she was unaware!

Bane's thin smile was cocked to one side. Folding long, lean arms defiantly across a narrow chest, he rested a bony shoulder against the wall. His small, round eyes, sunk in deep sockets, reminded Ura of a serpent's cold stare. But his hair was what had always unnerved her—pale, like the hair of any ice

**80**

dweller, with the exception of a thin, rust-colored line, which began at his left temple and ended at his nape.

Ura had never grown accustomed to the look of him or his aggressive temperament, and she had told him so more than once. So why was he always pestering her?

"What are you doing here, Bane?" Ura leveled him with a derisive glare as she came to her feet. "You know my father forbade you to call while he is away."

"No, he forbade me to be alone with you." Bane stepped nearer, closing the distance between them, until they were merely a few breaths apart. "And you are not alone, are you?" His beady eyes darkened. "Where is he?"

Ura stepped back, nearly stumbling on the fur beneath her. "Why do you care?"

Bane shrugged and a wicked gleam crossed his features. "I wish to see this dark giant for myself."

"He is there, resting." Ura pointed to the narrow doorway, leading to her brother's room, where she hoped the land dweller still slept. "Now leave him be."

Bane glared at the eel-skin covered doorway, his lip rising in a snarl, before turning his sharp gaze back on her. "They say you watch over him like a mother coddling a newborn babe."

Heat infused her chest and flamed her cheeks. Why did Bane's words upset her so? "He is injured. He needs care."

"What of my needs, Ura?" Bane hissed, stalking toward her.

"Go find some other fool, Bane," she replied, so tired of playing this game with him. "I do not want to marry you."

Ura stepped back again. Tossing a glance behind her, she found that she was almost backed up against the wall.

If it was at all possible, the sharp features on his gaunt face softened. He continued to approach her with his arms splayed wide. "You do not know your own heart."

Ura's back hit the wall as Bane closed the gap between them. Her heart raced, not from lust or love, but anger. How could this arrogant fool presume to know her thoughts?

"I know my heart does not pine for you! Now get out!"

Bane stood still. Shaking his head, he blinked hard, looking stunned and confused. Heaving a breath, he ran wiry fingers through his hair. "When Ryne returns with promising news, you will be yourself again."

"How do you know what my brother will find? Or if he will return at all?" Ura's words ended on a sob. Biting down on her fist, she refused to let the tears fall. She would not allow Bane to believe he'd made her cry.

"Is that why you tend this land dweller? Do you seek to fill the void in your heart left by Ryne?" Bane took a slow step forward.

Ura nearly retched at the feel of his cool breath on her cheek. "Leave me," she growled.

"No man understands you better than I, Ura. I know what you were doing the night you found the land dweller." He reached out, cupping her shoulder in a tight grip.

"Let go of me!" she shrieked, pushing his chest.

It was like sticking her hands through a hollow drum. She knew Bane had less girth than a starved skeleton, but she had no idea of his frailty until that moment. He weightlessly stumbled back, grasping her arm and pulling her with him.

This time, Ura jerked free with all her might. Her chest heaved with strained breath and her flesh burned with stinging intensity. Never before had she been so angry. Had Bane thought he could behave like a fool without reproach? Did he believe his family's name gave him the right to take freely what did not belong to him?

Bane caught himself on a nearby stool, just as he was about to tumble onto the floor. He stood upright, glaring at her with malice reflected in the stony depths of his tiny orbs.

Bane spoke in a low, venomous hiss. "You will not push me again, girl."

"You will not touch her again!" The deep bellow rattled the tiny cave with dizzying force.

Ura could hardly believe the land dweller was standing before them, his expansive shoulders filling the room as he leaned against a wall for support. Ura could see pain in his strained features.

"Ah, so he awakens." Bane bowed before Markus, his skeletal arms splayed wide as if he was paying homage to a goddess. All the while, his eyes glowed with amusement. "The mighty being from above!"

Ura paid Bane little heed for she could not take her eyes off Markus. He was not well and should rest, as she could easily defend herself against the likes of Bane.

"Markus, go back to bed. Your head has not healed."

"I am healed enough to pound my fist through his face should he touch you again," said Markus. His features were turned to stone, with the exception of his fiery gaze, which was locked on his adversary.

Bane stood upright and casually shrugged his shoulders. "Very well, I will leave, but I will be back." He flashed Ura a thin smile. "I do not trust you with this giant."

Ura heaved an exasperated breath as she watched Bane exit through the narrow opening, knowing he was off to tell his clan that he'd been threatened. Bane would do his best to make Markus's stay with her people unbearable.

MARKUS WATCHED AS THE bony man scurried through the narrow doorway. A souring in his gut warned him that he would be back all too soon, bringing trouble with him.

He held his breath as another wave of pain coursed through his head. Markus did not know if the pain was due to the fall or the anger that had nearly split his skull in two. When he saw the man clawing at Ura's arm, he had wanted to bash the fool's head against the nearest ice wall.

Markus chanced to look at Ura. She was watching him, her mouth turned down in a heavy scowl. He thought she must have been angry with him for some reason, until he looked into her eyes. It was then that he nearly lost his wits.

Ura held him in her wide, yet soft, silver depths. At once he thought of his mother whenever she looked upon Alec; the tenderness and love she showed him when he was ill or after one of Father's beatings. Ura motioned for Markus to sit on a low wooden stool.

Feeling the wall beside him with his good arm, Markus leaned onto the stool, cursing under his breath at the way his legs shook beneath him. After he'd sat and straightened his posture, he was almost at eye level with Ura. He was suddenly aware of the cramped chamber and the smell of sweet spices whenever she was near.

"I'm sorry for him, Markus." Her voice held a soothing edge.

Markus swallowed a lump that had originated in the hollow cavity of his chest. Emotions threatened to envelop him and it took all of his will to push back the avalanche. Men did not react to such feelings as tenderness. Coughing once into his hand, he cleared his throat, channeling his feelings into anger toward the man who had assaulted Ura.

"Who was that fool?" he asked.

"Bane," she sighed, "the first-born son of the House of Eryll." She blew a wisp of pale hair that had fallen across her forehead. "They are a very powerful family and Bane uses that power to his full advantage."

Markus knew all too well about bullies who abused their power. "So he thinks to bully you into marrying him?"

Her eyes widened. "How much did you hear?"

"Enough." He shook his head, trying to clear the dizzying rage that threatened to overcome him. "Don't listen to him."

"Has everyone I know been struck dumb?" she snapped. "I have said I will *never* marry him."

Markus winced at her tone, choosing to remain silent rather than argue. Ura was on edge, and he sensed it had less to do with Bane's intrusion and more to do with her brother. He couldn't fault her there. Ever since Markus awoke, his dark thoughts kept wandering to Alec's frail and bruised face. Who would care for his brother now that he and his mother were gone?

Markus covered his face and stifled a groan. Worrying over Alec was maddening when there was naught he could do until the blasted curse was lifted.

"Please don't be upset, Markus. I shouldn't have lost my temper."

Markus looked up to see Ura leaning over him, her eyes fraught with emotion as she settled a pale hand on his shoulder.

"You have not upset me, lass. I worry for my brother."

"You too?" Ura blinked hard, and her eyes watered over with unshed tears.

"Aye, he's all by himself with no one to care for him."

"As is Ryne." Ura stood and began pacing the small chamber while twisting the frayed end of her belt around a slender finger. "He left without a partner. Who will save him if he is in trouble?"

A heavy fog settled in Markus's head and he grasped the stool beneath him for support. Bane's accusation echoed in his skull: *I know what you were doing the night you found the land dweller.*

"What were you doing the night you found me?" he asked, his voice shaking.

Ura stopped pacing and there was a hopelessness in her eyes that Markus recognized. He had seen the same look in caged animals. It was then he realized what Ura had been doing the night she'd found him; she had set out to find her brother, but was forced to rescue Markus instead.

"He has been gone nearly a year. I could bear the waiting no longer," she groaned, raking fingers through her pale hair. "I went searching for Ryne. I thought to leave through the hole in the ice ceiling before they repaired it. Then I saw you lying there on a dragon's tooth." Her words seemed to be laced with resentment.

Markus's heart sank. She seemed to hold a grudge because he had come between her one chance to sneak away to search for her brother, for he was sure her father had forbade her to go. Though, in truth, Markus was glad she'd lost the chance to venture out alone. Ice Mountain was no place for a girl.

"Thank you for not leaving me to die." His voice breaking, Markus turned his gaze to the single, pale stone lying in the middle of the fur-lined floor.

"Did you think you could scale Ice Mountain?" Her tone was laced with disbelief. "Father said you were trying to reach the witch."

Markus had already given up trying to convince Ura and her father that Madhea was a goddess. Though fear prompted him to push any disparaging thoughts of her out of his mind, he couldn't help wondering whether Jon could be right. Was Madhea a witch, bent on making his life miserable?

"Aye," he replied. "I was trying to reach Madhea, to plead with her to break a curse."

Ura stormed up to him, fists clenched by her sides. "She will not listen, Markus. The witch has no heart. Why do you think my people dwell beneath the surface?"

Markus shook his head, trying to clear his mind of the fear that suddenly consumed him and threatened to strangle all thought and reason - fear of what Ura was about to tell him; fear of discovering that Madhea would never lift the curse.

His throat had gone bone dry and he struggled to speak. "I do not know why."

Ura scooped up the stone from the furs and cradled it in her grasp. Casting her gaze down, she ran her fingers over the stone's smooth surface for a long time before glancing back up at Markus.

She spoke slowly, her eyes clouding over as if she was recalling a dream. "Three hundred winters ago, our people lived above the ice, beneath the tall shadow of the mountain's peak. Every winter we held a festival in Madhea's honor and she would reward our people by not crushing us with avalanches. One winter our village was inflicted with a terrible pox. Many of our children died. Mothers and fathers were too grieved to honor the witch. Rather than show compassion for their suffering, she sent her dragon, Lydra, who entombed entire families in ice. Had it not been for those few who escaped with warming stones, my kind would have perished."

Markus swallowed back a knot of fear. Why would Madhea curse a people for refusing to honor her when their children were sick? Surely, there had to be more to the story, but he was too afraid to ask, lest he learn more of Madhea's dark deeds. Would such a goddess be willing to forgive him and break the hunter's curse?

Ura placed the stone, which was slightly smaller than Markus's palm, in his hand and his fingers buzzed beneath its weight. Then the stone did a remarkable thing: its pale hue turned to crimson and the heat from it warmed Markus's hand, nearly scalding his flesh. He jerked and gasped, tossing the stone into Ura's outstretched hands as if it was a fiery coal.

A rueful expression showed in the gleam of the girl's eyes. "My people were forced to come here and carve a way of life beneath the mighty glacier."

Markus looked at the stone with interest as Ura gently laid it back on the furs, its reddish glow fading until it was but a pale, innocuous ivory.

"Warming stone," she had called it. Such a thing would come in handy to heat his numb fingers while climbing. He would have to find a way to barter for one before he returned to the surface, although he had no wish to leave his icy refuge at present.

Markus blinked hard against the onslaught of dizziness. The fog in his skull grew thicker. Ura was right and he needed to rest, but he was tired of lying in bed. He briefly wondered what his father would have said at The Mighty Hunter being reduced to a bed-ridden invalid. He blinked harder, trying to cast out his dark musings.

"Your thoughts trouble you again." It was not so much a question, but a statement that Ura made as she bent down on one knee beside Markus. She peered into his eyes with a concerned expression.

"'Tis nothing, lass." Markus forced a smile as he tried to look earnestly into the depths of her pale eyes. He quickly averted his gaze, realizing the folly when his heart began to beat wildly. He scolded himself for acting the fool. He had no time for thoughts of love, not when the very real threat of death awaited him outside Ice Kingdom.

His impending doom made him think again of Ura's attempt to climb to the surface. She could've been killed, if not by the climb then by Madhea's wrath.

"What would you have done once you reached the surface?" Markus asked.

Ura shrugged as she sat down on the pale rug in front of him, crossing her slender legs at the ankles. "I hadn't thought that far." One corner of her mouth hitched up in a sideways grin. "Ryne is the only Ice Dweller who has ever ventured to the top in my lifetime."

Markus was in awe. Ura had never basked in the warmth of the sun or felt the cool breeze through her hair. She had never smelled the summer rain or reaped the fall harvest. It seemed to Markus that one could not live a full life without experiencing such joys.

At that moment he wished very much for a chance to take Ura to the surface, so he could watch her experience the wonders of his world. He imagined her standing in the meadow by his family hut, planting her bare feet in the soil and plucking flowers while the sunlight gleamed off the sheen of her pale hair.

*She would be a beauty,* Markus thought to himself.

His racing ideas stirred something within him, inspiring both sadness and joy. Before he could stop to think, he blurted out his secret desire. "If I survive this blasted curse, I should like to take you to the top."

"You would?" she breathed, her eyes widening with something akin to amazement.

"Aye," he answered, as he fought the urge to reach out and stroke her smooth cheek.

She rose up on her knees, determination set in the rigid line of her jaw. "I should like very much to go. I would see this melting glacier for myself."

Markus hoped the glacier was not melting as he wouldn't want Jon and Ura to lose their home. He feared for her safety if Ice Kingdom were to surface, as such a spectacle would not go unheeded by Madhea.

"Is that why Ryne went to the top? Because he fears the glacier is melting?"

Ura sighed, sinking back on her haunches. "Though many don't believe it, there is evidence that the glacier is melting. Ryne went to the top to find the source."

"And now you fear for him?"

She nodded, dropping her gaze to her hands folded in her lap. "He has been gone too long. I fear Madhea may have found him. Odu has told us the witch's grudge only intensifies with time."

Markus arched a brow. A familiar chord had been struck somewhere in the recesses of his memory, and he wondered if he had heard that name before. "Who is Odu?"

"He is the ice prophet. You will meet him when you are well enough. Father believes he can help you, Markus."

"What do I believe, child?" echoed Jon's voice in the opposing doorway.

"Father!" Ura jumped up and raced to Jon's side, planting an affectionate kiss on his cheek.

Jon wrapped one arm around Ura, returning a kiss on her forehead.

Markus cast his gaze down, feeling awkward as he witnessed their tender moment. How strange these Ice People were, he thought, wondering if all the fathers were as affectionate with their children.

"You are home sooner than I expected and your fishing fared well, I see."

Jon flashed a nearly luminescent smile as he held up a stringer of creatures that resembled fish wearing plates of armor. "I must skin these soon," he said.

Green slime dripped off the long, grey bodies. Jagged, silver, razor-like fins jutted out down the length of their crooked spines. Though he swayed in his seat, Markus couldn't tear his gaze from the lifeless, bulging eyes. Even fouler than the creatures' appearance was their smell. He shielded his nose from the pungent odor, fearing they had spoiled.

Before Markus could think to stop himself, he blurted out, "Those beasts are meant to be eaten?"

Jon chuckled as his gaze settled on Markus. "I have only stopped to check in on you both. I see Markus is strong enough to leave his chamber."

Ura pointed an accusatory finger at Markus. "I told him to stay abed."

Jon arched a silvery brow. "Defying your nursemaid already?"

Markus closed his eyes for a brief moment, trying to steady his head and regain his balance on the stool. He had no idea if the sudden wave of dizziness had anything to do with his fall or the thought of that coward, Bane, grabbing Ura. When he slowly opened his eyes again, his gaze traveled first to the girl and then to her father.

"I could not lie there while that dog was clawing her," he ground out through clenched teeth.

The mirth in Jon's eyes suddenly turned to stone and he looked sideways at his daughter. "Of whom does he speak, Ura?"

"Bane," she growled.

"Again?" Jon threw up his hands. "I must speak with his father."

A shrill burst of laughter escaped her lips. "We both know it will do no good."

Markus could feel the tension in Jon's shoulders roll off in waves. The air in the cramped room seemed to stagnate even more as the older man stared intently at the stone in the center of the room.

Finally, Jon's gaze snapped back to Markus, which made him look as if he had just awakened from a trance. "Since you can walk, perhaps you can accompany me while I skin these serpents. You've skinned a fish before, yes?"

"Aye," Markus agreed, "I have skinned many an animal."

Ura came to Markus's side, pointing at him as if he was an errant child. "He has only one good arm and his walk is not steady."

Jon leveled his daughter with an unwavering stare. "Then you may be his other arm and his crutch. He cannot recover if he does naught but lie abed all day. We've only a short distance to go to the cavern."

Ura stood motionless for a moment, her gaze locked with Jon's.

"Come, daughter." The firm tone in Jon's voice left no room for disagreement.

"Yes, Father," Ura mumbled.

She rushed into her brother's bedchamber and returned with two pale, furry boots with several small spikes protruding from the bottoms. She held them out to Markus. "Here, put these on."

He looked at the soles, which resembled hollowed-out hares, and scowled. He would not be paraded around Ice Kingdom with rabbits for feet! "I have my own boots."

"These are Ryne's old ice soles," said Ura, thrusting one into his hand, her stern gaze mimicking that of her father's just moments ago. "You'll need them." She bent on one knee and shoved the other rabbit sole onto Markus's foot.

With a resonating groan, he fought to stable his weight on the stool. "They are tight," he grumbled.

"Better than no soles at all. I don't want you falling on top of me out there." Ura covered her mouth, just after her lips had turned up in the slightest of smiles.

Markus was certain Ura was trying to conceal her amusement. He could only imagine his father sneering that he, The Mighty Hunter, had been reduced to wearing fluffy feet, but the humiliation was far from over as she proceeded to dress him. Ura helped him to squeeze his good hand into a tight glove and then she draped a large fur over his shoulders, swaddling his broken arm as if it were a newborn babe.

Ura helped him walk through the doorway as Jon held the dark, smooth covering to one side. Markus had to turn sideways and stoop down, and still barely managed to squeeze through.

The moment they stepped outside the dwelling, Markus was in awe of the winding path of ice on which he stood. It snaked past rows of doors and windows, and then down the side of the expansive cavern, where it dipped into obscurity, lost within the opening of a dark, narrow tunnel.

Markus drew in a sharp breath as he took in the view beneath the path which he realized was just an icy road hugging the side of a cliff.

Jagged prisms of shimmering, translucent ice, about five times the height and width of mighty lyme trees, towered above a crystalline frozen pool that was larger than any lake he'd ever seen. Small specks, which he guessed to be people, moved across the smooth surface, propelling themselves forward on narrow boards attached to their feet. These were not ants upon a pile of pine needles; these were people—hundreds or even thousands of them in a place larger than any village.

Many ice dwellers traversing the path stopped to stare at Markus and murmur amongst themselves. From the cursory glances he stole in their direction, the Ice People were small and lithe, like Ura, with pale eyes and an icy sheen to their hair. Few were tall like Jon and none were as wide as Markus.

He turned his attention back to the task at hand and filled his lungs with frigid air, so cold that it stung his eyes and made his icy bedchamber feel scorching in comparison.

It was when he took his first step that the folly began. Markus lost his footing and slid on the slippery surface before catching himself on a nearby wall, which was no easy task with only one good arm. He cringed as the Ice People passing by chuckled at his expense. He did not like being the source of their amusement.

To make matters worse, the fog in his head had been replaced by a steady, painful throbbing. Clenching his jaw, he stood while Ura anchored him by holding his arm. Jon came up behind him, and after peeling Markus's fingers from the wall, he grabbed his shoulder.

"Plant both feet firmly on the ice, son," Jon spoke into his ear. "The spikes will keep you from falling."

Markus did as he was told, forcing his foot down so hard that the ice beneath his foot made a terrible, high-pitched cracking sound, as if the ground was protesting against his weight.

"Mind how hard you step, Markus," Ura warned.

Paying her no heed, he did the same with the other foot and then smiled when his feet did not slip from beneath him. Markus tried to take another step, but faltered; his feet stuck in the ice. He growled as he tried to ignore the Ice People who were grumbling as they gathered around him.

Frustration fueled his ire as he struggled in vain to lift his feet from their icy grasp. Beside him, Ura broke into a fit of laughter and called him a "slog," which Markus assumed to be some sort of mindless ice animal. His ire rose.

"Mind how hard you step, Markus," said Jon, repeating his daughter's admonition in a mocking tone. He knelt behind Markus and, using a small pick, he split the ice trapping his feet.

Once freed, Markus grasped Ura's arm as his feet struggled for purchase. He thrust one foot down, though not as hard as before, and then another, and another. Before he knew it, he was walking on the ice without her support. A wide grin spread across his face.

The sound of clapping drew Markus's attention back toward the gathering crowd of ice dwellers lining the walkway. Sometime during his humiliating struggle, their numbers had doubled, and now they were applauding him as if he was a toddler taking his first steps.

Whether they were mocking or praising him, it made no difference. He had been brought low this day; The Mighty Hunter reduced to a babe. So confused was he by his tumultuous emotions, that Markus did not know whether to laugh or punch something. He clenched his fists and fought against the urge to strike one of their pale, mocking faces. Then, he shuddered at the realization that if he lost this battle with his temper, he would be no different from his father.

# Chapter Ten

"**D**oes he mean to eat those things, Ura?"

She was sitting so close to him that he could feel her cool breath upon his skin. Markus tried to shift his focus, but the girl beside him was somehow turning his brains to mush.

"We shall all eat them tonight, Markus," she replied.

Markus warily eyed the fish that Jon had laid out on the bloodstained stone table before him, though it was difficult to make out their forms in the dim light.

He had been brought through a dark tunnel to an even darker chamber, lit only by the soft glow of the few candles that had been set on the long filleting table, which could accommodate ten fishermen either side.

Markus and Ura sat on a bench carved out of an icy wall, watching as Jon skinned the fish. Jon had denied Markus's offer to help, saying he'd had enough lessons for one day. Markus was offended, for he could skin any animal in his sleep, and a cross-eyed fish would be no different.

"I've never seen such strange creatures," he said, making no attempt to hide the derision in his voice.

"You've never dwelt beneath the ice," Ura answered.

The vibrant, warm glow from the candlelight caught the reflection of Jon's skinning knife, sending a burst of light right into Markus's eyes. He turned his gaze from the fish. It was then he noticed that many of the other fishermen were not filleting their serpents. They were too busy gawking at him.

"Everyone is looking at me," he whispered.

"You are strange to them," Ura said in a far too indifferent tone. "Too big and too dark."

"Thanks, Ura," Markus growled.

She laughed and the cool rush of her breath struck him like a slap to the face. "Now you know how those poor, lazy-eyed serpents feel when you poke fun at them."

Jon walked up to them and told Markus to rise. He then shoved a foul-smelling, wooden bucket into his grasp. "Come with me to dispose of the entrails."

Markus looked into the pail and nearly vomited at the bloody entrails, which were dripping with green ooze.

Jon held the candle as they walked toward the edge of the gloomy cavern. He pointed toward a dark, watery pit carved in the ice floor. "I'm going over there," he told Markus, taking the bucket from him and handing him the candle instead. Then Jon leveled him with a stern look. "Stay here."

He watched as Jon dumped the entrails into the pit, making the water bubble and boil as if it had sprung to life. Markus jerked back, almost dropping the candle, so stunned was he by the violent fervor.

"What bubbles in that pit?" he called to Jon over the loud squeals rumbling from the water.

The man turned, clutching the bucket in both hands and walked back to Markus. The faint glow of the candle flames only served to illuminate the deep lines around his drawn mouth. "The Kraehn are feeding," Jon said.

Markus fought to quell the knot of dread rising in his throat. "What are Kraehn?" he asked, trailing Jon back to the filleting table.

"Fanged fish with razor-sharp scales," the man answered over his shoulder. "You never want to fall into a Kraehn hole."

A chill snaked up Markus's spine as he tried not to think about slipping across the ice and falling into one. The little monsters made Lydra seem tame.

"How do I know which holes have Kraehn?"

"They usually lurk in dark caverns," Jon replied, as he set his bucket down on the table and scooped some serpent meat into it. "The water around them will also be red or black."

"Why red or black?" Markus tried his best to stifle the note of fear that slipped into his voice. He understood that the red color was probably blood from the Kraehn's prey.

Ura appeared beside them. Gone was the hint of amusement in her somber eyes. "Red like the color of the blood from the animals that fall into

Kraehn holes; black like the color of Kraehn blood when they have no other animals to eat."

Curiosity piqued Markus's interest that the ice dwellers lived in caverns that housed such monsters. Surely, there had to be a way to rid themselves of this plague? "These Kraehn, why don't the ice people just kill them?"

Ura shrugged, acting as if living among violent, fanged fish wasn't anything unusual. "They eat our waste. This is why our kingdom is clean of filth. Besides, killing a Kraehn isn't easy."

"And don't be fool enough to try and catch one," Jon warned. "Take heed from the Ice People you meet who are missing hands and digits."

Markus had to work hard to shut his gaping jaw. The ways of these people were becoming stranger and stranger. To live inside the ice, and eat snotty dragon weed and ugly serpents was odd enough, but to coexist with man-eating fish was another. Humans were supposed to be at the top of the food chain, but he somehow feared that these fish had eaten more than just fingers and toes. Judging by the frenzied pace at which they ate, he reckoned an entire person could be devoured in the blink of an eye.

Markus shuddered and then looked up as two men cloaked in white furs approached him with resolute determination set in the hard angles of their pale faces. They had come here for him, of that he was sure.

"Land dweller," they said in unison as they stood before Markus, looking him over with scowls.

"Aye," he answered tersely.

"Odu wishes to speak with you," said one of the men. "You must follow us."

Jon laid a firm hand on Markus's forearm. "We will accompany you," he said. A slight smile parted his lips while he looked at Markus with luminescent eyes. "Do not fear."

Markus swallowed, pretending not to notice the fine trembling in his arms and legs, or the gnawing pain that settled in the pit of his stomach. "I am not afraid."

THE OLD PROPHET SAT cross-legged on a snowbear rug at the end of a luminous chamber. His white beard draped over one knee and gathered in a pile at his feet. As he gummed a bone pipe with an intricate pattern carved into the sides, a strange odor of pungent spices radiated off the prophet's fur robes.

Markus was less stunned by the oddity of the man sitting before him than by the low humming that reverberated around the chamber. Though the hum was by no means intense, its perpetual rattle unnerved Markus, thrumming deep inside the very marrow of his bones. He glanced around for the source, but saw nothing amiss, although the fur-lined walls also seemed to shake, as if the very ice around him was alive.

In the center of the chamber was a raised pool of water, from which emerged a misty vortex that gathered in a wide funnel, rising toward the ceiling.

Markus's gaze followed the swirling mist, and he gasped when he saw the razor-sharp iridescent ice crystals that jetted down from the ceiling, some measuring more than an arm's length. However, neither the prophet nor the Ice People who sat on furs against the chamber walls showed any alarm that these odd, glowing daggers were hovering above them.

The Ice People's only cause for concern seemed to be Markus, for they looked at him with narrowed eyes and mouths set in hard lines.

"Greetings, land dweller," said the prophet, beckoning Markus inside with a wave of his hand. He patted the fur beside him. "Come sit. Pay no heed to their stares. Ice People have not seen one of your kind in this lifetime, although it was not too long ago that we were all of the same race."

After Jon gently nudged his back, Markus took a hesitant step inside the chamber. As his weary gaze scanned the crowd of pale gawkers, he finally settled beside the prophet.

The old man flashed an almost toothless grin, and Markus was instantly reminded of Dafuar. He did not know if he should be comforted or alarmed by their similarities.

"They tell me your name is Markus," the prophet said.

Markus nodded. "Aye."

Then he continued to stare at the prophet. If it hadn't been for the translucent hair and skin, he could have been Dafuar's twin. The old man was so wrinkled that his age was beyond comprehension.

"Do not think to count the lines," the prophet spoke with a touch of humor in his voice. "You will be here all night."

"I'm sorry." Markus swallowed. "You just look so familiar."

The prophet hitched a bushy brow. "Do I?"

"Aye, you resemble another prophet I know."

A slow smile cracked the lines of the old man's weathered face. "How fares my brother?"

"Y-your brother?" Markus stammered.

"You speak of Dafuar, do you not?"

"Aye. He is your brother?"

The prophet shrugged a bony shoulder. "He is."

Markus's jaw fell open as he struggled to comprehend what the prophet had told him. "But Ura told me the Ice People have lived beneath the glacier for three hundred years."

Odu nodded. "We have."

Markus gasped. "But that must mean you're..."

"...very old," Odu interjected.

Markus gawked at the prophet for a long moment. What kind of magic had kept the two prophets alive for so long? Were they even men or were they witches? If so, how could he trust them?

"Great prophet," Jon called from the darkened doorway, "Madhea's dragon pursues Markus."

Odu's pale orbs narrowed at Markus. "Is this true?"

"Aye... I don't know." Markus shifted in his seat as he felt the weight of Odu's heavy stare upon him. "Last I saw the beast, she was buried beneath an avalanche."

"She will awaken with the thaw. It is not every day that the witch unleashes her dragon. What have you done to cause her ire?"

Heat infused Markus's chest and inflamed his face. He hung his head and spoke in a low whisper, "I k-killed animals."

"Killed them?" Odu asked. "You mean for food?"

"Aye."

Markus chanced lifting his gaze. Despite the heavy lines marring the old man's features, he could not mistake the disapproval in the prophet's eyes.

"You do not speak the whole truth." Odu leaned closer to Markus, speaking in a whisper that sounded more like a serpent's hiss. "Tell me now, boy."

Markus hung his head and spoke toward the white fur beneath his boots. "I hurt them."

"You abused them?!" The boom of the prophet's surprising tenor echoed throughout the frozen chamber, causing the icicles above them to hum in response.

The Ice People surrounding Markus gasped before an unsettling hush fell about the chamber.

Markus swallowed a lump in his throat as a cold rush of fear snaked up his spine. He had never considered killing woodland creatures to be abuse before. He'd thought of it as sport. But, as his hooded gaze briefly swept across several scowling faces, he was keenly aware of their disapproval.

What would the Ice People do to him? Would he be an outcast and branded a monster? Would they look upon him as he looked upon his father? Would Ura feel disdain toward him, too?

"I was distraught." His voice cracked as he forced out the words. "I knew not what I was doing."

"Very well." Odu waved Markus away with a flick of the wrist. "You may leave me now."

Though he was by far the largest person in the room, Markus felt much smaller than the hare he had disemboweled shortly before his mother's death. He rose slowly to stand on shaky feet, keenly aware of disapproving glares and whispers. More than once, he heard the words "giant" and "monster" muttered amongst them, leaving no doubt in his mind he did not belong in Ice Kingdom.

Just as Markus turned to go, Jon rushed forward. "Please, great prophet," he pleaded, "what should the boy do about the dragon?"

Odu held up his arms and two boys helped him to his feet. With stooped shoulders and legs that shook with every step, Odu walked toward the pool of swirling mists. He waved one hand through it, causing the cyclone to spin faster.

The prophet lowered his head, his gaze lost somewhere beneath the depths of the water. "He should seek out his heart." Odu's mumbled words lacked strength or conviction.

"His heart?" Jon shook his head before asking, "How will that stop the dragon?"

Odu lifted his head and leveled Markus with a stony expression. "Let the dragon be. Your land dweller has greater monsters to vanquish."

"MARKUS!" URA STRUGGLED to keep pace with him as he marched briskly down the icy slope. Luckily, he had to stop a few times to keep from falling, or else she was certain she would have never caught up with his long strides.

Just as he paused to catch himself from slipping on his backside, Ura reached out and grasped his elbow. "Wait! I wish to speak with you."

"Why?" Markus spoke in a low growl, not even turning to meet her stare. "Why, when you know now that I am a monster?"

Ura heaved a deep sigh. While he was big and clumsy, she knew he was no beast. "I do not think you a monster, Markus."

Markus kept his back to her and jerked his arm out of her grasp. "I saw the look in everyone's eyes - in *your* eyes."

Before he could flee again, Ura stepped in front of him. Though he kept his gaze averted, she could make out a shadow that cast a heavy gloom over his already darkened eyes.

"Are you sorry?" she asked.

He shrugged. "For what?"

"For abusing them."

Ura's breath caught as Markus slowly lifted his gaze to meet her own, revealing the pain reflected in the depths of his brooding eyes.

"I don't know that I can feel anything anymore."

She swallowed a lump that had formed in her throat. "Surely you have feelings. Surely you feel for something or someone. What about your brother?"

"I love him, aye." Markus nodded. "But not in the way he deserves. I am not a good brother. I am a monster."

Instinctively, Ura reached up and cupped Markus's cheek. For some inexplicable reason, she longed to feel his flesh beneath her own, but she was restricted by her heavy, eel-skin glove. "Monsters are heartless. You have a heart, Markus." She took a chance and placed her other hand on his chest. "I can feel it beating."

For a moment, Ura thought she saw a softness in his eyes before he screwed them shut. When he reopened them, his dark pupils seemed even more brooding than before.

"I am made of blood and bones, to be sure," he replied, with a cutting finality to his voice, "but the blood that pumps through my heart is cold."

Ura reached down and took his large hand in her own. He was not a monster; she refused to believe it.

He groaned as he shook off her grasp.

Ura fought to clutch at her chest and let him see what his denial had done to her. Her heart pained her, as if pierced by an arrow, and yet, despite his present treatment of her, she knew he had goodness in him. She guessed that someone had caused him to build this wall around himself.

"Who has done this to you? Who has hardened your heart?" she asked.

Markus tensed, his body looking as though it was encapsulated in ice. A look of pain crossed his features and he took a step back. "Ura, let us not speak of it."

"Markus," she pleaded, taking a hesitant step toward him, "please let me help you."

"Ura! You must come!"

She spun around at the sharp voice of her father and gasped when she saw the wild excitement in his wide eyes. "What is it?"

Jon raced away from her, while calling behind him, "Ryne has returned!"

# Chapter Eleven

U ra's brother was surrounded by Ice People in the gathering hall. Though Ryne still wore his hooded parka, he was always easy to spot, being tall like their father, who had already found his way over to his son.

Ura's heart swelled as she watched her father draw Ryne into a fierce hug. Leaving Markus to wait alone in the dark recesses of the large hall, she pushed her way through the throng to get to her brother.

"Ryne!"

Ura's father stepped aside, and Ura threw herself into her brother's arms while weeping tears of joy.

Ryne held her close, and for a long while all was right in Ura's world—the ice was not melting, brooding land dwellers were not falling from the sky, and ice dragons did not exist. All that mattered was that her brother was alive.

Though Ura cried out when Ryne pulled away from their embrace, her reaction turned to an astonished gasp when she saw how much her brother's face had changed. His skin no longer held its pale sheen and he looked as if he'd been rolling around in grime. Ura was even more astonished when she reached up and pulled down his hood. While his smooth strands of hair looked to be caked in dirt, she felt no grime when she ran her fingers through them.

"What has happened to you?"

He smiled, revealing ivory-colored teeth, the only part of his body that seemed to be immune to the change. "I've been touched by the sun. Do you like it?" he asked, ruffling his hair.

Ura jerked away and squinted at her brother. "Touched by the sun? How high did you climb?"

Ryne burst into a fit of laughter, and Ura didn't know whether to be pleased to see her brother was well or annoyed that she was somehow the brunt of his joke.

A loud grunt sounded behind Ryne. Ura jumped, before peering over her brother's shoulder to see a strange beast standing alone at the edge of the hall. The beast looked large enough to bring down a full-grown man. Ura thought its massive head must have come up to her waist. Most of its body was covered in pale, grey fur, except for the dark patches surrounding its silvery eyes. It wagged a bushy tail while dancing around on all four paws.

"Ryne," Ura asked in astonishment, "what is that creature?"

Her brother turned and whistled. The Ice People gasped and moved aside as the beast jumped up and skidded toward them, ramming into Ryne's legs before it came to a halt.

"Easy, boy," he chuckled, before turning to Ura. "Do not be afraid. His name is Tar. Land dwellers call him a dog."

Ura arched a brow. "Tar, the dog?"

Ryne nodded.

Ura warily eyed the creature named Tar. His pink tongue lolled to one side of his extended jowls while his tail was set in continuous motion. He shifted from one paw to the next, which Ura suspected was not from fear or anger, but from excitement. The most remarkable thing about the animal was the way he looked at Ryne with something akin to idolatry. Ura had long admired her older brother as well, and she had a feeling that she was going to like Tar very much.

"You may touch him," Ryne said. "He likes to be scratched."

Ura watched her brother scratch the dog behind the ears and marveled at his response. Such a simple gesture caused Tar to close his eyes and lean into her brother with a look of total contentment on his furry face.

When Ryne pulled back, Tar made a high-pitched whimper and looked at him with wide, pleading eyes. Her brother motioned for Ura to scratch the dog.

She knelt down before Tar, and tentatively reached out a hand to touch a spot behind his left ear. The animal responded by pressing his ear against her hand. Ura gasped at the feel of his warm fur.

"He's so soft!" she cried.

As she continued to scratch Tar, he let out a low moan that sounded like a predatory growl. Ura was amazed, but not alarmed. Though most of the animals she had known in Ice Kingdom were wild and vicious, if Ryne put faith in the dog then so would she.

Jon remained by their sides, but the rest of the Ice People continued to creep away. Mothers gnawed on their lower lips while clutching babes to their chests and fathers hid their children behind them.

Ura noticed a dark figure step out of the shadows and move closer.

"Markus, come feel his fur," she called.

Ryne's brow furrowed as he gazed at Markus. "A land dweller? Why have you come here?"

Markus shrugged. "I just dropped in for a visit."

To Ura's relief, the Ice People broke into laughter.

"He fell through the ice and nearly broke his neck," Jon answered in a somber tone.

Ryne's eyes widened. "Are you the one who brought on the dragon's curse?"

Markus raised his chin. "Aye."

"They speak of you in Kicelin," Ryne said. "They think you are dead."

Markus nodded. "That may come to pass soon enough."

Gasps from the crowd were followed by agitated murmurs.

Ura's heart leapt into her throat as an image of Markus encapsulated in ice flashed through her mind. She pulled back from Tar and rose on shaky legs. "Let us not talk of death now."

Jon cleared his throat and, splaying his arms wide, he spoke to the crowd. "Ura is right. My son lives." He stepped up to Ryne and placed a hand on his shoulder. "Tonight we feast and celebrate his return."

Several cheers erupted from the crowd. A few of the Ice People hesitantly approached Ura's family and offered their congratulations, while keeping wary eyes on Tar. The dog sat on his rear haunches and wagged his massive tail as his gaze darted from one person to the next.

After most of the community had dispersed, Ryne leaned toward Ura and whispered into her ear, "I'm famished. Land dwellers eat nothing but tough, stringy meat."

"Well, you are in luck," she replied. "Father has just skinned some lazy-eyed serpents."

Ura wasn't entirely sure, but she thought she heard Markus groan behind her.

WHILE MARKUS HAD HOPED they would dine in the solitude of Jon's quiet home, to his dismay the large chamber where they had found Ryne was also a dining hall of sorts. The round hall was not as well-lit as Ura's home, but it received a soft, pleasing illumination from above. Markus could not be sure, but it seemed that the ice crystals glowed just like the spikes in the prophet's chamber. The walls were draped in various furs while others were stacked in piles against them.

A warmth seeped into Markus's bones that was unlike anything he'd experienced so far in Ice Kingdom. It reminded him of nights at home beside the hearth fire, minus one drunken, raging father.

As more and more ice dwellers filed into the chamber and spread out furs in the center of the floor, Markus's senses were accosted by a strange odor, which wafted from the far side of the cavern. He knew the smell to be lazy-eyed serpents being roasted, and although his stomach ached for nourishment, he did not relish the notion of swallowing slimy fish.

To make matters worse, Markus soon discovered that wherever he chose to stand turned out to be someone else's sitting space and he was told more than once to move out of the way by a less-than-hospitable ice dweller. After much shuffling about, Markus was finally relegated to sit in a darkened corner near Ryne's mongrel, as if he couldn't be brought any lower this day.

The dog whimpered as he drooled over the fur beneath him, all the while keeping his sharp gaze on Ryne, who, alongside his father, seemed to be engaged in a heated debate with several older Ice People.

Markus groaned as he saw Ura approach with two steaming bowls of food. If it were at all possible, the dog beside him salivated even more.

"Here." Ura handed Markus a bowl of what resembled gooey serpent stew. "This time you will like it," she said, wagging a finger while glowering above him. "And, if you don't, you will eat it anyway."

Markus eyed the bowl suspiciously, his throat tightening at the sight of the slimy mush. Loathe though he was to touch the offending dish, Markus knew that Ura's offering was made with the best intentions, so he raised the bowl to his lips and sipped some of the broth. Accidentally swallowing a long serpent tendril, Markus nearly choked on the ooze as it slid down his throat, but for Ura's sake he drank it.

He tentatively looked up at her while plastering a smile across his face. "Mmm," he said with forced enthusiasm.

Ura scowled, looking rather unconvinced at his false display. "You land dwellers have no taste." She sat cross-legged beside him and took a hearty swallow of her stew.

*We do have taste. That is the problem.*

But Markus refused to voice his opinion aloud. Ura and Jon had taken him in and cared for him, and judging by the glares he received from the others, Markus knew he was lucky to have two friends in Ice Kingdom.

Tar drooled even more while he watched them with eager eyes. If Markus was not so hungry, he would have gladly given his food to the mutt. He warily eyed the stew again, deciding that his best option would be to plug his nose and swallow the whole bowl in several gulps.

Whimpering, Tar inched closer.

Markus's ire rose. He had never been overly fond of dogs and this beggar was no exception.

"What is this? Have you begun eating without me?" Ryne hovered above Markus and Ura, his brow marred in a heavy frown.

Ura smiled at her brother. "Your dog has been drooling all over the fur. Have you been starving him?"

"No." Ryne chuckled. "I have been collecting serpent fins." He pulled a handful of the scorched things out of his pocket and threw one to Tar. The dog leapt up and snapped up the fin in one greedy gulp. Licking his jowls clean, he let out a satisfactory bark while eagerly eyeing his master.

Ryne threw a few more fins into the air and Tar jumped up, catching each one with ease. The nearest ice dwellers stopped eating long enough to point and gasp as man and dog continued their tricks.

Markus watched with envy as Tar seemed to enjoy his meal. From the looks of the fins, they reminded him of dried meats. "Might I try a fin?" he asked.

Ryne frowned. "These scraps?"

"Aye, might I try one?" Markus struggled to keep the pleading whine out of his voice lest he, too, sounded like a begging mongrel.

Scowling, Ryne tossed him one.

Markus moaned with pleasure as he bit into the tough, crunchy meat. He chewed with haste and swallowed before holding out his hand for another.

"Oh, Markus," Ura cried, "that is disgusting."

Ryne shook his head. He dumped several fins into Markus's outstretched hand before tossing another one to the dog. "You land dwellers have no taste for good food."

Ura sighed. "That's what I've been telling him."

"And, you!" Ryne turned a mirthful gaze on the whimpering dog. "You shameless beggar. The least you could do is work harder for your scraps. Watch this," he said, winking at Ura. "Fetch!" he called out to Tar.

Ryne stepped back a few paces and then threw the fin a great distance, causing several ice dwellers to screech and swear as Tar leapt over their heads, scrambling for the bait.

"Amazing!" said Ura, leaning on her knees and clapping her hands. "Markus, did you see that?"

He shrugged. "I have seen many a dog do tricks."

Ryne looked at Markus with eyes narrowed to slits. "What have you against dogs?"

From what Markus had seen of mutts, they were only good for retrieving waterfowl, but he preferred the taste of venison or boar anyway. His father either shot or scared away the few foolish dogs that had invaded their homestead as they only sought to steal food.

"Other than the plague-infested vermin they carry on their backs? The drool and the smell?" Markus did not try to conceal the disdain in his voice.

Ryne snickered as he leaned over and patted Tar on the head. "What about loyalty, bravery, and companionship?"

Markus had to repress a laugh as he looked at the dog who was too busy gnawing on a serpent fin to even acknowledge his master's affection.

"My brother is all those things," Markus said, "so I've never had need for a dog."

"Oh?" Ryne folded his arms across his chest and leveled Markus with a smug expression. "Was your brother there to save you when you fell through the ice?"

"No, but neither was a dog."

Ryne shook his head. "If you would have had a dog—"

"He would have been killed by the dragon for his foolish temerity," Markus interjected.

"Tar saved my life," Ryne said, with an edge of finality.

Ura gasped, "You were almost killed?"

"Oh, several times," said Ryne, shrugging; his face a mask of indifference as if near-death experiences were all just natural occurrences. "As your land dweller can tell you, scaling ice and snow is no easy task. There was this one time when my rope broke and I fell into a crevasse nearly four men high. I was standing on a ledge and beneath me, where my picks had fallen, was a dark chasm. I thought I was done for."

Ura's pale eyes grew even wider. "How did you escape?"

"Tar found me." Ryne nodded toward the dog eagerly awaiting his next fin. "It took him almost an entire day. His paws were raw and bleeding. I knew he had to dig out much ice and snow to reach me."

"I love Tar," Ura breathed, wiping a bead of moisture from her eye. She leaned over and pulled a fin out of Markus's grip before tossing the meat to the dog.

"Don't feed him all of my food," Markus grumbled. Then he moaned even more when he noticed Bane approaching, followed by a handful of other serpent-eyed young men.

When Bane reached them, he spread his arms out wide. "How convenient these land dwellers are," he said, loudly enough to silence the other ice dwellers sitting nearby. "They retrieve and eat our garbage, just like the fanged Kraehn."

As Markus growled under his breath, he was startled by Tar snarling. His gaze shot to the dog, glaring at Bane with feral intensity. Well, at least he and the mutt shared a common interest, other than serpent fins.

Bane ignored the dog as he flashed a forced smile. "We are all relieved at your safe return. Your sister was most distraught in your absence." His lecherous gaze shot to Ura. "I've done all I can to comfort her."

Ryne angled his chin while squaring his shoulders. "My sister needs no comforting from the likes of you."

Bane's mask of insincerity fell. "Tell your dumb beast to stop growling at me," he hissed, reminding Markus of a slithery serpent.

Ryne regarded Bane for a long moment before breaking into a wide grin. "He's no dumb beast. He was trained to protect his family from unwelcome intruders."

Bane sneered back and then glanced at the dog. "His fur will make a nice rug."

"Touch my dog, Bane," said Ryne, his voice rising several octaves, "and you will find yourself skinned instead."

Many ice dwellers gawked at the pair as they exchanged malevolent glares.

"Guard him well," Bane snickered, "'ere he might end up as gnull bait."

With a roar, Ryne leaped up and snatched Bane by the collar of his hooded cloak.

Markus struggled to his feet and stood at Ryne's back, should he need assistance.

Bane cried out and shielded his face with his hands while his friends backed up several paces.

Jon stormed over, waving his hands wildly while shooing away Bane's companions. "Let him go, Ryne."

Ryne released Bane with a shove.

Bane stumbled backward, nearly falling on his backside before scurrying away, but Markus did not miss the look of hatred in his eyes before he turned his back.

Jon grabbed Ryne by the shoulder and spoke in a low growl, just loud enough for Markus to hear. "Bane is not worth it. You need no more enemies when you present your case to the Council."

Ryne heaved a groan before sitting beside Ura. "I have never counted on the Eryll clan. I do not expect their support now."

Markus and Jon sat down, across from the two siblings, so they formed a tight circle upon the fur. Tar sat beside Ryne whose narrowed gaze was lost among the crowd of Ice People.

Markus wondered if the mutt was still watching Bane. For a moment, he almost respected the dog's loyalty to his master, but then he surmised that he had probably only seen Bane as a threat to his food source.

Ura leaned into Ryne and grasped him by the hand. "What have you seen above the ice, brother?"

Ryne's somber expression traveled from his sister to his father. "The ice melts at an alarming rate."

Jon cleared his throat. "You have seen this?"

Ryne nodded. "The river leading from our glacier swells. Villages, which were once a safe distance from the water's edge, have been washed away and dams are breaking. I followed its path down to the ocean. The tides are rising."

Ura's mouth fell open. "What will happen to us?"

"I do not know how many more winters our kingdom will hold," Ryne said, "but we will need to surface before the foundation crumbles."

Ura's hands flew to her mouth. "The witch will destroy us all!"

Ryne pounded the fur with his fist. "Not if I destroy her first!"

Ura gasped, "Ryne, no! Do not say such dark things. She will kill you!" Her words ended on a shrill sob.

Jon's gaze shot to the ice dwellers, many of whom now stared at Ura while whispering to one another.

Markus repressed an urge to lash out at them. He was growing tired of their nosey gawking.

"Ura, be calm," Jon whispered.

She jumped to her feet. "Do not tell me to be calm!"

Ryne rose too, reaching for his sister's hand. "Ura," he said in a strained voice.

She shook off his grip as tears streamed down her face. Then she turned and ran.

Markus struggled to stand with his one good arm and watched helplessly as Ura disappeared into the dark corridor beyond the hall. Although he did not know his way around the icy fortress, he knew he should go after her.

Jon stood and planted his hand on Markus's back. "Leave her be. She will be back."

Markus turned to Jon, seeing only sadness in the older man's eyes. "Where does she go?"

From behind them Ryne answered, "A place where she can escape the weight of her sorrow."

If Ice Kingdom was truly melting, Markus guessed the weight of Ura's sorrows must have been great. He realized his own problems were insignificant in comparison to the plight of the Ice People.

Soon they would have nowhere to live, and what would Madhea do to them then? What would Madhea do to Ura?

# Chapter Twelve

Ryne followed his father to the Council's chamber. He glanced down at Tar, trotting beside him, and then at the land dweller, who trailed in their wake, clumsily treading the ice like a newborn learning his first steps. Every so often, Ryne and his father had to stop to give the brooding giant time to catch up.

*Why had Father allowed Ura to take in this stranger?*

From what Ryne had heard during his brief stay in Kicelin, the boy hunter had brought this dragon's curse on his head by abusing animals. Ryne thought the punishment fit the crime, not that the Ice Witch needed a reason to curse anyone. For his father's sake, Ryne had decided to tolerate his presence, but if the boy threatened any member of his family, Tar included, Ryne would not hesitate to strike him down.

Every muscle in Ryne's body tensed as they crossed the frozen dock and neared the boat that would take them across Crystal Lake to the Council's chamber. The lake sat at the heart of Ice Kingdom's darkest cavern, the ceiling of which was so steep and black that no one had ever dared to climb it. The cavern was illuminated by a few hanging ice crystals, which clung to the outer walls, and by the oarsman's lamp at the prow of the boat.

After removing their spikes, Ryne and his father stepped into the boat and sat together on the furthest bench. Without hesitation, Tar jumped in and settled on a fur-lined bench in the center.

Ryne looked at the land dweller with raised brows and an expectant glare. The boy's sun-kissed skin suddenly took on the hue of ice as he shuffled from one foot to the next, his gaze darting from the boat to the smooth body of water they would need to cross to reach the Council.

"Are you coming, Markus?" Jon asked.

Ryne laughed under his breath. The look in the boy hunter's eyes resembled that of a trapped animal.

The land dweller shook his head. "I doubt that boat would hold my weight."

"Nonsense, Markus." Jon chuckled and then pointed to the opposite bench. "This boat is sturdy."

It was true, the boy was large, but Ryne had seen up to six council members squeeze into the boat. Its bow was made of two hollowed-out tusks of a gnull and wrapped in its thick hide. Since it took a dozen hunters to take down the menacing beast, which was more than thrice the size of a giant snowbear, Ryne knew the boat was sturdy enough to hold the weight of the land dweller.

After a little more coaxing from Jon, Markus sat on the bench opposite them, his hands clenched by his sides and his body so stiff that he looked like a stone statue. He nearly jumped out of his seat when the oarsman pushed off and began paddling across the glassy surface.

While Ryne suspected the water's smooth, dark depths could appear frightening to an outsider, he had seen much bigger bodies of water. In truth, Crystal Lake was the size of a large pond, but its inky reaches knew no limits. None of his people had ever dared to swim more than a few feet below the surface, and then only for a moment as the frigid temperature was enough to kill a man within a few heartbeats. Many of the village fishermen had tried to gauge the water's extent, but their lines failed to reach the bottom.

Ryne watched with amusement as Markus's hands shook by his sides.

"How is it that a lake exists here when all around us is ice?" the boy asked.

"There is a thermal pocket beneath us, just warm enough to melt this pool of ice," Jon explained. As they crossed the center of the lake, he waved to a small pinpoint of light, deep below the surface. "See the light there?"

Markus swallowed. "Could this be why your ice is melting?"

"No," Ryne replied. "The thaw is not coming from within, but from outside."

Markus nodded before his gaze became transfixed on the water. "I've seen bigger lakes, but none so dark or cold." He shuddered and then rubbed his arms. "It is the calm that is most unsettling."

Ryne knew from his travels that many land dwellers were unsettled by the calm. "There's a village named Aloa-Shay, where the land meets the sea. They have a saying that goes 'only fools set sail in tranquil waters.'"

Jon hitched a brow. "Why is this?"

"The calm usually precedes the wrath of Eris."

"Eris? Who is she?" Jon asked.

"The Sea Witch," replied Ryne, not bothering to mask the disdain in his voice.

Jon's face twisted, making him look as if he had just swallowed raw serpent entrails. "Another cursed witch?"

"Yes, and some say she is even more vengeful than Madhea." Ryne remembered the spirit of the beautiful young woman he had seen from a distance. She had been cursed by Eris for her father's sins. Though she walked and talked and, by all appearances breathed as a mortal, she was nothing but wisps of air. Eris had stolen the girl's flesh and bones when she was only a babe.

Though Ryne did not know what sort of dark magic could rob a person of her body, yet allow her spirit to wander the land, he guessed that Eris's magic must be powerful. She was one witch that he had no desire to cross. When it came to Madhea, on the other hand, he'd gladly sacrifice his flesh and bones just to bring about her demise.

"We are here," Jon announced, which gave Ryne a reprieve from his dark thoughts, as the boat reached the dock.

Father and son helped Markus to his feet, and they all disembarked, followed by Tar.

Jon turned to Ryne. "After our meeting, we will retire to our dwelling. I wish to know all about your travels. In the meantime, please try to keep your composure with the Council."

Ryne felt a prick of annoyance at his father's warning. How could he be expected to keep his composure? Somehow, he suspected that the Council would deny his claims even if the ice beneath their soles turned to water.

When Jon placed a steady hand on Ryne's shoulder and leveled him with an expectant gaze, Ryne grunted his understanding. Yes, he would try, but he would make no promises when dealing with fools.

ENTERING THE BRIGHT, icy chamber, Ryne saw three men and two women, each stoic and silent, seated in a semi-circle of elevated, fur-lined thrones. They were flanked on either side by four beefy Guardians, peace-keepers of the kingdom, but more importantly, enforcers of the Council's edicts. Each Guardian wore thick pale tunics and wooly leggings. Strapped to their rust-colored belts were the largest knives Ryne had ever seen.

Elof Eryll, the Council Chieftain, sat in the center on the widest chair which was padded with the most furs to cushion his heavy weight.

Jon, Tar and Markus lingered in the shadows near the entrance. Ryne stood before the Council, although he was blocked by a glowing pit that held a bright warming stone and a table laden with many kinds of spiced foods. Ryne knew that running the kingdom was no easy task, but the Council did not suffer from lack of nourishment and comfort.

From the annoyed look in Chieftain Eryll's squinty eyes, he had been waiting none too patiently. Most likely, he was eager to stuff his bloated face with food, thought Ryne.

"And so he has returned." The Chieftain splayed his arms wide; a look of mock enthusiasm in his features. "Welcome home, son of the house of Nord-lund."

"Thank you." Ryne made a slight bow though it pained his pride to do so. These fools deserved no respect from him.

The Chieftain waved his hand. "Jon, bring your land dweller forward. I'd like a look at him."

His jaw fell open as Markus stepped forth. "My son did not lie. You are as big as a gnull!"

The land dweller's face flushed as he dropped his gaze to the floor. The Council members broke into laughter. The Chieftain's cousin, Ingred Johan, who had an angular face and a sharp nose resembling a bird's beak, squealed so shrilly that Ryne fought to shield his ears from the grating noise. Hearing Tar whimper behind him, he felt sorry for his dog, whose keen sense of hearing was so much better than his own.

The Chieftain jumped in his seat as his gaze narrowed on Tar. "Holy Elements! What is that beast?"

The other members gasped and Ingred shrieked again.

"His name is Tar," Ryne replied through clenched teeth. "He is no beast. He is my friend."

The Chieftain sat back against his throne, his hands visibly shaking at his sides. "He looks like some kind of vicious slog."

Ryne heaved a sigh. "I assure you, he is not vicious. Many land dwellers keep these animals as companions. They serve and protect their families."

"Is that so?" The Chieftain asked, scowling at Tar. "How do I know he means no harm to our people?"

Ryne dropped his gaze to his dog, who was too busy licking the fur around his anus to pay anyone much notice. He turned back to Chieftain Eryll, who had been watching the dog with a look akin to horror.

How was he ever going to convince these idiots that their foundations were melting? How would he impress upon them the gravity of their situation when the Chieftain was so easily distracted by a butt-licking dog?

Ryne's shoulders fell as he rubbed his fingers across his temple. His head throbbed and he knew it was not from the glacier kingdom's frigid air. It was the kind of headache that was brought on by stress. He bore too much responsibility at only two and twenty.

When would these old fools listen?

"Tar saved my life. He would never harm our people. You have my word."

The Chieftain's eyebrows dipped beneath his silver hairline as he harrumphed.

Ryne realized he would need to be extra careful and not give the Council any reason to kill his companion. He would not put it past the Chieftain and his vicious nature to want to cause his family pain.

"Jon!" The Chieftain's face contorted into one massive frown as he wagged a finger. "We heard you've already brought this land dweller to the prophet before introducing him to us."

"Odu summoned us," Jon explained.

"A summons you didn't have to answer," Chieftain Eryll replied with an air of indignity, "for only the Council has the power to issue one."

"I am aware of the Council Code, Elof."

Ryne did not miss his father's defiance in calling the Chieftain by his given name, even though his face and tone remained impassive. It bothered Ryne that his father appeared so calm at a time like this.

The Chieftain turned away from Jon's steady gaze, his face flushing, and placed his malevolent glare upon the land dweller. "What is your purpose here, boy?"

Markus's clenched fists shook as he spoke, "My purpose?"

The Chieftain made a grand show of turning in his chair and looking over each shoulder. "Is there an echo in these walls?"

Again, the other members broke into noxious laughter.

The land dweller tilted his chin. "I am just trying to heal, so I can climb to Madhea."

Chieftain Eryll shook his head. "Yes, I've heard about your fool plan to scale Ice Mountain and rid yourself of the witch's dragon."

Markus colored. "That is my plan."

The Chieftain broke into a wide grin. "Sounds like a lovely trip. Be sure to send her our greetings when you get there."

The piercing laughter from the members was almost unbearable. Tar whimpered and lay down while covering his ears with his paws. Though Ryne had no affinity for the land dweller, the Council's taunts pricked his ire. He had an overwhelming urge to rip off a sharp ice crystal and hurl it at the Chieftain.

After the laughter had died down, Chieftain Eryll leveled Markus with a sinister glare as his thin lips curled back in a feral snarl. "While you are here with us, boy, know this: we, here in Ice Kingdom follow a strict code, and those who disobey this code are dealt with by the Council." The Chieftain nodded toward the Guardians. "One act of violence against any of our people, and you shall be met with strict and severe justice. Do I make myself clear?"

Markus's eyes widened and his face paled, making him look more like a frightened child than a hulking giant. "Aye," he said in a weak voice.

"I suppose that is a yes?" The Chieftain arched back, never taking his heated gaze from Markus. "Nod if you understand me."

The land dweller swallowed and did as he was told.

Ryne didn't know whether to feel pity for the boy or disgust.

"Good. Now go hurry up and heal." Chieftain Eryll shooed Markus away with an indifferent wave of his hand. "You don't want to keep your beautiful witch waiting."

Much to Ryne's dismay, the squeals of laughter resumed. One member reached over and patted the Chieftain on his back as the arrogant slog puffed out his meaty chest with a triumphant, smug smile on his face.

As Markus stepped back into the shadows, Ryne could hear his father murmuring to him. While he couldn't hear what was being said, he knew his father would try to soothe the land dweller. When Ryne was younger, how he had relished his father's gentle hand whenever he came to him with cuts and bruises. Now he saw his father's coddling as nothing more than a reckless indulgence. He would have to speak with Jon before he turned the land dweller into a weakling.

"So, Ryne," the Chieftain said with a sneer, "tell us of your adventures above the ice."

*Adventures?*

Ryne clenched his fists by his side, trying his best to quell the flames of rage that kindled within. "I did not surface merely for an adventure."

"Ah." The Chieftain heaved an exaggerated sigh and slumped his soft body against the padded throne. "So more of your doomsday prophecies? Very well, then speak, for we have not gone to supper and I, for one, am famished." He patted his huge gut.

In that moment, Ryne knew his warnings would fall on deaf ears. "I do not know if what I have to say will do any good," he spat, "for it seems you've already made up your minds. But I must warn you all that the ice melts. Soon, our kingdom will be no more."

The Chieftain chuckled. "Ice always melts come spring. History has taught us it is the way of the seasons above the surface."

"Yes, but not like this." Ryne struggled to keep the anger out of his voice. "Entire villages along the river have been washed away."

The members gasped and whispered amongst themselves. Ryne was pleased by their startled reactions. Surely they couldn't refute his evidence.

But, even then, the Chieftain's booming voice silenced them all. "Do not be fooled by the boy's tales. He seeks glory for himself and to reclaim his family's status."

"That is a lie!" Ryne roared.

Jon grasped him by the shoulder. "Reign in your temper, son."

Ryne shook off his father's hand. He would not reign in his feelings. He was tired of begging the Council to understand, just as he was tired of the way his father bowed down to them.

"If it is status you seek," the Chieftain continued, "my son has already provided a way—an alliance with the house of Eryll." He heaved another sigh while rolling his eyes. "Though I cannot understand why he wishes to wed your sister when so many other esteemed families have offered their daughters."

"Esteemed families?" Ryne growled. "What good will esteem do you when you are dead?"

The Chieftain broke into a fit of laughter, and the other members chuckled alongside him.

"You are all fools!" Ryne stomped his foot, causing the ice beneath the padded floor to crackle. "My family seeks an alliance with none of you!"

"Very well, then." The Chieftain shook his head while waving Ryne away with a flick of the wrist. "The Council has heard enough of your doomsday prophecies, son of Nordlund."

As Ryne glared at the man who would sentence an entire kingdom to their deaths, rage like he had never known infused his skull. He wanted nothing more than to climb over the offering table and smash his fist through the Chieftain's fat face.

To make matters worse, Jon had done little to refute the Chieftain's accusations. But why? Why didn't his father stand up for him when he knew his son wasn't seeking glory?

Ryne turned to his father with an accusatory glare.

Meeting his gaze for a moment, Jon stepped forward. "My son speaks the truth."

The Chieftain laughed. "Then you are as big a fool as he is."

"If you do not believe him," Jon suggested, "send a party to the surface."

Chieftain Eryll's squinty eyes widened. "And sacrifice them all to the Ice Witch? Now I see where your son inherits his madness. I will not send any more ice dwellers to perish—a lesson you should have learned from your brothers and uncles."

Ryne had heard enough. He turned on his heel and marched out of the chamber before he did something they would all regret.

MARKUS TRIED HIS BEST to keep up with Jon and Ryne. He was getting better at walking across the ice, but it had been a long day and his legs were tiring from the strain of pulling each foot free with every step. They walked up a steep, dark tunnel, lit by the occasional glowing ice crystal.

Markus had no idea where he was or how to get back to Jon's dwelling. He only hoped he wouldn't lose his way. Jon was several paces ahead of him, and Ryne and his dog were even further along. Ura's brother had been in a foul mood ever since leaving the Council chamber. If it were at all possible, Ryne's cold silence had made the boat ride across the lake even gloomier.

"Ryne, slow down," Jon called as he stopped to wait for Markus. "The boy cannot walk as fast as us."

Markus cringed, wishing Jon hadn't pointed out his incompetence. He didn't want to give Ryne more fuel for his anger, so, despite the burning pain in his legs, he tried to move faster.

Ryne turned and marched back to them with enviable ease. Markus could not mistake the hatred bubbling beneath the surface of his eyes - the same look of disdain that Father had given Alec on numerous occasions.

"I am tired and wish to retire to my bed." Ryne nodded toward Markus. "Or does this sulking giant now sleep beneath my furs?"

Jon held out a hand. "Son, I ask that you reign in your temper."

"He has lived above the surface. I'm sure *he* has seen the thaw." Ryne pointed an accusatory finger at Markus. "You could have defended me, *land dweller.*"

Tar whimpered beside Ryne, looking from his master to Jon and Markus. Clearly, the dog was not looking forward to a confrontation.

Neither was Markus.

He swallowed as he worked to steady his trembling limbs. He did not want Ryne to drive him away now because he needed time to heal before he scaled Ice Mountain.

Markus shook his head. "I have seen none of what you speak."

Ryne stormed over and jabbed him in the chest. "Spring has come early this year or have you been too busy slaughtering defenseless animals to notice?"

Markus froze. Instinct told him to push back, but somewhere in the back of his mind he couldn't escape the nagging feeling of guilt; that he was a monster, just like his father.

"Ryne!"

Markus flinched as Jon stepped between them, glaring at his son. For some reason, Markus expected him to punch Ryne or, at the very least, push him to the ground. So, he was surprised when Jon gently pushed his son until he stepped away.

Ryne turned to his father, his features twisted in a look of pain. "You backed down to that Eryll slog when I needed you most!"

"Ryne." Jon heaved a sigh. "Swaying the Council takes time."

"We do not have time!" Ryne held out both hands and pointed to the icy walls around them. "Will none of you listen?"

He turned back to Markus and spoke in an accusatory tone. "Have you not traveled down the Danae to the neighboring villages and seen how the river swells?"

Markus shrugged. "I have only ever traveled to Kicelin."

"Then you are of no use to me, to any of us!" Ryne spat. "I sleep in my own bed tonight and you may make a bed on the floor." He turned and marched back up the tunnel, with the dog following behind him.

JON KNELT DOWN BESIDE Markus with a look of concern in his pale eyes. "Are you sure you will be comfortable?"

Looking away, Markus had wanted to say that the attention Jon lavished upon him was far more uncomfortable than a hard floor, but he kept quiet. After all, he was indebted to Jon and Ura for saving him and nursing his injuries. "I have slept on harder surfaces than this many a time on the hunt."

Markus was lying on a makeshift cot of raised furs on the floor of the chamber at the front of the dwelling where he had first seen Ura arguing with Bane. To his left were two door flaps; one led to Ryne's chamber and the other to what Jon had jokingly referred to as "the brewing room," but it was more like a cramped hole with a wooden bucket in the center. The family actually used the room to relieve themselves.

To Markus's right were two more door flaps. Markus assumed they led to the chambers of Ura and Jon. Facing him was yet another door, the exit to the dwelling, which was covered with a heavy drape resembling the slick coat of a fish.

Jon sat beside Markus and placed the warming stone next to him. "Here, this will keep you warm tonight. All you need to do is close your eyes and will it to warm you."

"Will it?" asked Markus, puzzled as to how he could make an object do his bidding.

"Imagine the stone is warming your bed," Jon said, picking it up and closing his eyes. Within a few seconds, the stone turned a glowing pink. Jon opened his eyes and handed it to Markus.

Markus was amazed as warmth radiated all around him.

"Now ask it to keep you warm tonight," Jon said.

Markus stared down at the glowing rock in his hand. "Do I ask it out loud?"

Jon shrugged. "You may say it to yourself."

Markus closed his eyes and murmured to himself, asking the stone to keep him warm. To Markus's surprise, it pulsated in his hand. Smiling, Markus slipped the warm stone beneath the furs.

"Do you sleep here, too?" Markus wondered, feeling slightly awkward that Jon was sitting beside him. The narrow cot of furs looked only big enough to sleep one person.

Jon shook his head. "No, I only wait for Ura. I will retire to my chamber when she returns. Do you mind waiting up with me?"

"Nay," Markus answered. For sure, he would not sleep until he knew Ura had returned safely.

Jon rubbed the deep lines etched into his narrow forehead. Markus thought how Jon seemed to care for his children; how he showed them love and patience even when they did not always seem to consider his feelings. If Markus had run off as Ura had done, or spoken as Ryne had, he knew his own father wouldn't have been so understanding.

"I think you are a good father," Markus blurted out, hardly realizing he was sharing his feelings with Jon before it was too late.

He paused, feeling the heat creep into his chest and face as he stole a glance at Jon. The man was smiling back at him, and he had that same caring look in his eyes that he gave to his own children.

Markus dropped his voice to barely a whisper. "My father would've beaten me to a pulp if I had spoken to you as Ryne had." Or, even worse, his father would've beaten Alec to a pulp and forced Markus to watch.

Jon leaned over and clasped Markus's shoulder. "A father need not beat his son to teach him a lesson."

Markus nearly choked on the rising tide of emotion that threatened to overwhelm him, thinking about the unfair hand that life had dealt him and his brother.

If his father had only been more like Jon, how different their lives would've been. Mayhap he wouldn't have felt the need to take out his frustrations on animals and he would have never evoked Madhea's wrath. Ura and Ryne did not realize their good fortune.

"I wish my father had been more like you," he said.

Jon leveled Markus with a knowing expression in the tight lines around his eyes. "Did he beat you often?"

"Nay, he beat my brother," Markus rasped, but could say no more.

"Alec?" Jon asked.

Unable to form words, Markus simply nodded. He leaned forward and clutched his chest, overcome by an arrow of shame that pierced his heart. What would Jon and his family think of him if they knew how Father had beaten Alec while he did nothing? Then he remembered Dianna's accusations that night of his celebration: that he would grow into a monster, just like his father. He had already brought a curse upon his family. His mother was dead; his brother alone and possibly dead as well.

"Do you miss him?"

Markus looked at Jon through a misty gaze. That was when he realized he'd been crying. He swiped at the moisture beneath his eyes and turned away, ashamed to have shown his weakness. "Aye, it pains me to speak of him," he replied, wishing Jon would leave him in peace, so he could bottle his dark thoughts and cease his foolish tears.

Behind him, Jon heaved an audible sigh. "You have a good heart, son."

A bitter laugh escaped Markus's throat as he glanced back. "I do not think so."

Jon dropped his hands to his sides as his eyes grew cloudy. "The icy fortress you've built around your heart will thaw as your wounds heal."

Markus peered down at his wounded arm, still bound in a sling.

"Not those wounds, son," said Jon. "Your father has wronged you and your brother, but that does not mean you must grow to be like him."

The soft sound of footsteps crunching on ice could be heard from outside the dwelling. As if they were of one mind, both men looked toward the door.

Jon rose and walked across the threshold. Pulling open the door covering, he peered outside and then turned to Markus with a slight smile. "In time, you will see my words are true."

URA WAS NOT SURPRISED to find her father and Markus waiting up for her when she returned home. While it brought her a measure of comfort to know she had a family who cared for her, she did not wish for any company right now. She only sought the solace of a warm bed and hoped they would not pester her with questions.

Father, having much experience gauging her dark moods, must have sensed her irritation. He simply kissed her on the forehead and wished her a good night before retiring to bed. Markus, on the other hand, glared at her from across the chamber where he sat atop a makeshift cot.

Markus was not her nursemaid, keeper or lover, so he had no right to look as if she owed him an explanation. She averted her gaze while crossing the threshold toward her chamber, and then swore when he stood up and blocked her path. She tried to swat him away, but he would not budge.

"Where have you been?" His tone was not stern or angry, but more like that of a wounded animal.

This land dweller was so puzzling. He was as solid as stone and as soft as moss. Ura heaved a frustrated sigh as she looked into his brooding eyes. "If you must know, I went to see Odu."

"The prophet?"

She nodded.

"Did he help you?"

Ura rubbed her aching temple, but it did little to purge her puzzling thoughts. "I go there seeking answers, but mostly I leave more confused than before."

Markus's darkened glare softened. "So why do you go?"

Ura sank onto the cot. She'd had such a wearying day. Her brother's homecoming should've been one of joy and celebration, but his troubling news only heaped more worry and sorrow upon her shoulders. That was why she had sought the prophet's guidance. Fool she had been to believe this time the swirling mists would give her answers.

Ura hung her head in her hands and spoke toward the fur-lined floor. "Sometimes Odu sees things, Markus; things that may come to pass. I thought he might know what is to become of us."

She heard Markus's sharp intake of breath as he sat beside her. "And what did you find?"

"More questions. More riddles. More possibilities," she growled, as the thick tension behind her skull threatened to break free. She wanted so badly to throw or hit something, or just run away.

Ura sat up and looked into Markus's eyes, and for the first time she allowed herself to wonder what life would have been like for the two of them if she hadn't once seen her own death in the swirling mists. Would she have allowed their touch to mean something more? She shook her head and purged all foolish thoughts of love.

"He sounds as frustrating as his brother," Markus grumbled.

When Ura saw Markus reach out to clasp her hand, she sprung to her feet. "Yes, but he means well." She paced the center of the chamber, across a snow bear rug, worn to a dull brown with age and use. "Did you know he was the one who saved the Ice People from Madhea?"

Markus arched a brow. "No. How?"

Ura stopped pacing and sank down onto the rug, her bones weary. Soon she would need to seek the comfort of her bed. "He was not from our village, but he came upon my ancestors soon after Madhea had unleashed her dragon. He brought the survivors to safety beneath the ice and gave warming stones to the four most powerful families."

"So there are only four stones?" Markus asked.

"Five. Odu has one."

Markus's eyes widened. "Your family is fortunate to be one of the few."

Ura swallowed before averting her gaze. "Before the Eryll Clan claimed the chiefdom, my family was once the most powerful in Ice Kingdom." She hated talking about her past and how her ancestors' sacrifice not only cost them their lives, but catapulted the Eryll Clan to power.

"What happened?"

Tears threatened at the backs of Ura's eyes. "My father was just a boy when my grandfather and uncles first set out to prove the ice was melting. They never returned. Odu believes the witch destroyed them."

"I'm sorry." Markus's eyes squinted as he tilted his head. "I don't understand. Even then the ice was melting?"

"Yes, but at a much slower rate than it is now, and then it stopped for a time."

Suddenly, Ura remembered the messenger who had come from the Council chamber with word of her brother's meeting, and she scowled as a new wave of anger surged through her. "When I was with Odu, word came that the Council refused to believe my brother's claims."

"Aye," Markus nodded. "The Chieftain said it was all a hoax to reclaim the family's glory."

Ura shot to her feet. A roar erupted from her throat. "That is a lie!"

"I know, Ura." Markus held out his hands in what looked to be a calming gesture. "I can see your brother is in earnest."

Ura turned down her gaze and clenched her fists at her sides, doing her best to regain composure. Letting her anger get the best of her would do her family no good.

"Thank you, Markus. It means a lot to me that you believe him." Ura inhaled a shaky breath. Looking back at him, her hushed voice sounded much like a plea. "Now, how do I convince my people that Ryne speaks the truth?"

# Chapter Thirteen

"Get up, land dweller."

Markus awoke with a start when his bed was jostled about. Just as he poked his head out from beneath the warm furs and into the frigid morning air, he was met with a big, sloppy kiss from Tar.

"Yuk!" Markus spat, waving the dog away. He looked up to see Ryne scowling at him.

"Hope you slept well. You will need your strength for training today."

"I did not sleep well," Markus grumbled. "When your dog was not trying to climb beneath my furs, he was making all kinds of noise. I've never heard a beast lick himself so often."

Leaning toward Markus, Ryne sniffed once and wrinkled his nose. "He prefers not to smell like an animal, which is more than I can say for you. Besides, what do you expect when you horde the warming stone beneath your furs?"

Markus wanted to reply that Jon had given him the stone because Ryne had forced him to sleep on the floor, but he knew that would only leave him open to more teasing. "You should have let your mutt sleep in your bed," he replied instead.

"I tried, but he kept returning to you." One corner of Ryne's pale mouth hitched into a mischievous grin. "I think he likes you, though I can't understand in all the Elements why."

Markus answered by scowling. Usually, one of his dark looks was enough to silence those who dared to mock him, but Ryne only laughed. Despite the frigid temperature in the room, Markus's blood began to boil. Even with an injured arm, he started conjuring images of knocking Ryne onto his backside.

Tar whimpered as he warily eyed both of them. Ryne knelt down and stroked him behind the ears. The dog ceased his whining and leaned into his master while wagging his bushy tail.

Ryne glanced at Markus. "Get dressed. Today is your first climbing lesson."

Markus's jaw fell open. "Climbing? I cannot climb with a broken arm." He instantly regretted the pleading tone that slipped into his voice as Ryne did not need another excuse to taunt him.

Ryne's brows hitched and his eyes filled with mirth. "Why, certainly you can," he said with rather too much enthusiasm, "though it won't be easy."

"This is madness, brother!"

Markus turned to see Ura standing in the doorway, her hair falling in cascading, crystalline waves; a sharp contrast to the fire in her eyes. Markus gaped at her, too transfixed by her beauty to speak.

Ryne stood and folded his arms. "It is madness to send him back out there as an unskilled climber, because I can assure you, sister, that when his arm is healed, this fool will attempt to scale the mountain again."

Ura shot him a look that could've melted stone. "Is that your plan, Markus?"

He slowly nodded. "Aye."

"Do you know that if you do not die on the climb to the top, the witch will kill you?" Her voice cracked.

"Mayhap she will," Markus reasoned, "but if I do not reach the top, her dragon will kill me anyway."

Ura shook her pale head. "Her dragon cannot reach you here."

"Aye, not as long as the ice is stable, but Ryne has already seen that it is not, and what of my village, Ura?" He slowly rose from his bed and faced her. "What of my brother? What will Madhea's dragon do to them in my absence?"

Ura did not answer. Though Markus could have been mistaken, he thought he saw a sheen of tears well up in her eyes. Why would she cry over him? Why would she cry over a monster?

Ura stepped around Markus to face her brother. "Where are you taking him?"

Ryne bent down and slipped on his ice soles. "To the Gnull Tusks."

Ura gasped. "Those spikes are too high."

Ryne stood and patted his sister on the back. "Do not fret, Ura. I will try not to let him die on his first day."

There was levity in Ryne's eyes that bothered Markus, but not nearly as much as it bothered Ura, who responded by punching her brother in the arm. She stormed back to her room without giving either of them a second glance.

"Ouch!" Ryne laughed, rubbing his arm. "This is my reward for teaching my sister how to fight." He picked up the worn, rabbit-feet ice soles and tossed them to Markus. "Put these on."

Markus scowled down at the soles. "I cannot with only one arm."

"Sure you can. My father and sister have softened you. Don't expect any coddling from me."

Markus grumbled and stormed off toward the brewing room. He made hasty work of relieving himself, returned to his cot and tried to stuff his feet into the soles with only one good arm. Markus swore as he struggled to slip on one boot. He leaned over, using the fingers of his broken arm to hold the sole in place. The movement caused his arm to ache, but he would rather go without soles at all than beg any help from Ryne.

After he finally finished the task of fitting into one sole, he looked up at Ryne as he reached for the other boot. The older boy was standing there, smugly smiling, leaning against the wall with his arms folded across his chest.

"By the time your arm has healed," Ryne said, "climbing will be easy work."

"Be back before luncheon. I will arrange a meeting with Odu," Jon said as he emerged from his chamber.

"Odu?" Ryne scowled. "What can he do for us?"

"He still has sway among certain members of the Council."

Markus's breath hitched as Ryne rolled his eyes at his father. "Not among the members who will decide our fates."

Jon merely shrugged as he grabbed the warming stone from Markus's furs. He placed it inside what resembled a small, clay oven, closed the door and then set a pot of ice on top. To Markus's surprise, steam rose up from it. Markus wondered how a mere stone possessed such properties to make broth boil. He wondered what other magical powers it had.

Jon then grabbed a handful of what looked like green slime and dumped it into the pot. Tar whimpered, and began salivating all over the fur-lined floor.

Ryne's eyes snapped to Markus. "Hurry land dweller, I've seen slogs faster than you."

Jon stirred the pot with a long, ivory-colored spoon. "You will need nourishment before you go."

Ryne shook his head. "We need to make haste if we are to beat the others."

In a way, Markus was relieved that he wouldn't be forced to eat green slime again. He thought about the meat sticks he still had in his pack. Though he knew he needed to conserve his own supply of food, the hollow, aching pain in his stomach reminded him that he hadn't eaten much since he fell into Ice Kingdom. Markus struggled to slip on the second sole before reaching for his cloak.

Jon did not lift his gaze from the boiling pot. "You will return before luncheon." Jon said it without inflection as he continued to stir the broth. Something in his unwavering tone said this was a command that was to be obeyed.

"Yes, Father."

Markus arched a brow, amazed Ryne actually showed his father some respect.

"Good," Jon added. "I have yet to hear what you have seen above the ice. I'm sure Odu wishes to know as well."

Ryne scowled at his father's back. "Why does he need my account when he has the swirling mists?"

Markus noted the slight fall of Jon's shoulders. "You know the mists do not always answer."

"Of course not! They only answer when it's convenient for him." There was no mistaking the venom in Ryne's voice.

Jon dropped the spoon into the pot and turned to Ryne. A look of pain flashed in his bright eyes. "He has always supported you, son. Why do you despise him so?"

Ryne pushed off from the wall and threw up his hands. "Because he is an old, babbling fool."

For a long, tense moment, neither father nor son spoke a word. Markus looked from one to the other. The void in the chamber seemed to widen with each cold stare and every shallow breath.

Finally, Jon heaved an audible sigh. "Do not say such things. Ura and I—"

"Put too much faith in his prophecies," Ryne spat. "I put my faith in facts."

Markus was still struggling to slip his cloak over his broken arm when Jon came to his aid. Though he could feel Ryne's scowl boring into both of them, he allowed Jon to help him finish dressing.

"Let us go, land dweller." Ryne swung a large sack onto his back before turning to his father. "We shall be back before luncheon. I will speak to your prophet, though I doubt it will do any good."

As Markus followed Ryne and his dog out of the doorway, he cast a furtive glance behind him. Jon was standing there, watching them go, looking ages older than he had the evening before.

Markus read sorrow in the older man's eyes; somewhat similar to the baleful look his mother used to give Alec after one of Father's beatings.

But, in that brief moment, Markus had seen deeper into Jon's soul than he had in a lifetime of living with his mother. What he saw in Jon was more than just sorrow, longing or despair. In his eyes, Markus saw a man haunted.

MARKUS CHEWED ON A meat stick as he struggled to keep pace with Ryne. As his eyes slowly adjusted to the dim light of the tunnel, Markus wondered how these ice dwellers could tell day from night while living in this chasm under the ground. He missed waking up with the sunrise and feeling its warmth on his face.

Taking another bite of his meat, Markus noticed Tar whimpering beside him, his eyes wide with longing. He laughed, watching saliva coat the dog's jowls and then harden to ice. So much for Ryne's assertion that Tar was loyal – he was only loyal to whoever held the meat sticks. Markus wished Tar would keep step with his master and wondered how long he would have to endure his bothersome begging.

"How much longer must we walk?" Markus asked, after he'd eaten the chewy meat. Wiping his hands on his pants, he showed his empty palms to the dog, hoping the mutt would go bother his master instead.

"Do not tell me you tire already?" Ryne called behind him. "You've yet to climb the Gnull Tusks."

Markus lengthened his stride, though he knew he risked falling. He channeled all of his concentration into digging his feet into the ice and then pulling them free again while he worked to steady his labored breathing. Finally, he almost caught up with Ryne.

"What is a gnull tusk?" Markus asked.

"A gnull is a beast; a vicious beast, thrice as large as a snowbear, with bloodshot eyes and two large tusks protruding from its mouth." Ryne made an animated roar before hunching up his shoulders and swinging his arms in front of his face.

Though Markus could not see his expression, he could hear a smile in Ryne's voice; he seemed to take pleasure in scaring him. Markus wondered if he had ever tormented Ura this much. After spending only one morning with this man who behaved like a child, he missed Alec's gentle words and kind smile. He was struck by an ache in his chest. How he longed to see his brother.

Markus shook his head, trying his best to purge any dark thoughts as missing Alec would not do him any good now. "So we are to climb these gnull's tusks?"

"They are two columns of ice, curved like gnull tusks. That is how they got their name."

Markus swallowed. "There are no gnulls there?"

"They reside mostly in the river."

"A river?" Markus jerked his foot clumsily out of the ice, missed purchase with the next step, and nearly fell on his face. "Beneath this ice?"

Ryne continued his steady stride, not seeming to care whether Markus had stumbled. "The Danae," he called over his shoulder.

Markus breathed a deep rush of air before refocusing on the task of walking on ice. "Danae Creek runs near my village."

Ryne stopped, allowing him time to catch up. From what Markus could see, their path descended into a darkened cave. Jagged ice crystals protruded from the mouth of the cave, making it look like the maw of a great beast.

Ryne folded his arms across his chest, a knowing expression in his smile. "Yes, the Danae River feeds into your creek."

Markus stilled as his gaze traveled to the ground. Just how thick was this ice and how precarious? "How is it that a river runs beneath, yet this glacier still stands?"

Ryne chuckled. "Our glacier is far more vast than you realize." His pale eyes darkening, he added, "But the Danae is rising. Even the Ice People cannot deny that."

Markus thought of the river and how it flowed from beneath Ura's kingdom to his village. If the glacier was truly melting, and the river swelling, then one day his village would be submerged as well. Markus thought of his home being washed away, with Alec, Dianna and her brother swept up in the flood. Then he imagined these beasts called gnulls swimming into his village.

"The Danae must be very large if gnulls live within its waters."

Ryne nodded. "There are several pockets of water beneath our glacier, some nearly as large as Crystal Lake."

A chill raced up Markus's spine and he suspected it had nothing to do with the frigid air. "Do gnulls live there, too?"

Ryne shrugged as Tar sidled up to him and nudged his leg. "The gnulls live in the deeper parts of the river; about three days' journey from here."

Markus willed the tension in his neck and shoulders to subside, though ever so slightly, and wished his arm was not broken. If only he was free from this blasted curse, so he could defend himself against any ice beasts with his bow.

"The gnulls do not surface?"

Ryne slipped his pack off his back and dug out a few serpent tails before tossing them to the dog. "Only when they are very hungry."

Tar's jowls snapped with a loud 'pop' as he caught each tail and devoured them without so much as chewing the meat.

Markus imagined one of the gnull beasts swallowing him in the same way.

"What do they eat?" he asked, fearing he already knew the answer.

"Kraehn, usually, but the gnull will eat anything they damn well please." Ryne's face hardened, his mouth set in a grim line. "It is best that we are always on our guard when we travel, and why we fish in packs."

Markus worked to close his gaping jaw. "But there are only two of us now. Do you not fear a gnull could overcome us?"

"Us? Why, no." Ryne flashed a sideways grin. "You would make a filling meal for a gnull, and Tar and I can easily outrun you."

Ryne turned and continued his descent into the cave with his dog at his heels.

Markus warily trailed in their wake.

THE WALK THROUGH THE pitch-black cave turned out to be much harder than expected, even though Markus knew he did not need to see to put one foot in front of the other. He tried to consider himself lucky that he had his ears to guide him. All he had to do was listen to the crunching of Ryne's boots ahead and the heavy breathing of the mutt.

Markus wondered how hunters were ever able to harvest their kill with such noisy companions. When the irksome dog was not whimpering, slobbering or chewing his behind, he was panting like a boar in heat. But, in all honesty, Markus welcomed the distraction of Tar, because the dog kept his mind off other things: dark thoughts of his father striking Alec; the crimson bullseye on his mother's stomach; and Alec alone and afraid, with no one to care for him.

The tunnel's frigid air also kept Markus in the present, though as he descended further into its icy grasp, he was not so sure it was a fair trade. Despite the exertion of traversing the ice and the burning pain buzzing across his sore muscles, as if fire ants had burrowed beneath his flesh, Markus was chilled to the bone. It was a cold unlike any he'd ever known. As he walked, he kept his head down to prevent his face being pelted by the wind.

*Wind! Beneath the ice!*

Markus had no idea from whence it came, but the tunnel was alive with the freezing air flowing all around him, mayhap even though him, for the wind seemed to breathe through every pore in his skin. As they finally emerged from the dark pit, he wanted to shout in relief, but even the shallowest of breaths burned his lungs.

Ryne turned to him, and Markus was shocked to see frost crystals had formed along his pale brows and nose. "I see you've survived the Icy Lung."

Markus simply glared at the man who had taken him through that frozen hell pit without warning.

Ryne bent over and patted Tar on the back, brushing crystals of his coat and face. Straightening up, he trudged ahead, leaving Markus no choice but to follow.

They were now on an incline and Markus's calf muscles screamed in protest with each upward step. But, as they ascended, he couldn't help but notice how the walls above them seemed to brighten, almost as if the sun's rays were permeating the cavern walls. Surely this could not be, as the ice would have melted.

Reaching the top of the steep hill, Markus gasped in awe. The dome-shaped cavern housed what looked like rows upon rows of plants, each one as tall as him—a garden amid the ice. There were several ice dwellers tending to the plants, scraping crystals off leaves and trimming the long, slender stalks.

The garden was far larger than Markus's family's little plot of soil beside their cabin, and the rows of greenery seemed to go on forever. He lifted his gaze and, once again, found himself in awe of the bright dome. Beams of light pierced its translucent surface and cast a dazzling glow over the plants below. How was it that this cavern had not melted?

Markus slowly followed Ryne through the garden, careful to keep his good arm by his side and not brush against the long, leafy stems. Ryne greeted a few ice dwellers as they went, but most of them shrieked when they saw Tar, despite Ryne's protests that the dog was harmless.

As they walked further into the garden jungle, Markus's senses were accosted by a sweet, pungent smell. The odor reminded him of the horrible dragon-weed broth that Ura had tried to force down his throat; the same slime that Jon was cooking on his stone hearth this morning. So, this was where the ice dwellers' main source of sustenance came from.

The further they traveled into the dragon-weed jungle, the more overpowering the smell. Gah! Markus wanted to wretch. How did these people stomach these plants? By the time they cleared the garden, his lungs were screaming in protest; not from the exertion, but from holding his breath.

After inhaling a huge gulp of air, Markus sighed in relief. Though the odor was still strong, it wasn't quite as powerful as inside the garden. Markus only hoped it wouldn't stick to his clothes and skin. He still had no idea how, or if, the Ice People bathed and he didn't welcome the thought of spending a whole season stinking of dragon weed.

It wasn't until Ryne shrugged the pack off his back that Markus spotted the two towering columns ahead of them. He let out a deep groan. How was a novice like he supposed to scale such obstacles, and with a broken arm?

Each tower was the width of a mighty lyme tree and must have risen to the height of forty men. Markus squinted. What appeared to be tiny insects on each column were actually climbers scaling the ice.

Markus spun around at the sound of Tar growling behind him. When he saw the smirking, skeletal figure of Bane Eryll approaching, he let out a low growl of his own. Bane was flanked by two equally ugly boys who looked no older than Markus. Though not as scrawny as Bane, his companions had the same beady eyes.

Bane strutted over, puffing out his chest. Markus had to repress a laugh as he recalled the image of the one scrawny rooster who ruled his mother's small nest of hens.

Bane turned up his chin and flashed a toothy smile at Ura's brother. "Greetings, Ryne, how fortunate that my brothers and I found you here." Dropping his cheerful countenance, he turned to Markus with a scowl. "Land dweller," he growled, before turning back to Ryne. "Where is your sister?"

"With our father," Ryne answered flatly, "although it is no concern of yours."

"Such a shame." Bane's voice contained a little too much exuberance. "I was hoping she would see me scale the tusks. Since you left, no man has been able to best me. I'd even be willing to bet that I can reach the top faster than you."

Ryne turned his back on Bane and rummaged through his pack. "I doubt Ura would care how fast you can climb and I am not here to race. I am here to teach Markus."

Markus blinked hard at Ryne. It was the first time Ura's brother had referred to him by his given name.

Bane let out a laugh that sounded more like the squawk of a bird. Markus was beginning to wonder if the man-boy was part fowl.

"You can't be serious!" Bane waved a hand at Markus. "You mean to teach this giant how to scale ice?"

Behind him, Bane's brothers chuckled.

Markus clenched his fists by his sides as he struggled to quell his growing ire.

"I do." Ryne didn't bother to look up as he began to examine the strands of a long rope.

Bane shrugged and cast a sideways glance at Markus. "I think you must be right. Why would Ura care how fast I can climb when watching this gnull fall on his ass will make a much finer spectacle?"

The brothers chuckled louder and Bane joined in with a few more loud squawks.

Pressure swirled inside Markus's skull like the violent ferocity of a winter storm trapped inside a canyon. He wanted nothing more than to release his anger and pound Bane into oblivion. As he struggled to control his rage, Markus was caught off guard by the sound of loud growling beside him. He glanced down at Tar, who was squatting down on all four haunches with his ears alert and fur raised along the ridge of his back. The dog's long canines were exposed, making him look like a fierce predator.

Ryne knelt by his dog and stroked his neck. "Easy, boy."

Bane backed up several paces, nearly knocking over one of his brothers in the process. "Is that beast rabid?"

"No." Ryne stood and leveled Bane with a glare. "He is just a good judge of character."

Bane's face hardened, but he said nothing as he strode past Ryne and toward the Gnull Tusks.

Markus heaved a sigh. It was going to be a long morning.

"NO, MARKUS, LIKE THIS!"

Markus swore under his breath. He had advanced up the tusk no more than a few steps. Ryne kept halting his progress to tell him he wasn't leaning into his spikes in the right way, but he could not do it. It felt too unnatural, not to mention uncomfortable. Markus would much rather hug the ice with his one good arm than rely on his legs to do so much of the work.

They had been at it all morning, and Markus was nowhere near reaching his goal. Ryne had belayed the end of the rope several feet above him. All Markus had to do was reach that belay point, but it was easier said than done when Ryne kept stopping his progress.

All the while, Bane had advanced up and down each tusk with ease. Markus thought that the boy-man's bones were probably as hollow as a bird's. His fingers were small and thin, and could fit easily into the small cracks along the icy wall. Bane was also lithe and quick, like a spider traversing a web. Markus hated him all the more for his skill and was certain he would easily be able to reach Madhea without injury.

To make matters worse, Ryne's mutt would not stop his incessant whining and barking. He stood on his hind legs below them, scratching at the ice wall as if he was begging to be pulled up. Despite Ryne's admonitions, Tar would not be quiet.

Ryne and Markus received their fair share of sour looks from other climbers. Many tired of Tar's barking and simply went home. In the end, Markus, Ryne, Bane and his brothers were the only climbers left. The dog continued to bark.

Bane must have finally tired of the noise as well, because Markus heard him mention turning Tar into a winter cloak before he and his brothers packed up and left.

Markus's legs were tired, and his soles and fingers were cramping. "Haven't we had enough for one day?" he asked.

"Quit your whining, land dweller," Ryne grumbled as he reclined back in his makeshift swing. Gripping a knot in front of him, he planted both feet on the surface of the tusk. Ryne looked so natural hanging from the side of the steep slope, as if he had no worries of his rope unraveling or the ice breaking.

Something about his careless indifference was unsettling to Markus. "Why do you call me land dweller to my face, but Markus in the presence of Bane?"

Ryne shrugged, before again yelling at Tar to quiet down. "I do not wish to give him the satisfaction."

"Satisfaction?"

Ryne studied Markus for a long moment in what appeared to be an assessing gaze. "Of knowing that I dislike you as much as he does."

Markus swallowed, not knowing how to answer. Despite the frigid air around him, warmth flushed his chest and face. Oddly enough, he couldn't summon the energy for a retort. Rather than feel anger at Ryne's admission, it pained Markus to know that Ura's brother thought badly of him.

"Is that as far as you've gotten?"

Markus looked down to see Ura standing a few heads below him. As if he couldn't have been brought any lower, now she would bear witness to his poor climbing skills.

Ryne chuckled before thumbing toward Markus. "This slog refuses to heed my advice."

Markus gritted his teeth; shame had been replaced by anger. If Ryne wanted to tease him, so be it, but he would not sit idly by and be made a fool of in front of Ura.

"Not when I know you'd like for nothing more than to watch me fall," he replied.

Ryne's sun-kissed face brightened as his eyes danced with merriment. "Of course, I don't want you to fall, not with my dog beneath you!"

Markus gritted his teeth. If they were not suspended several feet off the ground, and if Ryne was not Ura's brother and Jon's son, Markus would gladly pummel him.

"Father has sent me," Ura called. "He feared you wouldn't return in time."

Ryne nodded toward an ice crystal growing from a narrow shelf above them. "I have been watching the mites."

Markus looked up at the object, which glowed faintly at the tip. He did not understand how, but the ice dwellers seemed to use these suspended cones of ice to gauge the time.

"Is it time to go then?" he asked Ryne.

Ryne shrugged. "Almost."

Markus jumped at the sound of picks smashing through ice below him. He looked down to see Ura climbing up without a rope or a partner, her only tools being spiked boots and ice picks.

"What are you doing?" he gasped.

Ura flashed a dazzling smile. "I'm coming up!" Then she resumed her pace, as if climbing icy edifices was the most natural thing in the world for a girl to do.

Though Markus had been thirsty for some time, the remaining moisture in his mouth evaporated and he gazed at her, momentarily dumbstruck, with his jaw hanging open. "Y-you are scaling i-ice?" he rasped.

Ryne let out a low whistle. "Show this land dweller how it's done."

Markus turned on him. "You allow your sister to climb?"

Annoyance shone in Ryne's features. "Of course."

"But this is too dangerous for a girl."

Ryne smirked before nodding at Markus. "And yet you're up here."

In the next moment, Ura was between them. As he looked into her beautiful, vibrant eyes, Markus felt as if the wind had been sucked out of his lungs. "How did you get here so fast?"

Ryne snorted. "She can scale this entire column with no rope."

Markus watched with envy as Ryne swung on the rope toward his sister. She planted a kiss on her brother's cheek before continuing up the tusk.

Though Markus knew the spikes of his soles were firmly planted in the ice, his heart and gut felt as if they were plummeting toward the ground. Ura left the scent of cool spices in her wake as she lithely climbed up the incline.

"Ura, you could be killed," Markus called out weakly.

But it was too late. She was already several paces above him. A fall from that height would kill her for sure.

"No, land dweller," Ryne admonished, staring up at his sister with an expression akin to pride, "she is part mite."

While it pained Markus to watch her go, he had to admit that Ura's skill and finesse with a pick made Bane's maneuvers seem clumsy in comparison. She deftly plunged a pick into the ice and hoisted each leg up in what looked like one fluid motion.

He knew he was gaping, but Markus was too stunned to do anything about it. In what seemed a matter of minutes, Ura had reached the top and was quickly descending, just as smoothly as she had ascended the tusk.

Markus's chest ached as he followed her every movement. He could scarcely take a breath until Ura was safely back down. Only after she had passed between them again, and settled her feet back on the ground, did Markus resume the steady rise and fall of his chest.

"She is out of your reach."

Markus looked over at Ryne, who was studying him with a grim expression. Somehow, Markus suspected he wasn't referring to ice climbing.

# Chapter Fourteen

Markus couldn't believe he had followed Ryne and Ura to see Odu. Sitting inside the strange chamber that smelled like pungent spices made Markus uneasy. For once, he was grateful for the flea-ridden mutt that sat beside him, as he suspected Tar was the reason the other ice dwellers kept their distance. They sat cross-legged on worn animal pelts against the chamber walls, casting alternating stony glances at Markus and the dog while listening to the prophet.

Markus wondered whether these people had any intention of leaving. He had heard about followers such as these from his father, who had called them cults. In fact, it was said that Dafuar had such a following until he prognosticated the Great Famine.

At least this time it was Ryne who was under Odu's scrutinizing eye. Markus watched him, seated beside the prophet, from a safe distance.

"So, how fared your trip above the ice?" the prophet asked, before inhaling from his pipe.

Ryne waved at the raised pool of mist beside them. "Why don't you ask your mists, prophet?"

As Odu blew out a puff of air that seemed to fill the whole chamber, Markus's senses were again accosted by that strange, spicy smell.

"I would, but at times the mists can be just as stubborn as you." The prophet leaned over and handed the pipe to Ryne.

Scowling, he waved the pipe away. "I'm sure your little mites have already reported my findings to you."

"They have." The prophet tapped the ashes from his pipe into a small bowl, which looked to be nothing more than a shell. "But, I wish to hear it from your own mouth. Is it true that you have been to the ocean?"

Ryne nodded. "I have."

"You had no altercations with the witch or her pixies?" the prophet asked.

Ryne folded his arms across his chest and leveled the old man with a decisive glare. "No, prophet."

"What of the forest creatures?"

The slightest of smiles tugged at one corner of Ryne's mouth. "There were some strange ones, to be sure."

The prophet leaned closer, his white beard dragging the fur beneath his robe. "Were they kind to you?"

"I did not go above the surface to make friends." Ryne narrowed his eyes at the old man before turning toward the crowd. "The river is rising. I have seen it, though the Council refuses to believe me."

Odu leaned back, took a long drag from his pipe, and exhaled a curtain of smoke. "You must find a way to make them believe you."

"How? They are more stubborn than your mists." There was no mistaking the caustic tone in Ryne's voice.

The prophet waved through the cloud of smoke shrouding his face. "Take a party to the top," he suggested, not meeting Ryne's gaze as he leaned against the mound of furs behind him.

Ryne's face reddened as he clenched his fists by his sides. "The Council will not agree to it. They've refused me before."

The prophet sunk further into the furs and peered at Ryne through half-lidded eyes. "You do not need their permission if the men volunteer." He spoke with a sleepy, unaffected drawl.

"I could not rally volunteers last time," replied Ryne, his voice rising. "What makes you think I can now?"

Ryne's squinting gaze roamed Odu's chamber. To Markus's dismay, not one of the prophet's followers returned his gaze.

The prophet, seemingly oblivious or unconcerned by the cowardice of his followers, drawled in his sleepy tone, "You must do something, Ryne. Your house was once the strongest in all Ice Kingdom."

"I know that," Ryne spat.

Odu's eyes widened for just a moment before he lowered his lids again. "Your grandfather was a great chieftain. Do not dishonor his memory by doing nothing while your kingdom drowns."

"I have not been doing nothing!" Ryne jumped to his feet, his limbs shaking as his sun-kissed face reddened. "I risked my life to surface!"

Tar whined and shifted on his paws. The prophet's followers gasped and murmured. A few got up and left the chamber, while others scooted further away from Ryne and Odu.

The prophet merely folded his hands in his lap and smiled. His eyelids were now completely shut. "Not enough."

"Not enough? So, what should I do, prophet, even if I convince my people that the ice is melting?" Ryne's shoulders were rigid as he spoke. "Should I bring them all to the top? I might have escaped the witch's notice, but I can assure you I cannot lead an entire kingdom to the surface without drawing attention. Then what? For sure, she will send her dragon to freeze us all."

"Change is coming," Odu said as his eyes shot open. Raising one limp hand, he pointed toward the swirling mist beside him. "I have seen that much. The Ice People must learn to adapt or they will all perish."

Ryne threw up his hands. "So, what should I do?"

Odu sighed as he pulled a thick pelt from behind him and draped it over his bony legs. "You must become the man you are destined to be."

"This is why I hate coming here. Your parables are confusing. Do me a kindness, prophet, and never summon me again."

Ryne slammed his fist into a dangling ice crystal, and it came crashing to the ground just beside Odu's legs. His followers gasped and hissed, and a few of the men rose to their feet. The prophet did not flinch as he lay beneath his furs with a complacent look upon his wrinkled, worn face, before closing his eyes for a second time.

Markus narrowed his gaze on the shattered ice. What appeared to be tiny columns of glowing ants marched out of the crystal and began weaving their way under the furs and up the wall. It was one of the strangest sights he had ever seen.

After Ryne had stomped on what was left of the broken crystal, he stormed out of the prophet's chamber, with his dog trailing in his wake. Markus was sure the gawking ice dwellers were as shocked as he by Ryne's violent outburst. Mayhap they were not so surprised by the strange column of glowing bugs, which, oddly enough, had already crossed the jagged ceiling and were now tunneling into another formation.

So, this was how the ice crystals were able to glow: tiny, bright bugs had carved out their homes inside the ice.

For a moment, Markus was so in awe of the bugs that he nearly missed Ura's exit. He struggled to his feet and made haste as well. He had no desire to spend another moment with these 'cultists,' but he did plan on asking Ura more about the glowing bugs.

Markus had a hard time keeping up with Ura as she chased after her brother. Luckily, she was able to corner Ryne in a shallow alcove. Markus was still several paces away, but he suspected half of the kingdom could hear their heated debate.

"Ryne," Ura cried, "do not forget that it was the prophet who predicted the melting of the ice in the first place."

Her brother paced the small alcove while clenching his fists. "And what has he done about it? Nothing! Yet he expects me to convince our people."

"He tried to warn us once, and you know what happened to Grandfather and our uncles."

"He's the one who convinced our family to surface and look where that got them. Don't you see?" Ryne thrust his fist in the air. "He's an old fool! Now I'm a fool for believing in his prophecies as well."

"Don't doubt yourself, Ryne. Remember what the prophet said–'You must become the man you are destined to be.'"

"Great!" Ryne turned his back on Ura and growled. "Even my sister is quoting Odu."

Markus was only a few paces away and could not mistake the glossy sheen of tears in Ura's eyes as she turned from her brother. Markus stepped toward her, but she walked a wide arc around him, avoiding his gaze.

Markus's heart lurched as Ura walked away briskly, clutching a hand to her heart. He glared at Ryne, sulking in the corner of the alcove like a wayward child. Markus stormed up to him, determined to berate him for hurting her, but before he had thought of the right words, Ryne launched into a verbal assault of his own.

"Why are you not trailing after my sister?" he asked, flashing a menacing snarl as he spoke.

Markus refused to be baited by Ryne's taunts. Instead, he fired off his own reproach. "She cried for you when you were gone. I wish you could've seen the suffering in her eyes when she asked if I'd seen you."

Ryne's mouth fell open, but he made no retort as all color drained from his face. He gawked at Markus for a long moment before his wan face turned a dark shade of red.

Markus recognized the look in Ryne's eyes. It was the same look his father gave Alec right before a beating, but he didn't care. He was tired of playing the coward while watching others suffer at the hands of bullies. Markus had seen enough of that between his father and brother, and he'd be damned if he'd watch Ura suffer the same fate.

He turned up his chin and matched Ryne's dark scowl with one of his own. "If Ura was *my* sister, I would never yell at her."

Markus saw a flash of something in Ryne's eyes. Was it pain? Was it humiliation? Or was it simply another shade of anger?

Ryne worked a tic in his jaw for a long moment before the slightest of smiles cracked the hard angles of his face. "But she is not *your* sister, and I can tell your desire for her is anything but brotherly."

The accusation caught Markus off guard. Did he desire Ura? Markus did not have to give the question much thought: of course, he wanted the beautiful girl who saved his life. There was a connection when they touched, one that he could not understand. Somehow, he knew Ura was meant for him, but it would never come to pass, not with Madhea's ire plaguing him. Ura deserved a better fate than to be tied to a cursed boy.

Markus shook his head. "As you said before, she is out of my reach." Then he squared his shoulders as he willed the slightest trembling in his limbs to subside. He would not cower to Ryne, even if he was older and braver. "But you are not worthy of her, either. She deserves a better brother—one who loves her."

Ryne's smile vanished into a tight, thin line. The mirth in his eyes extinguished like a gust of wind snuffing out a candle. "Are you finished?" he asked between clenched teeth.

Markus nodded. "Aye."

"Good."

Within a few long strides, Ryne was upon him. Markus saw it coming, but he did nothing to deflect the blow. Though his face was nearly frozen and numb from the cold, Markus felt the pain instantly as warm blood seeped from his nose. His gut instinct was to cradle his broken nose in his hand, but he refused to give Ryne the satisfaction of knowing how much he suffered.

And, by damn, it hurt!

Markus considered striking back, but knew it would be foolish. Ryne was more sure-footed on the slick ice and he had two good arms. It was a fight Markus was sure to lose. Besides, what would Ura say if her brother came home bloody and bruised? Images of his mother's haunted eyes flashed through Markus's mind. He could not bear the look on her face whenever Alec came inside with a new bruise. He knew Ura loved her brother and he refused to put her through the same torture.

Beside them, Tar barked incessantly, his bushy head bobbing from one to the other, as if warning them to behave.

Ryne's face was within a chilled breath of Markus, so close that they were nearly touching, nose to nose. "No one loves my sister more than I," he growled. "And you can best believe that if the Council continues to refuse to heed my warnings, I will take my sister and my father to the surface, to some place far from here, before the witch unleashes her wrath on this cursed kingdom."

After Ryne turned on his heel and strode away, Markus finally gave into the urge to clutch his dripping nose. He was left with no choice but to follow in Ryne's wake as he could not remember the route back through the maze of ice tunnels. However, Ryne was out of sight as soon as he rounded the next darkened corner.

Luckily, Tar had waited. He padded up to Markus cautiously and nuzzled his knee before leading the way toward Jon's home. Markus was grateful for the dog's assistance as he followed on legs that suddenly felt heavy and weak. He did his best to pinch back the blood that seeped profusely out of his nose, but the break hurt to touch.

Markus did not know if the sting from his injury awakened his reasoning, but as he followed Tar's bushy, wagging tail, he realized that not all dogs were useless mongrels. Through the pain-induced haze that wrapped around his skull like a suffocating vice, Markus was able to form one clear thought—he liked that dog.

BY THE TIME MARKUS finally made it to Jon's home, the muscles in his legs were screaming in protest and his throbbing nose felt like it had grown three times in size. It took all of his remaining strength to push his way through the flap on the door, throw off his ice soles and stumble toward his cot.

Jon was standing by the small stove, brewing something pungent over the fire. He turned to Markus with a drawn brow. "What happened?"

Markus shrugged as he leaned back against the fur-lined wall, holding his nose with one hand. Though the blood flow had slowed, he still didn't feel it was safe to let go. "I slipped on the ice," he answered.

Without invitation, Tar jumped on the cot beside Markus and rested his head on his lap. Markus thought how he'd very much like to pet the dog behind the ears, but with one arm in a sling and the other clutching his nose, he had no free hands.

Jon sat down on the other side of the cot and gently pried Markus's hand away. "So, your nose broke your fall?"

"Aye," Markus said, not wishing to elaborate. If Jon knew that Ryne had caused this, mayhap he would send Markus away to avoid more strife. With nowhere to go, he couldn't risk losing his only shelter. He wasn't ready to leave Ura, either.

"An unlikely story," Jon replied, shaking his head. He rose from the cot and dipped a cloth in a steaming bowl of water that sat on the bench beside the stove. Returning to Markus, he pressed the material against his nose. "Let me tend to you."

Markus winced at the sharp pain that shot up his nose and then sighed as warmth from the cloth soaked into his bruised flesh.

"Hold this against your nose," Jon commanded. "I will make you a brew for the pain."

The man returned to the stove and grabbed a vial of dried herbs off a nearby shelf. He poured some into a mug and then ladled a spoonful of water in as well. Jon walked back to Markus and held out the steaming liquid. "Here, drink this, it will ease your pain."

Markus pulled his hand away from his nose and dropped the bloody cloth into his lap. Tipping the mug of medicine to his lips, he repressed the urge to gag as he gulped down the warm liquid. Luckily, he'd already had a bit of practice when ingesting the foul dragon-weed broth. That stuff tasted no better, he thought, as he placed the empty mug in Jon's hand and wiped his mouth with the back of his sleeve. Then he returned the warm cloth to his nose.

"Where is Ura?" Markus asked, grimacing at the nasally tone of his voice. "I do not wish her to see me like this."

Jon set down the mug on a small bench beside the cot and turned toward him. The lines of worry framing his pale eyes seemed more pronounced than ever before. "She is in her bedchamber. So is Ryne." He arched a knowing brow. "I don't suspect he will bother you again tonight."

Markus swallowed hard as he averted his gaze. Even though he didn't throw any punches, he feared Jon would try to punish them for fighting.

"The dog led you home?" Jon asked as he flashed a slight smile. Thankfully, he did not seem angry.

Markus released a pent-up breath. "Aye, he did."

"He is a good friend. Perhaps you will learn to like dogs."

"Mayhap I will."

Markus looked down at the dog, resting his head quietly on his lap. Tar met his gaze with wide, grey eyes and his bushy tail began to thump against the cot. Markus couldn't help but smile, although he inwardly berated himself for going soft over a mutt.

"Is the pain easing?" Jon asked.

Markus slowly nodded. "A bit."

The older man patted him on the shoulder before rising. "We will give the medicine a few more moments."

Jon returned to the stove and, with his back to Markus, he stirred the dragon weed.

Markus's stomach churned at the thought of swallowing even more green slime and he tried his best not to think of the torture to come. Averting his gaze, his eyes searched the small room. A candle on the table beside Jon's stove cast a faint glow across the iridescent patches on the walls around them, making the room appear bright and warm. The haze reminded Markus of the glowing bugs he'd seen in the prophet's chamber.

"I saw something odd today," he remarked.

Jon chuckled as he continued to stir the pot. "I'm sure you've seen many an odd thing in Ice Kingdom."

Markus agreed, wondering how many other strange sights lay in store for him. "When Ryne knocked over an ice crystal, there were these tiny, bright bugs."

"Mites," Jon explained.

"Are mites what light up Ice Kingdom?"

"Yes, and mites warm our fires."

Jon turned sideways and rattled the small chamber door beneath the stove. To Markus's amazement, the stove began to buzz. For the first time, he realized that thousands of hot insects were only a small door away from escape and he wondered if they were the stinging kind.

"I thought you used a warming stone to heat your fires."

"Ryne took the stone to bed, so tonight I'm using mites." Only a few families possess warming stones," Jon explained. "When you shake the mites hard enough, not only do they glow, they burn."

As if to emphasize his point, Jon shook the door harder, and the buzzing turned into a frenzy of pops. The stew on the burner began to steam and boil.

Markus was so fascinated by the bugs, he barely had time to grieve over the loss of his warm stone. No doubt Ryne took the stone to bed so that he had to spend a cold night on the floor.

"Burning bugs?" Markus asked.

"Yes, very hot." Jon wagged a finger at Markus. "Never touch them when they are angry unless you're wearing thick gloves."

"How is it that they haven't melted your entire kingdom?"

Jon turned his back to Markus again as he pulled the pot of broth off the burner and set it on the bench. "Slogs keep the mite population under control."

Markus scrunched his brow, thinking those slogs must have had innards made of iron. "So, slogs eat the burning bugs?"

Jon nodded as he poured the dragon weed into a large bowl. "Yes, the temperature doesn't affect the slogs. We also use mites to tell the time. When a crystal has half-melted and the dripping water has formed an equal-sized crystal below, that is how we know it is the noon hour."

Markus eyed the dragon weed, hoping the offering wasn't for him. Although his nose stung, he would still try to chew a few of his meat sticks. Markus breathed a sigh of relief when Jon pulled up a chair beside him and began slurping on the bowl of slimy weed.

"Strange how I never noticed those mites before," Markus said, watching Jon swallow a long tendril.

"Perhaps," Jon answered in between spoonfuls, "because your mind is always occupied with troubling thoughts."

"A dragon pursues me, a powerful goddess wants me dead, and my curse killed my mother–now it threatens my brother." Markus ended on a shaky breath as he struggled to hold back tears at the thought of his late mother and sick brother.

"What of your father? Do thoughts of him trouble you as well?"

Markus could no longer meet Jon's direct gaze. He turned away, preferring to focus on the subtle twitching of Tar's ears. "The only comforting memory of my father is the day he died, when I knew he could no longer hurt my brother and I no longer had to cower in fear at the sight of him."

He regretted the sound of despair that broke through the cracks in his voice, but while his father would have scolded him for going 'soft', he was tired of holding back his emotions.

Jon laid a hand on Markus's shoulder and squeezed until Markus was forced to turn back and meet his soft gaze. "How he treated your brother is not your fault," he said.

Pools of moisture threatened to spill out of Markus's eyes, and his throat felt tight and swollen. "Everything has been my fault. I am no better than the monster who sired me."

Jon dropped his hand to his side. "I did not know your father, but I do know that you have goodness in your heart. Ura and I can both see it. In time you will see it, too."

Again, Markus was compelled to look away. Jon's pity was too much for him to bear. He closed his eyes and silently cursed as a hot tear slid down his cheek. How could he ever grow into a man strong enough to face the challenges of Ice Mountain and Madhea's dragon if he cried like a soft female?

"I take it Ryne's meeting with Odu did not go well?" Jon asked.

Markus wondered whether Jon had changed the subject out of interest or pity. Either way, he was relieved to talk about something else.

"The prophet expects Ryne to save the kingdom, but offers him little help other than a few confusing parables."

Jon chuckled. "Yes, that is the way of Odu. I know Ryne is under a lot of duress, but that doesn't give him the right to hurt you."

Markus shrugged. "Others have fared worse than me. After bringing the curse upon my family, I deserve more than a broken nose."

Again, he was assuaged by guilt: guilt over his mother's painful death; guilt for abandoning his brother and leaving him to fend for himself; and guilt for unleashing the dragon who, when awoken, could wreak havoc on his village.

Most of all, Markus was overwhelmed with regret for needlessly killing animals. If he hadn't shot that rabbit in the gut, and all those other animals purely for sport, mayhap he wouldn't have brought on the curse. But it was too late for all that now. Markus only hoped that Madhea would see he was truly sorry for his crimes.

"Has the pain gone now?" Jon asked.

Markus pulled away the cloth and was surprised to find the throbbing in his nose had subsided. "Mostly."

His eyelids felt heavy and Markus wondered if it had anything to do with the potion.

Jon set down his bowl of broth and then stood in front of Markus. Markus winced as Jon grabbed hold of his chin with one hand and his nose with the other. Somehow, he feared this would hurt more than the initial breaking of his bones. Markus was vaguely aware of Tar whimpering beside him.

"Hold still and try not to scream," Jon said, and then jerked Markus's nose with a nauseating crunch.

Despite the warning, Markus opened his mouth to scream, but no sound came out. The blinding pain was so intense; it was unlike anything he'd ever known. For the briefest of moments, Markus realized how very much his brother had suffered at the hands of their father. How had Alec withstood the torture of broken and bruised bones day after day?

After a while, Markus was able to make the slightest of sounds from his gaping jaw, just before his world darkened.

TRAINING SESSIONS DURING the next several weeks were brutal. Ryne continued to belittle Markus's efforts, and with each step Markus took upward, he seemed to take three more back down. Why was he so deft with a bow and arrow, yet so clumsy when it came to climbing a simple slope?

If the days with Ryne were grueling, the nights with his family were even worse. The dark gloom that shrouded Ryne like a fog seemed even heavier when they ate supper.

Brother and sister barely spoke, and their father's thoughts were occupied elsewhere. Their family made for sad company, reminding Markus of the nights his family ate in silence following one of the many times Father beat Alec.

The depressing gloom of Markus's hosts only made him miss Alec more. Thoughts of his brother plagued him during the day, often distracting him when he should have been watching Ryne.

At night, Markus's mind would wander again to Alec, only he'd think of his mother, too, and how his foolishness had killed her. Guilt and depression consumed him, and on many mornings he'd wake up exhausted after only a few hours sleep.

As if Markus hadn't been tortured enough, Ura's presence whenever they found themselves momentarily alone unnerved him the most. The soft lilt of her voice, the accidental brush of her skin against his, or the way she looked at him with her large silver eyes, almost as if she could see into the very depths of his soul, was nothing less than torture. How he wanted this beautiful girl for his own, but Markus knew their love was never meant to be. Not when he was plagued by the curse.

Ironically, the only family member who managed to pull Markus out of his gloom was Tar. The dog had taken to sleeping with him most nights. Markus was getting used to the mutt's snores and the occasional times when he'd lick his nutsack or pass gas. Markus sometimes marveled at the fact that he'd actually learned to like an animal at all, but this change within him was nothing compared to the alteration in his outward appearance.

Jon had shown Markus his image one day in the reflective surface of a flat ice crystal. It was after they'd returned from bathing in one of the many warm springs found within the deep pockets of the glacier. He could hardly believe the pale and thinning boy with the slight crook in his nose was his own reflection. The color in his skin and hair had faded to an almost translucent, touched with a blue tint, just like the features of Ura and Jon. Even the hunter's mark on the side of his head had diminished to a pale blue.

Markus wondered how much more he would change before it was time for him to leave Ice Kingdom.

# Chapter Fifteen

"Wake up, Markus."

He slowly opened his eyes to see Ura smiling down at him, her pale curtain of hair cascading down one shoulder in a long braid. The small chamber echoed with the sound of her boot tapping against the floor.

"What is it?" Markus asked, as he struggled to sit up with his one good arm, the task being made even more difficult as he had busted open his shin on the Gnull Tusks the previous day.

Ura planted both hands on her hips while leveling him with a determined expression. "Ryne is in a foul mood today and I wish to go fishing."

Markus rubbed the sleep from his eyes. "Fishing?"

She nodded. "Yes, Father says I am not to go alone, so come with me."

"I thought we had to travel in large parties for fear of gnull attacks?"

"Gnulls?" Ura vehemently shook her head. "They cannot swim that far up river. It's too shallow where I fish."

"Your brother said they traveled to Ice Kingdom."

The girl flashed a lopsided grin before she burst out laughing. "And you believed him? I think mayhap Ryne was trying to frighten you."

"Aye," Markus grumbled, feeling a fool for believing Ryne's tale and an even greater one now that Ura knew he'd been tricked. "That is something he would do."

"It takes our hunters three days to reach the gnulls," Ura said, sitting down beside him and casually brushing her arm across his. "The river swells just below the edge of the glacier, before it separates into several creeks. That is where you will find the gnull colony."

Markus looked down at the spot where her skin had briefly made contact with his own, making his flesh buzz with energy. He tried not to think about her nearness as his heart raced. How did this girl affect him so, even when their conversation drifted to giant, tusked beasts?

Markus scooted away from Ura as he shook off the feel of her. He refused to draw out his torment by pining for a girl he could not have. "But your river is rising. One day the gnulls may be able to reach you here."

Ura's eyes widened. "I hope not. It takes many hunters to bring one down. If the gnulls reach Ice Kingdom, this part of the river will not be safe."

"Then let us hope your brother is wrong."

The thought of a gnull attacking Ice Kingdom, mayhap even Ura, sent a knot of fear through Markus's gut, especially as he, The Mighty Hunter, would be powerless to stop such a beast.

"My brother has been charting the water levels since he was a boy," she replied. "For the past six springs, the river has risen by a hand taller than before."

Standing, Ura grabbed a bowl off a nearby table and held it out to Markus. "Eat, so we may go." She nodded toward his bandaged leg. "Father has added herbs to the broth and it will ease your pain."

Markus accepted his dragon weed breakfast with a grimace. He was getting tired of eating this sludge every day, but the hollow ache in his stomach demanded nourishment and he hoped the herbs would calm the throbbing in his leg. Markus tipped the bowl into his mouth and gulped it down, expecting a violent reaction from his palate, but, oddly, the broth didn't taste as foul as it had before.

"Where do we go?" he asked.

"To the Danae," Ura replied as she sat beside him with her own bowl and began spooning dragon weed into her mouth. "You will see for yourself how the river swells."

Tar jumped off Markus's cot and spread his paws in front of him while raising his hind legs in a long, complacent stretch.

Oh, to be a dog and have no other cares in the world other than hunting for scraps and sleeping on a warm fur. For a moment, Markus envied the mutt. To his knowledge, dogs did not suffer from broken hearts. If they lost a mate, they simply found another. He hadn't heard of Madhea cursing animals either, so Tar would never need fear heartbreak, the ice dragon, or the wrath of the Goddess.

After they had finished their dragon weed and Tar had devoured several serpent fins, Markus and Ura prepared for their trip to the river. Ura carried a satchel slung over her shoulder and a long spear, made of what looked like an animal bone, with sharp, barbed hooks at the tip. Markus carried a pail. He also strapped his boning knife to his boot; not that he intended to kill anything, but he could at least make himself useful by fileting the dead fish.

Ura tried to give Markus a fishing spear, too, but he refused, knowing that, as part of Madhea's curse, he couldn't kill another living being. There would be neither fishing nor hunting for him this day.

Markus sighed as he glanced over at his unstrung bow and arrows, resting in the corner of the chamber. How long had it been since he'd drawn back a bow? How long would it be before he could once again feel the hum of the string as he released an arrow, or before he could fell, gut, and clean a beast for a stew? He missed being a hunter.

After they stepped out onto the long and winding tunnel, Tar slipped through the flap and followed behind.

Markus turned and pointed toward the door. "Go home, Tar," he commanded.

The dog looked to Ura and whimpered while dancing around on all four paws.

"It's okay. Ryne said Tar is to be my protector," she said before whistling to the dog.

Tar came bounding up to Ura. When she bent down and patted him on the head, he planted a big, wet kiss on her lips. She giggled, and then stood and wiped her face with the back of her sleeve.

As Markus watched the affectionate interaction between Tar and Ura, he found himself in the odd position of being jealous of a dog.

"A protector?" asked Markus. "What dangers lie at the river?"

But when Ura averted her gaze and began marching in the opposite direction, Markus had his answer. Tar was there to protect Ura from him.

THE TREK TO THE RIVER took much longer than the walk to the Gnull Tusks. The trio navigated winding tunnels, some so dark that Markus had to walk with one hand clutching Ura's satchel. Occasionally, he would catch sight of a creature covered in ivory fur hanging from an ice crystal at the top of the cavern. Having already seen a few of these slogs before, Markus knew them to be harmless, but he still didn't like walking beneath them in the dark. If they happened to be feasting on angry mites, one of the scorching bugs could easily slip and fall on his head.

The Kraehn holes were much easier to spot than Markus had initially feared, for whenever their small party reached within a few paces of a hole, the fish would bubble and snap their greedy little jowls in anticipation of food. While Markus and Ura steered clear of the Kraehn holes, Tar would whimper and walk an even wider circle around the predatory fish.

Markus was thankful that most of the journey was downhill. On this particular morning his mind felt muddled and focusing on the act of walking across the slick ice took extra effort. He suspected it had something to do with the herbs, but he didn't complain. He'd rather have a brain of mush than be constantly reminded of his aching shin.

Markus wondered if Mother had ever made a similar brew for Alec after Father's beatings. Then his thoughts would darken, wandering back to memories of his brother and regret for his actions that brought on the curse.

Markus's mood did not seem to affect Tar, whose bushy tail wagged in constant motion as he practically trotted across the ice. Even Ura walked with a hint of cheerfulness in her gait. Every so often, she'd stop to pet Tar while she waited for Markus to catch up. The mutt greedily soaked up her attention as he licked and nuzzled her hand. Again, Markus found himself in the position of being jealous of a dog.

Markus heard the river before he saw it.

"See how much the water rises?" said Ura, pointing into the distance.

Continuing his steady pace, Markus squinted in the dim light as the dark tunnel opened up to the most magnificent sight he'd ever seen. A river spanning at least ten men in width flowed rapidly through a mountain of ice, creating a cavern, whose crystalline walls jutted up toward the sky, and leaving an ice ledge of about five men in length on either side of the water. Shards of light burst through the curtains of ice that draped the walls and reflected off the water, creating a brilliant prism of color.

Markus inhaled the cool scent of fresh water and then breathed out a heavy sigh. Something about this place made him feel alive. Then he spotted fish jumping through the milky water. These were not the kind he'd seen before, with long bodies and jagged spines. No, these were plump fish with protruding, round eyes and shimmery scales. The most remarkable thing was that their fins flapped so quickly they buzzed, like the wings on an insect.

Tar barked and danced on his paws as his canine gaze eagerly followed the flying fish. It took several serpent fins to finally calm him, though Markus knew it only bought them a little extra time. For, as soon as Tar finished the fins, the mutt would resume his barking. Markus only hoped the dog wouldn't get too excited and fall into the river.

"What are those?" Markus asked, pointing at the odd fish.

"Soaring Perch," Ura answered as she shrugged her satchel off her back and clutched her spear in one hand.

Markus marveled at how the fish leapt from the water and seemed to be suspended in the air for a long moment before returning to the milky depths of the river.

"Do they taste good?" he asked, as the rumble in his innards reminded him that dragon weed and serpent tails were not enough to sustain his hunger.

"They are not sweet like Lazy Eyed Serpents," Ura answered.

Markus's mouth began to water. Mayhap these fish tasted like *real* food. The fish resembled the perch he had eaten from Danae Creek, although those didn't soar.

He watched as Ura tied one end of her spear to a long, thin string before anchoring it to a spike in the ice. Then she lifted the spear and clumsily heaved it at a fish. Markus grimaced as he watched her throw again and again, putting so much of her shoulder into the throw that he feared she would injure herself.

"Stupid fish!" She stomped her foot as she pulled the spear out of the water.

Markus repressed a grimace as he watched Ura trip clumsily over the spear before casting it to the ground.

"It isn't the fish—it's the way you throw."

Ura reached for the weapon and thrust it into his hands. "Here, you try if you think you can do better."

Markus looked down at the spear in his hand, before his gaze shot to the soaring creatures. Then he shut his eyes, envisioning the speed of the fish and the trajectory of his weapon. In his mind's eye he could see his arm release the spear and pierce the shimmery scales. Grasping the line, he jerked the rod back into his grip with the fish locked onto the barbed end.

This was what made Markus a mighty hunter: his ability to envision the kill before he released his weapon, for his kills always happened exactly as they had played in his mind.

Markus's hands began to tremble as he fought the urge to hurl the spear at a fish. How he longed to hunt again. But this longing was quickly replaced by regret as the image of his mother's bloody innards flashed in his memory. No, he would not kill. He would not lose Alec too.

Markus released a slow and shaky breath. "I cannot kill, but I can do better. Here, let me show you."

Turning, he hurled the spear into a wall. It lodged in the ice with a loud, snapping sound. He then unsheathed his knife and began digging the spear out of the ice.

Ura came up beside Markus while he worked. "My brother told me they called you The Mighty Hunter up above."

When her cool fingers brushed against his hunter's mark, he instinctively jerked away.

"I'm sorry," Ura said, before stepping back. "Does your scar pain you?"

Markus lowered his knife and turned to her. "I don't feel it, Ura. It's just that your touch startled me."

His scar shamed him. It was funny how he had always been proud of the mark. The villagers often pointed to it whenever they lavished him with praise, but now it only served as a reminder of how he had abused his blessing, which was now no more than a curse.

"Your scar looks like a bow waiting to be drawn. Is it true, then?" she prodded. "Were you a mighty hunter?"

"Aye," Markus mumbled.

"Show me," she said, before pulling out her boning knife and carving a circle into the ice wall. "Go, stand back there." She pointed to a small mound of crushed ice at least forty paces away and tapped the circle with her knife. "Let's see if you can hit the target."

Markus finally dislodged the spear and grumbled as he trudged away. Upon reaching the mound, he turned and raised the spear, noting its heavy weight and determining how much thrust he would need to hit his target. Markus aimed the spear at the ice; the vision of him penetrating the target quickly worked itself in his mind.

"You might want to move," he called to Ura, more out of courtesy as he would never really hit her. Once she had stepped away from the target, Markus pulled back, aimed, and threw.

URA RACED TOWARD THE lodged spear and let out a low whistle. She couldn't help but gawk at Markus as he walked toward her. Physically, he had changed dramatically since falling into her kingdom. Markus was much leaner now, and his dark hair and eyes were just a few shades darker than her own. But, despite his new outward appearance, Ura had to remind herself that she knew little about him.

"How did you do it?" she asked.

He turned down his gaze as his pale cheeks took on a rosy hue. "My aim always strikes true, Ura." He turned his back to her and began cutting away the spear.

"Amazing," she breathed the word at his back. "You are truly gifted, Markus."

When he turned to face her, there was no mistaking the flash of pain in his eyes. "Nay, I am cursed. If I hadn't been born with this gift, I wouldn't be here now."

Ura stepped around him and placed a gentle hand on his forearm. She gasped at how the slightest caress of her skin against his sent a jolt down her spine. "Would it be selfish of me to say I'm glad you're here?"

Markus slowly pulled his arm away as the rosiness in his cheeks spread across his face and neck.

Ura cursed herself for being a fool. He recoiled from her touch and did not show her the same interest. Besides, what right had she to flirt with this land dweller when she had seen her fate in the mists—the avalanche that would crush her bones and rob her of breath? He would leave her soon anyway, and most likely never return. Ura knew the witch would not forgive Markus, but that mattered little when he lacked the skills for climbing ice.

Ura turned her back and wiped the moisture from her eyes. Odu had told her that Markus was sent to her for a reason. While she had no idea what that might be, Ura knew she should make sure the short time he spent with her was not wasted on futile fantasy.

"It's funny how you throw the spear with such ease, yet you scale ice so clumsily," she remarked.

"I don't think it's funny at all," Markus grumbled behind her.

Ura turned back to him at the popping sound of the spear breaking free of the ice, and she nodded toward it. "Perhaps you could apply the same principal to climbing as you do to hunting."

Markus arched a pale brow. "How so?"

"If your aim always strikes true, why can't you envision yourself as the spear and the peak of the tusk the target?"

Markus looked down at the weapon in his hand as if he were seeing it for the first time. "I've never thought of it that way."

Ura inwardly smiled, hoping her advice had helped him in some way. "Try it the next time my brother takes you climbing."

A wide grin split his face. "I will."

Her heart skipped a beat at Markus's smile. Odd, but she could not recall him smiling until now.

"Good," she replied. Turning on her heel, she marched back toward the edge of the river. "Let's go catch some fish."

Ura pulled a heavy net out of her satchel. "This is what we use to catch slogs before they extinguish all of our light crystals." She tied the net to the end of her spear. With the wide, bone hoop, she aimed to net one or two large perch.

Markus walked up beside her and leveled her with a sideways grin. "That's cheating."

Ura flashed her best mocking smile. "Would you prefer some more dragon weed for your luncheon?" She couldn't help but laugh as Markus's features twisted. "I thought so."

She wasted no time when she spotted a fish flying her way. She scooped it into the net and quickly flung it to shore. Holding the net face down, she watched as the creature flapped against its confines.

Tar dropped his serpent fin and bounded up to Ura, barking at her and the fish.

While she had caught the perch this way many times before, Ura always marveled at its strength. She knelt on the spear and held down either side with her palms, but it still wasn't enough to quell the fighting fish.

"Markus, help me!" she cried.

"I can't!" he called back, a high-pitched note of despair in his voice.

No matter how firmly Ura held the spear, the fish bucked toward the water, dragging her with it. Just as they neared the water's edge and she thought all hope was lost, Tar bounded on top of the net and chomped down on the fish. The creature went limp as blood seeped out of the dog's sharp fangs.

"Drop the fish, Tar," Ura instructed.

The dog merely whimpered as it held its catch tightly in its jowls.

"The fish is dead, Markus. Can you help me now?"

"Aye." He let out a sharp whistle while clapping his hands. "Come here, Tar."

The dog backed up, dragging the fish, net and spear along with him.

Markus followed while continuing to clap. "Come, boy."

Tar whimpered and backed up again. Then he turned on his heels and ran for the tunnel.

"Stop him!" Ura shrieked. She didn't know whether to be angry or amused.

The dog sped off with her kill, the spear clanking noisily behind him as he vanished into the darkness. Markus lagged behind while dragging his wounded leg.

Ura chased after Markus, watching as he made several futile attempts to grab the end of the spear.

"Give it back, you mangy thief!" Markus hollered before he was finally able to grab hold of the weapon.

Tar stopped and turned, still clutching the fish and net in his jaw. Ura hoped the dog hadn't done too much damage to her net. It had taken her weeks to weave it.

"Drop it, Tar. Drop the fish!" Markus bellowed.

After the dog flashed them with pleading grey eyes, Ura finally gave in. "Oh, let him have it. Just get my net back."

Markus rolled his eyes while yanking on the spear. "How do I explain to this stupid mutt that he may keep the fish, but surrender the net?"

Finally, after a long, tense standoff, Tar dropped both objects. He whimpered while licking fish blood off his lips.

Markus lifted the net off the mangled fish and then handed the spear to Ura.

Tar danced around, eagerly eyeing the prize.

Markus's shoulders fell and he shook his head. "Eat it, Tar."

The dog yipped once before pouncing on the fish.

Ura examined her net, which was, surprisingly, only ripped in a few places. "I can mend this when I return home. The rips are not very large. I still think I can catch another perch."

"Let us go then while the mutt is eating," Markus grumbled.

Ura edged closer to him and, against her better judgment, she tentatively laid a hand upon his arm. "That was very nice of you, letting Tar have the fish."

"You told me to let him have it. If it were up to me, I would've given the perch to the krachn as the meat was ruined anyway." Markus scowled at Tar before turning his dark gaze back to her.

Though Ura knew Markus pretended indifference, she could not mistake the longing in his eyes. She took a chance and squeezed his arm, and when he did not pull away, she leaned in closer. He smelled of rich scents, mayhap the spices he used to cure meat. "It was still kind of you to give it to him," she breathed.

Markus's eyes darkened and Ura knew that longing had been replaced by need. Her spear fell to the floor with a loud clank before he pulled her against his chest. Ura knew it was wrong. They were not destined to be together, but she couldn't deny the wild beating of her heart as she tilted her lips toward his.

His mouth had barely brushed hers before he pulled back. "This is wrong, Ura. I must leave soon and I will not be the one to break your heart."

She clutched his shoulders as tears formed at the rims of her eyes. "It is too late, Markus."

MARKUS STRUGGLED TO find the will to let go of the beautiful girl. He was a cursed boy. He knew he did not deserve to be holding her in such a way, and yet, he could not deny the ache in his heart at the thought of letting her go. And now, as her eyes pooled over with tears, Markus hated himself for surrendering to his foolish impulse.

At the sound of Tar's menacing growl behind them, Markus released Ura and spun around.

Bane and his brothers emerged from the shadows, each looking like they wanted nothing more than to thrust one of their spears through his chest.

Bane raised an arm and pointed a finger at Markus while continuing his rapid stride. "Keep your hands off my girl!"

Tar jumped in front of Bane, the fur on his back standing on end, and the boy halted his advance. His two younger brothers and another beefy-looking boy stopped behind him.

"Call off your brother's mutt, Ura," Bane hissed, "before he meets the pointy end of my spear."

Ura gasped before whistling to Tar. The dog held his ground, blocking Bane's path while snarling like a rabid animal. Bane lifted his spear and thrust it into Tar.

As the dog howled in pain, Markus raced toward Bane and slammed his fist into his chest. The force of the blow knocked the spear out of the boy's grasp and sent him crashing to the ground. Not until Bane had skidded across the slick ice and into a darkened corner did Markus hear the bubbling frenzy.

*Kraehn!*

Markus raced after Bane and dove to the ground, latching onto his leg just as the wisps of the boy's pale hair were shredded by the demonic fish.

Bane screamed as a Kraehn jumped up from the pit and bit his ear. Markus pulled him away and then spun around on the ice, kicking the voracious predator back into its hole.

Markus was vaguely aware of a sharp pain shooting up his side and into his broken arm. His skull felt foggy, and he realized he must have hit his head when he dove for Bane. Somewhere in the distance, he thought he heard Ura crying.

Bane's brothers had swarmed around them. The beefy boy stood over Markus, glaring down at him with beady eyes similar to Bane's. Markus clutched his side and watched while Bane was lifted to his feet.

"Land dweller," Bane growled while clutching his bloody ear, "meet my cousin, Ven." The cousins exchanged knowing grins before Bane added, "Ven, meet the land dweller."

With that, Ven swung his foot toward Markus's broken arm. Markus jerked back as the spiked heel of a boot cut across the bandages protecting his arm. He howled as his flesh ripped open. His brain slipped further into a fog and his vision blurred. Somewhere in the distance, Tar whimpered and Ura cried louder. Why were they crying? What had happened?

Then two hands hooked beneath his armpits and dragged him across the ice. Somewhere behind him, a strange mixture of sounds grew louder, like a thousand snapping turtles in boiling water.

Then someone bellowed in the distance. "What is the meaning of this?!"

Markus shook his head at the sound of Ryne's booming tenor. He'd angered him on many occasions, but never had he heard such a volatile edge to his voice. He struggled to sit up, despite his dizzying skull, and the pain shooting up his side and arm. Ryne was standing just a few paces away, clutching a spear with whitened knuckles.

Bane stepped backward and pointed at Markus. "This land dweller was pawing at your sister. We meant to teach him a lesson."

"By feeding him to the kraehn?" Ryne demanded, before pointing to the whimpering dog lying on his side. "And what happened to Tar?"

Bane's brothers shifted from one foot to the other while their gazes darted about the room. Ura was hovering over Tar, having already wrapped a makeshift bandage around the wound in his shoulder.

Bane turned toward Tar and sneered. "Your dog tried to attack us while I was saving your sister."

Ryne's jaw fell open. "What?"

"That's a lie!" Ura cried. "We kissed, Ryne, nothing more."

Her brother turned a scowl on Markus. The look in his hooded eyes was one that promised retribution. "You kissed my sister?"

Markus nodded as a knot of regret seized his chest.

Ryne pointed his spear at him. "You, I will deal with later."

Then Ryne turned toward Bane before throwing his spear to the ground. "You," he bellowed, "I warned you what would happen if you hurt my dog." He pushed up the sleeves on his cloak and bared his fists. "Throw down your spear and fight me like a man."

"Ven," Bane cried as his beady eyes shifted toward his cousin.

Ryne laughed as Ven stepped forward. "I knew you'd never be man enough to marry my sister, Bane Eryll. I will pummel you after I'm finished with your cousin."

Markus struggled to his feet. Though injured, he would try his best to help. He stifled a nervous laugh for he knew that once Ryne was through with Bane and Ven, he would be next.

He didn't know whether it was the foul smell that coiled around his senses or Tar's sudden shift in movement that alerted him, but when the hairs on the back of his nape stood on end, his hunter's sixth sense told him something was amiss.

As a deep, menacing rumble sounded behind Ura and Tar, Ryne and Ven turned while gripping their spears.

Bane's mouth fell open. "Gnull!" he shouted. He raced behind Ryne and Ven before disappearing down the tunnel in the opposite direction.

Tar staggered to his feet, growling, while Ura scooted against the tunnel wall. Bane's brothers stood rooted to the spot, both staring toward the mouth of the tunnel with their mouths agape.

Two enormous tusks emerged from the shadows, followed by the most menacing beast Markus had ever seen. Covered in pale, fine fur, the creature was at least thrice the size of a snow bear. Large folds of heavy skin hung over its four, fin-like feet. As the beast slowly advanced toward them, the ground shook as his flesh smacked the floor. But the tusks were the most daunting aspect; long enough to drag the ground as its head scraped the top of the tunnel.

Ryne and Ven aimed their spears at the gnull while rushing forward and yelling. The creature answered with a roar that shook the icy walls and rocked

Markus to his core. Tar jumped in front of Ryne, heedless of his own injury as he risked his life to protect his master. All the while, Markus stood helpless, knowing he could do nothing to help Ryne and hating himself for it.

One of Bane's brothers broke to the left, crouching against the wall beside Ura. The other brother dropped his spear and continued to gape at the beast, despite Ryne and Ven yelling at him to flee.

Markus fought the urge to turn away as the gnull reared back and came crashing down on the boy, snapping him in half with his massive jowls. The boy's legs fell to the ground as the creature swallowed his torso in one gulp.

An enraged cry broke from the other boy as he picked up his spear and threw it at the gnull. It bounced off one tusk before falling to the ground. As the beast swung his head, the boy screamed and threw himself against the wall, coming within a hair's breadth of being swept away by a tusk.

"Stay down, Gunther!" Ven yelled.

Ryne and Ven continued to raise their spears above their heads while stomping their feet. They must have known two spears were no match for a gnull and would only anger the beast further.

But if they were trying to scare it away, it wasn't working. The monster showed no intention of backing down as he scooped up the dead boy's legs and swallowed them.

Gunther let out a shrill cry, but made no more advances. Meanwhile, the gnull took a thunderous step toward Ryne and Ven, followed by another.

Tar barked madly, dancing in wild circles around the beast and nipping at a large fin or a bit of flesh. The dog proved too fast for the gnull, which swung its head clumsily, but never made contact.

Markus's heart hammered. He could no longer see Ura as the beast had advanced past her and Gunther, trapping them against the wall. With Ryne and Ven yelling, and Tar attacking, Markus hoped it was enough to divert the beast's attention away from Ura.

Markus followed Ryne's lead and backed up a few more paces, nearly tripping over Bane's spear. Instinct told him to seize the weapon. He leaned over slowly and gripped the rod with his good arm. Mayhap he could injure the animal, just as he'd done with the ice dragon, but Markus feared such an injury would only make the beast more dangerous.

Just as Tar ran another rapid circle around the gnull, the beast missed the dog again and swung its head into a wall. A loud crack resonated throughout the chamber.

Markus's breath hitched. He braced himself, waiting for the tunnel to cave in, and then sighed with relief when the walls held, even after the beast had turned his body to dislodge a tusk from the ice. Once it had broken free, Markus could not mistake the sound of Ura's panicked scream. The gnull was now facing the wall where she was hiding.

Ryne and Ven unleashed their weapons, which sank into the gnull's meaty flesh. The beast turned on them and cried out in anger, before shaking his blubbery folds. After the spears fell to the ground, the creature reached out a massive fin and ground the spears into the ice.

As the gnull turned back to the wall where Ura was hiding, instinct fueled Markus's movements and he jutted forward, thrusting his spear into the beast's head.

The gnull roared and thrashed, slamming into one wall and then another, as if it were trying to dislodge the spear. Then the monster heaved a big, blubbery breath before all of the fleshy ripples on its body began to shake. Its massive head crashed to the floor first, followed by the rest of its body, its girth filling the entire width of the tunnel.

Markus's knees gave way when he realized what he'd done. He'd killed Alec.

RYNE HEAVED A SHAKY sigh of relief at the sweet sound of his sister crying from somewhere behind the beast. Ura was alive! He cautiously walked up to the gnull and poked it with the broken end of a spear.

Tar sniffed the beast while nervously skirting around it.

When it made no movement, Ryne called out to Ura. "Are you safe, sister?"

"Yes!" she answered. "We're at the mouth of the tunnel."

Ryne eyed the monster before calling back. "Do not go near the river. There could be more gnulls. I may need to scale this beast to reach you."

Ryne fanned his face while trying not to breathe in the noxious stench from the dead gnull. He cringed as he noticed strange slimy creatures crawling about the blubbery folds.

Ryne recalled what he'd brought with him in his pack: only the warming stone and tools to measure the depth of the river. He glanced at Ven. "I have no picks or gear. I will need your help with this."

Ven nodded and pulled some rope from his pack.

Ryne clutched one end of the rope and tied the other around Tar's waist before issuing the command, "Go to Ura, boy."

The dog jumped on top of the gnull with surprising ease and dug his sharp claws into the beast's fur as he climbed over the top.

Blood was seeping out of Tar's bandage and Ryne knew he would have to tend his dog's wound soon, but, for the moment, he wanted nothing more than to hold his sister close. It had taken nearly losing Ura for him to realize that he'd been behaving like a stupid slog. After being apart from his sister for so long, he'd returned only to unleash his foul mood upon her.

Ryne turned at the sound of muffled crying behind him. The land dweller had fallen to his knees, clutching his waist while hunched over. Tears streamed down his face as sobs wracked his body. Ryne wondered if the boy believed the hunter's curse had killed his brother. The witch's magic had never affected the people in Ice Kingdom and Ryne hoped the same would be true for Markus.

His breath stilled as a loud, splintering crack resonated overhead. Ryne had heard such a sound before, when he and Tar had almost been buried by an avalanche. The noise continued for a long, tense moment and was followed by a heavy booming sound somewhere in the distance.

Markus had crept up beside Ryne. Clutching his arm in a tight grip, he gasped. "Avalanche."

"Where?" Ryne cried. "There is no snow here, only ice."

Somewhere on the other side of the gnull, Tar yipped, and Ura and Gunther screamed. Ryne nearly lost his footing as the ground beneath him quaked with violent force.

After the tremors had subsided, Ryne's limbs froze with fear. Ura's screams were no more. Even the muffled roar of the river had been silenced.

What little light had filtered in from the mouth of the tunnel was now extinguished. Only a few ice crystals illuminated the gloom.

Ryne swore as he lunged for the gnull, feeling around until his boots made purchase with the slick folds of hide. Not knowing whether Tar was buried beneath the snow, Ryne only hoped the rope would hold until he reached the other side.

Behind him, Ryne heard the shredding of fabric. Feeling a pull on the rope, he knew Markus was behind him. Ryne paid little heed to the stench of the beast, or the slime on its slippery flesh, as he struggled against the rope and pulled himself forward. His only thought was that he had to save his sister.

Reaching the other side of the gnull, Ryne cried out at the sight before him. Tiny shards of light illuminated the space just enough to reveal that the other end of the rope was buried under a mound of snow and ice, which reached almost to the top of the tunnel entrance.

"Ura!" Ryne screamed. He pulled the warming stone out of his pack and pressed it against the packed snow.

*Warm,* he begged the stone, *please.*

As the stone slowly turned a glowing pink, the snow around it began to soften. Frantic, Ryne dug out the wet snow with his gloved hands. Ven joined them. He pulled out an ice pick and dug out larger chunks. Markus did the same with his blade.

They found Tar first. The dog whimpered as Ryne pulled him free. Ryne spared only a moment to brush ice and blood off his dog before resuming his tunneling.

Images of Ura's crushed, lifeless body raced through Ryne's mind as tears coated his face. He had to reach her. He couldn't lose her, but despite help from the warming stone, it was taking them too long to tunnel through and he had yet to see any sign of his sister.

Ryne jumped at the forceful bark behind him as it ricocheted off the walls and inside his skull. He turned to see Tar standing on wobbly legs, a look of feral determination in his canine gaze.

Ryne moved aside for Tar, and watched in amazement at the dog's voracity as he tunneled a gaping hole with his large paws. Even Markus and Ven stepped aside, slack-jawed as they watched the dog work. Though the wait seemed interminable, it took Tar a matter of moments before he reached Ura's pale wisps of hair. He jumped back and barked once.

"Good boy, Tar!" Markus cried as they all began to pick away at the snow.

When Ryne saw a small arm draped over Ura's chest, he knew the boy was beside her. Finally, he managed to pull his sister's body free. He laid her upon the ground as Markus and Ven worked to free Gunther.

"Ura!" Ryne called as he smoothed a hand over her brow, but she made not a sound. Her pale body was stiff and cold. Ryne placed the warming stone over her abdomen and then pressed her gloved hands against it.

"Ura!" he cried again, shaking her shoulders. "Please wake!" He could not lose her!

Markus climbed beside Ryne and nudged him aside. "She needs breath."

"How?" Ryne sobbed.

"Move," Markus commanded.

Markus clutched Ura to his chest and slanted his lips over hers. It was then that Ryne noticed Markus had removed the sling from his arm. He watched with bated breath as the boy blew into Ura's mouth and then laid her on her back and pumped her chest with his hands.

What was Markus doing to his sister? Was this some trick he'd learned up above? The boy leaned over Ura and breathed into her mouth once more, before pumping on her chest yet again.

Markus pulled away and wiped a bead of sweat from his brow. In that instant Ryne heard a small gasp escape his sister's throat. It was only then that he allowed himself to exhale a pent-up breath of air.

Ura was alive!

Ryne noted the shallow rise and fall of his sister's chest as a moan escaped her lips. He had no idea the extent of her injuries, so he sent a silent prayer to the Elements, begging them to spare her life. Then Ryne glanced over at Markus, who was wiping his eyes with the backs of his hands.

"Thank you for saving my sister, Markus."

The land dweller answered with a nod as more tears streamed down his face. "My mother used to do this for my bro..." With his voice cracking, he screwed his eyes shut.

Ryne cast a glance behind him and noted that Ven held his cousin in his arms. Though the boy seemed as limp as a bear pelt, he was breathing.

"We need to get my sister to a healer," Ryne told Ven and Markus. "I will need your help to get her off this gnull."

Markus nodded, before rising on shaky legs. That was when Ryne noticed the motionless body lying on the ground.

"Tar!" he cried.

Fresh blood oozed from the dog's wound as he lay on his side. His body appeared lifeless, with the exception of a weak thump of the tail when Ryne called his name.

Markus placed a hand upon Ryne's shoulder. "We will carry Ura down the gnull and then I will come back for Tar."

Ryne simply nodded, unable to say more as his throat choked with emotion. Then he sent another prayer to the Elements, begging them to save his companion, the dog who so selflessly risked his life to save them.

# Chapter Sixteen

Markus clutched Tar to his chest while he trudged up the tunnel's incline, following Ryne who carried his unconscious sister. Markus's sore legs screamed in protest with each painful step, but he would not falter. The dog had fought so bravely despite his loss of blood. Markus knew the Goddess would not heed his prayers, so he sent a silent prayer to the Elements that Tar and Ura might live.

Markus knew he would be forever indebted to Tar; not only for his courage in facing down the gnull, but for saving Ura's life. Now that Alec was gone, Ura was the only person still breathing whom he truly cared for. Though it pained him to know the danger he brought to her, Markus could not deny it now—he loved her.

Markus also realized that because of this love, he had done the unthinkable and defied Madhea's curse. For that, he knew he would never take another breath without feeling the heavy weight of sorrow pressing upon his chest. He would never forgive himself for bringing the curse upon his family and allowing Alec to die. In Markus's eyes, he was nothing more than a monster, a curse upon those he loved.

Despite his fresh wounds, the break in his arm had healed. Markus needed to go to Madhea and beg her to break the curse, or die trying. He could not live among the Ice People any longer and put them at risk. If he had to kill again, he feared Ura would be the next to die.

So consumed was Markus by his deep thoughts that he did not hear other people approaching until they were almost upon them. A large hunting party raced through the tunnel, with Jon at the head, and Chieftain Eryll and his son, Bane, right behind him.

Jon rushed up to Ryne and laid a palm on his daughter's forehead. "Ura! What has happened?"

"She was buried in an avalanche," Ryne explained as he eased his sister into Jon's arms. "She breathes, Father, but she does not wake."

"Where is the vicious beast?" Elof Eryll asked with a raised brow.

Ryne answered him with a dismissive wave. "You have come too late. Markus has already slain the beast with one spear."

The Chieftain's eyes bulged. "How could this be true?"

Ryne leveled him with a thunderous look. "I speak the truth, just as I always have, and let you remember this day." He pointed an accusatory finger at Bane. "Your coward of a son fled, leaving his brothers to face the gnull alone. If it hadn't been for Markus and my dog, *both* of your young sons would be dead."

The Chieftain dropped his spear as his hand flew to his meaty chest and his gaze swept over them all. "*Both* of my sons? Ande! Where is Ande?!"

Ven stepped forward while cradling the Chieftain's youngest son. "He was eaten by the beast."

"What? What! Ande!" The Chieftain fell to his knees while covering his face with his hands.

Markus knew it was unkind to think so, but the way Chieftain Eryll's chins and chest heaved while he wailed reminded him of the blubbery gnull.

Bane marched up to his cousin. "How could you let him die, Ven?!"

Ryne stepped forward. "You would blame this on Ven? He refused to run when the gnull attacked, unlike you!"

Jon turned on Bane as his eyes darkened. "You told us they followed you out."

Bane stepped back while casting a nervous glace at the others. "I thought they did."

Bane's brother lifted his head from Ven's chest and waved a shaky hand. "He lies! Bane left me and Ande to face the beast while he ran away screaming."

"And this is who you've chosen to rule in your stead when you retire?" Jon hissed at the sobbing Chieftain before squaring his shoulders. "I will not serve a coward."

Ryne stood by his father's side and they shared a look of understanding. "Neither will I," he said, scowling down at Chieftain Eryll before leveling the other hunters with a direct gaze.

"Abandonment is punishable by law," Jon added. "Bane must face trial."

Bane let out a strangled cry before collapsing on the ice.

Two other hunters walked behind him and jerked him to his feet. They continued to clutch his arms, despite his protests.

The Chieftain struggled to stand. He glared at Jon and Ryne, before thrusting a meaty fist in the air. "I have already lost one son this day!"

Jon heaved a sigh while shaking his head. "It is the law, Elof, and you are bound to follow. You will summon the Council and your son will be judged for his cowardice."

Then he glanced down at Ura, sleeping in his arms. "Now I must take my daughter to a healer." He pushed past the Chieftain and briskly walked up the incline.

Markus, Ryne, and Ven followed while the crowd of hunters parted to make way for them. Markus shook his head as Bane wailed. The coward got what he deserved.

Just as they passed through the crowd, the Chieftain's voice rumbled behind them. "There will be no Council meeting today! I need time to grieve for my son."

Jon and Ryne spun around as if of one accord. The son looked to his father, who answered with a slow nod.

Ryne stormed over to Chieftain Eryll and jabbed a finger in his meaty chest. "You are the Chieftain! You do not get that luxury. Summon the Council or we will summon them ourselves! Or do you wish to wait for more gnulls to attack our children?"

With that, Ryne marched back to his father. Markus followed behind, sparing only a cursory glance at the Chieftain, who was now back on his knees, sobbing like a baby.

MARKUS'S MIND WAS IN a haze as he followed Ryne and Jon through the winding ice tunnels. He had no idea where they were headed, and it took all of his focus just to put one foot in front of the other.

Thankfully, Ryne had taken Tar from him, just moments before Markus thought his arms would surely break. But the burning in his limbs was nothing like the pain in his heart. He could not escape the vision of Alec falling to the ground with a gaping hole in his head. Just as he had killed the gnull, Markus knew his brother had suffered the same fate.

It wasn't until Markus smelled familiar, pungent smoke that his gaze shot to Ryne. Why had they come to the prophet?

As Jon approached the flap to Odu's chamber, he turned to Ryne and leveled him with a stern gaze. "Say what you want about his prophecies, but he is the best healer in the kingdom."

Surprisingly, Ryne nodded. "I agree, Father."

Markus wondered at the transformation in Ryne. He suspected it had something to do with him nearly being eaten by a gnull.

After walking through a short tunnel, they emerged inside Odu's chamber.

The old man rose on wobbly legs and motioned Jon to approach. "Come, come. Lay them upon the furs."

Jon, Ryne and Ven laid the injured down, and then knelt beside them. Markus clung to the shadows, not knowing where he belonged.

Odu laid a bony hand upon Gunther's brow and looked into his wide eyes. "How do you feel, boy?"

Gunther visibly swallowed before answering, "The gnull ate my brother."

The prophet bent his head as his eyes softened. He placed a hand upon Gunther's shoulder. "I am sorry." Turning to Ven, he said, "The boy has no serious injuries. He is just in shock."

Ven's lower lip quivered as he bowed. "Thank you, prophet."

Next, Odu moved to Tar. The dog's tail thumped against the furs as the old man ran bony fingers down his back.

Odu lifted his gaze to meet Ryne's. "The animal is strong. My apprentices will clean and bandage his wound. He will recover."

Ryne heaved an audible sigh before casting a nervous glance at his sister. "And Ura?" he asked in a voice that cracked with emotion. "Will my sister live, prophet?"

When Odu frowned, Markus thought his heart fell through his stomach.

"It is too soon to tell," Odu answered and bent over her chest. He straightened up, shaking his head, which made his lengthy, white beard sway with the movement. "Her breathing is shallow."

Markus watched Ryne work a visible knot in his throat. "She was crushed in an avalanche."

The prophet nodded solemnly. "I know."

Jon raised a brow. "You saw it?"

"This past winter," Odu answered, "on one of the many times she begged me to help find her brother. After the mists revealed the avalanche, she did not look into them again."

Jon rose slowly to his feet, bearing down upon Odu with a thunderous expression. "You knew of the avalanche? Why did you not tell me?!"

Odu ran his hands along Ura's extremities. "It was not for me to tell," he answered plainly.

The murderous look in Jon's eyes was frightening, even to Markus.

"Father?" Ura whispered.

Markus gasped as he looked down at her pain-stricken face.

Jon fell to his knees and reached for his daughter's hand. "Yes, child, I am here."

"Tar and Gunther?" she rasped.

Jon nodded. "They live."

"Markus and Ryne?"

"We are here," Ryne said, clasping his sister's other hand.

"I could not breathe," she said with an audible strain in her voice, "and it was so cold."

"Are you pained, child?" Odu asked.

"It is still hard to breathe, but the pain is subsiding."

"Jon Nordlund, you and your son have been summoned before the Council," barked a male voice from inside the prophet's dark threshold, "and Ven Johan and the land dweller, as well."

Jon frowned as he looked at the Guardian standing in the doorway and then back to his daughter.

"Ura needs rest," said Odu. "We will examine her for breakages, but I think the danger has passed now."

All of the men heaved a collective sigh of relief. The heavy gloom that had settled over Jon's darkened eyes seemed to melt away as he bent over and kissed his daughter's forehead. Ryne, likewise, kissed the other side of her temple.

Markus's heart warmed when Ura weakly smiled.

When Jon stood, Markus followed his lead. Though he was relieved that Ura would live, he was not looking forward to another visit to the Council when all he wanted to do was mourn the loss of his brother in private.

RYNE WAS DISGUSTED, but not surprised at the chaotic scene in the Council chamber. Ingred Johan towered over her cousin, Chieftain Eryll, and screamed obscenities while he wept into his hands. The other Council members had risen from their thrones and were arguing passionately amongst themselves. Several of the hunters were also there, yelling and waving their hands at Bane, who huddled behind a wall of four Guardians.

Everyone stopped and stared as Ryne's party entered the chamber. Ingred left the Chieftain's side and rushed to Ven, pulling him against her bounteous chest while sobbing into his hair.

"Mother, I am fine," Ven said as he struggled out of her embrace. His pale skin darkened before he cast a wary glance at Ryne.

Ingred stepped back from her son and squared her shoulders while looking directly at Ryne. "Son of Nordlund," she said. "We were wrong not to listen to you. Tell us what we should do about the melting ice."

"How dare you speak for me!" Chieftain Eryll pounded a meaty fist against the arm of his throne. "I am still the Chieftain."

Ingred turned toward him with raised brows. "Do you still insist that your son should not be judged?"

"He was frightened. He's just a boy." The Chieftain's bottom lip trembled as he spoke.

Ingred's wide nostrils flared as she turned up her nose. "Ryne Nordlund is two-and-twenty winters!" she said, waving a hand at him. "This man has traveled to the surface and back, and Bane is a year his elder!"

Chieftain Eryll's expression fell, his fleshy cheeks rippling with the movement. "The Nordlund clan is impoverished and used to such hardships."

Ingred planted both hands on her hips. "My son, who is five years Bane's junior, stood his ground against the gnull. Your son is a coward and must be judged, and if you stand in the way of the Council, I must vote for your abdication as Chieftain."

A collective gasp echoed around the room.

Chieftain Eryll's face took on the color of an overripe apple. "You would turn your back on a member of your own family?"

Ingred folded her arms across her chest. "As your son did to mine and his own brothers."

Another Council member, Willa Eriksson, a middle-aged, petite woman, shook her head as she broke away from the group. "We trusted in your leadership, Elof Eryll. We believed you when you said the ice was not melting. Now look what has happened."

The Chieftain clutched a hand to his chest and rose slowly on wobbly legs. "I have already lost one son this day. You would add insult to my suffering?"

Ingred glared at Chieftain Eryll before turning to the other members. "I call for a vote of abdication. Who among the Council will support me?"

Slowly, the members began to raise their hands until every last one had sided with Ingred.

Willa moved to stand beside her and turned to face the two male Council members. "I call for Ingred Johan to rule as temporary Chieftain until the people elect another. Who among the Council will support me?"

The two lone men beside the dais again raised their arms and Elof Eryll wept into his hands.

Ingred angled her chin and marched up to Elof, before bearing down on him with a scowl. "As my first order of business, Guardians please remove Elof Eryll from the chamber."

Two of the men flanked Elof and hooked their hands beneath his shoulders. They heaved his large body up and proceeded to drag him from the dais. Elof made no effort to stand or help the Guardians bear his heavy weight. Instead, he cried like a baby as they dragged him from the chamber. His sobs could be heard echoing off the walls long after he had been removed.

Ryne heaved a disgusted groan. How had this man risen to become their kingdom's Chieftain?

"Guardians," Ingred announced, taking her position on the Chieftain's throne, "please bring Bane Eryll forward so that he may be judged."

The two remaining Guardians lifted Bane to his feet, but he proved no more useful than his father and crumpled back to the floor in a heap of sobs. The Guardians had to drag him. They deposited him in front of the new Chieftain before taking a few steps back.

Long tendrils of snot hung from Bane's nose as he cried into the ice.

Ryne groaned again and, much to his pleasure, he heard Ven swear beside him. Ven had always been Bane's heavy-fisted hound. Ryne hoped the boy had now learned a lesson.

"Bane Eryll," boomed Chieftain Johan's deep, yet feminine voice, "you have been accused of abandonment. How do you answer?"

Bane answered by sobbing even louder.

The Chieftain leveled him with a beady-eyed glare. "I will take that as a guilty plea. The Council will adjourn to decide your fate. You will know on the morrow." She waved to the two men standing behind Bane. "Guardians, please place him in a holding chamber."

Bane cried into his chest as the Guardians dragged him away.

"Land Dweller," Ingred commanded, "please step forward."

HARDLY AWARE OF HIS own actions, Markus immediately moved to the front of the chamber when the new Chieftain called him. The gloom that originated in his heart had seized his chest like a vice and shrouded his mind in a heavy fog. Why couldn't they just let him mourn his brother in peace?

Ingred tilted her chin and slowly looked him over. Despite her sharp, beady gaze, there was a touch of kindness in the tilt of her mouth. "We are told that you brought down the gnull with one spear."

"Aye," he replied with a shrug.

Ingred's mouth tilted the slightest bit more in what appeared to Markus as an unfinished smile.

"For that we thank you," she said. "The Ice People will be eternally indebted to you for your bravery. If there is anything..."

"You will come up with a plan to find safety for your people," Markus interrupted with a sharp edge to his voice. The sacrifice he had made today could have been avoided if there had been such a plan in place. "If the gnulls can reach you now, Madhea will reach you soon."

Ingred's subdued smile vanished. "We will consider a plan for Ice King-dom."

Ryne stepped forward, standing shoulder-to-shoulder with Markus. "You must do more than consider, Chieftain Johan, if you do not wish our people to perish."

"What do you suggest I do, Ryne?" she asked, with a hint of annoyance in her voice.

"Send a party with me to the top," Ryne pleaded. "We will find a safer home for our people."

Ingred's expression fell as she coursed a hand through the pale roots of her hair. "Such a task would require volunteers."

Ven Johan stepped forward. "I'll go."

Ingred gasped and jumped to the edge of her seat. "My son! Not you!"

Ven puffed out his chest while clenching his fists by his sides. "I will not stand by while others make sacrifices for our people." He looked Ingred squarely in the eyes while tilting up his chin. "I am going, Mother."

One of the hunters came beside Ryne. "I will go, too."

"And I," answered another.

Ryne could hardly believe his good fortune: three volunteers to go with him to the top! Such a party would be small enough to elude the witch's no-tice, hopefully, but big enough to defend themselves against snow bears and other monsters.

The Chieftain settled back in her throne and folded her hands in her lap, looking far more solemn than she had just moments before. "Ryne Nordlund, you have your party."

Ryne bowed slightly. "Thank you, Chieftain."

Ingred then leaned forward while grasping her knees with whitened knuckles. "I am trusting you, not only with my son's life, but with the lives of our people." Her features hardened as she glared at Ryne through slitted eyes. "Do not fail us."

# Chapter Seventeen

Markus followed Jon back to Odu's chamber while Ryne stayed with the Council to discuss preparations for the journey.

All of the prophet's followers had left, leaving the luminous chamber virtually empty. Even Bane's younger brother was gone. No doubt, his family had come for him.

Much to Markus's surprise, Ura was sitting up and drinking broth. He noticed that the dark circles beneath her eyes and the sharp angles of her face had softened. Tar was sleeping beside her, his legs stretched out as he snored loudly into the furs. Markus smirked as the dog began to bark under his breath. Mayhap he was dreaming of fighting a gnull.

Jon sat on the other side of Ura and kissed her forehead, before clasping her hands in his own. She kissed him back on the cheek. Then, turning from her father, she gaped at Markus. "You do not wear the sling."

Markus stood beside Jon and held up his hand. He spread his fingers while turning over his arm. "My bones are healed."

Her eyes darkened. "You will leave us soon then?"

He nodded. "Aye, I must."

So much had happened since they had shared a kiss earlier that day, but now, as Markus looked into Ura's clouded eyes, he recalled the memory of her lips against his. What he wouldn't give for their lives to have turned out differently. What he wouldn't give to be able to stay with her.

Ura's bottom lip trembled. "If the witch should spare you, will you return to me?" she asked in barely a whisper.

He nodded again, his throat feeling too choked up with emotion to let him speak. Ura wanted him to stay. If only he could forsake his honor and duty, and stay with her forever.

"You will not go to your brother?" she asked.

Ura's words cut through him worse than any insult or injury, reminding him of the reason he had embarked on his quest to reach Madhea and how he had failed to keep his brother safe.

"My brother is dead, Ura," he said, dropping his gaze. Tears streamed down his face and, despite the weight of the stares from Jon and the prophet, Markus refused to hide his emotions any longer. The person who meant most to him in this world was gone and it was his fault. What did a few tears matter now?

"You brother is not dead. I have seen him."

Markus jerked his head up to see Odu pointing a finger toward the swirling vapors.

"The mists show you my brother?" Markus asked as a trill of hope surged through his veins. How could this be?

Odu waved him over. "Come, look."

Markus struggled to his feet. Within a few long strides he, was standing beside the prophet, staring down into the raised pool of water. Several grey stones, many larger than Markus's fist, protruded from the shallow depths. Pale wisps of air danced around them, making the mists seem alive.

A thought struck Markus: the wisps *were* alive, for they moved with a purpose. Soon, they all coalesced together and imprinted a faint image onto the surface of the pool. Markus's jaw slackened as it became more defined.

The picture was of Alec stacking wood beside a hut. Amazingly, his brother looked healthy and strong, not like the person he'd left behind. This had to be some kind of trick as it was not the brother he knew.

Markus turned to Odu with a scowl. "This is an illusion."

Odu shook his head. "A young witch took him in and healed him after you left." Then he pointed to the image of a familiar-looking woman, thanking Alec for bringing firewood.

"Witch?" Markus asked as he gaped at the girl he had once admired. "Dianna? She is no witch."

"She is, and a very powerful one. She has been blessed by the Elements."

Odu waved a hand around the swirling smoke as he gazed intently upon the image of Dianna adding wood to her cooking fire. "I think that is why the mists favor her. For the past fortnight, they have shown me little else."

But Markus was unconvinced. "My brother walks upright. He looks strong. How is it he lives?"

"As I said, the witch healed him. He lives with her and her brother." Odu's eyes softened as he turned his gaze on Markus. "He speaks of you often. He misses you."

Markus swallowed. Could it be true? Was Alec alive and well? "Why didn't Madhea kill him when I felled the gnull?"

Odu smiled. "The witch's magic cannot touch you here."

"Will you still go to the witch?" Ura called.

Markus spun around. Ura was staring wide-eyed at him, her brow furrowed and her mouth drawn. Jon sat beside her, clutching her hands within his own, and the lines framing his eyes were more clearly defined than before.

Markus read the plea in Jon's haunted expression, but he could not be swayed. He had to reach Madhea.

He shook his head. "I have no choice, Ura."

"Your brother is safe." Her bottom lip trembled as her eyes watered over with unshed tears. "*You* are safe."

Markus's chest clenched and his throat constricted. He did not wish to make Ura cry, but he could not forsake his brother. "The dragon will awaken soon. What will Lydra do if she cannot find me?"

"She will destroy your village and Kicelin," Odu said with a cutting finality to his voice. "If she cannot find you, the Ice Witch will seek revenge, perhaps on your brother."

Ura cried out and covered her face with her hands. Her body shook with convulsions as she wept aloud.

"Ura, please." Markus was beside her in an instant. He knelt down and reached out to her, but she broke from her father's grasp and backed away from both of them.

"The witch will kill you!" she cried.

"Not if he kills her first!"

Markus spun around to see Ryne standing in the doorway.

Tar groaned through a loud, sleepy snort and then jerked his head up. His tail thumped as his master stepped into the prophet's chamber.

"W-what?" Markus stammered.

Ryne's booted steps rang out across the cavern walls as he marched toward them. He pointed a finger at Markus's chest. "One shot with your arrow and you could end her reign."

"Brother," Ura gasped, "this is madness."

"If anyone has the power to kill the witch, it is Markus," Ryne spoke through a clenched jaw.

"Is that true, Odu?" Ura looked up at the prophet, who was still standing by his pool of mists. "You said he was sent to us for a reason."

Odu nodded. "I did."

"Then what is that reason?" Ura asked.

"The boy must seek out his heart and find the answer."

Ryne grumbled beside Markus, muttering something about "confusing parables."

Ura turned to Markus and grasped his hand in her own. With pleading eyes, she asked in a breathy whisper, "What does your heart tell you, Markus?"

Dropping Ura's hand, he turned his gaze toward the furs. Markus could not look at her or at anyone else, knowing what he had to say. For he knew that neither she, Jon nor Ryne would be pleased with his decision.

"My brother lives, though only moments ago I thought him dead. His life has been plagued by sickness. He is strong now, a man. If I fell the witch with my arrow, the curse will kill him. What right do I have to take my brother's life when he has only just begun living?"

"What of the lives of the Ice People?" Ryne spat. "What of the women and children she will kill once the ice melts? What of Ura's life? Did you save her only to watch her perish?"

Markus's heart clenched before it began pounding out a wild rhythm. Images of Ura being forced to surface and then struck down by the witch's dragon flashed through his mind.

"No," he answered weakly, still not sure of the sagacity of his plan. "I will plead for Madhea to forgive the Ice People as well."

Ryne threw up his hands. "When will you listen? She will forgive none of us!"

"I have to try!" Markus cried.

Ryne shook his head before turning first to his father and then Odu. "If he will not kill her then I will go. I may not be as skilled with a weapon, but I am a far better climber."

"No. This, Ryne, is not your destiny." The prophet's tired gaze fell back to the mists. He ran a hand over the stones. An image wafted up from the pool. It was a picture of Ryne leading a band of ice dwellers down the side of a rocky mountain. "You are the only ice dweller with knowledge of the surface. You must find a way for us to escape when the ice is no longer stable."

Ryne leveled Markus with eyes narrowed to slits. "When she refuses you, for she will refuse you, have your weapons at the ready."

MARKUS EMERGED FROM the dragon weed crops with a fresh respect for the Gnull Tusks, but also a new understanding: he would climb to the top and he would not fail. He pulled picks from his satchel and strapped on his longer, ice-climbing spikes. The rope and crampons would be left behind. He didn't need a harness or anchors. All he needed was faith in his ability.

Markus tilted his head and scanned the length of one mighty tusk, which tapered to almost a point at its peak. He closed his eyes and envisioned himself as a human arrow, shooting to the top with dexterity and speed, just as Ura had told him.

Reaching up, Markus planted his picks above his head, making solid contact with the ice. He grabbed hold of them and followed suit by planting one foot in the ice and then the other. He didn't think, he just acted, as if on instinct, focusing on the thrust of his body as he propelled himself toward the top.

RYNE COULD HARDLY BELIEVE his eyes. Markus had climbed straight to the top of the tusk, moving quickly and smoothly toward its peak. What had transformed the boy that he could shoot up like an arrow piercing its target? Was it simply that his arm had now healed? Or was it something more?

Ryne realized now that he had misjudged the land dweller. Though he still wanted to pound his fist through Markus's face for kissing his sister, Ryne knew Ura would not be alive if it had not been for him.

But Markus had the chance to save Ura a second time; one more final act of courage. Was Odu right? Had this boy been sent to them for a reason? Would he deliver their people from the malevolent clutches of the witch? Or would Markus's courage falter when the Ice People needed him most?

After Markus had moved swiftly back down the tusk, Ryne stepped back and crossed his arms over his chest, eyeing the boy intently. When Markus turned to him, his lips curved into the slightest of smiles and his cheeks reddened, reminding Ryne that the land dweller was still just a boy at heart.

"I climbed to the top," Markus said proudly, waving a hand toward the tusk.

"So I see," Ryne answered. He was careful not to lavish any praise on Markus. Not until he knew whether the boy had the courage to do what was right.

For the briefest moment, their gazes locked. But during that time, the look in Markus's eyes belied his conflicted emotions. Ryne could read his fear and indecision, but he also saw something more; perhaps a fire deep within. Ryne prayed to the Elements that it was true.

"Well?" Ryne watched as Markus placed his picks into his satchel.

"Well what?" the boy asked as he slung his bag over his shoulders.

Ryne wondered why, after everything he had faced in his life, his hands began to tremble now. Was he afraid the boy hunter would refuse to help them? What would he do then? He had already come too close to losing his sister—he couldn't lose her to the witch now.

Finally, Ryne cleared his throat as he willed his limbs to stop shaking. "Will you risk the lives of an entire kingdom to save the life of one man?"

Markus turned up his chin and leveled him with a defiant glare. "Not just one man—my brother."

"And when the witch refuses to forgive you?"

Markus's shoulders dropped. "I-I don't know."

The boy's indecision pricked Ryne's ire. "Coward," he spat.

Markus's eyes widened. "What?"

Ryne marched up to the boy and jabbed a finger in his chest. "You have the power to take her down. You have the power to end her tyranny, Mighty Hunter, and yet you cower behind indecision."

Markus jerked back and his wan face colored. "I do not cower!"

Ryne clenched his fists, repressing the urge to strike out. "Then do what is right!"

With that, he turned and marched back through the dragon weed crops and toward the Icy Lung, where the frigid air would be a welcome distraction to his dark thoughts. For, if Markus refused to help him, the weight of saving the Ice People would fall entirely on Ryne's shoulders.

# Chapter Eighteen

**M**arkus woke from a fitful night's sleep and rubbed his eyes. The previous night had been the longest of his life. Between the sounds of Ura's muted cries and the wild racing of his own heart, which pounded like a drum in his head, Markus could scarcely keep his eyes closed. Today he was going to leave the Ice People.

Today he was going to leave Ura.

Though loath to go, Markus knew he had to. His brother was counting on him. So many times during the night his troubled thoughts had wandered to Alec. His brother had been to him what his parents had not: a loving mentor and a caring friend. In return, Markus had given him nothing but grief, refusing to heed Alec's sage advice and abusing the forest creatures while thinking of no one but himself.

He had behaved like a monster. But his heart had now changed. He knew he didn't have to grow to be like his father. Nay, all he wanted was to be a man like Alec. If only Madhea would give him the chance to prove it.

What if she didn't give him that chance and refused to heed his pleas? Would he risk his brother's life and shoot Madhea? Could his arrow fell the Goddess or would he only stoke the flames of her ire? And what if she forgave him but refused to forgive the Ice People? How far would he go to protect Ura?

Markus's only comfort during the night was that Tar slept with him. The dog had made a miraculous recovery after being wounded in the shoulder and buried under an avalanche. He had crawled back into Markus's bed by the day's end, and even resumed his nightly habit of licking his nutsack and chewing his anus.

The mutt had been a welcome distraction. Despite his disgusting habits, Markus was relieved that his friend would live. Tar had come to mean so much to him, yet to think, not long ago, how he had despised all animals. How wrong he had been.

"Wake up, land dweller. It is time for us to go."

"Ouch!" cried Markus, jerking up after Ryne threw his heavy satchel onto his legs.

Markus looked up to see Ryne was already fully dressed and scowling down at him, so he picked up his bag and threw it at the man's feet.

Dodging the projectile, Ryne burst into laughter. Tar jumped off the cot and landed in between them. He growled at Ryne and then at Markus, before issuing a warning bark.

Tossing back his furs, Markus jumped to his feet, determined to enact revenge on the man who was always taunting him. Didn't he have enough weight on his shoulders? Why did Ryne always seek to compound his troubles?

But Markus already knew the answer to his question. Ryne was angry with him because he had refused to kill the witch.

As Markus charged across the small room, closing the distance between them, his feet suddenly slowed and he moved with less purpose. He could hardly blame Ryne for hating him, not when he hated himself. What right had he to save just one man when an entire kingdom depended on him?

Markus stopped within an inch of Ryne and looked at the pained expression in his silver eyes. Markus had barely noticed before, but now that Ryne's sun-kissed skin and hair had paled to an icy translucence, he looked more like Ura, the sister Markus knew Ryne loved with every breath in his body. How could he hate the man who loved Ura so?

Ryne tilted his chin and looked squarely at Markus, the tendons in his neck bulging beneath his translucent skin.

The tension that sparked between them was palpable. Markus swallowed. If he threw the first punch, Ryne would fight back, and then what? Markus would be no better than a brute acting on impulse. No better than his father, hurting the people he should have been defending.

"Is this how I am to remember the two of you before you leave me?"

Markus spun around at the sound of Ura's small voice behind him. She was standing in the doorway, clutching the wall with her hands, looking fragile and vulnerable. She was not fully healed and she'd risen from her bed to find them fighting.

The heat of shame crept into Markus's chest and inflamed his face.

"I'm sorry, sister." Ryne stepped forward. "We have disturbed your rest. Please, let me help you back to bed."

"No." She waved him away while still holding onto the wall with one hand. "I wish to see you off."

"But you have not fully healed." Ryne led her by the arm to Markus's cot. "How do you feel?"

Ura's lip trembled as she looked first to Markus and then back at Ryne. "Like the very foundation on which I stand has already given way and I am falling into the abyss."

Ryne shook his head and clutched her hands within his own. "I will not let that happen."

Ura's eyes pooled over with moisture. "You cannot make those promises, Ryne."

"I can promise that I will do everything in my power to keep you safe." Ryne put Ura's hands to his lips and kissed them. "A promise I made to our mother the day she died birthing you, and a promise I intend to keep."

"It is not *my* safety I worry for, Ryne." Tears spilled down her face as she spoke. "It is yours."

"I will be careful, just like last time."

"You were fortunate last time. Odu said the witch has a swirling mist, too, and that she can see far below the mountain."

"I know this, Ura, and I promise I will be careful."

"What about you, Markus?" she asked.

Markus shifted on his feet when Ura turned her attention toward him, especially as Ryne was watching him as well. He felt awkward enough after witnessing their tender exchange.

"You need not worry about me," Markus said, feeling ashamed. He did not deserve her concern.

"But I do, Markus. Who will console me when you are both gone?"

Markus's heart broke when Ura looked up with glossy eyes.

"You will have Father," Ryne said.

Ura shook her head as her shoulders slumped inward. "Father's depression is darker than mine."

Ryne's mouth fell open. "Father's depression?"

"He suffered when you were gone, Ryne." Ura wiped her eyes as more tears spilled over. "He hides his pain now, but last time you left, Father was a shadow of the man you knew."

Markus turned as he heard a rustle outside the front door. Jon emerged from behind the flap. His mouth was drawn into a deep frown, and his eyes were framed with dark circles and heavy lines.

"Well, Bane has been sentenced," Jon said grimly.

Ura released Ryne's hands and gripped the edge of the cot. "What was his judgment, Father?"

Jon glanced from Ryne to Ura, and then heaved a sigh. "He has been outed."

Ura's trembling hands flew to her mouth.

Whatever 'outed' meant, Markus knew it wasn't good. "Outed?" he asked.

"Forced to surface," Jon answered, pulling down his cloak and raking his fingers through his hair.

"Will he be allowed to return?" Markus wondered.

Jon shook his head. "No. A team of Guardians has already taken him to the top."

Though Markus knew Bane deserved to be punished, he couldn't help but feel badly for him. It wasn't long ago that Markus had been sentenced for his crimes too; not by a council, but by Madhea, and Markus had learned his lesson. If he was fortunate, he would be allowed to return to his brother and, eventually, mayhap he could return to see the Ice People as well. Bane would not have that chance.

"There is more." Jon's voice dropped as he lowered himself onto a stool. "Elof Eryll is dead."

"Dead?" gasped Ura.

"He suffered a fit of the heart during the night. His wife has fallen ill as well." Jon averted his gaze and stared down at his fists in his lap. "They do not think she will recover."

"I feel badly for the Eryll clan now," Ura said in a breathy whisper.

"Do not feel badly, Ura." Ryne placed a hand on his sister's shoulder. "They suffered rightly for their son's cowardice."

"You are wrong," Markus snapped. "Bane's sins are his alone. His entire family should not suffer for them."

Markus recalled the sound of his mother's agonizing screams. She had died because of him. He thought of Alec, who had been a good brother and warned him of his cruelty, but Markus had not listened. They should not have suffered for his mistakes.

Ryne narrowed his eyes at Markus. "Bane's parents raised a coward."

"But, what of his brother, Gunther?" Markus asked. "He did not flee the gnull and now his family is gone. Should he be made to suffer as well?"

Ryne blinked hard and looked away. Markus only had a momentary glimpse of Ryne's face, but it appeared that the fire in his eyes had been doused.

"No," Ryne groaned as his shoulders fell, "the boy should not be made to suffer."

In that brief moment, Markus hoped Ryne finally understood how he felt about Alec and why he did not want to sacrifice him to Madhea's curse.

"Ryne, Markus, we need to prepare for your departure," Jon said. "We should say our goodbyes now. Ura cannot make the walk to the Dragon's Teeth and I doubt we will have a chance once we reach the crush of people."

When Ura buried her face in her hands, Jon walked over to her and knelt by her side. "Daughter, we must be strong, for both of their sakes."

But even as he said it, Markus could not mistake the gloomy shadows circling Jon's eyes. Here was a man plagued with grief and worry over his family.

Ura lifted her head and wiped her eyes with the backs of her hands. "Yes, Father."

Jon stood and Ryne followed. They stared at one another for the longest time before Jon placed a hand on his son's shoulder. "For the sacrifice you are about to make and for the sacrifices you have already made for our people, I am proud to call you my son. You are a boy no more, but a brave and noble man."

Ryne frowned before the hard angles of his face solidified into a mask of stone. Only his eyes belied his emotions: a storm appeared to be raging within those grey depths. "I am my father's son. I'm sorry it took me this long to see it."

Jon answered by grabbing his son in a fierce hug.

"Do not worry for me, Father," Ryne said against the man's neck.

"As futile as telling the glacier not to thaw," Jon chuckled before releasing Ryne and quickly wiping the moisture from his eyes.

Ryne swallowed before angling his chin. "I will be safe, I promise." Then he knelt before his sister. "I have not been a good brother to you," he said in a hushed whisper, just loud enough for Markus to hear.

"No," said Ura, shaking her head vehemently, "you have been a great brother. Everything you do, I know is to keep our family safe."

Ryne reached up and cupped her pale cheek. "I love you."

She reached her arms around his neck and kissed his forehead. "And I you, brother."

Markus was hardly aware of the moisture that had spilled over his eyelids until Jon stepped in front of his clouded vision.

"Here, Markus, you will have a greater need of this than us." Jon placed a small sack, secured with a long cord, in Markus's hands.

His mouth fell open when he peered into the sack. "Your warming stone? I cannot accept this."

He tried to give the gift back to Jon, but the man took the cord and hung it around Markus's neck. The heavy sack pressed against his chest.

"You must," Jon said sternly. "You will not survive the climb without it."

"But your family's honor?" asked Markus. Jon and his family had already given him so much. He couldn't take from them the remnant of their once high status.

Jon shook his head. "We do not depend on a stone for honor, Markus." He placed a hand across his heart. "Our honor is in here."

Markus's gaze shifted to Ryne, who was now standing and watching them intently. "Won't he have need of the stone as well?"

Ryne shrugged. "It is warm where I am going. Besides, Ven will carry his family's stone."

Markus was even more shocked by Ryne's reaction. He knew Ryne despised him, and rightly so, so why didn't he seem to mind that Markus was taking their stone?

"Take it, Markus, please," Ura pleaded.

"But..."

Jon turned to his son, heedless of Markus's protests. "Ryne, you must show Markus the way to the witch's lair before you break at the pass. You must also remind Markus how to use the stone."

Ryne answered with a slight tilt of the head. "Yes, Father."

Markus looked at the sack hanging around his neck and clasped it within his grasp. It was cold to him now, but he had seen its power. He knew it would prove to be quite useful on the freezing journey toward the top.

"If I should survive, I will return it," he said.

A slight smile tugged at the corner of Jon's mouth. "I know you will."

"Thank you for this, and for everything," Markus said to Jon as he struggled to keep the emotion out of his voice. "I wish my father had been more like you."

The sharp edges around Jon's eyes softened. He reached out to Markus and pulled him into an embrace. "I'm sorry your father was unkind. You and your brother deserved better," he said into his ear. "I know I've told you this before, but you have goodness in you. You do not need to follow the path of your father."

Markus relished the warmth of Jon's hug before pulling back and meeting the man's gaze. "I know this now. Thank you for helping me to believe it."

Jon broke into a broad grin. "A man's greatest strength is his heart. Do not be afraid to use it."

Markus nodded. "I won't."

Jon turned to his son and clasped him around the shoulder. "Come, Ryne, let us walk. Markus can catch up."

After Ryne and Ura had exchanged a final hug, father and son were both out the door, and Markus was left alone with Ura. Had Jon wanted to leave them alone together?

Markus spun around to find that Ura was already standing only a breath away. She reached out and grasped his hand in her own, before slipping something soft and feathery into his palm. "Here."

Markus looked down at his hand and gasped. "Your hair, Ura?"

"Yes." She nodded while batting pale lashes.

Markus hardly knew what to say as he stared down at the silky lock. This gift she'd given him was a treasure beyond words. His mouth suddenly felt parched. He had to swallow hard before summoning the courage to speak. "If I should survive..."

"I will wait for you," she answered.

Markus shook his head. He didn't deserve Ura and he knew it down to the marrow in his bones. But some part of him, some selfish part, wanted to claim her for his own. "I have nothing to give you."

"There's only one thing I want," Ura said in a breathy whisper, and she leaned up and kissed him.

As Markus pressed his lips against hers, deepening the kiss, he realized that he did have something he could give Ura. He could kill the witch. But did he have the right to trade his brother's life for hers?

# Chapter Nineteen

Markus realized that just about every ice dweller in the kingdom had come to see them off as he followed Ryne, Tar, and Jon through the crush. Ven and the other volunteers were waiting for them on a dais carved out of ice. Ingred, the new Chieftain, was there as well, looking down at her people with her mouth set in a grim line. With her giant nose, she resembled a hawk guarding her nest.

Ven offered Ryne and Markus a hesitant smile as they climbed the steps to the dais. Markus was glad to see Ven's transformation. He, too, had learned that cruelty served no purpose.

Markus's gaze swept the columns behind them. There were many, some as tall and wide as Markus, with pointy spikes at the tips. Others were giant prisms reflecting myriad colors of light as the thin curtain of ice above them mirrored the sun's rays.

So, these were the Dragon's Teeth and where Ura had first found him. The tallest tooth was as wide as a lyme tree at the base. Markus craned his neck as he struggled to gage the width of the tip, which looked to be no larger than he was.

Markus swallowed hard, realizing just how lucky he'd been to survive the fall into Ice Kingdom. He hoped he wouldn't repeat the same mistake and lose his grip on the mountain. His sense of dread only made the wait more agonizing. He wished to be off.

Tapping his boot, Markus looked around anxiously. The Chieftain and Jon were engaged in a deep discussion with Ryne and the others. Tar stood beside his master, whimpering as he scanned the crowd. The ice dwellers below were abuzz with chatter.

A hand grabbed his shoulder, making Markus clench his fists and spin around. He breathed a sigh of relief. It was Odu, stooped over an old cane, his spine so crooked and bent that he looked to carry an invisible weight on his back.

His bushy eyebrows pinched together. "You look troubled, boy hunter."

Markus bit back a sardonic laugh. "You could say that." How could he not be when he was about to exchange his shelter for an unknown fate? He might never see Ura or Alec again.

The prophet shook his head as he lifted his gaze to the ceiling. "There is something more to this curse."

"What?"

"The witch cares nothing for animals." The prophet tapped his cane on the ice, making a loud, splintering crack. "Do you think she spared the livestock and pets when she first set her dragon upon the Ice People's ancestors? And what do you think she does with that dragon when she has no need for it?"

"I-I don't know," Markus stammered.

"She locks the monster up in a chamber of ice, sealed by a veil of magic."

Markus's limbs froze over with fear. If Madhea cared nothing for animals, why did she send her dragon for him? Why did she place a curse upon his head that would kill his mother and threaten his brother? His muscles tensed and his throat tightened.

"Then why curse me?" he asked with strained breath.

"That is the question." Odu waved a bony hand at the side of Markus's face. "It's almost as puzzling as why you were born with that mark, for it took great magic to gift you with such skill."

Instinctively, Markus's hand flew to the side of his head. His father had told him that Madhea had blessed him with the Hunter's Mark. Had she meant to curse him instead?

"If it is not over the animals then I have done nothing to anger her. Madhea has no other reason to curse me."

"So it would seem." Odu reached into his pocket. "If you survive the encounter with the witch, would you pass this on to my brother? I haven't written him in more than three hundred years. I think a letter is long overdue."

Odu handed a rolled-up scroll to Markus, who took it with a trembling hand. He ran his thumb over its soft texture.

"Eel skin." Odu's mouth hitched up in a nearly toothless grin. "Parchment is so hard to come by down here."

The prophet turned from Markus and slowly made his way toward the Chieftain.

Markus stuffed the scroll into his fur-lined pocket and let his hand linger there for a moment. Then he traced the silky texture of the lock of Ura's hair with the pad of his thumb, hoping the lingering memory of her would ease the trembling in his fingers.

Could Odu be right? Did Madhea care nothing for the woodland creatures? If so, what grudge did she hold against him?

The group broke their tight circle and the Chieftain walked toward the edge of the dais. As she lifted her hands into the air, palms facing outward, a hush fell over the crowd.

"Oh, Heavenly Elements, hear us now," she called, turning her gaze up to the ceiling. "Please keep our sons safe from harm and veiled to the witch's eye. Bless them with wisdom, strength and, above all, courage in the face of adversity, so that they might return to their families safe and whole. We ask this in the name of Water, Land, and Sky. Amen."

Ingred bowed her head and everyone else followed, including Markus. He now respected these ice dwellers who prayed to the Elements and not to Madhea, for he was beginning to realize she truly was no goddess. She was a witch, an evil witch.

Markus wondered at the wisdom of his plan to scale Ice Mountain in the hope of winning Madhea's forgiveness. He was almost certain she would neither break the curse nor forgive the Ice People. She would kill him. Later, when Ura and her people were forced to surface, she would kill them as well.

Just as the crowd began to raise their heads, Odu pushed forward and stepped beside Ingred. The towering Chieftain gasped and then scowled down at him, but the prophet offered no apology. He only shrugged.

Tapping his staff on the ice, he cleared his throat. "Hear me, oh Heavenly Elements. I ask one more favor. Please give the land dweller the strength to follow his heart."

Soft murmurs rolled through the crowd as all eyes turned on Markus. When he lifted his chin to meet their expectant stares, Markus realized what he had to do; what his heart had been telling him all along. He must kill the witch, even if he had to sacrifice his and Alec's lives to do it.

# Chapter Twenty

*The Ice Witch*

It took the group the remainder of the morning to scale the Dragon's Teeth, mainly because they had to help Ryne haul Tar and their pack of spears. The dog was not happy with his harness and the further he was lifted from the ground, the louder his whimpering. When they finally reached the top of the spike, Ven held his stone up to the ceiling.

Markus watched as the ice above them melted away, and then he shielded his eyes as he was pelted with a splash of cool water. Luckily, he had layered his head and face in warm gnull fur. Small holes were cut into the 'mask' so that only his eyes, nose and mouth were exposed to the Elements. Zier's shield covered most of his back. The water splashed off it and onto the ice below him.

Ryne and the others had dressed warmly, too. Markus could barely make out the whites of their eyes as they all wore similar, protective furs over their faces.

Ryne and another hunter were the first to surface, pulling Tar and the spears behind them. The rest of the climbers followed, one by one, through the hole. They latched onto a nearby ice wall, clambering a short distance until they reached a rocky ledge.

Ven was the last to surface. He clutched a pick in each hand and the sack holding his stone dangled around his neck. Once he had latched onto the wall, Ven anchored himself in place and tied in with a rope, before leaning over and removing the sack from his neck. He then dangled his stone above the hole in the ice.

To Markus's amazement, the sack began to glow a pale blue and the hole sealed itself back up.

"How did he do that?" Markus asked Ryne.

"It is a freezing stone, too," he answered. "It is how our climbers repair the ice."

Markus squinted as the light around the stone faded to nothing. Ven draped it back around his neck.

"I thought it was a warming stone," Markus said as he watched Ven make his way up the wall.

"That is what we call it," Ryne replied as he patted his whimpering dog's head. "We have more use for its warming properties."

Markus looked down at the stone around his neck. How could such an innocuous-looking rock hold such power? Surely it was infused with strong magic. "So it can turn any temperature?"

"Yes, if your will is strong." Ryne turned and nodded toward several massive columns of ice in the distance. "Once we reach the ice towers together, you will continue your ascent and we will go down."

It took several more hours for the group to reach the safety of a small snowfield, above which the ice towers loomed. Ryne freed Tar from his harness and the dog bounded through the snow, wagging his tail in excitement.

Markus's arms and legs were burning from the strain of the climb, so he found an exposed rock to sit on while he rubbed his sore muscles. He dared not moan as Ryne's task had been much harder. Ryne and another climber had hauled Tar behind them, neither complaining about the dog's weight.

When Ryne whistled, Tar bounded up to him and sat at his feet. His tail wagged with such voracity that it carved a channel into the snow behind him. Ryne patted the dog on the head and then tied a rope around his neck. He walked toward the rest of the group with Tar at his side.

"We must break here," he said, "but only for a short time. If we stay too long, we risk being spotted by the witch." Then he nodded toward the sack around Markus's neck. "Take off your stone, Markus."

He did as he was told. Clutching the sack in his gloved hands, he looked up expectantly.

Ryne knelt beside him, close enough that Markus could see the frost covering his lips and nose.

"Pull out the stone and take off your gloves," Ryne ordered.

Markus's mouth fell open. He did not wish to expose his fingers to the Elements and risk frostbite when he still had a long climb ahead of him. "But it is cold."

"Do it," Ryne snapped.

Markus reluctantly set the stone on his knee and pulled off his gloves. His fingers, already numb from the chill that had seeped through the material, started to burn.

Ryne nodded at the stone. "Hold it in your hands. Close your eyes and 'will' the stone to warm you."

"But I already know how to use it," Markus argued.

"This is different," Ryne said. "You will need to use more concentration while climbing." Ryne held the pale stone in his hands and it turned a bright crimson. Then, he passed it to Markus.

No sooner had Markus taken the stone from Ryne then the warmth subsided. It was once again a cold, pale rock. Though his joints ached from the effort of wrapping his fingers around the stone, Markus clutched it in his hands and closed his eyes. He imagined the warmth returning and within seconds the numbness in his fingers began to subside. Amazingly, the stone not only warmed his hands, but the heat infused his arms and chest as well.

"Ahhhhh," Markus moaned as he basked in the warmth that enveloped him.

"It is a simple stone, is it not?"

Markus opened his eyes and looked down at the magical rock in his hands. Surprisingly, it was still glowing. "Aye," he answered.

"If you think hard enough," Ryne added, "you can will it to turn any temperature."

Looking up, Ryne nodded toward the ice tower looming beyond the snowfield. "That is the highest tower on the mountain. It will lead to an ice wall." His eyes darkened as he fixed Markus with an unwavering stare. "Straight up the ice wall is the summit to the witch's lair."

Markus nodded with understanding. His mouth had suddenly gone dry and he was unable to say more. He had known this day would come, but, still, a jolt of terror coursed through him, for though his destination remained the same, his purpose had changed. Markus would not ask the witch for forgiveness. He only prayed that her death would release him from the curse and Alec's life would be spared.

Ryne pulled the stone from Markus's chest and dropped it into the sack, before draping it around Markus's neck. "Wear it close to your heart and it will keep you warm while you climb, as long as you will it." Ryne's voice then broke and he dropped his gaze to the ground.

Markus struggled to understand the sudden shift in the man's temperament. Was it sadness he heard in his voice? Did Ura's brother actually care for him?

"I am going to do it," Markus said. His heart began to quicken as he voiced his decision, knowing that once he told Ryne, there would be no turning back. "Kill her."

Ryne's wide gaze shot to Markus. In that moment, the two shared a look of understanding.

He leaned over and grasped Markus's shoulder. "Let us not speak of it here."

Markus licked his parched lips and nodded his understanding. Ura had said Madhea had her own swirling mists, so she could easily be watching them now.

Ryne squeezed Markus's shoulder once before dropping his arm to his side. He averted his eyes, but not before Markus saw the storms brewing within their depths.

"I am sorry I have been hard on you," Ryne said.

Markus shook his head. "You were right to judge me harshly, but I am not the same lad who fell into your kingdom months ago."

When Ryne turned to him, Markus could see his lopsided grin through the small crack in his fur mask. "No, you are not," he agreed with a touch of humor in his voice, "and if you survive the witch, you will be welcome to drop by again."

Markus laughed and Ryne soon joined him. Tar showed his approval by wagging his tail as his gaze darted between them.

"I know that would make Ura happy," Ryne said.

Markus could not contain his smile, knowing that Ryne had finally approved of his love for Ura. "Aye, it would make me happy, too." As he spoke, warmth flooded his chest and he suspected it had nothing to do with the warming stone.

Then, without warning, Ryne charged at him. Markus stepped back, but it was too late. Tar grunted beside them and then broke into a low whine. Before Markus realized what was happening, Ryne was hugging him.

"May the Elements bless you," he said into his ear.

Markus hesitated only a moment before returning Ryne's embrace. "And you as well."

When Ryne pulled back, there was no mistaking the sheen of moisture in his eyes. "Thank you, Markus."

Markus feared that he, too, would start crying if he said another word. He nodded his understanding to Ryne, before bending down to pat Tar behind the ears.

"Take care of yourself, boy," Markus said in a voice that was tight with emotion. Then he reached into his satchel and pulled out a dried serpent fin. With a yelp, Tar snatched the fin in his jowls, before practically swallowing it whole.

Before Markus could stand, Tar jumped up and knocked him on his backside. Markus gasped as the wind was knocked out of his lungs. Then the mutt was upon him, planting a big, wet kiss on his lips.

"Tar!" scolded Ryne, pulling his dog off Markus.

Standing up, Markus laughed and brushed the snow off his legs. Odd how a few months earlier he would have been disgusted, but Tar's show of affection only caused Markus's heart to ache more. He would truly miss that dog.

RYNE AND HIS PARTY made their way across the snowfield as Markus trudged alone toward the base of the ice tower with a heavy heart. Though most days Ryne's constant belittling had been difficult to bear, Markus was going to miss him. But, mostly, he would miss Tar. He heaved a sigh as he watched the group slip further and further away.

The wind had started to pick up, bringing snow flurries with it, reducing Markus's visibility even more. He squinted as he watched the figures disappear. He thought he saw Ryne's silhouette turn and wave before disappearing.

Markus tried to push any disparaging thoughts from his mind. Though he could not see to the top of the tower, which was obscured by fog, he knew he'd have to traverse a great distance to reach Madhea; far more than climbing a simple tusk.

THE CLIMB UP THE ICY tower was nothing like scaling the Gnull Tusks. A blistering, relentless wind pelted Markus's face with snow and ice, obscuring his vision. A heavy fog shrouded his view of the top, making it hard for him to visualize himself as an arrow shooting himself upward when he had no idea where upward ended.

After scaling the tower for what seemed like hours, Markus's muscles ached and his throat felt raw. Worst of all, the structure offered no ledges and very few cracks for support. Markus's only lifelines were the picks and his sheer will to survive, but even that was waning. He would need to rest soon. If he didn't find a ledge, he would have to tie himself in and pray the rope held.

The warming stone had proven of little use. When Markus willed it to soothe his aching bones, not only did it suffuse his body with warmth, but it also melted the ice around him, making the wall unstable and slippery. How had he ever believed he could climb to the top of this tower? Even with all of his training, scaling such a monolith was proving too difficult.

Though Markus tried his best to purge any disparaging thoughts from his mind, he knew if he could not find shelter by nightfall, he wouldn't survive until morning.

Just as Markus reached up to dig another pick into the ice, he felt a slight tingling in his bones. Rationalizing the sensation as a result from fatigue, Markus pulled himself up and raised another pick, but the tingling strengthened. He dug a pick into the ice again, thankful that the tools were tied securely to his wrists. Mayhap he just needed to rest for a moment.

Holding his position, Markus leaned his knees into the wall while resting his fur-lined forehead on the surface. But the tingling sensation increased, so much so that it began to hammer out a buzzing staccato in his ears.

When the shield on his back and the ice wall itself began to vibrate as well, Markus realized the buzzing was coming from another source. His heart leapt into his throat. What was causing such tremors? Was the ice shifting? Was the tower breaking?

Markus lifted his head and cried out. Hundreds, mayhap thousands of tiny winged beasts, no larger than a child's fist, were diving toward him. Their bodies were a pale grey, but their large eyes were an ominous red. The bright orbs shone menacingly as the creatures bared sharp teeth and attacked the ropes securing him to his picks.

"Go!" Markus screamed.

The beasts buzzed louder, their high-pitched squeals sounding like demonic laughter.

Markus clutched at his picks with all his might, although the menaces had already torn through his ropes. Then his soles slipped. The creatures were gnawing at the leather straps that bound the spikes to his boots! Markus screamed as his feet fell out from under him and he dangled from the icy wall.

As if that wasn't enough, the demonic monsters began to gnaw the ice around the picks as well. Markus released a pick and waved it at the little beasts, which quickly flew out of his reach. One even bit down on Markus's hand and he screamed as the flesh tore open. Then he lost his grip on the picks.

Falling through the air, Markus lashed out at the creatures, even as they dove after him. The air rushed from his lungs as he plummeted toward the ground. Unexpectedly, he was jolted upright. The swarming creatures had latched onto his arms and legs, and the face of the mountain passed in a blur as Markus swiftly flew heavenward.

What were these beasts and where were they taking him? Were they Madhea's mites? Was she waiting for him at the top? If so, what was she planning to do to him?

# Chapter Twenty-One

The flying menaces unceremoniously dumped Markus onto a hard floor before buzzing into a dark portal on the opposite wall. A beautiful girl with long, coppery curls swung a metal grate over the opening before securing a lock on the handle. The monsters squealed against the door, but they appeared to be trapped.

Markus struggled to his feet and peeled off his mask as the girl turned toward him. She was a beauty, dressed in a flowing, white dress. It clung to her shapely legs before pooling around her ankles and disappearing beneath the haze of a low mist that blanketed the entire floor.

She gazed intently at him from beneath thick lashes. There was a smile in her tapered amber eyes, which unnerved Markus, for something in her look was familiar. This beauty couldn't possibly be the evil witch who had cursed his family.

"M-Madhea?" Markus stammered.

"No." She shook her head and her thick locks glided across her shoulders with the movement. "I am not she."

"Who are you?" asked Markus, taking a hesitant step forward while warily eyeing his surroundings.

The spacious, cave-like chamber resembled the dining hall in Ice Kingdom. It was brilliantly lit by several pale blue and white crystals suspended from the ceiling. A handful of small alcoves dotted the chamber, from which a deep tunnel led at the furthest end. Just beyond the tunnel entrance sat a throne, lined with plush furs.

Markus's breath hitched as he recognized the raised, stone-lined pool of water in front of the throne. White mists pooled over the depths and blanketed the luminous chamber. A vortex of spinning vapors rose up to the ceiling.

Markus's gaze darted back to the girl. He had to be in Madhea's lair. Who else would have a pool of mist?

"Who are you?" he asked again.

She looked back with wide eyes. "I am Jae, servant to Madhea."

*A servant to the witch!*

Markus instinctively reached for the bow slung across his back. "Why did you save me?" he asked, never taking his wary gaze off of the girl.

"Come," she replied, stretching out a hand to him. "I will show you."

Markus knew not why, but he had an urge to trust Jae. Something about her smile belied the same kindness that Jon and Ura had shown him, but how could he trust a servant of the witch? Markus eyed the girl's outstretched hand while stepping a wide circle around her.

Jae's smile momentarily dropped when he refused her hand, but she shrugged and walked toward the pool of mists. She stood opposite him and peered down into the pool of water, before spinning the vapor with one wave of her hand.

"Swirling mists tell us our past, our present and what could be." Jae pointed to the figure of a man standing in the center of a small hut. "See there."

Markus blinked hard and shook his head, hardly believing what he was seeing. The man looked like him, only he didn't have the Hunter's Mark on the side of his head. As he studied the man's profile, he realized that the image in the mists was a younger version of his father.

A fair-haired toddler, who looked too much like Alec, bounded up to his father. Markus nearly fell over when he saw the man scoop the boy up in his arms and kiss him. The child answered with a giggle. As his father continued to kiss the child, his chuckles turned to boisterous laughter.

Could this be true? Was Father once kind to Alec? If so, what had caused his heart to harden?

Alec began to cough and Father held him against his chest until it subsided. A woman appeared. She looked much like Markus's mother, only not as thin and frail. When she took Alec from his arms, Father turned from her, but not before Markus saw the sheen of tears in his eyes.

"My father?" Markus asked.

"Yes," Jae nodded.

"But he is..."

"Kind." Jae flashed a smile that didn't quite mask the sadness in her eyes.

Markus shook his head as a heavy gloom settled in his heart. This kind man couldn't have been his father. "This is an illusion."

"No," replied Jae as she slowly walked around the pool toward Markus. "He was kind once, until Madhea put a curse upon his heart."

Markus's jaw fell open as a jolt of dread shot up his spine. "Why?"

She looked away from Markus, turning her gaze to the swirling mists. "Because he would not stay with her."

Markus shook his head. "I don't understand."

Jae heaved a sigh before fixing Markus with a direct gaze. Her voice cracked as she spoke. "Alec had been born frail and sick. He was dying. Rowlen tried to scale the mountain and plead to Madhea for help."

Jae's eyes narrowed as her voice turned sour. "Madhea saw him through her swirling mists and had the pixies bring him to her, not out of pity, but out of lust. She promised him that she would put a spell on his son to ward off death, but only if he spent the night in her arms."

Markus sucked in a sharp intake of breath. He remembered that Zier once told him his father was the only man who had ever scaled Ice Mountain. The trader had been known to weave an exaggerated tale or two, so Markus had mistakenly asked his father if the rumor was true. It was the only time Rowlen had ever struck him.

Now Markus wondered if he'd touched a nerve that day. Mayhap he had conjured up old memories that his father was trying to forget—the night he'd slept with the witch. Could Jae be telling the truth?

"The next morning," she continued, "Madhea begged Rowlen to stay, but he refused. Rowlen held her to her promise of one night for his son's life, but just as the pixies were about to carry him down the mountain, she put a spell on his heart. From thereon he hated his son. As for the babe, he did not die, just as Madhea promised, but she did not put an end to his sickness. If anything, she prolonged it, making his life as miserable as death."

Markus's jaw hardened. He clenched the arrow in his hand so tightly that he nearly snapped it in two. Ryne was right, the witch needed to be killed!

"There is more." Jae cast her gaze down as her voice dropped to barely a whisper. "Madhea conceived a child during her night with Rowlen."

A child? That would make Markus a brother to the witch's offspring. How could he bear the thought of having such a sibling? His mouth suddenly went dry. Licking his cracked lips, he willed the tension that coiled around his neck to subside. "What became of the child?"

When Jae lifted her gaze back to Markus, he could not mistake the vortex of emotions that clouded her eyes. "I am her," she said.

"You?" Markus gasped. "You are my sister?"

"Yes."

"But you said you were her servant." Markus wondered what kind of parent would force her child into servitude, but he already knew Madhea was capable of cruelty.

Jae shrugged. "She treats me as such. I did not inherit her magical powers. I am useless."

"I'm sorry." Markus took a step forward and reached for his sister's hand.

Jae clasped his hand in her own and looked into his eyes before flashing a dazzling smile. "Do not be. When I learned that you were my brother, I longed to meet you. I'm so happy you are here."

Markus couldn't help but feel pity for her. All of his life he had been ashamed to have a monster for a father. What must Jae's childhood have been like with an evil witch for a mother? Suddenly, the thought of the girl being his sister wasn't so bad. Jae was a victim of her parentage, just as he had been. Could this be why she sent the pixies to pull him from the mountain? Had she meant to help her brother defeat the witch?

"Do you know why I have come here?" Markus asked.

"I saw you in the mists, telling the trader that you were going to beg my mother's forgiveness." Jae tightened her grip on Markus's hand. "It will not work. When you were born with the Hunter's Mark, Madhea had not meant to bless you. She knew that one day you would bring upon the hunter's curse, and she wanted to punish our father for leaving her."

Markus's heart hammered against his chest. Releasing his sister's hand, he stepped back. Should he tell her that his plan had changed and that he meant to kill Madhea? How would she react? Would she help him to kill her own mother?

"I'm sorry, Jae, but your mother is evil. She needs to be destroyed."

"No!" Jae's hand flew to her mouth. "You can't destroy her. She can conjure deadly thunderbolts." She lowered her hands, clenching them by her sides. "Appeal to the Elementals. It is the only way to stop her."

"Who are they?"

"My sisters," Jae answered, "but born of magic. They are not cruel like my moth..."

"I knew I should have smote you when you were a babe! Useless mortal! Traitorous bitch!"

Markus turned to the source of the shrill voice that echoed off the chamber walls just as a blinding flash of light almost knocked him off his feet. Instinctively, he swung his bow into his grip and nocked an arrow while skidding to his knees behind the raised pool of water. In that moment he saw his sister's lifeless body on the floor. Smoke rose from a charred hole in her chest. Markus cried out before gagging on the pungent odor of Jae's burnt flesh.

A cackling, winged woman flew down beside Jae and kicked her head with a bare foot.

Markus leapt up and released his arrow. "You are a monster!" he yelled.

The woman laughed and waved a wrinkled hand, slowing the arrow to a near standstill. She opened her palm and a bright bolt of lightning shot out, turning the arrow to ash.

"Keep your distance, boy hunter," she warned, holding out her smoking palms.

The glowing, pale robe that flowed around the woman's bony body did nothing to soften her ugly features. Scraggly, grey hair clung to her scalp and cascaded down her back like dead vines. Her mouth hung in a permanent frown and her emerald eyes were framed by dark, heavy circles.

She had to be Madhea.

The witch had killed her own daughter and Markus's only sister. He would make her pay. Markus nocked another arrow, but his heart sank as the winged witch circled him. How could he possibly destroy a flying witch who could shoot thunderbolts from her hands?

"You've grown pale," she sneered, while leveling him with a smug expression. "Been dwelling among the Ice People, have you? They cannot hide from me forever and when I find them they shall pay for helping you!"

Anger surged anew through his skull. "I will kill you!"

Markus released another arrow and, just like before, she turned it to ash.

"Who do you think gifted you with the power to kill, you stupid boy?" she shrieked, lifting her palms.

Markus jumped behind the raised pool of mist just as Madhea released a thunderbolt. Rocks tumbled down around him, followed by the rush of frigid water.

"My mists!" the witch cried.

Markus rolled away and his arrows clanked to the floor, just as another thunderbolt shot out. Dodging it, he leapt to his feet and scrambled behind the stone wall of an alcove.

Markus reached into his quiver and found only one arrow left. Pulling back his bowstring, he peered around the wall. From what he could tell, Madhea was bent over the destroyed pool of water, but the swirling mists had scattered, obscuring almost everything in the room. He could no longer see his sister's body and Madhea's winged form was just a blur.

But the one thing that did catch his eye was a glowing crystal above Madhea's shadow. Mites! Markus aimed his arrow and struck at the core of the crystal. Light scattered as the ice shattered.

Madhea let out an agonizing scream. Her wings buzzed noisily as she shook her arms and jumped up from the mists.

Even through the dense fog, Markus could feel the heat of the witch's angry glare. Gasping, he ducked behind the wall and searched for an exit, but there was no escape. Markus unsheathed the knife from his boot and backed against the wall, just as the witch flew above him. Red, angry welts were forming along her pale arms.

"You shall pay for hurting me, boy hunter! You are a fool, just like your father!"

With all his might, Markus threw his knife, aiming for Madhea's cold heart, but it dissolved when struck by her magic. The witch let out an ominous hiss before a blinding, white force knocked Markus's head against the wall. An agonizing scream pierced his ears just before his world darkened.

MARKUS AWOKE WITH A thick fog in his head. Somewhere in the distance, he could hear the faint sound of women crying.

"Jae! She is dead!"

"The mists have been destroyed!"

"What has happened?"

Markus slowly opened his eyes. Though it was difficult to see, the misty haze was beginning to clear. He could vaguely make out two winged women fluttering over Jae's body.

"Oh, the poor girl," sobbed one of them.

"Our mother has gone too far this time," the other said, pointing somewhere near Markus.

Markus struggled to sit up, though his chest ached and his extremities were numb. Finally, he managed to lean his head and shoulders against the icy wall behind him. There, just beyond his feet, lay Madhea. Crusted blood coated the old witch's temple, and her arms and face were covered in raised, red welts.

Markus clenched his teeth as the winged women flew toward him. His gaze shot to the opposite tunnel and he thought about fleeing, even though he feared the women would strike him with thunderbolts. It mattered not. His legs felt like dead weights and he could scarcely twitch a muscle, let alone walk.

The women fluttered down to Madhea and knelt by her side. Markus sucked in a sharp breath. They were beauties and, from what he could tell, almost identical, except that one had pale blonde hair and the other a soft, strawberry shade.

"Is she alive, Kia?" asked the fair-haired one, smoothing her fingers across Madhea's brow.

"She breathes, Ariette, but barely," answered the other as she bent over the witch.

"She was struck by her own thunderbolt," gasped Ariette.

"How?" Kia asked.

"Look there." Ariette pointed a finger. "The boy wears a stone!"

Markus glanced down at the sack dangling around his neck. There were several rips in the leather pouch, revealing the glowing stone inside. Panic seized his chest as the women fluttered beside him.

"Where did you get this?" Kia's lips pulled back in a snarl as she waved a hand at the stone. The flapping of her translucent wings reminded him of the frenzied buzz of a hornet's hive.

Markus sat up on his elbows. His tongue was swollen and heavy inside his parched mouth, and he had to clear his throat to speak. "It was a gift."

Kia's eyes narrowed. "Who gifted it to you?"

But Markus refused to answer. Madhea did not need another reason to curse the Ice People.

"The Ice People gave this to you, didn't they?" Ariette asked. "I *knew* they were using magic to escape Mother's eye."

Markus clenched his fists as every muscle in his body tensed with fear.

Kia exchanged wide-eyed glances with her sister. "How many more do they have?" she asked, her strawberry-colored hair falling over her shoulders.

Kia wore a loose robe, just like her sister, but what alarmed Markus was the huge blade tucked into her belted hip.

"I-I do not remember," he stammered. No use trying to pretend the Ice People didn't have stones. Markus knew these women had already read the truth in his eyes.

Struggling to sit up straight, Markus pushed his back against the chamber wall. Feeling was starting to return to his numb limbs.

The two sisters shared another look of understanding before turning their gazes back to him.

"Now we know why Mother could never find the Ice People in her mists," Ariette said. "The stones shielded them from her magic." Arching a brow, she looked the boy over with an assessing glare. "Who are you and why have you come here?"

"I am Markus, son of Rowlen." He paused when the pair gasped and covered their mouths with their hands. Jae had said her sisters could help him and he assumed these women were they, but he still didn't dare divulge his true reason for seeking out Madhea. "I came to break the curse and to beg Madhea to call off her dragon," he replied.

Kia's face flushed as she glared at him from beneath pale lashes. "You are the cruel hunter?"

Markus vehemently shook his head and instantly regretted the dizzy wave that overcame him. "I am cruel no more. I have learned my lesson. I swear it."

Ariette flew down and knelt before him. She leaned forward and looked intently into his eyes as if she were reaching into his soul. "There is truth in your face, but we cannot stop Lydra. She only obeys our mother."

Markus's head began to spin as if the very foundation on which he sat was about to collapse. He had come all this way, all for nothing. Now his sister was dead and the curse was still not broken.

"B-but my sister said..."

Ariette shook her head. "Jae is not your sister."

"Stop, Ariette," her sister scowled. "You've said too much."

The woman looked up at Kia with a pleading gaze. "The boy must know. No one else can overcome Mother's magic but her."

Kia's wings slumped as she dropped to the ground and knelt beside her sister.

"When our true sister was born," Ariette said to Markus, "we stole her from her cradle and traded her for another babe in your village."

Markus sucked in a sharp breath. "Why?"

"Mother would have twisted our sister's mind and used her magic against us," Ariette said. "Our sister will have even greater magic. We have seen it in the swirling mists."

"Has not Madhea seen this as well?" Markus asked. "Won't she know you've fooled her?"

Kia shook her head. "The swirling mists are rebelling. They no longer reveal all to her. Mother's magic is waning. The Elements are gaining strength and fleeing her grasp."

"The melting ice," gasped Markus, his gaze darting from one sister to the other.

Ariette folded her hands in her lap. "Yes. Once the ice melts, Mother will have no power."

"Then mayhap we should let it melt," he said.

There was an edge to Kia's outburst of laughter. "You do not know how vast this ice is. The whole world would be underwater."

Ariette nodded. "Yes, and the more power our mother loses, the more power the Sea Witch will gain."

Despite the chamber's frigid air, Markus's temperature rose. Even if he did destroy Madhea, his people would still be beholden to her evil sister. "I've heard there was another witch."

Kia's nostrils flared. "Eris, Keeper of the Sea, and she is more malevolent than our mother."

"Our sister is the only way." There was a note of desperation in Ariette's voice. "She must destroy our mother and take her place as the Sky Goddess."

Markus ground his teeth as he struggled to rein in his temper. "Why can't you do it?" he asked the pair.

Kia's wings snapped open and she took to the air. She scowled down at Markus. "We are not powerful enough to destroy Mother. Even if we were, Eris would seize control of Ice Mountain."

Markus's ire grew. He, a mere mortal, was willing to risk his life and fight Madhea, so why couldn't these daughters overcome both witches themselves?

He coursed his fingers through his hair with a groan. "Then who is my sister? Who is this witch destined to kill Madhea?"

A moan beyond Markus caused Ariette to jump. She spun around while taking to the air. Kia clutched the blade on her belt. After flying toward their mother, the sisters looked over their shoulders at Markus.

"Our mother awakens," Kia hissed as she flew back to Markus. "You must leave. Guard your stone well. Madhea must not know you have it."

Ariette fluttered forward while twisting her fingers. "Mother will think her thunderbolt smote you to ash."

Kia turned to her sister. "I will release the pixies and have them take Markus to his people." With that, she flew into the mist.

Markus struggled to rise on shaky legs. He watched Ariette flutter around while twisting a knot in her robe.

"What of Jae?" he asked her.

Though the girl was not his true sister, he still felt a sense of guilt over her death. She had saved him from the mountain and paid for it with her life. How many more people would die on account of him?

The lines in Ariette's brow softened. "Jae has been a good servant. We will see to it that her soul passes to the Elements."

She glanced over her shoulder before turning back to Markus with glassy eyes. "I hear the pixies coming. You must go and never return or my mother will kill you for sure."

# Chapter Twenty-Two

As the pixies flew swiftly, the mountain passed in a blur, causing Markus's head to spin. The freezing wind whipped against his exposed flesh, numbing his lips until he could no longer feel them. He shut his eyes and prayed to the Elements to help him survive the descent. Then he willed the warming stone to glow. Soon, heat infused his chest and eased the burning chill.

After several tense moments, the pixies came to a halt, pulling tightly on Markus's clothes until his breeches wedged up his buttocks. Squirming against the pressure, he looked down to see the grassy ground only a few feet beneath him. Tremors from the buzzing pixies rattled his dizzied brain. They squealed and squawked before letting out high-pitch laughter.

The creatures dropped him on the ground and flew away. Markus landed on his feet, but stumbled before falling on his backside. He lay on the grass for a long moment, feeling dazed and confused as he stared up at the bright spring sky. Once the fog had shaken from his mind, he slipped out of his satchel and rolled off his shield.

When he came to his knees, Markus dug his fingers into the ground and relished the feel of the damp soil against his skin. Oh, how he missed home. It was odd how only that morning he had been scaling Ice Mountain, thinking he'd never live to see his home again.

Sitting up, Markus smiled at a squirrel staring intently at him from the bottom of a nearby pine. The animal must have been as dazed as he upon seeing a boy survive a drop from the sky. Markus spied a pine nut nearby, partially hidden beneath the soil. He unearthed it and rolled it to the squirrel. The creature snatched it up and squeaked his delight before scurrying up the tree.

Markus struggled to his feet, brushing ice and dirt off his breeches. He slowly unwrapped the fur mask from his head and tossed off his heavy cloak.

He arched back his neck and cried out with joy before breathing in a deep gulp of fresh air.

That's when he saw her standing beneath the branches of the pine, gaping at him while clutching a bow in one hand.

Dianna.

DIANNA STARED FOR A long moment at the blue-colored man who had been dropped from the sky by tiny, winged creatures. Who was he and why had he come here? For good or evil? Was he one of Madhea's servants, sent to wreak destruction on her people?

She watched with fascination as the stranger fed a nut to a squirrel and then cried out as he stretched his arms up to the sky. But when the man turned his gaze on her, Dianna thought her knees would buckle. She knew him. She had seen his features before, of that she was certain.

Dianna jerked back with trepidation as he took one step forward and then another.

She nocked an arrow and lifted her bow. "Halt!" she called.

The stranger stopped and splayed his hands wide. Dianna noted how his limbs shook.

"I mean you no harm, Dianna."

Her heart pounded out a wild staccato. "Who are you and how do you know my name?"

As the figure drew closer, Dianna was momentarily struck dumb. Though he was lean and tall like the mighty pine tree, there was a boyish glint in his features. Was this man really just a child?

"Do you not recognize me?"

She arched a brow at the familiar ring in his youthful voice. "Should I?"

"Aye, you should." The stranger nodded. "I am Markus."

"CENTER YOUR AIM, DES. Flex your shoulders and put your back into it."

Alec pulled back the boy's shoulders while gently lifting the hand clutching the bowstring. Des aimed at the target and released his arrow. It landed just left of the bull's-eye.

"Excellent shot, Des!"

Beside them, the boy's dog, Brendle, yipped his approval.

Des's shoulders fell. "No, it wasn't."

Alec patted him on the back. Despite his encouragement, the boy was still unsure of himself. "Your arrow landed on the target," he told him.

"But not in the center," Des whined.

"Don't worry." Alec leaned over and ruffled the boy's mop of hair. "With practice, it will."

Des's eyes lit up. "Do you think I'll be as good as your brother?" he blurted. Then he slapped his hand over his mouth. "I'm sorry," he added, dropping his hands to his sides. "Dianna told me it pains you when I speak of him."

"It does," Alec answered, his chest tightening, "but my heart will ache for him no matter what."

Though Alec tried to conceal his sorrow from Dianna and Des, he cried for his brother every day. Markus had to be dead. Alec had never seen or heard of the dragon since that day. He guessed that Markus must have let the beast destroy him rather than shoot it and allow Alec to die.

On the eve of his brother's birth, Alec had vowed to Madhea that he would give his last, dying breath to make certain Markus did not grow into a monster, but he had failed. He had failed the Goddess and himself, but, most of all, he'd failed his baby brother. For that, Alec despised himself, but, if truth be told, he also held the same feeling for Madhea. Though he would never voice his thoughts aloud and risk bringing on another curse, Alec hated her with every breath in his body.

Markus was just a boy. The Goddess did not need to punish him so severely. She need not have killed their mother. Besides, where was Madhea when his father had brutally beaten him day after day? Why hadn't she cursed his father for his cruelty?

All this had led Alec to believe that the Goddess cared nothing for the people of Adolan, and he was tired of paying homage to such a heartless witch.

"Alec, are you okay?"

He shook the fog from his head and looked down to see Des staring up at him with a slackened jaw. The boy pointed up at his face. "Your cheeks are turning red."

Alec averted his gaze. He did not wish to dwell on more dark thoughts of his brother. "I need to chop wood for the fire and you should get back to your studies before Dianna returns home."

Des scrunched his brows while scratching his scalp. "But we have enough wood to last us through next winter."

"I know, Des." Alec nodded toward their small hut. "Now go to your studies."

The boy hung his head, turned on his heel, and dragged his feet toward the hut. His little dog, whose tail was set in constant motion, followed him inside.

Alec walked over to the woodpile and picked up the axe. He placed a large log on the ground and cut into it with a splintering crack; all the while his thoughts continued to wander. He needed to chop wood. Not only because the exercise revived his strength, but because he knew he wouldn't stay much longer, and he wanted to leave Dianna with something to show his appreciation for all she'd done for him.

She had saved his life by healing his illness and infusing his body with a strength he'd never known. For that, he would be eternally grateful. If the villagers were to discover Dianna's power, they would condemn her as a witch and demand she be offered on the pyre to the Goddess. But, to Alec, Dianna was not a witch. She was a blessing.

While Alec would like nothing more than to live out the rest of his days with Dianna and Des, there were too many daily reminders of his dead brother and cruel father. Whenever Alec happened on Markus's favorite hunting glen, just beyond the ridge by Dianna's hut, a pain would twist his gut as he was overcome by feelings of guilt. Many a time he thought he spied the reflection of his father's dark eyes or heard his ghost call his name within the shadows of the nearby forest.

Alec knew he could not remain in his ancestral village for long. He had already spoken with Zier. Now that Alec was growing stronger, he had decided to accompany the trader to the sea in the early summer. Zier had told him of a small fishing village, where the salty air and smell of the ocean seeped into his skin and filled him with renewed vigor.

Alec thought he would very much like to feel this salty air and gaze upon the vast ocean. Most of all, he needed to escape this place that held so many dark memories.

"We have company!"

Wiping a bead of sweat off his brow, Alec turned to see Dianna striding briskly toward him. Beside her walked a blue man! Alec blinked hard and then shook his head as he looked into the man's pale eyes.

Alec's axe fell from his grip as his arms and legs suddenly felt weak. The man's slanted smile... his pale mop of hair... the faint scar on his forehead...

"M-Markus?" Alec stammered.

"Aye, brother." The blue man replied, opening his arms wide. "It is me."

Alec was barely aware of his own actions as he staggered toward his brother, whose skin was such a pale shade of blue to be almost translucent! But nothing else mattered now that Markus was alive.

"Brother!" Alec cried, grasping him in a fierce hug.

As the two men held each other for a long time, Alec wept against Markus's shoulder and he was surprised to hear his brother's muffled cries as well. He'd rarely known Markus to shed a tear.

Finally, Alec pulled back and looked into his brother's face. "I thought you'd been killed by the dragon."

Markus shook his head. "No, I escaped. I've been dwelling among the Ice People."

Alec's gaze swept across his brother's features. "Your skin and hair have changed."

Markus heaved a sigh. "That is not all that has changed. My heart has changed as well."

When Alec saw the sincerity reflected in the pale pools of his brother's eyes, he nearly wept with joy. "Can it be?" he asked.

Markus grasped his brother's hand and placed it over his heart. "Everything you taught me about kindness to animals, I finally understand. I'm sorry it took the witch's curse for me to learn my lesson."

Alec gasped. "Do not call the Goddess a witch!"

Markus's eyes darkened. "I call her many things, but, aye, she is a witch and a cruel one at that."

A strangled cry escaped Alec's lips. Madhea would destroy him for sure.

"Do not worry, brother, she cannot hear me now." Markus reached beneath his heavy cloak and pulled a small sack from around his neck.

"Has the curse been lifted?" Alec asked.

"Nay," said Markus, opening the sack and holding out a pale rock in his hand, "but I wear a sacred stone that shields me from her eye."

"Sacred stone?" Alec arched a brow as he eyed the smooth, flat rock, which was slightly smaller than Markus's palm.

"Aye, look." Markus closed his eyes and held out the stone. Soon, it turned a bright crimson.

Alec's jaw dropped.

Dianna walked up beside him and gasped. "How odd," she said, peering at the stone. "What is that strange noise it makes?"

"Noise?" asked Markus as his brows drew together in a frown, making him look just as puzzled as her.

"Aye." Dianna arched back and warily eyed the stone. "Almost as if it is whispering. Don't you hear it?"

Markus shook his head. "Nay, it only glows. It doesn't make any sound."

Suddenly, an ear-splitting roar shook the very ground beneath their feet. Dianna jumped before unsheathing her bow. "I hope you heard *that* sound."

Alec gaped at his brother. "The dragon? She still pursues you?"

"Aye," Markus answered as he bunched his hands into fists at his sides. "The beast has awoken."

"Brother, we must flee," Alec said with a strained breath, as a pain stronger than he'd ever known struck him in the chest. Had he been reunited with his brother only to lose him again?

Markus slipped the stone back in its pouch before turning to Alec. "I must face down this thing myself."

"But brother," pleaded Alec, grasping Markus by the arm, "you cannot kill!"

IT PAINED MARKUS TO see the look of despair in his brother's eyes, but he had no choice—he hadn't come this far only to be killed by Madhea's dragon.

He reached out to Alec one more time and wrapped him in a fierce hug. "Do not fear, brother." Markus struggled to keep the emotion out of his voice as he spoke against Alec's ear. Every muscle in his body tightened. "The stone protects us from the curse. This beast nearly wiped out an entire village. She must be destroyed."

"Are you mad?" Alec pulled out of the embrace. The look in his glassy eyes was one akin to horror. "You cannot go after a dragon!"

Markus didn't have time to argue. If he didn't stop Lydra soon, he suspected she would attack the village. He nodded toward the small hut. "You and Dianna go inside where it is safe."

Markus turned on his heel and ran in the direction of the dragon's roar, toward the first place he knew Lydra would look once she awakened and the last place he ever wanted to go to again—home.

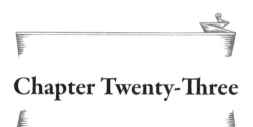

# Chapter Twenty-Three

Alec watched in disbelief as his brother ran toward peril once again. Gone. Markus was gone and he had done nothing to stop him.

Dianna came up beside him as Markus disappeared into the forest. "Does he think a mere stone can stop a curse and that an arrow can fell a dragon?" she asked, her voice laced with disbelief.

When Dianna voiced his thoughts, Alec knew he had to take action. He refused to let his brother face this monster alone. "Go inside with Des," he commanded.

Alec didn't wait to gage her response as he swung around and scooped up the axe from the woodpile. Determination fueled his movements as he sprinted toward the forest.

"Alec, you will be killed!" Dianna called behind him.

Alec steeled his resolve as he ran. He knew Dianna was right and he might very well die, but he'd be damned if he let his brother face this dragon alone a second time.

MARKUS BURST THROUGH the clearing with his bow drawn. The sight before him stole the breath from his lungs. The beast had her back to him, her huge hindquarters protruding in the air while her head was embedded inside the hut of Markus's family.

He watched the dragon's giant, spiked tail wave circles in the air while she tore through his home with her massive snout. Markus's heart sank. The small hut, containing the loft he had shared with Alec, was now destroyed.

Anger surged through him as he ground his teeth and he exhaled a shaky breath. Centering his aim on the beast's big buttocks, he fired his arrow.

Wood splintered and thatch snapped in two as the dragon roared and jerked up her head.

Markus had already nocked another arrow. This time he didn't plan to aim at the wings or buttocks. This time, he would shoot to kill.

As the beast turned her ominous red eyes upon him, Markus almost lost his resolve. His limbs iced over, not just from fear, but from the chill that shrouded the dragon like a heavy fog and stole all warmth from the spring air.

Thoughts of Alec and Ura flashed through Markus's mind. He would not allow the dragon to defeat him. He would live to see both of them again. Suspecting the scales covering the beast's torso would be too hard to penetrate, he had to aim for the throat.

Just as he was about to release the arrow, the dragon's tail swept him off the ground and sent him flying onto the roof of the skinning shack. Markus broke through it and landed on top of the cutting table with a thud. He gasped as a sharp pain shot up his leg.

A low, heavy growl sounded outside. Markus watched in horror as, board by board, the skinning shack was stripped away by a pair of massive talons. He reached for his bow, but it wasn't there. Markus cried out when he spied it, dangling next to the gaping hole in the ceiling, though he didn't know if he'd be able to draw back a bowstring anyway. His body was so numb from the chill of the dragon's breath that he could scarcely bend his fingers.

The dragon's red eyes shone through the cracks in the shack. Markus knew the beast was prolonging his death, toying with him in the same way a cat played with a mouse. He refused to die like this. He had come too far to end up as nothing more than gristle between Lydra's teeth.

Markus struggled to his feet and, despite the stiffness in his hand, he grabbed a large boning blade off the table. In the past it had been used to cut up snowbears and other tough meat. Though Lydra was much bigger than a bear, the blade would have to do.

"Hey! Over here, you big, ugly monster!"

Markus's throat constricted and he barely managed a sob when he recognized the tone of his brother's taunts. Why had Alec come?

Now they would both be killed!

Markus burst through the door of the skinning shack just as the beast turned away, and he saw his brother standing on the edge of the clearing. Alec hurled an axe at the monster's chest. It bounced off her thick scales and fell to the ground with a thud.

Alec jumped as the dragon unleashed a stream of deadly current, but he didn't move fast enough. He was frozen within a heartbeat, entombed in an impenetrable, icy arc as his body glided through the air. The agonizing sound of Alec's final cry hung suspended in the stagnant air, and for one interminable moment in time, Markus's heart stopped beating.

DIANNA COULD NOT STOP the flow of angry tears as she raced through the forest, dodging roots and branches that seemed to jut out of nowhere and slow her chase. How could Alec have risked his life so foolishly?

Even though Dianna used her healing powers to ease the heaviness in his chest, Alec had still not recovered all of his strength, yet now he thought himself strong enough to fight a dragon? He would be nothing more than a sacrifice—an offering to the bitch goddess, Madhea—and he expected her to do nothing? Just wait inside the hut?

During the short time that Alec had lived with her and Des, he'd become more than a friend to them. He had become almost as beloved as her brother. She'd be damned if she was going to wait around while he sacrificed himself on a fool's quest.

Dianna wondered if she was an even bigger fool. Armed with only a bow, she knew she would be no match for a dragon. Her only hope was to stop Alec before he reached the monster.

As she neared the clearing to Alec's childhood home, her heartbeat quickened. Though, as part of her magical gifts, she had been born impervious to the Elements, she recognized the chill that shrouded the forest like a heavy fog: the dragon was near. She hoped Markus and Alec would be able to sustain such cold.

The loud roar of the dragon, followed by Alec's anguished scream, made Dianna skid to a halt. She tried to quell the knot of panic that rose up in her throat.

Great Goddess! Alec had already met his fate!

MARKUS HURLED HIS KNIFE at Lydra's wing. It cut a hole through a translucent membrane before flying out the other side. The dragon howled as she spun around. Plumes of thick vapor rose from her flared nostrils. The beast pulled her injured wing against her side before hunching down on all four claws. With serpentine grace, she moved toward Markus as a deep, menacing growl emanated from her throat.

Markus cared not for his own safety. All that mattered was that his brother was dead and the beast must pay. He clutched an arrow behind his back. He only needed Lydra to get close enough so that he could lodge the weapon in her throat with his bare hands.

"Come closer, dragon! Look me in the eyes!" Markus cried, slapping his chest. "I dare you!"

Markus tightened his grip on the arrow as the beast moved closer. Her tongue flicked across massive, ice-encrusted jowls as she leveled him with an ominous red glare. Markus's teeth began to chatter and his innards shook with a chill that seeped into his bones. He tried to roll the tension from his shoulders as he flexed his burning muscles. He would not fail.

Just as the dragon lowered her head and was almost upon him, Markus heard the cry of a woman. "Stop! Leave him be!"

Dianna! Markus's pulse quickened. No! He would not let another person die on account of him!

Lydra jerked up her head and spun around, revealing Dianna, standing beside the ice spout that held Alec's frozen form. With tears streaming down her face, Dianna angled her chin and raised her bow.

"No!" Markus screamed. "Run, Dianna!"

But Dianna didn't budge as the dragon advanced on her.

Markus leapt into the air, wincing as he landed on the beast's spiky tail. With no time to think about the pain shooting through his limbs, Markus drove his arrow through her leathery hide.

Lydra howled and whipped him through the air. Markus's head felt as if it would implode after he landed on the soft grass. He rolled over, trying to shake the fog from his skull as pain lanced through his arm, but what he saw when he looked up made him cry out in rage. Alec's frozen form hovered above him.

As Markus's eyes shot from Lydra to Dianna, the breath was stolen from his lungs. Fists planted at her sides, she stood before the dragon, which cowered before her.

*USE ME. I CAN FREE the boy from the ice. Hurry!*

Dianna's sharp gaze shot to Markus and the glowing stone hanging inside the threadbare purse around his neck.

*Did that rock just speak to me?* she wondered.

The amber light from the stone pulsated in response.

Dianna took a hesitant step toward Markus, while keeping one eye on Lydra.

The dragon shut her eyes, giving the impression that she had extinguished the lights in her red orbs. Then the monster let out a low and mournful wail while trembling on the ground.

Dianna took another step toward Markus as he cried against the arced column of ice in which Alec was buried.

"Markus," she said through shaky breath, "give me the stone."

He looked at her with wide, watery eyes. "Why?"

She impatiently wagged her fingers. "Just do it!"

Markus removed the stone and placed it in her grasp. Despite the chilled air, Dianna's hand instantly warmed.

*Hold me against the boy,* the stone beckoned.

She reached up and pressed it against Alec's blurred form. Miraculously, the ice began to melt.

Lydra whimpered louder. Dianna glanced at the dragon. The beast was now flat against the ground, shielding her eyes with her paws.

Dianna paid no heed to the frigid water that splashed down her arm and splattered across her forehead. The chill from the darkest winter's night had never seeped into her bones. This water was no different.

Alec tumbled into his brother's arms as the final layer of ice surrounding him melted. Markus wrapped his arms around him while murmuring into his ear. With tears streaming down his face, he laid Alec's prone body on the grass and pumped his chest before breathing air into his mouth.

Markus's cries became more frantic as he continued to press Alec, whose skin was a pale blue; his body motionless.

*Place me upon the boy,* the stone said.

"Move aside, Markus," Dianna commanded.

He pulled back and looked at her with a quivering lip. "Please save him," he begged through a sob.

When Dianna laid the stone upon Alec's chest, it began to pulsate; its crimson glow spreading until the warm light encompassed his entire body. As the light slowly faded away, Alec was on his side, coughing water into the grass. Markus sat beside his brother, rubbing a hand down his back until his coughing subsided.

Dianna could not contain the joy that bubbled up in her throat. Alec was alive! But her laughter quickly died when her gaze shot to Markus.

He clutched Alec to his chest while pointing at her with a shaky finger. "You are our sister. *You* are destined to kill Madhea."

# Chapter Twenty-Four

Draped in several layers of fur, Des and his little dog had fallen asleep by the fire, shortly after Markus had relayed his story about the time he'd spent with the Ice People. The boy had been more impressed by the tale of the gnull attack than with the snoring dragon, which now slept outside their hut.

After Markus was certain that Des was lost to a deep slumber, he relayed the rest of his adventures, including what he'd learned from Jae and her sisters.

Dianna shed a tear for Jae, and then her face hardened when Markus told her that Madhea and Rowlen were her parents. Alec leaned over and wrapped an arm around his sister, and she exhaled a long breath before reaching up and planting a kiss on his cheek.

Markus averted his gaze, not wanting to intrude on their moment of sibling affection. Even though he was Dianna's brother as well, he didn't feel he deserved her love. He watched the flames dance in the hearth, casting shadows around the small room. Despite the warmth from the fire, it was not enough to drive the chill from his bones. He doubted the night would get any warmer, thanks to Dianna's new pet.

She pulled away from Alec and shook her head and limbs, as if she was purging herself of the taint of her parents' blood.

Alec's expression turned from shock to horror when Markus explained to him that their father's cruelty had actually been a curse. He kicked his empty bowl of stew into the hearth before jumping to his feet and storming off into the night air.

Markus had sensed that Alec would not handle the news well. "I should go after him," he said to Dianna.

She shook her head. "No. Many times, when he was plagued by dark thoughts of you or Rowlen, Alec would disappear for several hours, only to return at morning light. I tried to follow him once and he was not happy with my intrusion."

Alec had suffered too much during his young life, not just physically, but emotionally as well. If it hadn't been for Dianna's healing powers and friendship, Markus believed his brother would surely have perished while he was gone.

Markus swallowed the rising tide of emotion that threatened to overwhelm him. "Thank you, Dianna, for caring for him in my absence."

She laughed. "You do not need to thank me. He is my brother." Her gaze softened as she reached out and clasped his hands in her own. "As are you."

Markus looked down at their joined hands and a shudder stole up his spine. To think that he'd once desired his own sister. Thankfully, now Markus felt only brotherly affection toward Dianna, though it would not have mattered as she had never shown him any interest other than scorn, and rightfully so.

"You were right to call me out that night during my celebration," he said.

"Let us not talk of it now." She squeezed his hands before pulling away. "You've learned your lesson. That is all that matters."

Dianna looked down as the stone in her lap began to glow. "Her name is Sindrí," she said, picking it up. "She claims to be my cousin."

Markus swallowed, hardly believing what he was hearing.

"Sindrí says her mother was Kyan, Goddess of the Land," Dianna explained, turning the glowing stone in her hands. "Madhea turned Kyan and her daughters to stone."

Markus clenched his teeth as his gaze tunneled onto the rock. All this time, this innocuous-looking object had possessed a soul; a soul which Dianna had awakened. Though Markus could not hear Sindrí speak, he believed his sister. No wonder the stone was able to deflect Madhea's magic. It had the power of a goddess.

"Sindrí says her mother was a good goddess," Dianna continued, staring down at the pulsating rock. "She wants to help us defeat Madhea, but we must find her mother and sisters."

"How many stones are there?" Markus asked.

Dianna paused. "Seven."

"The Ice People have five. Does she know where we can find the others?"

Dianna shook her head. "No."

Markus swore, for he now knew what this meant. While he'd managed to deflect the witch's curse and escape the dragon's breath, his ordeal was far from over. If Dianna was prophesied to bring an end to Madhea's reign, she would need help; not only to find the stones, but to defeat the witch as well.

"COME, LOOK!" DIANNA burst into the small hut. Frost hung off the tips of her hair. "Lydra has made Des a slide!"

Markus followed Alec outside. To his amazement, the small patch of soil surrounding Dianna's hut was covered in rising waves of ice. Des squealed with delight as he sat on top of Zier's shield and slid down one wave after another.

Alec scratched his head while sipping a cup of warm tea. "This is all very odd."

"Aye," Markus laughed, "and somewhat disturbing."

Dianna held out her arms as a broad smile lit up her face. "Would you rather she was turning you into icicles?"

Alec shook his head while he blew steam off his cup. "No, once is enough for me."

Des's little black dog yapped and tried to chase him, but ended up skidding across the ice on his hindquarters.

Lydra sat at the edge of the icy wonderland, looking as complacent as was possible for a demonic-eyed dragon, while she licked icicles off her massive claws.

It was then that Markus heard the faint sound of barking coming from deep within the forest. He turned to his brother. "Do you hear that?"

Alec held a hand to his ear. "It sounds like a dog."

Des's pet must have heard it, too, because he skidded across the ice and onto the grass before taking off at a full run toward the forest.

"Brendle!" the boy screamed as he struggled to rise from the shield. "Get back here!"

The animal hadn't even reached the tree-line when a massive, furry beast came bounding toward them.

"Tar!" Markus cried as he sprinted toward the dog.

But Tar didn't have eyes for Markus. He charged past the little yipping dog and straight at Lydra.

"No!" Markus cried. "Tar! Heel!"

Tar stopped at the edge of Lydra's tail and pulled back his lips in a snarl while growling menacingly. The beast looked down at the dog as a deep rumble rose up from her massive chest.

"Lydra!" Dianna commanded. "Don't hurt the dog."

The dragon's wide-eyed gaze switched to Dianna. The beast whimpered once before turning her back on Tar and lying down upon the ice. The dog continued to bark, but the dragon paid him no heed as she waved her tail through the air.

"Tar," Markus called, bounding toward the dog, "it's okay."

The mutt took one look at Markus, yelped and then knocked him to the ground before smothering him in wet, sloppy kisses.

"Enough, boy," Markus chuckled, while grasping the back of Tar's neck and pulling him into a hug. "I'm happy to see you, too."

"Hold your weapons!" Dianna ordered authoritatively.

Markus looked up to see Ryne and his traveling party advancing upon them with spears at the ready.

He struggled to his feet while keeping hold of the rope around Tar's neck. "Ryne!" he shouted, waving his hands. "It's okay, she won't hurt you."

Ryne stopped in his tracks, his mouth hung open. "Markus?"

"Aye," Markus laughed, as he pulled on Tar's rope and approached them.

"What are you doing here?" asked Ryne, his voice laced with disbelief. He waved a trembling hand toward Lydra. "With a dragon?"

Markus bent down and scratched Tar behind the ears before breaking into a wide grin. "It's a long story."

Ryne looked at him with an expectant glare. "I'm listening."

EVERYONE GATHERED AROUND the hearth inside Dianna's hut, with the exception of Des, who stayed outside to play with the dragon. Every so often, the sound of Lydra grunting or blowing curtains of ice caused Ryne and his party to twitch and throw wary glances toward the door.

Markus had to admit that the dragon still unnerved him. After all, only yesterday she had tried to turn him into a block of ice. He filled Ryne in on all the details of his journey, including the real reason why the Ice People were protected from the witch.

"How did you come to believe that the ice repels the witch's magic?" Markus asked.

Ryne shook his head while frowning into his cup of tea. "I don't know. It's what we've always believed."

The others in his party nodded their agreement.

"Well, now we know it was the stones," Markus said. He nodded toward Dianna, who was sitting beside him. "My sister says there are two more, and we need to find them if we are to defeat Madhea and the Sea Witch."

Ryne stretched his long legs beside the hearth. "We will inquire about the stones on our journey." His pointed gaze shifted to Markus. "In the meantime, my people have been left with only three stones since you and Ven have the others. I wonder if three will be enough to shield an entire kingdom from the witch's eye."

"I have wondered that, too," replied Markus, raking his fingers through his hair. His eyes moved to Alec, sitting on the other side of Dianna, and he hoped his brother would be accepting of his plan. "I will return my stone to your father."

Alec's mouth fell open. "You are going back to the Ice People?"

"Aye, brother," he nodded. "You must come with me."

Since learning of the stone's role in shielding the Ice People from the witch, Markus had known that he had to take the stone back. Besides, as his fingers wound around the lock of hair in his pocket, he realized he couldn't be gone from Ura long. He already missed her sweet smile.

Alec's shoulders fell as he shook his head. "I am stronger brother, but not fully recovered. I wish to go to the sea where the air is warm. Zier has offered to take me this summer."

Markus clenched the warm mug in his other hand as his focus centered on Alec. "Then we must part, brother?" he asked in a trembling voice. He had not planned for this, certain that Alec would accompany him.

"I'm sorry, Markus." Alec waved a hand at Ryne. "Can't one of your men take the stone back?"

Ryne opened his mouth to speak, but Markus interjected, "I wish to do it myself."

Alec's jaw dropped and there was no mistaking the hurt in his eyes. "Why?"

Markus bit on his lip as he struggled for the right words. Heat flamed his face when he saw that all eyes were upon him.

"Is there a girl?" asked Alec as one corner of his mouth hitched up in an impish grin.

Markus's gaze shot to Ryne, who, thankfully, was looking at him with mirth in his eyes.

"Aye, brother," Markus murmured. "There is a girl."

To his amazement, Alec broke into laughter, soon echoed by the others.

Dianna nudged Markus and flashed a teasing smile. "I'm just thankful it isn't me anymore."

With that, the chuckles in the room intensified. Markus couldn't help but join in the merriment, even if the jest was at his expense. He'd suffered many hardships these past months and it felt good to laugh again.

Their laughter quickly died as an eerie sound came from outside. The rolling rumble shook not only the walls, but rocked Markus to the core. A few others shared nervous glances. Ven and Ryne leapt to their feet while glaring at the door.

Dianna waved a dismissive flick of the wrist. "It's only Lydra," she said with casual indifference. "She is laughing, too."

Ryne slowly sat back down, but Ven remained standing, his back ramrod straight, hands fisted at his sides.

"Sister, what will happen when the villagers learn of your pet?" Alec asked Dianna.

She shook her head. "I don't know. I can't very well send her back to Madhea, to be imprisoned in the ice and only released to destroy villages."

"You must take her far away from the witch's eye," Markus suggested.

Dianna tilted her head as her brow marred into a deep frown. "But you told me her mists have been destroyed."

"That doesn't mean she cannot build more," Ryne interjected.

"Des cannot ride astride her." There was a note of desperation in Dianna's voice. "He will freeze."

Alec leaned over and patted his sister on the knee. "I will take Des with me."

Dianna's eyes widened and her voice became more shrill. "That will not be until the summer. I cannot leave him here until then. What if Madhea sends her demon pixies?"

Ryne stood and stretched his arms. "They may travel with us. We are heading to Aloa-Shay now."

Dianna frowned. "Aloa-Shay?"

"A village where the river meets the sea," he replied, placing his mug in a nearby basin. "It means Haunted Waters."

"Haunted Waters?" Dianna gasped. "I cannot allow my brother to go through such perils."

"I have been there," said Ryne, "and the village is peaceful."

Alec clasped Dianna's hands within his own while looking intently into her eyes. "You are my sister, which makes Des my brother as well. I will protect him at all costs. You have my word." He squeezed her hands before releasing them.

Dianna's shoulders slumped and she heaved a sigh. "Thank you." Then her glassy eyes swept the room. "So where do I take the dragon?"

"There is a trade route from Aloa-Shay to The Shifting Sands," Ryne said as he sat back down beside the hearth. "It is beyond the reach of Madhea and her sister." He raised a finger and pointed toward the small window. "Fly east from here, over the mountains and beyond the sea, and you will reach it."

Dianna tilted her head. "The Shifting Sands?" Her voice was laced with doubt.

Ryne shrugged. "It is a vast land, from what I hear, with many clans who live in caverns beneath the ground. They trade spices with Aloa-Shay." He leaned nearer to Dianna, his eyes narrowed. "I have also heard that a great dragon lives among their people."

Dianna jerked back. "A dragon?"

Ryne nodded. "He is a deity of sorts. I think they should be more willing to welcome another dragon." After Dianna nodded her agreement, Ryne turned to Markus. "You must give the Eryll clan some news about Bane."

"Bane?" Markus straightened his shoulders. "Have you seen him?"

"No, we found only his cloak." Ryne's mouth was set in a grim line as his eyes darkened. "It was caked in blood. Snowbear tracks were nearby."

A deep gloom settled in Markus's heart. Though Bane was cruel and a coward, it was not long ago that his own character had been similarly flawed. "I know Bane deserved to be punished, but I feel sorry for his family."

Ryne sighed as he leaned back in his seat. "As do I."

Markus glanced at Ven. His face remained impassive with the exception of a single tear that slipped over the rim of his eye.

"When will we all see each other again?" asked Markus, looking around the room.

"In a year's time," Ryne replied. "We should meet between here and Aloa-Shay, at the edge of Werewood Forest, far away from Madhea's eye. I need time to find somewhere safe for my people. Our glacier will not hold forever."

"Aye," Markus added, "and when it melts none of our villages will be safe."

"Sister," Alec said to Dianna, "mayhap you could find a haven for us in the Shifting Sands."

"I will look," she said, before slowly rising to her feet.

The others rose as well.

"Until next spring then," Ryne said to the group. "We must be on our way. How soon can you be ready, Alec?"

"I will pack my things," Alec replied, before turning somber eyes on Markus. "I fear that even if we try to hide, we must eventually face down this witch. If Dianna is destined to take her place, she will need our help."

"Aye, she will," Markus added.

The others voiced their agreement.

MARKUS WATCHED HIS sister fly away on her dragon with a heavy heart, not just because he worried for his sister, but because he'd have much to explain to the Ice People after Dianna had convinced him to give her the stone. Though he was loath to part with the Ice People's treasure, he realized she needed it more than they did, especially since the stone had told her she'd need to find them all if she was to defeat Madhea.

Once again, Alec and Markus stood face to face, exchanging emotional goodbyes. Ryne's party was waiting for Alec at the clearing.

"It is not fair that we have just been reunited only to part again," Alec spoke through a shaky voice. Reaching out, he clasped Markus on the shoulder and his lips curled up in a subtle smile. "But I am proud of the man you have become."

"Your support was what helped me through my trials. You are the reason I am alive today. Thank you for your faith in me." Markus's voice cracked with emotion before he hung his head. "Even when I was a monster."

Alec cupped Markus's cheek while shaking his head. "You were never a monster to me, brother."

Markus embraced his brother, as a few tears of both sorrow and joy slipped down his face. Aye, he would miss Alec, but at least their parting was on his terms, and he would make sure he saw him again next spring.

"I will miss you," Markus said, pulling away to look into his brother's eyes once more. How much different their last parting had been, with Alec's face disfigured by cuts and bruises.

"And I you," Alec replied, squeezing Markus's shoulders before dropping his hands to his sides. "Stay safe."

Markus shrugged Zier's shield off his back and handed it to his brother. "Will you give this to Zier when he travels to Aloa-Shay?"

"Aye." Alec hoisted the shield into his arms and slung it across his back. "This might prove useful on our journey."

Markus smiled as he watched his brother handle the heavy weight with ease. He hoped Alec would grow much stronger on his journey to the sea.

After they had parted and walked a while, Markus spared one last glance at his brother, who had reached the other side of the clearing. He was not surprised to see Alec stare back at him before he disappeared into the forest.

Markus felt inside his pocket for Odu's letter. As he did so, his hand came to rest on Ura's lock of hair. He would deliver the letter to Dafuar and then visit his favorite hunting glen.

The tulips would be blooming this time of year. Markus's heart warmed as he envisioned Ura's smile when he handed her a bouquet of spring flowers.

THE END

# Spirit of the Sea Witch

*Spirit of the Sea Witch*, *Keepers of the Stones, Book Two* is available now!

\*\*A scorned woman's revenge burns hotter than a pyre. The vengeance of a goddess is more destructive than a thousand fires.\*\*

Desperate to escape the wrath of the vengeful sky goddess, Madhea, a group of brave young explorers flees to the sea in search of safe haven for their people while the apprentice witch, Dianna, steals away Madhea's dragon to the Shifting Sands. Though they are an ocean apart, the future of humanity lies in their entwined fates. Before they can defeat Madhea, they must stop the vindictive sea goddess, Eris, from destroying the world.

Dear readers,

I hope you loved Markus's story as much as I enjoyed writing it. And now I ask that you do me a HUGE favor. Please go to where you purchased this book and leave a review. If you enjoyed Markus's story, please tell your friends, too. I also love hearing from my readers @ tara@tarawest.com.

# The Beginning of Time

Edited by M. Edward McNally.

In the beginning there was chaos, with no division between the land, sea, and sky. Only the Elements reigned: air, soil, fire, and water, colliding in discord, making Tehra a volatile, miserable planet. The Elements were unhappy with the constant state of unrest and change on Tehra. Since none of them could exist together in harmony, they knew they needed something stronger and more powerful to rule over them and bring peace to the planet.

The Elements called upon the vast magic of the universe and created the Tryads, immortal keepers of the Elements. Their names were Madhea, keeper of sky and spirit; Kyan, keeper of land and breath; and Eris, keeper of water and life. But the Elements made one fatal mistake. They used magic, and only magic, to create the sisters. The Tryads were not of the Elements, and so they had little regard for the safekeeping of the planet, save for one of the sisters, Kyan, who loved her land and the people who inhabited it.

The Elements had believed the Tryads would rule Tehra peacefully, keeping the distinction between air, land, and water, and ending all chaos. The Elements, being simple in nature, had not planned for avarice and greed.

Eris, keeper of the fin folk, was unhappy with her station below the surface of Tehra. She did not enjoy living among sea creatures and being tethered to an unsightly fish tail. She felt slighted by her air-breathing sisters who lived above her.

Madhea bemoaned spending her days among the sky creatures, peering down at life below. Her land sister lived with beings called humans who had built a shrine in her honor. But the bird folk gave Madhea no such special treatment. Thus, she wished for nothing else than to shed her wings and take her sister's place as ruler of the human world.

Kyan, keeper of the land, felt no such resentment toward her sisters. She had fallen in love with Orhan, a handsome mortal. Together, they had conceived six daughters, each one the exact likeness of her mother and bearing magical powers. Kyan knew of her sisters' envy, but did not fear them because, along with her daughters, she was more powerful than Madhea and Eris combined.

If Kyan had one weakness, it was her love for Orhan. Though he had wealth, power, and love, he was still unhappy with his lot in life. He desired sons. Kyan, as a daughter of Elemental magic, could only conceive a likeness of herself. In order to give him sons, she would have to use a different magic, a dark magic — one that came not from land, sky, or water, but from the darkest recesses of the soul.

Kyan loved her husband and could not deny him his ardent wish, so she birthed him twin boys, Dafuar and Odu. But something changed within Kyan after she'd called upon the dark magic. Her soul had been compromised and her powers weakened. Her daughters' magic had been tainted as well.

Madhea was the first to seize upon her sister's weakness, flying fast from the heavens and striking Kyan and her daughters with great thunderbolts, sending their souls into the great abyss and reducing their human forms to mere stones. Heartbroken and distraught, Orhan fled with his young sons to the shelter of the Shifting Sands.

When Eris learned of Madhea's treachery, she rose up from the waters, demanding her fair share of the land. Madhea refused, and thus began a war between the two sisters. Madhea pelted the waters with thunderbolts and hurled great gusts of wind. Eris retaliated with monstrous waves that eroded the soil and swept away entire villages.

All the while, the Elements mourned the loss of Kyan and the ongoing destruction of their planet. The world had become chaos once more — something that the Elements had sought to prevent by creating the Tryads. Now they had to act before Tehra was lost forever.

As each sister was consumed in destroying the other, the Elements manipulated wind and water and pollinated their wombs. Eris and Madhea each bore six daughters, the Elementals, who grew into adulthood before the first full moon. And though the Elementals had inherited their mothers' magical powers, they were children of the Elements as well, and owed their loyalty to them, and thus to restoring peace and tranquility.

The Elementals forced their mothers to sign a truce. Eris was made keeper of the sea, as well as all of the islands and shorelines. Madhea would rule the sky and the mountains. The land in between was given to Dafuar and Odu. But though Kyan's sons were immortal like their mother, the dark magic used to conceive them had robbed them of their inherent magical powers. They feared they would not make good keepers.

The Elements presented Dafuar and Odu with seven sacred stones; each stone had once been the body of their mother and sisters, and they possessed great power. Through these stones, Dafuar and Odu could rule as keepers of the Elements. But soon it became evident that the sons had inherited their human father's weaknesses, for though they lived forever as immortals, they aged as men. Their bodies became more weathered and decrepit with each passing year, and their memories began to fade.

The Elements, fearing Eris and Madhea would find a way to seize the stones from Dafuar and Odu, stole the stones, hiding them in the darkest recesses of Tehra. The Elements then divided the remaining land between Madhea and Eris.

Dafuar and Odu left their homes and wandered the land for ages, searching for something they'd lost, not remembering it was the stones they sought. They lived a cursed life, wise but unwise; immortal, but old and frail.

Although Madhea and Eris were tethered by the Elementals, their powers grew. Displeased with the shrines built to her by the mortals, Madhea built one to herself; a giant palace of ice, rising up from the ground and reaching as far as the heavens. Eris built a palace out of fire, which rose up from the ocean; a towering cylinder, shrouded by plumes of smoke and guarded by molten lava.

The two sisters had become so transfixed in building their shrines and strengthening their magic, that they had forsaken their duties as keepers of The Elements, paying little heed when ice storms and cyclones ravaged the land and people. The Elementals, likewise, had no time to manage sky, land, and water, as they were most often preoccupied with their mothers.

Slowly, once again, Tehra began to crumble. The ice melted, the wind howled, and the land shook. The Tryads and the Elementals had failed to protect the Elements from chaos. Now, the people's only hope of saving their planet lay in hiding, within the powers of the sacred stones.

# The Shifting Sands

Edited by M. Edward McNally.

SINDRI SHIELDED HER eyes as the heavy beating of Tan'yi'na's wings doused her with a thick plume of sand. She had been dreading this meeting with her mother's dragon, but as Kyan's eldest daughter, it was her duty to try to soothe the great beast. She knew the dragon would not be happy to learn of the birth of her brothers.

Though Tan'yi'na rarely left Kyan's side, Sindri's mother had sent her dragon on a fool's errand, just long enough to distract him while she conceived and birthed her sons. It had taken only a fortnight for Kyan's dark magic to work. And now, Sindri feared for the safety of her family. The use of dark magic never came without price.

The dragon landed with a thud, nearly throwing Sindri off balance as the ground shook beneath them. He pulled back his heavy golden wings, shaking them once as a bird would ruffle its feathers, spraying Sindri with even more sand.

Sindri coughed on the residue which had coated her mouth and nostrils. She blinked several times while wiping the dust from her eyes.

*I must speak with my goddess.* The dragon's command boomed inside her skull.

She looked up at Tan'yi'na, whose large golden eyes were bearing down on her while his fanged jowls turned in a harsh scowl.

Her heart hammered against her chest. She had never known the dragon to be angry. What would he do if he learned the truth? "M-mother is sleeping," she stammered.

*Are the rumors true, Sindri?* The dragon's voice was laced with accusation. "Did Kyan bear sons?"

She nodded slowly before answering. "Yes."

So Tan'yi'na already knew. At once, she suspected her mother's pixies. The wretched little vermin were known more for their desire to cause strife than for their loyalty.

Something akin to loathing danced in the dragon's gaze. *There is a darkness cloaking you, Sindri. Tell me now, did your mother use black magic to conceive her sons?*

She had not the courage to answer as she turned her gaze toward the soft mist of dust that swirled around her toes.

*Why did you not stop her?!*

She turned to Tan'yi'na with pleading eyes. "I tried, but Father wanted so badly to have sons."

The dragon answered with a solemn shake of the head. *She has compromised her magic, and her daughters' magic as well. Kyan's sisters will take advantage of your weakness.*

Her mouth fell open. She had not thought of her aunts. But why would Madhea and Eris wish to harm their own sister? Sindri would certainly never inflict sorrow on any of her sisters. But something in the dragon's woeful gaze made her heart sink like a stone.

"What do we do?" she pleaded.

Tan'yi'na heaved a sigh before turning his gaze to the heavens. *There is nothing we can do. The Elements trusted you with the safekeeping of their planet. I doubt even they can save you now.*

IMAYA PUSHED AN ERRANT strand of golden hair behind her ear as she slowly turned the salamin roasting over the fire. She then slathered more palma jelly across its scales, a ritual she had performed since her mother had died eight years ago while birthing Imaya's brother, Renì. Her family ate salamin and palma almost every day except on the days when Father was too drunk to go fishing. Then, Imaya would be forced to dredge up riverweed for the family meal. When she was able to sneak a few extra coins from Father, she would buy spices from the trading boats. The spices made everything taste better, even riverweed. But the family coffers were empty again, because father had been too drunk to haul in his fair share of fish. There would be no new spices for a while.

She scowled down at her father, who had passed out on a small cot beside the fire. Though he had his own bedchamber in the large hut he had built for their family, he had not slept in his bed since the night Mother had died. Actually, he had refused to do much of anything since Mother's death, leaving Imaya and Renì to fend for themselves.

At only seven-and-ten summers, Imaya had a heavy burden to bear, trying to keep her father sober and out of fights, and protecting her brother from the bullying taunts of other children. Most girls Imaya's age had begun their own families, but Imaya had no time for courtship when she had so many other responsibilities. Besides, the young men in the village had made it clear they did not wish to form an alliance with Imaya's family. Though Imaya had heard the rumors many times before, just the thought of it made her heart break anew. They feared Imaya would birth them sons like her brother.

Though others called Renì clumsy and dumb, to Imaya, her brother was a blessing. He could sense things that other people could not. Renì could predict a storm days before even the slightest wisps of clouds dotted the sky. Renì also knew the best time to harvest fish and the best places to find them. It was as if Renì had a connection with the Elements. Imaya knew her brother was a special boy, and she resented any villager who thought otherwise.

Imaya jumped as the door was thrown open and Renì burst inside. She could feel energy radiating off her brother, like the frenzied wind from a summer storm, as he spun a circle around her skirts.

"Come see! Come see!" he looked up at her with his one good eye.

She looked down at her brother and smiled. Though he looked much like her, with golden skin and hair and large amber eyes, the entire left side of his body appeared to be wilted, like a flower petal that had been plucked and one half left out in the sun. His left arm was practically useless, while his eye on that side remained permanently shut. His leg was good for balancing, but not much else, as he was forced to drag it behind him whenever he walked. But despite his deformities, Imaya thought her brother was beautiful, for he filled her heart with joy whenever they were together.

She pulled the salamin off the flame while wiping her hands on her smock. "What is it, Renì?"

He jumped up and down on his leg while waving his arm wildly. "Fishies, fishies, on shore everywhere!"

Then he dragged himself over to his father's cot and rattled it with his knee. When their father didn't' respond, Renì bent over and screamed loudly in his ear. "Da, come look!"

Imaya laughed into her palm as her father snorted loudly and then rolled off the cot in a tangle of furs and limbs. He sat up and peered over the cot with a dull look in his eyes. His matted greying hair was sticking up in all directions. He groaned while rubbing his head as his gaze shot to Imaya, who offered him no sympathy. A grown man should not have spent the day wasting away when there was work to be done.

Father smoothed a hand across his weathered and dirt-smudged face as he looked up at Renì. "What is it, Son?"

"Water gone!" Renì shouted with a wild excitement in his eyes. "Fishies flopping." Then Renì began jerking about while puckering his lips as if he were a fish out of water.

The hairs on the nape of Imaya's neck stood on end as her limbs iced over with fear. "What happened to the water?" she breathed the question to her father.

"I don't know." Father shook his head. "But I'm bringing my net."

THE FURTHER THEY WALKED across the barren shoreline, the louder Imaya's heart pounded out a drumbeat in her ears. All around them was chaos. Fishermen greedily scooped flailing fish into their nets while children chased each other down the sandy slope. It was as if a crack at the bottom of the ocean had drained all of the water. Plant life and coral were exposed to the elements, baking in the summer heat. Imaya shook her head as she observed how the other villagers seemed unconcerned that their water had vanished. But where had the water gone? Were these stranded fish truly a gift from the Elements, or a portent of darker things to come?

"What has happened?" Father asked Sol, another fisherman, who lived by the ocean's edge with his wife and four healthy sons.

Sol was one of the few fishermen in the village who actually talked to Father, but his words were usually laced with insults. He was larger than father by nearly a head and wider, too, so father usually took Sol's barbs with a grin, not wanting to lose his teeth in a brawl with the beefy fisherman.

"I don't know." Sol shrugged while hauling his net of fish up the bank over one broad shoulder. "One moment the water was here, and the next moment, it was gone."

Imaya swallowed while latching onto her father's arm. "This is not natural."

"What are you waiting for, Tunnuk?" Sol said to her father as he laughed heartily. "Fill your net before they are all taken."

Renì drug himself up beside Father and tugged on his other arm. "Danger, Da, danger!" Renì nudged his limp hand toward the empty shoreline.

"Father," Imaya spoke with a trembling voice. "Renì, is right. Since when has the Sea Goddess given us such a bounty? Never does she reward us without price."

The people of Imaya's village worshipped the benevolent Land Goddess, Kyan, but her sister, Eris the Sea Goddess, was known for her vengeful and jealous nature. Imaya would not put it past the witch to try to cause harm to Kyan's followers.

"Danger, Da! Big water!" Renì let go of his father and jutted his finger toward the horizon.

"Listen to Renì, Father," Imaya implored. "He is never wrong about such things."

Father looked at Renì for a long moment before his shoulders slumped and he nodded his agreement. Then he turned toward the other villagers and shouted. "We must get to higher ground! Hurry!"

Sol strode back down the incline with an empty net slung over his shoulder. "What are you babbling about?" he chuckled.

"There is danger coming." Father raised a shaky finger toward the horizon. "My son can sense these things."

A broad grin split Sol's sun-kissed face before he swept an arm toward the flailing fish. "There is enough fish here to feed my family for an entire season, and you think I'm going to listen to a drunk fool and his freak son?" He laughed out loud and nearby fishermen joined in his merriment before returning to their frenzied harvest.

The lines around Father's eyes tightened as his skin took on the hue of sunbaked coral. He clenched his fists by his sides before jutting a foot forward.

"Father, no!" Imaya reached out and clenched her father's arm. "He's not worth it." She motioned toward the barren landscape before them. Any moment, and she knew Renì's prediction would come to pass. "We don't have time!"

Father stepped back before picking up Renì and hoisting him on his shoulders. Imaya turned and followed her father before casting one more wary glance at the villagers, knowing they would all perish for their foolish greed.

"Where are you going?" Sol called at their backs.

Father turned and spoke with a heaviness in his somber voice that Imaya felt in her own heart. "To higher ground. I suggest you do the same."

Sol and the other villagers answered with more laughter.

THE WALL OF WATER BORE down on the village swiftly. Imaya tried to shield her ears from the terrified screams of the villagers below, but it was no use. The memory of her town's destruction would be eternally etched in her mind.

"Hurry, Daughter!" her father called down to her as he continued ascending the treacherous terrain with Renì's small arms wrapped around his shoulders.

Imaya slipped on loose rock and cried out as she nearly lost her footing. It was then she chanced a look down at the devastation below. The monster tide toppled huts and boats and everything in its wake. Water swirled beneath them, continuing to rise at an alarming rate. She feared that the steep slope they were climbing would not be high enough.

When she neared the top of the cliff, her father held a hand down to her and hauled her up. She fell against his chest and sobbed, unable to look again at the devastation below. The villagers' screams had been silenced, but the violent sound of water battering the landscape continued to fill her heart with sorrow and dread.

"Imaya crying," Renì sniffled from behind their father.

When her father pulled her back and looked into her eyes, Imaya saw strength reflected in the amber depths that she had not seen before. "No time for tears, Daughter," he said as he wiped the moisture from her cheek with the pad of his thumb. "We must keep moving before the water rises."

Father pointed to the crest that loomed above them. Kyan's magnificent temple was perched on the highest point overlooking their small fishing village of Aya-Shay, a village that was no more. The temple priests had named the village several centuries ago. Aya-Shay: Blessing by the Sea. The irony made Imaya want to weep anew.

She trudged up the incline toward the temple, wincing as the rocks and dry grass chafed her bare feet. She silently sent a prayer to Kyan that the goddess would keep them safe. If she and her family had a chance of surviving this cataclysm, it was within the sacred walls of Kyan's temple.

AS THE WATER HAD SWARMED the temple steps, they had climbed to the top of Kyan's temple, hoping that their goddess would protect them, but the water had continued to rise. Imaya and her brother now sat huddled together, wet and frightened, while the sea raged around them. Father paced the top of the temple, scanning the horizon for any sign of hope. Imaya feared she did not know how long the temple would hold before they would be completely submerged. And then what? There was nowhere else higher for them to run. She and her family were trapped, and they were rapidly running out of time.

Dusk had fallen, shrouding the watery landscape in an eerie blanket of crimson and gold. Soon it would be nightfall. Imaya feared she and her family would die a dark and lonely death, sucked into the bleak abyss, like pawns in Eris's fit of vengeance. She knew such devastation had to be the work of the bitch goddess.

But why, she wondered, had Kyan not risen up against her sister? Why had Kyan not offered aid to her people?

"Do you see that?" her father said in a harsh whisper as he pointed to an object floating toward them.

She squinted against the setting sun. "What is it?"

Father shielded his eyes. "It looks like a boat." Then he turned to his children. "Stay here with your brother. I will try to swim to it."

Fear welled up in her throat as she cried out. "Father, no! You will drown."

The tide was too fast. She had already seen roofs of huts and toppled masts of fishing boats float rapidly past them. Father would be swept away in the current as well.

Father laid one calloused hand on Imaya's shoulder. "The water is rising, Daughter. It is our only hope." The look of desperation in his narrowed gaze was replaced by something more.

Again, she read strength in her father's eyes, and for a fleeting moment, she actually believed that her drunk and useless father might save them.

And then in a flash he was over the side of the temple, splashing against the current as he swam toward the drifting mass in the sea.

She cried out and clutched her brother tightly.

Renì looked up at her and cupped her cheek with one small hand. "Father, live. Wind save Father."

Imaya watched in amazement as the mass floated right toward their father, pushed across the oncoming current as if it were being propelled by magic. As the object neared, she realized it indeed was a small fishing vessel that could hold maybe ten passengers. Father seized a rope hanging from the side of the boat and pulled himself inside.

Then, as the boat was propelled dangerously close to the side of the temple, he tossed the rope to Imaya. "Grab it!" he called out. "Hurry!"

She quickly grabbed the rope and pulled the boat toward the side of the temple, the strong current fighting against her efforts and threatening to snap the rope in two. The water had risen much higher now, nearly submerging the entire temple beneath its tide.

"Come to me, Renì." Father held out a hand.

Her brother climbed inside with surprisingly quick movements.

Then Father held out his hand to Imaya. "Now you."

She swallowed a knot of panic as she looked into her father's somber eyes. For so long she had never been able to depend on him, and now she was trusting him with her life. Who was this man before her and could she continue to have faith in him?

The water had risen higher, lapping at her feet now. Imaya knew it was only a matter of time before her foundation crumbled and she was left with no choice but to climb in the boat. She sent prayers to both Kyan and the Elements before she placed her hand inside her father's and let him pull her aboard.

In the next instant, their boat was rapidly pulled into the vast current. She held her brother close, burying her face in his hair while praying even more fervently that the Elements would somehow guide them to safety.

"DAUGHTER, WAKE UP."

Imaya woke from a fitful slumber and peered up into her father's surprisingly stoic eyes. Odd how she could not recall a day when she had seen such clarity in his gaze.

Her own eyes swept the horizon. She was surprised to see the waters were calm and smooth, almost like the surface of her mother's coral-handled looking glass.

Renì was already sitting up, his little back propped against the side of the boat while he sucked the juices from a palma fruit.

Her mouth fell open. "Palmas?" she asked her father.

Father flashed a lopsided grin before nodding toward a pile of fruit at the bow of the boat. "I found a palma pod floating in the water."

For the first time in what felt like ages, Imaya smiled at her father. She launched herself into her father's arms and planted a kiss on his weathered face before kneeling beside Renì. When he offered her a fruit, she bit into the succulent, sweet flesh before lifting it toward the Elements.

"Oh, Heavenly Elements," she called toward the clear summer sky, "thank you for this blessing."

But when Imaya turned her smiling eyes toward her father, her heart sank at the fear reflected in the drawn lines of his mouth.

"Keep praying, Daughter," he said as he nodded toward the placid waters. "We are not out of danger yet."

That was when she realized they were in even greater peril than before. There was a saying among the fishermen of her village: *Only fools set sail in tranquil waters.*

Eris's giant man-eating carnivus plants that rose up from the bottom of the sea had eaten many a wayward fishing vessel that had strayed from the trading route.

The calmer the water, the more likely the plants were to strike, which was why some seamen would rather risk facing the wrath of Eris's storms than be caught up in a nest of carnivus plants. Few had ever faced a carnivus and lived to tell.

Imaya sent another prayer up to the heavens. That was when she noticed the small sail that propelled them forward. Painted on its canvas was a giant, inky black eye.

"I do not recognize this boat," she said to her father. "Where do you think it came from?"

"Eris's fleet." Father's tone was grim.

Imaya's limbs went cold at the mention of The Sea Goddess's name.

*This vessel belongs to the goddess! What will she do to us if she discovers we've taken it?*

"W-what?" she stammered.

"Look there, her symbol." Father pointed to the sail. "Her dragon's eye."

"Naamaku," she barely breathed the words. Eris's sea dragon, even more menacing and powerful than the carnivus plants. Then a thought struck her.

Was this boat a gift from the Elements, or a trap set by Eris? "What if Eris sent this boat and we are riding to our doom?" she asked her father.

But Father did not answer. She gaped at him as all of the color drained from his sun-kissed face. His body appeared to be set in stone, as his gaze was transfixed on something in the water.

Imaya slowly rose on wobbly legs and stood beside her father. She stifled a scream at the sight before her. Their boat was surrounded by dozens of gaping maws, some twice the size of their vessel. They floated in the water, not aimlessly but with purpose, as long, serpent like tongues protruded from between their razor-sharp teeth and whipped wildly through the air.

Shards of splintered wood were stuck to their scissor-like teeth, remnants of their prior destruction.

"Oh, dear Goddess!" Imaya cried, as her legs nearly gave way beneath her.

"Look there." Father pointed to the bow of the boat.

She was stunned to see the massive heads of the plants bobble away from the boat's path, as if they were parting to let the vessel pass.

"Why aren't the plants attacking?" she asked her father in a hoarse whisper.

Father shook his head, never tearing his wary gaze from the water. "Perhaps there are enchantments on this boat?"

"Dragon eye!" Renì shouted as he pointed to the painted sail.

She hissed at her brother to be quiet, but despite his outburst, the carnivus plants still kept their distance. And then the realization struck her. The dragon's eye! Did the plants believe this boat to be the dragon? That would explain why they were afraid to attack. She noted how the wooden planks of the boat were painted a bright green, just like the scales of the fabled dragon. This boat was no enchantment. This boat was an illusion.

So many times, Imaya thought, she and her family had narrowly escaped death. But how? Were they truly blessed by the Elements? And would they always be so fortunate?

AFTER SEVERAL DAYS at sea, Imaya and her family landed at a strange port. Or rather, what was left of the port, for it seemed Eris's monster tide had wreaked destruction on this village, too.

Sunbaked and tired, Imaya barely dragged herself from the boat as she reveled in the feel of the wet sand between her toes. After Father hoisted Renì on his shoulders, they walked through the devastated village. Her heart sank at the realization that her family would not find food or shelter when so many others were without as well.

Although most of the village had been leveled, she was surprised to see people along the shore, sifting through the wreckage and mourning the loss of their town. She had never seen a place so wondrous. Behind the narrow beach was a vast cliff that seemed to stretch to the heavens. Had the villagers been able to climb the cliff before the monster tide had reached them? If so, how did they know Eris would send the wave?

The people here were darker than Imaya's family, with skin the color of mahogany and black hair piled in rows atop their heads. The men wore long, loose robes and the women wore similar garments along with crowns of fine fabric that cascaded down their backs.

A few stopped to stare at Imaya and her family, but most were too preoccupied with recovering their lost possessions. Then she noticed a long caravan of people marching through the wreckage. Massive, four-legged furry creatures with awkward humps on their backs, laden with many goods, trailed behind the caravan.

The tall, broad-shouldered stranger leading the caravan caught Imaya's eye. Though he had the physique of a grown man, he had a youthful gleam in his eyes. A small child sat atop his shoulders. She had to look twice at the child, for though the left side of her dark face was smooth, her right side was wilted.

Her father hailed the stranger, who broke from the group and walked over to them. Though his gaze was focused on her father, Imaya blushed when he stole a glimpse in her direction. She had to steady her trembling limbs as he neared them. His dark face was smooth and his lips full. Though he wore a long robe like the others in his village, his sleeves had fallen back to expose well- toned arms. When he slanted a smile in Imaya's direction, she realized he was beyond beautiful. Her blush deepened as she looked down at her torn and stained dress. What must he think of her?

"Where have you come from?" the young man asked her father while the girl perched on his shoulders bounced her dangling leg. Though he spoke with a thick accent, she easily understood him. He sounded much like the traders from the Shifting Sands.

"Aya-Shay," Father answered. "Our village was destroyed by a great wave."

"Then you are very lucky to be alive. I am sorry we cannot offer you more of a welcome. The same has happened to our port." He swept his hand toward the trail of people and animals behind him. "Our caravan travels now to the Shifting Sands."

"The Shifting Sands?" Father turned to her. "Imaya, we have traveled across the sea!"

"Imaya." The young man spoke her name in a throaty whisper, as if he savored the taste of it. "I am Ammon." He pointed to himself and then nodded to the child on his shoulders. "This is my sister, Nala."

"My father, Tunnuk, and my brother, Renì." Imaya motioned toward her family as she felt her chest and face inflame with heat.

To Imaya's amazement, Renì began making hand gestures toward Nala. The girl answered him back with gestures of her own. It was as if they shared their own special language.

"Do you know the source of this tide?" Her father asked Ammon.

Ammon's dark eyes narrowed. "Madhea and Eris were at war."

"The Sky and Sea Goddesses were at war?" Father rasped. "But did not Kyan stop them?"

Ammon's face fell as he slowly shook his head. "Our benevolent goddess is dead."

"Dead!" Imaya's hand flew to her chest. "This cannot be!"

"It is true." Ammon's eyes softened as his mouth turned down. "Her great dragon, Tan'yi'na, has spoken to my people. She weakened her powers with dark magic and was destroyed by Madhea."

"Dark magic?" Father asked, his voice laced with incredulity. "Why would Kyan do such a thing?"

Ammon shrugged, and again he stole a fleeting glance at Imaya. "We were told love was to blame."

"Love?" Imaya shook her head, hardly believing what she was hearing. How could such a powerful goddess be destroyed by love?

Father turned toward Imaya and laid a gentle hand on her shoulder.

When she looked into her father's watery, woe-filled eyes, she had to swallow the rising tide of emotion that threatened to overwhelm her.

"Love has caused many of us to do foolish things." Father's voice cracked as he spoke. "I sacrificed eight years of my life, and of yours and Renì's lives, to mourn the loss of your mother. It took nearly losing you both for me to realize I had been behaving like a fool."

She could do nothing but gape at her father in awe. For so long she had wished for him to become the strong man she once loved. Could it be true? Had Father finally had a change of heart?

"Kyan's family was not so lucky," Ammon said with cutting finality. "Madhea has killed the daughters of Kyan as well. All that is left of them are seven stones."

"Oh, Heavenly Elements!" She gasped. "There are no benevolent goddesses left! All the world will perish."

Ammon heaved a sigh before turning his gaze to the heavens. "Let us hope the worst has passed for now."

"Until the goddesses decide to wage another battle," Father said.

"That is why we are fleeing to the home of the great golden dragon." Ammon waved toward the towering cliffs behind them. Then he fixed Father with a direct stare before flashing another smile toward Imaya. "You and your family are welcome to accompany us."

Renì and Nala both began to kick and squeal wildly.

Ammon chuckled while patting his sister's leg. She leaned over and whispered something in his ear.

Then Ammon turned toward Imaya, a knowing expression in his dark eyes. "Your brother speaks to the wind."

"Wind speaker?" she breathed. Imaya had once heard about the wind speakers from the village priests. They were magical folk who spoke to the Elements. That explained so much about her brother. Renì was more than just a special child. He was blessed by the Elements! "My brother warned us that the tide was coming but the other villagers refused to listen."

Ammon shook his head. "Then they were all fools. Our harbor may have been destroyed, but my sister saved every last villager before the tide struck. Nala is never wrong about such things. She speaks to all of the Elements." He tilted his head and kissed his sister on the cheek.

Imaya couldn't help but smile at the exchange between Ammon and Nala. "Your sister is very special," she said.

When Ammon turned to her and flashed a broad grin, Imaya thought her heart would burst with joy. "As is you brother," he answered.

At that moment, Imaya knew that she and her family had finally found a land where they belonged.

# Witch Flame

Edited by M. Edward McNally.

Special thanks to my glitterific critter partner, Shéa MacLeod for her support and feedback.

# Chapter One

The sun was fast setting and Feira was hungry and tired. She had been walking for days, following the rustling of leaves as the Elements led her further away from home. Kneeling on top of a patch of snake moss, she pulled a water bladder off her shoulder while breathing in the heady air. It was warmer near the shoreline and the air smelled more alive than the stagnant fog of the forest. Feira reveled in the feel of the sunshine on her face. Her home had been so dark compared to this place.

*Aloa-Shay,* the wind had whispered. *Village by the sea.*

Feira had not lived near a village since her family had fled to the forest when she was a small child. She only hoped the people here would be kind.

She almost gave into the temptation to lie down and bask in the soft glow of the setting sun, but Feira dared not close her eyes lest she conjure images of her mother's bloody and torn body.

If Feira hadn't wandered away to pick *cotulla* blossoms, if she had only stayed by her mother's side...then her mother would still be alive, and Feira would not have needed to flee the forest. But even Feira, with all of her powers, was not strong enough to take on an entire colony of giants.

Biting down on her knuckles, Feira stifled a sob. It would do no good to give in to tears now, not when she still needed to find a shelter for the night. When Feira pulled her hand away, flakes of charred flesh flitted down toward the moss. She pulled several strands from the ground and rubbed the cool plant between her fingers. Her hands barely pained her, but the regrowth of new skin was starting to itch.

The Elements grew impatient, tossing dust in her hair and whipping her skirt about her ankles. Feira reluctantly rose on shaky legs, though she did not know how much longer she could walk.

"Who are you?"

Feira spun around and sucked in a sharp breath as she looked up at the old woman who stood not a few paces in front of her.

*Wind speaker*, the breeze hissed in Feira's ear. Not as powerful as a witch, but more closely related to her kind than mere mortals. Odu had taught her that much, before he'd wandered away one bleak winter morn, never to be seen again.

Feira hesitantly stepped forward, eyeing the woman with trepidation. Her bronze, leathery skin was covered in so many lines and dark spots, she resembled an old, weathered map. Gnarled hands that looked more like claws, clutched the rounded top of a twisted and bent walking stick. She wore no covering to conceal her nearly bald head, which was dotted with only a few fine tufts of white hair. The rest of her was draped in a heavy brown robe. The only other adornment on the woman's body was a large silver ring with a bright ruby stone in its center. Despite the old woman's frightening appearance, Feira was compelled to trust her, for she sensed compassion and understanding deep within the woman's heart.

After all, the Elements had led Feira here for a reason. Though Feira was only a child, she'd been gifted with a wisdom beyond her nine winters. She knew this woman would help her.

"I am Feira," she said while straightening her shoulders and leveling the old woman with a direct stare. "Who are *you*?"

"I am Akahi." The old woman leaned further over her bent cane while squinting her eyes. "Feira is an odd name. Where did you come from?"

Feira nodded north, beyond the jungle and toward the direction of the cool winds. "The Werewood Forest."

The old woman gasped. "The dark forest? No, child, you did not come from there." She shook her head while clucking her tongue. "Where is your mother?"

Feira swallowed the rising knot of sorrow that welled up in her throat. She wiped her watery eyes with the backs of her hands. "She went to the Elements." Her voice sounded small, even to her own ears.

The deep lines embedded in the woman's twisted face seemed to soften. "What of your father?"

"He forgot about me." Feira's shoulders fell as she recalled the day Odu had walked out of their small hut without sparing either of them a second glance. Mother had crawled into her bed, crying beneath the furs for days. The time had come for the old man to continue his quest. What he was after, Feira did not know, and neither did Odu for that matter. But he said he'd know when he found it. Of one thing Feira was certain: she would never see the man she'd called her father again.

The woman edged closer to Feira. "What has happened to your hands?" She nodded toward Feira's blackened fingers.

Feira shrugged. "Flame came out of them."

The woman's mouth fell open, and for a long moment, she simply stared at Feira. "Flame? Do they pain you?"

"Only a little," she said as she stuffed her fingers into her pockets. Feira knew her hands looked hideous, and the weight of the woman's stare made them feel even more so.

"Can you do more than make flame come from your hands?" The woman asked, her voice laced with incredulity, and something more—fear.

Feira looked up at the woman and nodded, afraid now that if she said too much, she'd drive the woman away.

"Can you heal broken things?"

Feira nodded again as she thought of the barn that had caught fire after a winter storm. Her mother had sobbed for the loss of the structure, so Feira had toiled an entire fortnight, healing the wood board by board. If only she'd been strong enough to heal her mother, but she was in too many pieces. Feira had only enough time to kill the giant before more of the monsters descended.

The woman leaned even closer, so that Feira could smell the sweet and pungent scent of her breath. "Can you lift things without touching them?"

Feira answered by pulling one charred hand out of her pocket. She pointed at a small boulder and called upon the Elements. The boulder shook and trembled as the air around it grew thicker, lifting the object above the ground. Feira lowered her hand and settled the stone back in its resting place. She turned her gaze upon the woman, who was looking at her with dark, wide eyes.

"Come with me child." The woman latched one of her gnarled hands onto Feira's shoulder. "You are not safe out of doors." Then she turned her soulful gaze toward the sky. "Oh, Heavenly Elements protect us. If the Goddess finds this child, we are both dead."

# Chapter Two

Feira was just sixteen summers when a booming knock shook the door of her foster mother's small hut. She knew it wasn't her foster mother, as Akahi had left just moments ago to pick berries and would not be back until evening. Feira quickly dropped the wooden spoon into the cauldron of Akahi's special healing brew and rushed to the door.

What she saw before her nearly made her knees buckle—her beloved Tumi, draped over his brother's shoulder, with a cracked and bloodied skull.

Tumi's mother, Katriana stood beside her sons. She looked at Feira with keen eyes and a twisted scowl. "He calls your name, but says nothing else," she said in a voice that was surprisingly devoid of emotion.

"Bring him inside," Feira beckoned. "What has happened?"

"He was struck by a palma. Foolish boy," Katriana growled as she followed them inside. She looked around the modest room with derision in her cold eyes before plopping down on a nearby stool and helping herself to a cup of Akahi's wine. "I told him to be careful around those heavy fruits. Now who will take care of me if he is dead?"

Feira pulled back the furs of her own small cot. "Lie him down here," Fiera said to Tumi's brother, while trying her best to stifle her rage at Tumi's heartless mother.

Tumi's beefy brother, Nuk, who had been born a mute, answered with a grunt. He dropped Tumi onto the cot without care and stepped back, a vacant expression in his hooded gaze.

Feira often marveled at the differences between Tumi and his family. His mother and brother had rich, golden skin and flowing chestnut hair like many inhabitants of the nearby seaside village of Aloa-Shay. Tumi's skin was dark, and his hair an unruly mess of black straw that he had to weave in a tight braid, else it would spring wildly from his head.

Feira leaned over Tumi and brushed her hand across his brow. His eyelids fluttered open, but his pupils had receded somewhere in the back of his skull. Sticky blood clung to his matted hair and skin. One corner of his temple had been crushed. Feira shook her head as silent tears cascaded down her face. Most likely, he'd been trying to chop down a palma pod so that he could add more coin to his greedy mother's purse. The large palma pods that hung from tall trees could yield hundreds of small, sweet fruits. But the pods were heavy, and falling palmas had killed more than one hapless villager. Feira wondered how Tumi had managed to speak her name, or anything at all with such an injury.

She bit her bottom lip while stifling a sob. Tumi would die without her care, but if Feira healed him, she knew she would be marked as a witch. No mere doctoring could bring someone back from the brink of death.

Her gaze shot to Tumi's mother, who was looking at her expectantly with that serpent cold gleam in her eyes. More than once, Katriana had accused Feira of bewitching her son. Now the cold bitch would have proof that Feira was a witch, for Feira knew she could not take another breath if her true love was gone from this world.

Feira was only glad her foster mother wasn't here to see what she was about to do. Elements save she and her mother, once Katriana knew the full extent of Feira's powers.

# Chapter Three

Feira pushed aside a curtain of leaves as she stepped inside the abandoned temple that had once served as an altar to a fallen goddess. The massive stone pillars which supported the structure were now cracked and covered by an overgrowth of vines and moss. The dark sanctuary was lit only by narrow shafts of light that crept in from the holes in the walls and ceiling. The villagers of Aloa-Shay avoided the temple, fearing it was haunted, but Feira had never felt more at peace than when she was among the crumbling statues and decaying walls of her secret meeting place.

Feira's heart skipped a beat as she smiled down at her true love. Tumi was lying on a woven mat, his body propped up on one elbow. A threadbare tunic was pulled tight across his broad chest. His long, black braid, intricately woven with golden Fau feathers, hung over one shoulder. His dark eyes and complexion were such a stark contrast to Feira's pale skin and flame-colored hair, which was why she thought he complemented her, not just in spirit, but in body as well.

His full lips were pulled back in that same wolfish grin, the smile Feira had loved since they were children. Only in Tumi's eyes, Feira read his hunger, reminding her that they were children no more.

When she knelt on the mat, he pulled her against his chest while slanting his lips over hers.

"*Mi Oaña*," he murmured against her skin, as he traced a finger down her arm.

She sighed against his mouth before pulling back. If only it were true. If only she was his Oaña, his destiny. But Feira knew fate had other plans in store for them. Tumi's mother would never allow their union, and if they disobeyed her, Katriana had threatened to expose Feira as a witch. Feira might be able to battle the village priests, but she'd never win against the deity they served, the Sea Goddess, Eris.

Tumi's brow creased as he looked at her with a sullen expression. "Why do you pull away from me?"

Feira turned her gaze down, speaking softly as she twirled a frayed end of her skirt around her finger. "Your mother says I've bewitched you."

He wrapped his arms around her while feathering kisses across her temple. "She is right," he breathed into her ear. "You have bewitched me."

Feira knew she mustn't prolong her misery any longer. Though she loved Tumi, it was unfair to bind him to her when they could never complete their union. "No. We mustn't." Even as she pulled away, she regretted the loss of his touch.

"But I love you," Tumi said with a crack of despair in his voice. He cupped her chin with his calloused fingers, forcing her to meet his gaze. "And I know you love me."

One look into Tumi's molten eyes, and Feira knew she was lost. She couldn't help the emotions that overwhelmed her as she burst into tears. "Your mother will out me as a witch."

"Do not cry, Oaňa." Tumi wiped the tears off her cheeks with the pad of his thumb. "Even if we have to leave Aloa-Shay, we will be together."

"No." Feira shook her head. "I cannot leave Akahi."

Tumi heaved a sigh while smoothing his hand across his brow. "Can you not see that Akahi is ready to pass to the Elements? These herbs you feed her only prolong her life, but they do not make her well. Let her go, and run away with me."

Feira swatted him across the chest before jumping to her feet. "That is selfish, Tumi!"

Tumi stood, shaking his head as he bore down on her with a scowl. "No more selfish than prolonging the misery of a sick old woman."

With a rigid spine, Feira turned from him. Even though she was angry with Tumi, somewhere in the recesses of her mind, she feared his words were true. Was she only prolonging Akahi's misery? Did the woman whom she'd loved as her own mother wish to pass on to the Elements?

Feira flinched when Tumi's strong hands rested on her shoulders.

"Oaňa, please forgive me," he implored as he turned her toward him. "Look around you. Where are all the fathers and grandfathers? What fate is the life of a fisherman on Eris's waters? Even if we stay here, even if my mother allows us to marry, you could be a widow before our first babe is born."

Feira swallowed a sob as she shook her head. "Do not say that."

"It is true," Tumi said with an edge to his voice. "This is not the life I want for you. This is not the life I want for our children." Then the hard angles of his face softened and his voice dropped to barely a whisper. "Leave with me."

Feira's breath hitched when she saw the love reflected in Tumi's eyes. "Where will we go?"

Tumi turned his gaze toward the East. "Across the sea to the Shifting Sands."

"The Shifting Sands?" Feira stepped back as she sucked in a sharp breath. "No, Akahi cannot make such a journey."

"When will you understand?" Tumi spoke through a groan.

Without warning, a strong wind whipped Feira's hair across her face and tousled her skirts.

*Help me, Feira.*

Feira's eyes widened. "I must go. Akahi needs me."

Just as she turned to run, Tumi grasped her arm, a look of concern marring his brow. "I'll come with you."

"No." She pulled away. "You cannot risk being seen with me. I will return on the morrow."

But even as she ran toward her home, she wondered if she would see him again. Something in the urgency of the rustling leaves warned her that danger was fast approaching.

# Chapter Four

"**W**ell, hello, my sweet flower."

Feira's chest heaved as she looked up at the soldier who was blocking the door to her hut. The man was nearly twice as wide as her Tumi, with skin a rich mahogany and long, black matted braids that cascaded down his back like dead ivy. Dressed in bronze-plated armor bearing the insignia of the horned broot whale, Feira knew this was no ordinary soldier. This was one of Eris's warriors.

Had she sent him to kill her?

Slowly, Feira unclenched her fingers while keeping her wary gaze on the warrior. "Who are you? Where is my mother?"

The man's blood-red lips curled back in a feral smile, exposing two rows of jagged, yellow teeth. Feira read the lust in his eyes as he jutted one foot forward and lunged for her. She quickly ducked under him, dodging his grasp, only to barrel into another massive chest.

The man wrapped his meaty arms around her, crushing her against him. Before Feira could even react, he'd tossed her over his shoulder.

"Let me go!" she screamed while pounding his back. "Akahi!" she called to the wind. "Where are you, Mother?!"

"I found her first," the soldier behind them growled.

"You will get your turn after I'm through," her captor answered.

"Akahi!" She screamed again, but the wind did not answer.

Panic seized her chest at the sight of two more warriors exiting from her hut.

"What have you done with her?!" She pounded her captor's back even harder.

Her captor answered with a deep, sinister chuckle. "Search the hut for more food and then burn it," he said to the others. "I will bring her back when

I'm finished." Then he turned and walked back toward the forest with long, urgent strides.

Tears were cascading freely down Feira's face, and for a moment, she could not think beyond the numbing pain which seized her limbs. She closed her eyes and silently called out to her mother, but the air around her was stagnant, lifeless.

Akahi was dead.

The realization sunk low in Feira's chest like a heavy stone. Then the stone began to smolder, burning brighter, until it was a scorching fire. She stopped pounding against the soldier as she extended her fingers over his metal-plated armor covering his back.

And she released her flame.

The armor melted in an instant, sending him to his knees as he cried out.

Feira stumbled away from the man as he writhed in pain. Lifting her hands into the air, she arched her fingers until they resembled claws of fire. Flame shot from her hands and pierced the man's body, burning him with such intensity, he was reduced to nothing more than a pile of ash and flecks of molten metal.

Anger fueled her movements as she surged forward. Carried on a cloud of flame and smoke, she burned every last soldier who had dared hurt her mother.

FEIRA FOUND AKAHI LYING inside the hut with a fatal stab wound to the chest. Feira worked quickly, placing healing herbs upon the wound, crying out to the Elements to send back the spirit of her mother before she passed over into the Veil of Light.

Feira placed more healing herbs upon her mother's wound. She closed her eyes, searching for her mother's wind, sobbing as she cried out Akahi's name. But she was met with no answer. "Oh, Heavenly Elements," she cried, "why have you forsaken me?"

The Elements answered with a flicker of light, and then something more, a teasing breeze upon the nape of her neck. Feira's breath hitched, as she waited, hoping, praying, for her mother to return.

"Feira," her mother's voice echoed upon the breeze. "I must go to the Elements."

"No!" Feira screamed through a sob.

"Dear one, my time has long passed. You must flee, child, to the Shifting Sands where the goddess cannot find you. Go now," her mother implored, "before it is too late."

And then the breeze had vanished and the light along with it, until there was nothing left but dead air and darkness.

Feira opened her eyes and looked down at Akahi. She jumped with a start as the door to their hut blew open. A strong gust of wind whipped around her before encircling her mother. The cyclone spun so rapidly, Feira had no time to blink before Akahi's body had vanished, carried away by the wind, leaving behind nothing but the old woman's ring made from the bright red lava stone.

*Wear it in remembrance of her,* the wind whispered.

# Chapter Five

*G*o to her. She needs you.

Tumi nearly fell out of the palma tree as the breeze whistled the urgent plea in his ear. Never before had he heard the voice of the wind. But he knew the Elements had been speaking to him. Feira had told him how she and her mother relayed messages through the wind before.

He hastily climbed down the tree's branches, ignoring the pain that seared through him as thorns cut open his bare feet. Once he hit the ground, he raced toward the direction of Feira's hut. He only hoped he wasn't too late.

Tumi found Feira staggering down the small path that lead from her home to their village. His legs suddenly felt heavy and weak as he stopped in his tracks, looking at her with wide eyes. When she looked up at him, his heart seized at the haunted emptiness in her gaze. At that moment, Tumi knew their lives would never be the same.

Feira's hands and face were blackened with soot. Her hair was disheveled as tears spilled over her red-rimmed eyes.

"Oaňa! What has happened?" He held his arms open.

She fell against him, sobbing into his chest. "Eris's soldiers attacked my hut. They killed Akahi."

"I'm sorry." Tumi smoothed a hand through her hair and kissed her brow. He was overcome with guilt as he remembered how earlier he'd told Feira to let the old woman go. Now Feira's mother was dead, and Tumi cursed himself a heartless fool for his ill-timed words. Then the thought struck him as he looked down at the moss which clung to her skirt and hair. Had these soldiers raped his beloved as well? White hot rage inflamed his body and threatened to split his skull in two.

"Did they hurt you?" he barely breathed the words, more afraid of his reaction than the answer.

She pulled back as she spoke through a sob. "No, but they are all dead." She pointed to just beyond the swell of jungle trees.

It was then he saw the plume of smoke rising up from the canopy. Tumi's relief was only momentary, for now he knew they must flee. If the townspeople were to discover the carnage, they would mark Feira as a witch.

"The spice vessels leave for the Shifting Sands today. We must go before the Goddess discovers you."

Her mouth fell open as her eyes watered over with fresh tears. "You will go with me?"

Tumi nodded as his heart hammered out a wild staccato in his chest. "I will follow you anywhere."

IT DID NOT TAKE LONG for Tumi to secure a position as a crewman on the spice ship, *Sate'a Najmeh, The Bright Star*. Of the three spice vessels that had survived the voyage to Aloa-Shay's port, *The Bright Star* was in sore need of new sailors.

Tumi learned from the spice traders that Eris's soldiers had not come in search of Feira. Eris had sent her army to wage war against the Sky Goddess, Madhea, whose imposing mountain throne of ice lay north of the Werewoood Forest. A suicide mission, to be sure.

Several war ships had beached on the shores West of Aloa-Shay. One ship had even attacked *The Bright Star*, killing most of the crewmen before seizing the precious spices for themselves. The soldiers Feira had killed had only been a small party of scouts, as thousands more warriors were pouring onto the shoreline.

The sooner the spice vessels left the harbor, the better, as they were anxious to return to the safety of the Shifting Sands. Tumi only hoped Eris's soldiers would not invade the town of Aloa-Shay. He briefly thought of those he left behind, including his mother and brother. His whore mother had always been cruel, reminding him almost daily that he was a bastard child, conceived during one of her many trysts with the spice traders.

"You are dark and ugly," she would tell him. "Like the bastard who sired you."

When Katriana was in a particularly foul mood, she would order Tumi's older brother, Nuk, to beat him. Though Nuk was mute, there was no mistaking the twisted gleam of excitement in the larger man's eyes whenever he pounded into Tumi.

Tumi's shoulders fell at the realization that he would not miss his family. His only remorse was that he knew his mother would not grieve his absence, only the loss of the coins he provided.

Tumi had never known love from a woman until he'd met Feira. He had just come from harvesting a palma pod the day he'd met her. She'd been picking healing herbs in the jungle. Though Tumi was only a boy at the time, he had instantly fallen in love with the beautiful girl with the golden eyes, alabaster skin and flame-colored hair.

She had rubbed cooling herbs on his bruises and cuts, as cutting down the thorny palma fruits was painful, and sometimes deadly, work. But his mother did not care for his safety, so long as she had money to buy flowing dresses and pretty jewels.

As Tumi and Feira's friendship blossomed, so did their love for one another. Soon, she had revealed to him that her powers extended beyond the knowledge of healing herbs. She could ease his pain by smoothing her hands across his sore and tired muscles. He marveled at the soft white aura that shrouded her fingers while she worked.

Then she revealed to him an even darker secret. Her healing hands had the power to kill, and she'd harnessed that power before, scorching a mighty giant when she'd lived in the dark and dangerous Werewood forest.

Tumi made a blood promise never to reveal Feira's secret, for if the village priests were to learn of her witch flame, Feira would have been killed. The jealous bitch goddess, Eris, whose man-eating plants were the reason so many fishermen had lost their lives at sea, would not tolerate the existence of witches. Though Eris's island throne was across the sea, her reach extended to the shores of Aloa-Shay and the neighboring villages. The Goddess had decreed that any woman showing the slightest sign of power was to be executed, and towns that were thought to harbor witches would be eradicated by her army.

Luckily, Tumi's mother had wandered off with a handful of spice traders from another ship, so he was able to trade the family's store of palma pods in exchange for Feira's passage on *The Bright Star*. Then, they could leave this unforgiving land and its bitch deity for good.

The traders rarely allowed female passengers, but *The Bright Star* was in desperate need of goods, as they had no more spices to trade. One large palma pod could yield several hundred hearty fruit, which replenished the crewmen on their long journeys, and was a valuable food source to the people of the Shifting Sands.

Of the five ships that had set out from the Shifting Sands, only the *Quamar 'a Nor, The Moonlight,* and the *Nor 'a Sans, Rays of the Sun,* had survived along with *The Bright Star*. Two other spice vessels had perished in a storm. Trade vessels usually only set sail during rough weather, for they feared Eris's *carnivus* plants more than the mightiest gales. These plants rose up from the ocean's floor, and their giant maws were large enough to snap a ship in two. Though these monsters served to protect Eris's volcanic island home, they ate anything in their path. They appeared to be multiplying, for their destruction stretched far beyond Eris's volcanic lagoon, out into open waters.

Tumi's gaze sought his Oaña as he helped the crewmen load the vessel with goods. She was sitting in a darkened corner of the ship, knees pulled to her chest and face shrouded beneath the heavy hood of her cloak. Her shoulders shook, and Tumi knew she was mourning the loss of her mother.

His heart ached, for he knew he could do nothing to comfort her. Tumi sent a silent prayer to the Elements that his beloved would find happiness in their new life among the people of the Shifting Sands.

# Chapter Six

Feira spent her days serving the sailors food and water. In the evenings, she prepared special herbs for the sick and weak passengers. She made her bed upon the deck of the ship, ignoring the leers of one bold sailor who dared come near. But he soon learned to keep his distance when he wandered too close to her bedroll. She'd conjured a smoke hot enough to singe the hairs off his body.

Murmurs of witch and sorceress did not escape her notice, but the sailor bothered her no more. Shortly after sunset, Tumi would collapse beside her after long days of washing and polishing the deck. Feira would cover them with her cloak and secretly use her healing fires to soothe his sore muscles. On one particularly calm night, the crewmen were all on edge. Few slept as they kept watch on the dark and placid waters with cannons, spears and torches at the ready.

There was a saying among the villagers of Aloa-Shay, "Only fools set sail on tranquil waters."

Feira had not understood the full weight of this parable until she'd experienced the eerie stillness of that fateful night.

Feira slowly stood from her bedroll and walked toward the side of the ship while gazing out onto the water. The other ships looked to be nothing more than massive black skeletons against the backdrop of the pale moonlit night, as they eerily cut through the smooth seas with nary a splash. A sailor stood at the stern and bow of each boat, each wielding a bright torch while scanning the ocean.

And then, despite the stagnant air enveloping Feira like a thick shroud, a breeze blew across the deck, tousling her skirts and whipping through her hair.

*Beware, child. The monsters are near.*

Feira sucked in a sharp breath as a loud crack, followed by terrified screams, sounded from *The Moonlight*. She watched in horror as a monstrous, bulbous head full of teeth latched onto the stern of the boat and spun it in a half-circle.

Crewmen on *The Bright Star* were in a frenzy, barking orders and hurling spears as their ship spun toward *The Moonlight*.

Tumi had rushed toward Feira and turned to her with a crazed look in his eyes. He grasped her wrist and pulled her back toward her bedroll. "Stay away from the water's edge, Oaňa." Spear in hand, he raced to the side of the boat.

The boards beneath Feira's soles shook as cannons were fired. But when the smoke had cleared, *The Moonlight* was already on its side as three more monstrous carnivus plants attacked it. Sailors who'd fallen into the water met a swift end, as several smaller carnivus plants devoured them whole.

More cannons were fired. More spears were thrown. The jowls of two large carnivus had been blown open, but for every monster that had been shot, two more seemed to take its place. Feira's heart sank as she heard a horn sound a retreat. *The Moonlight* and all of its crew would perish.

A jolt sent Feira sprawling onto the deck. She heard the splintering crack before she saw the monster's head climbing up the side of the boat. With a deep, feral hiss, it reared back its head before smashing a gaping hole on top of the deck. Coming within a breath of Tumi, the beast ensnared two armed sailors, making easy work of devouring their flailing bodies, spears and all.

"Oh, Heavenly Elements, protect us," Feira cried before rising to her feet and lifting her hands in the air. Spirals of flame arced off each fingertip into the night sky, before spinning toward the water and striking the plant with a thunderous clap. Feira raised her arms higher, calling on the Elements again as ten more spirals shot out of her fingers, coating the water's surface in a sea of flame.

The monsters emitted strange, guttural squeals, as one by one, their charred bodies slumped back beneath the water's surface.

As Feira looked down at her charred fingertips, she was vaguely aware of sailors scurrying to repair the damaged hull. Tears streamed down her face as she realized what she'd done. Now everyone in the Shifting Sands would know her for a witch. Was there nowhere she and Tumi would be safe?

# Chapter Seven

Feira had no time to lament her fate, not when she had to treat the surviving sailors that had been pulled from the water. Rather than apply herbs on those men that were gravely injured, Feira used her healing fires. Everyone on board had witnessed her display, so there was no sense in hiding her powers.

After the crewmen had done their best to repair *The Bright Star*, Tumi stayed beside Feira, helping her attend to the injured.

It was well into the morning hours before Feira had finished treating the last victim. Surprisingly, the ship's captain insisted she and Tumi seek rest in his personal sleeping quarters. After sleeping for several nights on the hard deck of the ship, Feira could not refuse the offer of a soft feather bed.

As Feira lay in the cradle in Tumi's arms, for the first night in many moons, a sense of peace washed over her. These crewmen from the Shifting Sands, they had not treated her with disdain after learning of her powers. Though most of them kept their distance, Feira had been treated with nothing short of respect and awe by the few sailors who were bold enough to come near.

Perhaps, Feira thought, she'd find acceptance among the people of the Shifting Sands.

FEIRA AND TUMI BOTH shot up in bed at the sound of the deafening roar that shook the walls of their cabin.

Monster!

She and Tumi shared wide-eyed looks of horror before scrambling to the floor. Before Tumi could stop her, Feira was out the cabin door. With extended fingers, she spun around and lifted her arms, ready to confront whatever beast was attacking their vessel.

What she saw not only rendered her speechless, but motionless as well.

Tumi came barreling into her, and then, he, too, gaped at the sight before them—a magnificent golden-hued dragon, whose wingspan easily encompassed the length of their ship.

Even more shocking was the reaction of the crew members on board. The ship had docked in a harbor, and the traders were carrying their cargo down a long plank, which just so happened to be positioned under the crook of the creature's wing.

And not one of them seemed to be alarmed.

Feira's gaze shot back to the dragon, who was looking at her with what could only be described as a smirk tilting his heavy, fanged jowls. Her gaze searched the rest of his features, but she could discern no malice shining back in his gold-flecked eyes.

An ocean breeze flitted through her hair. Warm, crisp tendrils of air soothed the prickles on her arms and nape.

*Friend*, the wind whispered.

*Friend?* Feira gasped. *A monster? How could this be?*

But the wind only answered with a lilting laugh before it blew past her, ruffling Tumi's tunic and unkempt hair.

Tumi swatted at the air before shifting closer to Feira's side.

Just then the ship's captain stepped forward. He bowed low to Feira before sweeping an arm toward the monster. "The Great King wishes to speak with you."

"The Great King?" Feira rasped as she slowly lowered her arms. All the while, she kept a watchful eye on the dragon.

The captain nodded while bowing lower. "He was once servant to our fallen goddess, Kyan. Now Tan'yi'na, the magnificent golden dragon, is supreme ruler of the Shifting Sands." The captain slowly backed away, leaving Feira and Tumi to face the dragon alone.

Feira swallowed the rising lump of bile in her throat, all the while trying her best to still her quaking limbs. "*You* rule the Shifting Sands?" she asked, unable to mask the tone of disbelief in her voice.

*Do not fear me, child. I have come to honor you, as only the descendent of Kyan could have so much power.*

Though the dragon's lips did not move, the deep voice resonated in Feira's skull.

She gaped at the monster. "Kyan?"

Something akin to merriment danced in the dragon's gaze. He pulled back his heavy wings, shaking them once as a bird would ruffle its feathers. Feira gasped in wonderment as plume of dust rose up from the dragon's body. Tiny flecks of gold particles floated through the air and then coated the ship in a fine powder.

*The Land Goddess, your grandmother.* The dragon's wide nostrils flared as more flecks of gold rose up from its snout. *I can scent her in your blood. You are a daughter of Odu, are you not?*

Feira nodded and watched in awe as shimmery particles coated her hair and hands. She looked over at Tumi, whose dark skin was now a glinting bronze.

"Odu was my father's name," she said, "but he left me when I was a child."

The dragon's laughter was deep and rich. *The sons of Kyan tend to wander. They have been roaming this world for hundreds of years.*

"Hundreds of years?" Feira gasped. "How can this be true?"

The dragon lowered his massive head, and his wide gaze bore down on Feira as if he was reaching into her very soul. *You have much to learn. In time, you will understand why the Elements brought you to us.*

Feira swallowed hard before sharing anxious glances with Tumi. "So we are welcome here?" she asked the dragon.

*My children*, the dragon answered, *you are more than welcome.*

Tumi reached out and laced his hand through hers. Feira could not help but smile at her *Oañu* as her witch flame flooded their hearts with warmth.

# GLOSSARY

Adolan – A village below the glacier, and far below the peak of Ice Mountain.

Alec – Markus's older and sickly brother, who is blessed with wisdom beyond his years. He looks after Markus, but is not strong enough to defend himself against his father's brutal beatings.

Aloa-Shay – A seaside village, several weeks' journey from Adolan.

Ande Eryll – Bane's brother and Elof's middle son.

Ariette – An Elemental, she is Madhea's daughter and Kia's sister.

Bane Eryll – Oldest son of Elof Eryll. Vindictive and selfish, he constantly pesters Ura to marry him. Their clan is the most powerful in Ice Kingdom.

Crystal Lake – A large lake at the center of the glacier.

Dafuar – Ancient prophet and son of the fallen Goddess, Kyan. He dwells in Adolan and his twin brother is Odu.

The Danae – A stream beside Adolan. It branches off from The Danae River, which flows beneath the glacier.

Desryn (Des) – Younger brother to Dianna, the witch huntress.

Dianna – A young witch huntress who lives in Adolan. She criticizes Rowlen for beating his son, Alec, and Markus for not defending his brother. Dianna is sister to Desryn, whom she has cared for since their parents died.

Dragon weed – The primary vegetation for the Ice People. Very nutritious, but slimy.

Dragon's Tooth – A large 'spiked' tower of ice.

The Elementals – Daughters of the Elements and of the goddesses. Six Elementals serve Madhea and six serve Eris.

The Elements – The creators of Tehra, and the source of magic for the witches and Goddesses.

Elof Eryll – The Council Chieftain of Ice Kingdom and Bane's father. He turns a blind eye to the melting ice, more concerned with stuffing his face than protecting his people.

Eris – Goddess of the Sea. Also known as the sea witch, she is Madhea's sister.

Gnull – Large predatory ice creatures (think prehistoric walrus) that are very dangerous and a threat to the Ice People. However, they are prized for their blubbery oil, which is used as candle tallow. Gnull fur is used for clothing, and their bones are used for weapons and crafting boats.

Gunther Eryll – Bane's brother and Elof's youngest son.

Ice Kingdom – City within the glacier.

Ice Mites – Light bugs that dwell in frozen crystals, giving the ice formations a glowing appearance.

Ice Mountain – A towering column of ice that stretches beyond the Heavens, built by Madhea as a shrine to herself. She dwells at the top of Ice Mountain with her daughters, the Elementals.

Ice Shield – A thin layer of ice shielding Ice Kingdom from the outside world.

Ingred Johan – Council member and Elof's cousin. Her son is Ven Jonan.

Jon Nordlund – Kind ice dweller, and father to Ura and Ryne.

Kia – An Elemental, she is Madhea's daughter and Ariette's sister.

Kicelin – Village at the base of Ice Mountain.

Kraehn – Fanged fish that dwell beneath the icy river. They devour just about anything, even people, in a matter of moments.

Lazy Eyed Serpents – Ugly, long eel-like fish. Though their meat is soft and slimy, serpents are the main food source for the ice dwellers.

Lydra – Madhea's dragon, which breathes impenetrable ice.

Lyme tree – A tree large enough for a gathering hall to be built within its branches. Found at the base of the mountain and surrounding the village of Adolan.

Madhea – An evil goddess sometimes referred to as the Sky Goddess or the ice witch.

Markus – The boy hunter who brought on The Hunter's Curse. He is the son of Rowlen and brother of Alec.

Odu – Ancient prophet and son of the fallen Goddess, Kyan. Twin brother to Dafuar, he dwells in Ice Kingdom.

Orhan (O-Ran) – Kyan's mortal husband, and father to Odu, Dafuar and their six daughters.

Pixies – Small, flying, fanged creatures with razor-sharp teeth, long claws and red eyes. With a penchant for creating mischief and an appetite for blood, they answer to the bidding of Madhea or her daughters.

Rowlen Jägerrson – Alec and Markus's cruel, drunk father.

Ryne – Ice dweller who tries to convince his people that the ice is melting. Jon's son and Ura's brother.

The Sacred Stones – Seven stones, each one possessing the spirit of the fallen goddess, Kyan, and her six daughters.

The Shifting Sands – A land with a hostile, dry climate, which serves as a sanctuary from the witches.

Sindrí – One of Kyan's daughters turned to stone by Madhea.

Slog – A slow, lazy ice animal, very similar to a modern sloth. Eats ice mites.

Soaring Perch – Fat, winged fish that swim in The Danae River, beneath the glacier.

Snowbear – Similar to a Polar Bear. These bears can be found all along the glacier, Ice Mountain and, occasionally, south of Adolan.

Tar – Ryne's loyal dog companion. Think of an Alaskan Husky.

Tehra – Their world.

Ura – Ice dweller. Jon's daughter and Ryne's sister.

Ven Johan – Bane's beefy cousin who does his bidding.

Werewood Forest – An enchanted forest, halfway between Adolan and Aloa-Shay.

Zier – The dwarf trader.

# Books by Tara West

**Eternally Yours**
Divine and Dateless
Damned and Desirable
Damned and Desperate
Demonic and Deserted
Dead and Delicious
**Something More Series**
Say When
Say Yes
Say Forever
Say Please
Say You Want Me
Say You Love Me
Say You Need Me
**Dawn of the Dragon Queen Saga**
Dragon Song
Dragon Storm
**Whispers Series**
Sophie's Secret
Don't Tell Mother
Krysta's Curse
Visions of the Witch
Sophie's Secret Crush
Witch Blood
Witch Hunt
**Keepers of the Stones**
Witch Flame, Prelude

Curse of the Ice Dragon, Book One
Spirit of the Sea Witch, Book Two
Scorn of the Sky Goddess, Book Three

# About Tara West

Tara West writes books about dragons, witches, and handsome heroes while eating chocolate, lots and lots of chocolate. She's willing to share her dragons, witches, and heroes. Keep your hands off her chocolate. A former high school English teacher, Tara is now a full-time writer and graphic artist. She enjoys spending time with her family, interacting with her fans, and fishing the Texas coast.

Awards include: Dragon Song, Grave Ellis 2015 Readers Choice Award, Favorite Fantasy Romance

Divine and Dateless, 2015 eFestival of Words, Best Romance

Damned and Desirable, 2014 Coffee Time Romance Book of the Year

Sophie's Secret, selected by The Duff and Paranormal V Activity movies and Wattpad recommended reading lists

Curse of the Ice Dragon, Best Action/Adventure 2013 eFestival of Words

Sophie's Secret, iBooks Breakout Book Award

Hang out with her on her Facebook fan page at: https://www.face-book.com/tarawestauthor

Or check out her website: www.tarawest.com

She loves to hear from her readers at: tara@tarawest.com

Made in the USA
Las Vegas, NV
22 January 2021